VE... DESIRES

<u>BOOK YOUR PLACE ON OUR WEBSITE AND MAKE THE READING CONNECTION!</u>

We've created a customized website just for our very special readers, where you can get the inside scoop on everything that's going on with Zebra, Pinnacle and Kensington books.

When you come online, you'll have the exciting opportunity to:

- View covers of upcoming books
- Read sample chapters
- Learn about our future publishing schedule (listed by publication month *and author*)
- Find out when your favorite authors will be visiting a city near you
- Search for and order backlist books from our online catalog
- Check out author bios and background information
- Send e-mail to your favorite authors
- Meet the Kensington staff online
- Join us in weekly chats with authors, readers and other guests
- Get writing guidelines
- AND MUCH MORE!

**Visit our website at
http://www.kensingtonbooks.com**

VEILED
DESIRES

TRACY MACNISH

ZEBRA BOOKS
Kensington Publishing Corp.
www.kensingtonbooks.com

For my Grandmothers:

To Grandmom, who has more names than the Queen:
Amy Lilly Florence Mary Theresa Wolfe McGilloway,
and who everyone knows as Molly.
A lovely English rose with her own Irish hero.

To the memory of my much-loved,
deeply-missed Mommoms,
Marie Theresa McClintock Nish,
the strongest, most selfless woman I have ever known.

And to Mommom Fricker,
Marie Antoinette Trauger Fricker,
who loves books, high heels, and lipstick
just as much as I do.

Acknowledgments

The author's sincerest thanks and best wishes to:

My mentor and friend, Brent Monahan, who can be counted on for rigorous instruction and relentless truth; My agent, Mary Sue Seymour, a truly lovely person; My editor, Audrey LaFehr, whose enthusiasm for my first novel made me strive to be better; My dear friend, Joan-Marie Budner, who read the manuscript in all its many variations and never lost her enthusiasm—thank you for your invaluable insights; Tracy Tappan, my Rome correspondent, for honesty and friendship, a rare and wonderful combination; Peter Schulman, who loves my characters as much as I do; Bill Kent, ZenMaster Writer, whose approach to the act of writing is as noble and inspiring as it gets; And Jamie Howell, whose writing proves that great talent simply IS—you are a modern-day Prometheus, the fire is in your hands, my friend;

My fun and fabulous sister Aislinn, who also happens to be my very best friend;

My son, Ethan, who despite his belief that my books are "probably boring girl stuff," is still proud of me—the feeling's mutual, kid;

And always, always, always, to my husband, Randy, my German—thank you for loving me.

"All human actions have one or more of these seven causes: chance, nature, compulsions, habit, reason, passion, desire."

—Aristotle (384–322BC)

"Listening causes me to find the existence of truth behind the veil."

—unknown ninth century philosopher

Chapter 1

Barbados, 1774

The noise of cannon fire greeted Rogan Mullen and his crew as the *Paradise* sailed into Barbados's inner harbor along the peaceful western coast. On his return from the wild shores of the Americas, the island looked tinier than in his memory: the beaches whiter, the water a deeper turquoise. Grasping the ropes of the rigging, he swung down from the mizzenmast, dropped one of the sun-bleached sails and handed over a line to a waiting sailor.

"Find out who knotted that, aye?" Rogan instructed. "If we'd hit a squall, that line wouldn't have held."

"Aye, Sir," the sailor replied, as he wound the rope into a tight, neat coil.

Crewmen shouted to each other, the sounds of their voices punctuated by the shots of another cannon and the cries of seagulls and the crowd that gathered. All the island came alive when a ship returned home, the locals anxious for news from other parts of the world, and also for the goods the ship would bear.

The captain of the ship strode over to Rogan and stood

beside him, the stub of an unlit cigar firmly clenched between his teeth. "A good voyage."

"Aye," Rogan agreed. He gestured to the rigging high overhead. "I saw sloppy work up there. You'll need to find the weak link before we set sail again."

"Will do," the captain said with a nod. "Other than that?"

"All is well. I'm pleased." Rogan clapped the man on the back and nodded, his eyes sweeping over the ship, taking in the shiny black paint, the polished brass, the clean, orderly decks. "You've done well."

The crew lowered the remaining sails as the brig coasted to the pier and slid into berth. The anchor dropped with the rattling scream of thick metal links and hit the bottom of the cove. With a heave-ho, ten crewmen dropped the gangplank into position with the resounding crack of wood on wood, and then took to securing the hawses. Within minutes the ship came even more alive, as islanders clambered aboard and crewmen rushed to disembark, everyone milling about chatting and calling out to one another. The din of voices grew louder, mingling with the cries of the seagulls wheeling overhead, the clatter of the rigging being secured, and the creaking of the tall masts.

Rogan leaned against the rail of his ship. He employed his own crew, his own captain, and saw to the trade himself, loving the bustle of the various port Exchanges, the hot feel of trading tickets in his palm, the thrill of barter and sales.

The sun warmed his shoulders with a pleasant heat, and he breathed in the scent of home: the salty fresh air mingling with the food from the docks, the slight reek of rancid fish from the fishing boats docked alongside them, and the sweet odor of fermentation wafting from the vegetables and fruit piled in crates, spoiling in the hot sun.

A few of the pretty island girls came aboard the ship, the sound of their giggles floating around them. They wandered over to Rogan as a tight bevy of four, fetching from heads to heels, their bright kerchiefs tied over their hair and their sun-tanned, bare feet peeking from their colorful skirts. The boldest of the bunch, Greta, took a step apart from their pack. She breezed a bit closer to Rogan, her color riding high on her cheeks as she approached him.

"Good to see you, Rogan." Her voice was full of laughter, and her long, thin toes curled against the wooden deck. She clasped her hands behind her back and leaned forward so she could tilt her head up coyly as she looked into his emerald green eyes. "Where have you been all this long year?"

Rogan grinned down at them, causing a fresh eruption of giggles. He arched a brow. "Oh, here and there, Greta. Now tell me, did you marry the foolish Smith boy?"

A bright flush crept up her neck, turning her pink cheeks a darker rose as indignation crept into her tone. "No. He went to sea, and asked me to wait for him."

"Well, I did say he was foolish, aye?" Rogan pointed out. "You're too pretty to be waiting on a boy, Greta."

She leaned closer and touched his arm, placing her hand on the large bulge of his muscle. "Maybe I was waiting on a man, Rogan."

Rogan laughed easily at her lack of subtlety and reached down to tuck a stray curl into her kerchief. He knew her parents, two quiet, hardworking Germans, and had known Greta since she was born, well enough to know she was a hopeless flirt. "You'd only break my heart."

"That might be so, but you would enjoy the process."

"I likely would," Rogan agreed, glancing around at the throng milling on and off the ship, saw that it was thinning. It was time to disengage himself and be on his way, now that the bulk of the crowd had died down a bit. He grasped her hand and bowed over it, pressed a light kiss against her warm skin. "But I'm afraid I cannot risk it."

He turned and walked away, heard a whisper and a fresh

round of girlish giggles, and he grinned. It was good to be home.

Greta tore herself from her group and ran after him, reached out and tugged at his sleeve. "Oh and Rogan, do tell me what's in the letter."

"What letter is that?" Rogan asked, distracted. His attention caught on a cracked keg leaking rum onto the deck. He gestured for a mate to attend to it and then met Greta's eyes once again.

"Only the talk of the island after Kieran did nothing but boast of it for months." Her eyes grew sly and her lips drew into a smirk. The rivalry between the two girls was epic, and Greta found herself in the position of being first to dispense the information. "The finest vellum, a bold red seal, and the crest of the most powerful duke in England."

A mate called out to Rogan from high in the rigging, stealing his attention once again. Rogan gestured to the pier and then back to the forecastle, using sign language to answer the man's question before addressing Greta. "I'm sure you'll hear about it. Nothing stays quiet on this island for too long."

He took her hand once again and brushed his lips over it as his eyes saw to it the man in the rigging got his instructions right. "Good day."

Dropping Greta's hand he turned once again. This time he managed to escape.

One of the old men on the pier spied Rogan. He gripped his cane and called out, "I'll send word you're here. They'll be chomping to see you, son."

Rogan waved down at him from the ship's deck. "No needs, Harry. I want it to be a surprise, aye?"

Harry nodded and waved him along, grinning toothlessly. Rogan grabbed a trunk from his cabin and hoisted it onto his shoulder, making his way from the ship, greeting people as he passed them, shaking hands, thanking them for the welcome. As much as he had needed to get away, it felt good to return. Better than he'd thought, as he saw the familiar faces of the islanders, the rugged limestone cliffs of the landscape, and heard the cries and noises of the docks.

Rogan made his way down the gangplank, worked through the throng to where Julius was hunched over an open pit, roasting a young boar. The man had done so every day for as long as Rogan could recall, wrapping the meat in sugarcane strips and basting it with a sauce of coconut milk, rum, and secret spices until the outside was charred black, the meat inside so succulent it melted in the mouth. He shook Julius's hand and gestured to the meat, the rich scent making his mouth water. "Is it ready, I hope?"

Julius grinned wide, his teeth blinding white against the black of his skin, and took out a huge knife, cut a slab and set it on a plate with a piece of bread and a helping of the sauce. He handed it to Rogan, who set down his trunk and accepted it gratefully, along with a pint of warm ale. Standing in the shade of a huge palm tree, he drank deeply and ate the meat, then set the dirty glass and plate into a crate set aside for that purpose. He leaned against the tree and sighed deeply.

"My thanks." He reached into his purse for a few coins. "A year is too long to go without your cooking."

Julius waved away his payment. "Missta Rogan, ya put that beck, now."

"Thank you, Julius," Rogan replied, regretting the manners that prevented him from pressing money on the man. The islanders were as warm and gracious as they were poor, but to insist on paying would be offensive. So Rogan opened his trunk and pulled out a long scarf he had purchased in a coastal town of the Carolinas. Made of fine cotton, it was so soft and sheer it felt like silk, dyed pale pink and embroidered with silver thread. There had been a lovely woman selling them, and Rogan had purchased one in every color to give as gifts. "For your wife, then."

Julius accepted the scarf, his wrinkled face beaming. "She'll love it, Missta Rogan. Thank ye."

Rogan shook the man's hand and picked his trunk back up, hoisted it once again onto his broad shoulder. "Now don't mention you saw me, aye? 'Tis a surprise."

Julius nodded and set to wrapping the scarf in a banana leaf where it wouldn't get splashed or ruined, and sent Rogan on his way with a promise of silence.

The day gleamed brilliantly, the afternoon sun hot and bright overhead, the songs of the wood doves a melody in the white cedar trees as Rogan followed the familiar paths to his home. The trails undulated, hilly and uneven, with winding rough walls of coral rising around him like a medieval stronghold in places, spreading back out in others. Hibiscus, frangipani, and jasmine grew in tangles of bushes and vines, their scents heavy in the salty air. Shade and sun dappled the path as he walked in the shadows of palm trees and huge ferns. Vines draped gracefully from the bearded fig trees, dangled to brush against his arms as he passed.

Rogan looked at the flowers that clustered around him, the blue lotus, begonias, and desert rose, but he scarcely saw their untamed beauty. He saw flowers twined in the hair of a woman with skin the color of toffee, seductive amber eyes that promised, a sultry body that delivered. He remembered soft dark hair, long and tangled from a swim in the ocean, spread out to dry on the sand as she lay naked in the mouth of a secluded limestone cavern, and her mouth, curled at the corners as she dared him to make love to her right then, right there. His muscles tensed, bunched, and his blood heated. But it was not remembered lust for the woman he felt. That had faded. Changed into something completely different.

He kept going. Just as he'd done for the year past. Kept going, pressed forward. No looking back.

The thick growth hedged in on him, darkening the trail for a few yards. He needed to lower his trunk and duck down as the vines draped thickly from the fig trees, the fecund scent of earth blending with the fragrance of the flowers and ripening fruit. He emerged from the vines, parting them like a curtain as he stepped out into the bright sunlight, the trail open and maintained now, the house in sight.

The Mullens' home rose up graciously from the lush foliage that surrounded it, a large, sprawling home of sun-bleached woods and creamy limestone, the orange tile roof gleaming under the glaring sun. The wide verandah in the front was welcoming, bordered with flowers and shaded by trees. Birds darted all around, wood doves, bananaquits, and finches, the soft sound of their flapping wings mingling with their songs. And there on the verandah, rigidly formal in a high-backed chair, sat his younger sister, Kieran. She sipped a cup of tea as she read a book.

Rogan set down his trunk and crept around the house, careful to not make a sound. He drew closer to her, his footsteps as quiet as a cat's, came up near enough that he could smell the fragrance of her tea and the scent of her perfume, sandalwood and jasmine. She lifted her cup and brought it to her lips slowly, completely absorbed in her novel. He crouched down and picked up a pebble, tossed it high so it landed in her teacup with a plop, sending a tiny geyser splashing on her face.

Kieran gasped, dropped her book and tossed her cup, which upended, causing the tea to slosh all over her gown as the porcelain smashed on the wooden floor. She turned to face the intruder, her eyes wild. "Rogan!" she half yelled, half choked.

Rogan bounded up the steps and picked up his sister, twirled her around once and then grasped her by her shoulders, held her out for inspection. With her shiny auburn hair, stormy blue eyes, and the fine, fair features of her mother, she was even more beautiful than his memory of her. "Look at you, Kieran. Just as pretty as ever." He took out his handkerchief and wiped the tea from her face. "Where's Mum and Da?"

Kieran snatched the cloth from her brother's hand and began blotting the tea from her gown, muttering something about silk and stains and childish men, and then gave up, too happy to see her brother to pretend annoyance with him. She handed back the square of linen and answered him, her English as precise as the king's court. "I believe they are in town. No doubt they already will have heard you're home by now."

"I swore everyone to secrecy, though we both know how well a secret is kept on this island."

Kieran stood back, looked her brother up and down, from his wavy black hair, to emerald green eyes made even brighter by his darkly tanned skin, to his tall, rugged build. He looked different to her, rougher, leaner, his nose slightly crooked as if it had been broken and mended. His skin had grown tougher, leathery, and a few skinny scars gleamed whitely on his jaw amidst the burnished shades of skin and stubble. "You're as dark as a savage. Did you not wear a hat even once?"

"Admit it, Kieran. You missed your only brother."

Kieran pointed to the splotch of tea on her elegant bodice of lace and buttery silk. "I admit nothing."

"Admit it, or I won't give you your presents."

"Presents?"

Rogan laughed at her sudden change of demeanor. "What kind of brother travels for a year and does not return bearing gifts?"

"Not my brother," Kieran replied happily. "Come inside, Rogan, and I have missed you. We all have."

Rogan jogged to where he had left his trunk, picked it up and rejoined Kieran as they went indoors. The house hadn't changed in the slightest since the year before, the spacious rooms decorated in the tones of the beach itself, warm browns, pinks, and creams, with quiet shades of blue in the paintings on the walls, and potted plants splashing dark, glossy green boldly against the walls. A huge Persian rug of the same hues graced the pale wooden floors, an invitation for one to remove one's shoes and be comfortable.

Just as he had feared, Rogan couldn't avoid seeing his wife everywhere. She was there, on the settee, laughing with Kieran. At the dining table, gesturing with her soup spoon as she told a crazy story from her gypsy childhood. On the floor, wiping up a drink she'd spilled because she'd been laughing so hard it had tipped from her hands, the tears of her laughter still leaking from the corners of her eyes as she sopped up the wine.

Mentally shaking off the memories and the compulsion they created, he opened the lid of the chest and began to rummage through the contents for his sister's gifts. Kieran took the seat left out especially for her, high-backed and stiff, as the proper corsets and stays she insisted upon wearing did not permit her to sit on the soft, upholstered pieces. He handed her one bundle at a time, and she opened chocolates from Belgium, soaps from Paris, a bolt of soft blue silk from England, and finally a necklace of finely made gold links that suspended a beautiful sapphire pendant. She held the riches in her lap, her eyes round and wondrous.

"I thought you were in the Americas."

"I was. 'Tis an amazing place, Kieran. Wild but civilized, with towns that have imports from all over the world, both goods and people."

"I would love to see it," she said wistfully, touching the necklace. "There is a whole world out there, Rogan. I would like to see even just one part of it."

"England."

She looked up to him, her face sharp and pained. "Yes. England."

"Perhaps one day."

Kieran lifted the soap to her face and inhaled its fragrance, then touched the silk, so fine it felt like a cool breath on her skin. "I have dreamed of running away."

Rogan felt his body tighten. He left his seat, came and knelt in front of his sister. "Kieran, you will listen to me. You will not run away."

"Of course I would not," Kieran assured him, trying to feign nonchalance. "'Twas a jest."

Rogan took her by the shoulders and gave her a hard shake. "I'll tie you up and lock you away first. A city is not a place for a woman alone, and a ship with two hundred sailors aboard it is even less so, aye?"

Kieran opened her mouth to speak but was interrupted as her mother, Camille, rushed in. "Kieran? Is all well? There's a smashed teacup on the verandah and your book—"

She gasped and ran to her son, threw her arms around his neck, nearly knocking both of them to the floor, tears of joy instantly flowing. She pulled back, looked at him, and then squeezed him again, tight. Finally Camille let go a bit, leaned back and regarded her son. She took in his every detail, from the face that was like her husband, Patrick's, the look of an ancient Celtic fable, to the green eyes that were the mirror-image of her own.

"I have missed you, Rogan." Fresh tears sparked in her eyes. And then she swatted his arm gently. "You could have sent word that you were coming home. You're like to kill an old woman with this sort of surprise."

He grinned down at his mother, the reckless grin so like his father's it had helped him escape a scolding countless times while growing up. "You'll never be old, Mum."

Camille reached up to smooth her hair, as dark as Rogan's but for some streaks of silver. "'Tis nonsense, of course, but my vanity appreciates your effort." She reached out to touch his hair, her fingers lingering on the black waves, before she cupped his cheek tenderly. Her thumb brushed over the scars, but she would not inquire. He was his own man, and she'd long ago learned to let him be. "So good to see you, Rogan."

"Well, I wouldn't be a good son if I didn't come home in time for my parents' thirtieth wedding anniversary."

She smiled at him, her face soft with love for her husband, her son, and her daughter, the family they'd become, the family she had always longed for. "You remembered."

"Of course. I have gifts, too."

Camille held up her hand. "No gifts until Patrick is home and we've heard all about your travels. Right now, though, I'll make tea and we'll talk."

"Where is Da?"

"He is still in town; he had a meeting with the governor regarding some new trade laws. He's due home soon, though."

Suddenly, as if stung by a bee, Kieran leapt to her feet. "The letter!"

A frown touched Camille's brow. She'd been uneasy ever since that letter had arrived months ago. "Not now, Kieran. Rogan has not even had tea, yet."

"I don't need tea, Mum, thanks." He turned to Kieran. "What letter?"

" 'Tis from England, and it bears our uncle's ducal crest. I will get it, Rogan. Wait here."

In a rare display of undignified enthusiasm, Kieran raced from the room, and returned moments later, breathless from running while wearing a corset, brandishing a creamy envelope of thick parchment, the waxy seal a bold red circle pressed with a crest. She handed it to Rogan and took her seat again, leaning forward, her eyes intent on her brother. "Open it," she urged.

Rogan broke the seal and unfolded it, read it through, and looked at his mother. "You haven't heard anything else from your brother?"

"No. This arrived for you, and I set it aside. What does it say?"

Rogan read it again. "It says my cousin, Kenley, Lord Jeffrey's son, has died."

Camille let out a little sigh of sadness, that her only remaining brother had lost his only son. And just as quickly, she said a quick prayer of gratitude that both her children lived and thrived when so many others did not.

"That's not all it says, is it?" Kieran pressed, knowing the look on her brother's face meant there was much more to the letter.

In answer, Rogan handed the letter to Camille. She reluctantly took it and sat across from Rogan. She looked at the letter, frowning slightly as she saw the impression at the bottom, the Bradburn ducal crest. She shivered, and as she read the letter, she felt her legs and arms go heavy with shock, her heart a thick thudding in her chest. Camille looked back up to her son, his green eyes as verdant as her own, the Bradburn eyes.

"What does it say?" Kieran demanded.

Rogan tore his eyes away from his mother's, not wanting to see the fear and denial evident on her face. "It says that by the laws of primogeniture, I am next in succession."

Silence hung over the three of them like a storm cloud until Kieran broke it, stating the obvious, but what none of them had yet absorbed. "You will be a Duke." She looked dazzled, in near-breathless awe. She stood in a flurry of silk. "And I will be a Lady."

Camille leapt to her feet as well, the parchment still in her hands. A quick vision of London flashed through her mind: the darkness, the decadence, the depravity. "No. No!"

"Yes," Kieran insisted. Her small white hands smoothed her fine English gown. "Primogeniture."

"No," Camille repeated, her voice hard even though she spoke quietly. She knew precisely where her daughter's ambitions lay, and she rushed to disabuse Kieran of any illusions. "'Tis *male* primogeniture. You are still the daughter of a disgraced lady and a commoner."

"I am the niece of a great duke, and someday I shall be the sister of the Duke of Eton. If I go to London with Rogan, who would deny me the respect due such a position?"

"Everyone," Camille said flatly. "You deceive yourself, Kieran. The memory of Londontown is long amongst the peers, and though they might be kind to your face, they would mock you behind your back. Make no mistake: No peer would deign to marry you. No matter who your brother is, you are still the granddaughter of a hanged duchess and the daughter of disgraced lady. You bear my ignominy."

"You don't even sound sorry for it," Kieran accused bitterly.

Camille smiled then, her eyes going soft with the memory of herself and Patrick when they were young, the love that had been like life itself, so urgent and necessary. Of what they had found in the most unlikely of circumstances, their splendor among shadows. "No, my Kieran," she said, unable to keep the wistfulness from her tone, "I am not sorry for one minute of it."

Kieran turned to her brother, her face earnest, her eyes bright. "Rogan, what will you do? Will you go to London?"

Rogan shrugged carelessly. England's manners and mores did not appeal to him. The wealth did, however, and his curiosity had certainly been piqued. And no matter where he decided to go, he needed to go to sea again, away from all the memories that the island bore like stigmata. "I don't know, Kieran. Maybe."

When Kieran failed to get a suitable response from her

brother, she turned back to Camille, taking a different angle. "Mummy, please. You know how much this would mean to me. If Rogan goes, may I please go with him?"

"You don't understand, love. It isn't as you think, all glittering parties and masquerades. It is open, stinking sewers, disease and darkness, crime and corruption. I would not lie to you, Kieran. It is as I say."

"Just because you were not happy there doesn't mean I shall not be."

Camille felt the stirrings of real anger at her daughter's stubbornness. "It is a parent's responsibility to provide what is best for her children."

"I am no child!" Kieran shouted, unable to rein in her frustration.

"You certainly sound like one, raising your tone to your mother," Patrick commented as he entered the room. And then his eyes lighted on Rogan, and he grinned. "So, the rumor is true."

He rushed across the room and grabbed his son, pulled him into a strong embrace, and clapped him on the back. "Good to see you, son."

"Da." Rogan gripped him hard in response. Patrick was over sixty, but still fit, his muscles roped and hard from physical work and good health. Rogan hugged his father solidly, not letting go. "Good to see you, too."

Patrick pulled back, held his son by the shoulders and met his eyes. "We'll talk later, aye? It's going to be a good night for it."

Rogan nodded once, looking forward to the evening when he and his father would sit on the verandah with a glass of whiskey and conversation. Such talks had kept them close, and across the past months, Rogan had missed them.

Kieran sat back down, unwilling to put a further mar on the day. She could not, however, prevent herself from staring at the letter in her brother's hand. She caught her mother looking at her and registered the meaningful glance that meant they would discuss it later.

The rest of the afternoon was whiled away with laughter, memories shared and stories told, past and present. Patrick opened a bottle of wine as the sun lowered, and then another with dinner. They dined on turtle soup and fresh bread, fruits and cheese, and when Rogan sat back, his hunger for food and family had been sated. He took his time giving them their gifts, watching Camille's eyes light up with every bundle she opened, pleased with Patrick's delight in the gifts Rogan'd brought for him.

And when night fell Rogan joined his father on the verandah. The stars sparkled and the moon hung plump and low in the sapphire sky. All around them the air breathed, soft and warm and fragrant.

Patrick took a small sip of the mellow whiskey before he set it aside, leaned back in his chair, and stretched out his long legs. " 'Twas an interminable year without you, lad. Fine to have you home again."

"I wouldn't have missed your anniversary."

"And that touches your mother's heart, for sure. I haven't seen her so happy in a long while."

"I'm glad for it."

Patrick leaned over a bit and placed his hand on Rogan's shoulder, his long fingers gripping tight. "You won't be staying long, will you."

It wasn't a question, because both men already knew the answer. "I can't, Da."

"Aye, I understand. She was a good girl, and we all miss her."

Rogan fell silent, took a deep draw of whiskey. His blood sang a song he could not respond to, his body tense with urges that would have to be controlled. Another gulp of whiskey slid down his throat, burning, warming, loosening.

"You'll go to England, then?" Patrick asked.

Rogan shrugged. "'Tis good as anywhere. I admit, I'm intrigued." He turned to his father, saw the reflection of the moon in his eyes. "Wouldn't you be?"

"I suppose, aye. I've a favor to ask of you."

"Anything, Da."

"Take Kieran." Patrick cocked his head, sighed. Pain touched his features and he shook his head slowly. "She is restless here, and isn't like to be happy if you go without her. It will be incredibly hard, letting her go, but I worry she'll take matters into her own hands and run off."

"Aye," Rogan murmured his agreement without giving away his sister's confidence. But he worried about his own secrets coming to light. He'd have to be careful, he told himself. "I worry for that, too. Better to send her with me where I can watch over her, than to have her buying passage on some frigate. She's stubborn. Too stubborn."

"Indeed," Patrick agreed, and then he laughed. "So much like your mother, she is. Strong, with minds of their own. No wonder they butt heads, aye?"

"But don't tell Kieran she's like Mum, eh? She's like to bite your head clean off."

Both men chuckled and then fell silent. Rogan sat back, cleared his throat. "Will Mum be all right, then?"

"In time. Truth is, Kieran is two years older than Camille when she knew her own mind so well. She'll not like it, but she will understand it. And aye, she'll be fine." Patrick smiled, a bittersweet expression. "I can see you both as you were as children, clear as yesterday. And look at you now. It isn't easy letting your children go, but 'tis a pleasure like nothing else to watch them become themselves."

Rogan reached out then and touched his father's arm. "You could tell me I'm like you, Da. I'd take it as the compliment it is." He asked for approval, wanting it, even though he knew it was not entirely deserved. He should be stronger, he admonished himself. Better able to cope.

Patrick covered his son's hand with his own, gave it a hard squeeze. "You're a better man than me, laddie. Such strength and grace you've shown in the face of what you've lost. I'm proud of you, Rogan."

Rogan looked up again to the sky, and was grateful for the darkness that his father couldn't see the expression on his face. Memories of the year gone by tore through his mind, split-second images, of blood, sweat, and pain. Things he could not speak about, that would not be understood. His father's pride burned like a brand on his soul, undeserved, unwarranted. What would Patrick really think if he knew, Rogan wondered.

As if reading his thoughts, Patrick spoke.

"I know you've changed, lad. I see the differences in you."

"I've not changed more than anyone would have, aye?"

Patrick didn't answer at first, but took his time as he always did, choosing his words with care. Rogan worried his father would question him about the things Rogan could not hide and would not discuss. Things exposed in inevitable ways: the tightness in his voice, the look in his eyes that could not be easily hidden, revealing his terrible, private pain, and the scars that marred his face and hands.

"Aye, maybe," Patrick remarked slowly. He lifted his whiskey glass, swirled it twice before setting it back to his side without drinking. His gaze drifted upwards to the night sky. "But you're not just anyone, and more a concern to me."

"I'm doing fine, Da. As well as can be expected."

"Aye, you'll be fine, sure."

The patient answer had Rogan silenced, marveling at the way his father could say so much with so little, and the easy, slow lilt in his tone that implied doubt and assurance in the same breath.

Rogan sighed and gulped more whiskey, wishing for the pitching roll of his ship, the crude banter of the sailors, the wild danger of the sea. Beneath those wishes prowled a another desire, one that would have to be contained while he visited his parents. It would not be denied for long, though.

England seemed a fine enough place, the wealth a good enough reason. And there had been the talk of London amongst the sailors, places Rogan wanted to see for himself, where his deeper needs could be satisfied. Rogan decided to see to the re-outfitting of the *Paradise* immediately.

Chapter 2

London, England, 1774

The bodies of hanged thieves and murderers dangled in chains from a public gibbet, their decaying flesh and exposed entrails dripping down their bloated legs, forming noxious puddles of slime that pooled into the ruts and holes on the street beneath them.

Running along the Strand, street urchins and footpads ducked in and out of alleyways, oblivious to the mutilated bodies that hung as a deterrent to the rampant crime, their dirty faces pinched and intent on any potential quarry. They spent their time looking for the slightest sign of inattention or weakness to prey upon, perhaps nicking a handkerchief, a hat, or a cane, or, if they were truly fortunate, a purse.

All around the streets teemed with activity, the unpaved roads rattling with the heavy traffic of coaches, carts and sedan chairs, splashing filth and foul liquid from the deep grooves and puddles onto those who dared to walk the streets.

A carriage of obvious quality but discreetly devoid of adornments pulled to the side of road, the footmen and guards jumping down to the street below and rushing to the door, their weapons ready, their wits quick. They hurried to attend to the occupant who alighted, flanking him so no passersby might perceive his identity.

Their man wore all black, a heavy cloak draped around his shoulders, the collar pulled high against his face, a hat low on his forehead, concealing all but his eyes. They shepherded him indoors, ignoring the lascivious offers of the prostitutes who littered the Strand.

The interior of the house belied its humble exterior and location. It sported tufted leather chairs and deep Turkish rugs. The heavy window hangings of wine-colored, tasseled velvet were closed tight to the outside, obscuring the bolted shutters that guarded against unwanted entrance. Pipe smoke hung in the air, a thin, swirling fog, scented with the cherry bark of the fire, with damp wool from the cloaks drying on hooks, the musky odors of the men who sat around a gaming table, and the spicy whiff of harlots' perfumes.

"Late again, Cousin," Lord Simon Britton chided, and all the men laughed.

Lord Jeffrey Bradburn, the tenth Duke of Eton, shrugged out of his cloak and doffed his hat, depositing them on the last empty hook. To the left of the fireplace stood a table laden with spirits and wines. He poured himself a tall glass of gin, took his seat at the table, sipped deeply and then sighed with relief and delight. Getting to his private club always filled him with a groin-tingling sense of dread and decadent anticipation.

"It is impossible to be on time when traveling through this cesspool we call home," Jeffrey declared emphatically. "Now, what have I missed?"

Simon gathered up the cards and began to shuffle the deck, his watery eyes lit with alcohol and the light cast by candles and fire. He rested a hand on his crotch as he remembered the previous hour. "The first round of lovelies has come and gone, chap."

Jeffrey sighed and licked his lips. Then a disturbing thought came to him. "My prize was not among them?"

"No, good fellow. She's still upstairs."

Jeffrey glared around the table, silent until each of the men had met his gaze. "I have your word that not one of your blackguards touched her?"

He waited as each of the men assured him that they had left the girl alone. After all, why press the unwilling when there were so many who were eager to please?

"Is tonight the night?" Samuel, the Duke of Westminster, asked, his feral face mirroring the excitement of all the men.

The group had formed their extremely private club years before, their own house of lords, meeting once a month to exchange information, play cards, drink gin, and enjoy a steady parade of scantily clad women. And the women were professionals, with whom the men were free to indulge the limits of their fantasies.

Jeffrey, however, never, ever touched the women. His obsessive awareness of the filth and disease of the prostitutes allowed him only to indulge in watching the others sport. When his need became too great, he would allow one to service him with her hands. His own hands and mouth he kept to himself, and saved his darkest desires for the mistresses he kept in his home.

This night, however, was special. Tonight, Jeffrey would take home a new plaything. The stepdaughter of Lord Britton, an engaging woman twenty-one years of age who, Simon assured him, had experienced no men other than Simon himself.

Jeffrey had been keeping a close eye on Simon, seeing to it that the man seemed free of the pox or any other communicable affliction. All seemed well enough, and with a little flourish of his hand, he set down his glass of gin, picked up his hand of freshly dealt cards, and gave a little bow. "Indeed, indeed. Tonight I shall take my winnings home."

"I give you credit, chap," Simon commented casually, sorting through his hand of cards. "The girl is a vigorous minx. As sorry as I am to let her go, 'twas a fair round of cards, and well played by you." Simon ran his palm over his chin, where the girl had bitten him quite smartly and left a scar that would never fade. "She has fangs, though. You are warned."

Jeffrey shrugged broadly, laid down his cards and displayed a full house. "A few trinkets and a well-placed slap, and they all come around."

Simon snorted, folded his hand, and shoved his money over to Jeffrey. "So says you, mate."

"Indeed. I've had many mistresses, and most far too willing. I daresay the challenge of an unwilling wench piques my interest more than one who's quick to bed."

"Do you not mean you prefer one quick with the heel of her boot and a slap of her own?" Samuel asked dryly, eliciting more laughter from the other men.

Jeffrey leaned back in his chair, smoothing his immaculate brocade coat so it wouldn't wrinkle or crease. He looked around at the men, and winked. "Only if I deserve it."

"All this talk of sport gets my blood up," Simon said. "What say you, men? Are we ready for another round?"

Samuel didn't answer, but held his hands above his head and clapped loudly, signaling to the women upstairs that the men had had enough cards and conversation.

"Send down my prize," Jeffrey called, his own blood beginning to race at the thought of the night ahead of him.

The card game he'd won last month had been huge, as Simon lost hand after hand, doubling his bets in an effort to recoup his losses only to lose yet again. The other men dropped out as their purses grew empty and Jeffrey had taken all the spoils, until finally Simon matched all the coin he'd lost to Jeffrey against his stepdaughter, Emeline.

Never before had there been a more exhilarating round of cards; never before had he dared so much, stood to gain another human being. A young woman of intoxicating beauty and charms. He had admired her at Simon's home and at their private house of lords, never even daring to dream she might someday belong to him.

His heart pounded as he heard footsteps and giggles coming from the top of the stairs. He wiped his sweating palms on his handkerchief and dabbed his perspiring upper lip. The stories Simon had told him about the wench inflamed Jeffrey's imagination. She couldn't be more perfect.

Down they came in a parade of exposed flesh and freshly powdered faces, lips painted red and eyes lined dramatically black. One by one they circled the men, reaching out to steal a caress, to run a finger across a waiting cheek, moving slowly enough that they could be fondled as they passed.

The mood of the men changed, their breathing grew heavy, and as if under a hex they all stood, ready to move to the next room, following the women into the room they had designed for pleasure. One by one and two by two, the men paired off with the women, some choosing to watch for a while, some choosing to participate immediately.

Jeffrey stood by the gaming table and waited. At last she descended the steps, taking them slowly as she came into his view, first her ankles, then her legs, her waist, and finally the full length of her.

He was breathless. Even lovelier than he remembered her, she possessed the body of Venus and the face of Paris's Helen. High cheekbones and full lips, dramatic brows arched over eyes the deep, dark blue of midnight. And her hair: it framed the perfection of her face with a beauty all its own. Left to hang to her waist in waves, it glowed a deep, warm honey in the light of the candles.

She stood at the base of the stairs, folded her hands in front of her and met his gaze full on, matching his lusting look with her own regard, her face inscrutable, her posture dignified. Though she stood silent, she radiated something indefinable.

Jeffrey felt the lure of her. He ran a hand through his pale hair, dabbed again at his upper lip. The sounds of pleasure in the next room only heightened his excitement, the blood so thick in his throat he could hardly speak. "You are exquisite."

She lifted her chin and said nothing, for his compliment did not please her, but rather the contrary. Had she the choice, she would have chosen to be born flat of chest and plain of face in order to avoid male attention.

He approached her, noticing her uncommon height, how she nearly stood shoulder to shoulder with him. He leaned over and put his nose to her hair, inhaled her scent, sweet, clean and complex, like honeysuckle and warm summer nights. "Did you bathe today?" he asked.

Again she declined any response.

Using his handkerchief, he lifted her hand, studied it intently, noting the cleanliness of her skin and her neatly trimmed fingernails. He let go of her hand and lifted the skirt of her plain gown, taking care to inspect the condition of her calves and feet, looking for any swelling that might indicate dropsy or sores that could tell tale of leprosy or syphilis. But he saw only finely shaped legs and thin feet encased in simple leather slippers.

The moans in the other room increased, and he felt his ardor match theirs as he looked over this woman who now belonged to him. He again used his handkerchief to touch her, this time tilting her jaw to force her to meet his eyes. "Your silence is charming, and a rare quality in a woman, but mind yourself, dear. You belong to me, and silence or no, 'tis a fact unavoidable."

She met his eyes evenly, her face still expressionless. He let go of her jaw and walked around her in a circle, taking in the elegant length of her neck, the mesmerizing nip of her tiny waist in proportion to the swell of her hips and breasts. "You are magnificent."

He came to stand in front of her once again. "Open your mouth," he instructed.

Emeline held onto what remained of her tattered pride, wrapped it around her heart like a blanket, and remained silent. Opening her mouth, she let him look inside as if she were nothing more than a horse for sale. And in the privacy of her mind, she assured herself that it did not matter what he did or what he thought, that she knew who she was.

Jeffrey inspected closely, saw no rot on her teeth or sores on her gums. Her tongue appeared to be free of pustules and the thick coating that often accompanied illness. "Fine, excellent. You may close your mouth, dear."

He took his handkerchief and dabbed again at his brow and upper lip. She got his blood up, all right, and he wanted to see the rest of her.

But not here; not now. He'd not have her exposing herself more than necessary to the other women and men.

"Go upstairs and fetch your things. We will leave now." Jeffrey rushed to the table and gathered up his winnings, went to the doorway and looked around through the tangles of naked limbs for Simon, catching his eye as he sported with one of the whores. Jeffrey inclined his head to the door and winked.

As Emeline came back down the stairs he saw she held only one small bag. "Is that all of your belongings?"

She didn't reply, but nodded her head ever so slightly.

Jeffrey raised his brows in surprise. He hadn't realized his cousin had denied her so much. Well, he thought, the greater her needs, the easier to control her. He'd have her begging for jewels and gowns in a fortnight, and it would be wonderful to allow her to earn them.

Simon appeared in the doorway, completely naked except for a woman's robe, which he held carelessly against his private parts, revealing as much as he concealed. He strolled out, a smirk on his full lips. "I would say goodbye to my lovely stepdaughter."

Dropping the robe, he grabbed Emeline and held her in his arms, embracing her as he would a lover, ignoring her struggles. He pressed his lips against her ear and whispered, "Do not worry, Emeline. I shall visit you very soon."

She pulled her head back as if she would spit in his face, but she did nothing except stare at him, meeting his eyes with the contempt she felt for him burning in her own.

Jeffrey took Emeline by the arm and pulled her from Simon's grasp, wanting to have her alone. "Come along, dear."

They made it to his carriage without incident, and once they were safely ensconced in the plush interior and on their way he watched her in the light of the lantern. She sat across from him, indifferent to his regard, her posture perfect, her jaw held up and out, defiant and proud. She looked to him like the women of medieval legend, her bone structure speaking volumes of the Nordic invaders who came across the sea and laid claim to the land.

She met his eyes in the swaying carriage, the deep, dark blue enigmatic and yet distantly apathetic. Her silence began to grow tiresome, and Jeffrey began to wonder if he should have accepted Simon's bet. "Perhaps you will enjoy being my mistress, Emeline."

Emeline held tight to her composure as stirrings of fear in her belly and trembling hysteria tugged at her lips, and she wondered if Jeffrey would be as vicious and violent as

Simon. "You are thinking 'tis an improvement on being my stepfather's whore?" she asked.

And her voice, softly rich and a touch husky, went straight to his belly and started a warm glow. He considered the bet well taken. "In a word, yes. You will find that you are not badly used in my home."

She shrugged almost imperceptibly, but he noticed, so closely did he watch her.

"It does not matter to you?" he asked, careful to keep his voice neutral so she wouldn't revert to silence again.

"Nothing matters," she replied flatly.

He pondered this for a few minutes as they rumbled along the road, the cobblestones and deep ruts making for a tremendous amount of noise and bouncing. The lantern swayed on its hook, and the flame guttered and flared as the oil sloshed about. In the uneven light she turned from carved statue to mysterious witch, depending on how the light lit her face.

"You are married?" she asked.

"I am."

"Your wife will not mind my presence overmuch?"

Jeffrey relaxed a bit as he saw some of the cause for her worry. "Quite the contrary, my dear. Anna welcomes my mistresses. You will be treated as no less than a guest in our home."

Emeline raised a brow. She'd thought long ago that nothing could surprise her. "She does not love you at all, then?"

"Love me? Heavens, no. But she does love being a duchess, of that I can assure you."

Inside Emeline waged a war of duty and dread. She watched the duke as carefully as he inspected her, though her reasons for studying him could not have been more different from his. She cared very little for his appearance, though she did feel relieved that he was not grossly fat or covered in a rash. He had an attractive face, with whitish-blond hair and pale blue eyes; the kind of look that, while not unappealing, would be easily forgettable. At least she desperately hoped so, because she knew for an absolute certainty that the face of her stepfather, Simon, would forever be imprinted on her brain.

Still, she watched Jeffrey, looking into his eyes, reading him with the innate knowledge she possessed but did not relish. She saw him clearly, his darkness and dissolution. He wore the expression of perpetual dissatisfaction that often accompanies great wealth, a bored petulance worn thinly over desires long unsatisfied.

"You are so lovely," Jeffrey remarked again, continuing to stare at her like a man wondering what parts of her woman's body he wanted to pinch and penetrate first. It made her want to squirm but she held still, fully controlled. Like an actress onstage, she knew her part and played it to perfection.

Jeffrey rarely risked moving in the carriage, since the swaying of it threatened to pitch him into an unceremonious heap on the floor. But he felt a need to be near her. The look of Emeline had him wanting to caress her, and he could not wait. She seemed so clean to him, pure in a way. He did not even fear touching her. He held to the little sill under the center window and launched himself across the space between himself and Emeline, shifted his body so he pressed beside her, her thigh warm and firm under her skirts as he pressed his own against hers.

"I thought I had everything I had ever hoped for," he murmured, as he reached out to touch the softness of her golden hair. "And then I won you. You are a prize beyond imagining, my dear. So beautiful. So alluring. And you are all mine. My Emeline."

It was too much, his touch, his presence, his odor, all of it. Too much, and her spirit rebelled. She slapped his hand away from her hair. "I am not *your* Emeline. I belong to no man."

At last, Jeffrey thought, here was the minx Simon had boasted about. He laughed and pulled her to him, his greater strength easily overcoming her struggles as he held her arms at her sides and threw his leg across her thighs. He pressed his face in her hair, breathed in deeply the scent of honeysuckle and summer nights, so pure, so clean. "My sweet Emeline," he cooed, and laughed harder as she flushed with anger in the lantern light.

Emeline pushed against his arms, pulling back away from his mouth, not wanting him to be able to press his lips to her skin.

Tears of frustration nipped at the backs of her eyes, but she forced that pointless expression of emotion away, forcing her whole body into submission. She steeled her inner self, reached deep for the only methods she knew for controlling a man. And then she tried to find the courage to use them on Jeffrey, a stranger who would rape her if she did not use her wiles.

Jeffrey pulled her even closer, buried his face into her hair and shook his head like a dog. When that failed to bring her around, he licked her neck, the long slim column of it, and then bit her just under her earlobe. "My sweet Emeline," he repeated, hoping for it to spark another response.

When nothing of that nature worked, he shrugged and shifted his body, took his leg from her thighs and reached down to the hem of her skirt, began pulling it up slowly. "Emeline, Eme-mine," he began to sing, "what are your skirts hiding?"

Just as he got to her thighs, revealed them creamy white and trembling above the hose of her stockings, her hand clamped down on his wrist, her fingers caressing the underside, where his pulse rapidly throbbed, fast as a jackrabbit.

"This is not what you need, Your Grace," her voice said huskily.

Jeffrey's head snapped up, met her eyes. "It is not?"

"No. There are other needs. Darker needs." She held his gaze as her fingers stroked the soft, thin skin over his pulsing veins.

"Emeline," Jeffrey breathed. "What are they?"

Emeline smiled a seductress's smile, a slow, tantalizing curve of full lips that parted, moist and full of promise. She read Jeffrey well, and knew what she needed to do to stop him from forcing himself on her. If she could possess him with desire, she could control him. And once she had him under her control, she could dominate him. But first, she would have to make him crave her as breath itself.

"They are the pleasures that await you, when you and I gratify compulsions too long neglected." Her fingers traveled inside his shirtsleeve, stroking farther up his arm.

Jeffrey hung suspended and still under her spell, heat and awareness tingled beneath her touch. When had anyone ever touched him with such intent? he wondered. He leaned closer to her. "Do you know?"

"I do. I know what you want." Emeline's smile grew secretive.

Jeffrey reached out to cup her face, to kiss her lips. But the carriage shuddered to a stop and shattered the moment. He cursed at himself under his breath as he dropped her skirts to the floor and sat up straight, once again the dignified duke.

The girl was too good, a veritable sorceress. She put him under her power with frightening ease, Jeffrey realized. He would have to teach her a few lessons about how he liked his play.

Jeffrey decided that he would lock her away, keep her only for himself. He envisioned her hidden in solitude, the door barred so only he could enter. Her beauty would be a secret treasure for him alone to plunder, his the only face she would be permitted to see.

He was the master, and she his mistress.

"Come along, Emeline," he coaxed, his tone one that he might use with a small child. "'Tis time to take you to your new home."

Chapter 3

London, England

Rogan stood at the taffrail of the *Paradise*, watching with awe the amount of traffic in the Thames. Boats, barges, skiffs, sloops, and great ocean-greyhound ships plied the waters, many angling for an opening to pull alongside its banks. Sailors, harlots, merchants, and tradesmen teemed on the streets and docks, unending waves of humanity heaving along the riverbanks as far as Rogan's eye could see.

Night fast approached. Everyone seemed frenzied to get their ships set down, and the crew manning the *Paradise* was no exception.

The ship rocked and lurched into a slip at Wapping Dock that Rogan thought looked too tight. The tall masts above his head creaked and groaned as the sails were dropped and secured; pulleys in need of greasing emitted shrill squeaks. The wrenching, rattling scream of thick metal chain links accompanied men cursing and urging each other to push harder, work faster. With the help of men on the docks the hawses were fastened to pilings and the gangplank was dropped into place. The noise of the throngs grew deafening, overridden by the calls and shouts of the crew, many of whom tried to catch the attention of a harlot. Rum flowed amongst the sailors in celebration of a successful voyage.

Rogan handed a sealed note to the first mate, clapped a hand down on the man's shoulder and glared into his eyes. "No whores or pubs until after this note is delivered."

The wizened sailor peered up and into Rogan's handsome face, but saw no good humor in the burning green eyes, only the promise of punishment if he did not do as instructed. "Aye, Sir. After." That said, he rushed down the gangplank with his rolling gait, his bowed legs seeming detached from his hips as he hurried away.

Rogan sighed, wanting to believe that his note would be delivered with the proper haste. He watched the man until he disappeared into the crowd on the docks.

The sun rode low in the darkening sky, a burning orange orb descending over the great river. Rogan watched the fiery ball sink, the gloaming sky a sight to behold. As the sun dropped behind the ships, it back-lit the traffic in the waters. The opaque, churning black Thames gleamed brilliantly beneath their hulls, and turned each man and woman aboard into nothing more than faceless, moving shadows aboard ghostly galleons.

Rogan shook his head to break his own trance, turned, and walked at a quick clip to his sister's cabin, trying to ignore the unaccustomed reek of London. It combined dead fish rotting in the filthy water, coal fires, human waste, and offal of every sort imaginable, into one pervasive stench that Rogan feared would make his sister all the sicker.

After a week at sea Kieran had taken ill with vomiting that at first Rogan thought was seasickness. When it continued for three days, he began to worry. His worry intensified when she worsened with a dry fever that made her mumble in her sleep and thrash about. Things hadn't improved; before Rogan's eyes red spots broke out on her skin. He feared smallpox, until they turned into the oozing, itching pustules of chickenpox. Over and over again, his wife's sickness replayed in his head as he tended his sister, and he prayed he would not fail again.

The ship's doctor, whose skills lay more in treating injuries than illnesses, had wanted to bleed Kieran. When Rogan had staunchly refused that treatment, the doctor threw up his hands in resignation. He had no other remedies to offer. And so Rogan had taken over the care of his sister, and therefore, the weight of the outcome as well.

While he tended to her, Rogan wished the sickness were a beast, a living thing he could hit and punch and kick, something he could kill with his bare hands, tear apart and leave a bloody dead mess at his feet. But those desires he kept inside, safely chained and bound under his control.

He knocked and entered her cabin, his heart lurching at the sight of her lying in her bunk, nearly every bit of exposed skin covered in seeping blisters, her misery written in the expression in her sunken eyes.

Her maid, Jane, who slept in the opposite bunk, stirred as he entered. She'd been helping Rogan take care of Kieran, but was plainly exhausted from the burdens of nursing and her own intermittent seasickness. He gestured for her to lie back down, to keep resting.

"We tied up," he told Kieran. "You made it to London."

"Brilliant," she mumbled, and with an effort she turned to her side, shut her eyes, her breathing heavy with the exhaustion of moving. "When I die you can put me in the ground instead of the sea."

"You will not die."

"Don't be so certain."

"Nonsense. 'Tis the chickenpox, not the plague."

"People die of chickenpox." Kieran opened her eyes and looked at her brother. "You can die from much less."

Rogan didn't reply, couldn't argue that fact. The catarrh

had swept their island two years before, killing several adults and nine children, and afterwards the flux had followed, claiming three more babies. And he knew from his mother that it was not unheard of for a person to go to bed with a sore throat and never wake up again. Illness threatened death every time it struck, and Kieran's high fever scared the hell out of Rogan, for it was the same sort of fever that had killed his wife. But he wouldn't let his fear show. "'Tis time for you to drink your tea."

The tiny, potbellied stove in the corner warded off some of the chilly dampness, and Rogan had at the ready a cast-iron pot filled with steaming water. Carefully following his mother's written instructions in the valise she had packed full of remedies, hc prepared a drink of catnip tea and molasses, which was reputed to lower fever. It didn't seem to be working. Still, he stirred the thick, sticky mixture until the molasses dissolved, and then went to his sister's side, feeding her little sips from the spoon until it was gone. He pressed cold, damp cloths to her forehead, noticing the bones in her face and shoulders, so close now to the skin as she wasted with sickness.

Kieran blinked, her eyes bleary. "I am trying to live, Rogan."

"I know, and look at you, drinking all your tea. You'll be better tomorrow."

"Rogan?" she murmured, "if I die, tell Mum and Da I am sorry."

"I sent word to Uncle Jeffrey." Rogan forced his voice to sound calm, ignoring her talk of death. "I expect him to send a carriage for us before noon tomorrow. I requested he bring his most trusted physician."

Kieran nodded slightly, unable to muster any more strength for speaking.

Rogan returned to the valise his mother had packed, searching through her notes for another remedy he could try to lessen Kieran's fever, praying she would live until the morning. The beast prowled through Kieran's body, taunting Rogan with its strength and power. *I could kill her*, it taunted. *Take her away forever, just like the other one you loved. And there is nothing you can do to stop me.*

Tension ran through his body, tightening his muscles like tensile bands of steel. He wanted to hit something, make it hurt. Let it hit him back, feed the pain, drown the fear. Only then did he feel any sense of control, no matter that he knew it to be the most potent illusion of them all.

Rogan had himself and his sister ready at dawn, their cases packed and waiting by the gangplank. He'd seen to Kieran's needs, helping the maid who could not lift her mistress's weight on her own. With Jane's help, they clothed her in a clean dressing gown, wrapped a thick cloak about her, tucked her feet into warm woolen socks and soft leather slippers, all the while careful to not dislodge the crusts on the sores. He didn't want a single moment wasted when the coach arrived; Kieran needed treatment more than he could provide. More than anything else, she desperately needed to escape her cramped bunk and the dampness of the ship and be ensconced in a clean, dry bed where she could get proper rest.

Rogan stood at the rail, watching the crowds of people coming and going, saw three ships depart on the morning tide. He looked on as lovers embraced each other one final time before one of them took to a ship. His own loneliness tugged at his heart. Stands selling ale and hot food did a brisk business, he noticed, nearly as well as the pickpockets Rogan watched, doing their bump and snatch, quick, clever fingers dipping into pockets even as they helped a person back to their feet.

Finally he saw emerging from the throng a shiny black carriage with a gold ducal crest on its side, the tall iron-banded wheels with gold spindles rattling to a stop in front of their gangplank. Liveried drivers and footmen rode upon the coach, resplendent in matching suits of sedate black. A fine team of eight horses, their coats a glossy brown, fitted with black leather reins, pranced nervously in place as if eager to be back on their way. The spectacle flaunted wealth unimaginable to nearly every citizen of the city.

Rogan called out to a few members of his crew and gave them instructions to load all his belongings on the carriage. He hustled down ahead of them to meet his uncle, but stopped short as the footman held up his hand.

"The Duke was unable to meet you here himself," the footman imparted. "However, His Grace generously sends his physician." He opened a door. Out stepped a man about fifty years of age, his generous belly squeezed into a waistcoat three sizes too small, his face as wide and red and shiny as an apple, a leather satchel in his hand.

"Good day, my lord. I'm Cecil Fleming, and I look after your family's health." He gestured to the ship. "Let's have a look, shall we?"

Something in the man's demeanor bothered Rogan, a casual heartiness that belonged in a tavern, not by a bedside. With a single nod and frown, he led the way to his sister's cabin, determined that he would not leave her alone with him.

When they entered, Rogan noticed that the normally unpleasant smell of her sickroom had turned even more sour, and saw that Kieran had vomited again, this time making it into the pail he'd placed by her bed for that purpose. Rogan took the bucket and set it outside the cabin, pulling the door closed behind him and the doctor.

"It's the chickenpox, all right," Cecil proclaimed with authority.

"'Tis been a fortnight with a fever, and while it lessens

in the day, it is hot enough to cause delirium at night. The sickness ought to be abating by now, should it not?"

Cecil shrugged as broadly as his tight jacket would allow. "Adults get the worst of it, it seems. The children get through, but 'tis the adults who truly suffer." He bent and tugged on Kieran's chin, pulling her mouth open so he could peer inside, saw the blisters on her gums and tongue. "Ah, and in the mouth, too." He made clucking noises in his throat. "That's a shame, isn't it?"

Cecil straightened and opened his satchel, pulled out a long, thin razor and a shallow wooden bowl. Kieran glimpsed the razor and began to quietly cry. The doctor shrugged again, his manner careless. "I'll bleed her and we'll see."

"See what?" Rogan demanded, taking a few steps so he stood between his sister and the doctor.

"See if she lives, of course. Nothing else to be done, really. We let out the bad blood, release the foul humors, and God sees to the rest."

Rogan turned and lifted his sister into his arms with a fluid motion. Holding her slight weight with one arm, he reached into his purse and drew out a few coins, tossed them to the doctor. "Touch her and even God won't be able to help you. Buy your way home; if this is the extent of your abilities, you're not needed further."

Cecil puffed up like an angry bullfrog and began lecturing about the duke and his orders, but Rogan didn't pause to listen. He gestured for Jane to follow, turned, and strode from the cabin, Kieran's face buried against his chest. He carried her down the gangplank, yanked open the door to the carriage without waiting for assistance, and placed his sister inside, taking care to cover her with a lap rug before handing her maid up as well. He hung outside the door and stared into the faces of the surprised drivers. "Take me to my uncle's home. The good doctor will be finding his own way back."

With raised brows they did as instructed, each of them looking to the other in wonder that a man of his station should behave in such a way, and to leave the fine doctor behind, too. The driver shouted to the horses; the carriage lurched into motion, escaping the noise and bustle of the docks and clattering through the busy streets of London.

Kieran lay across from Rogan in the carriage on the bench seat, her eyes closed. Beneath the angry, red blisters, her skin was pale as death. Once again, Rogan prayed for her to survive the day.

Turning away from the heartbreaking sight, Rogan looked out the tiny window, seeing the city in its simultaneous ugliness and magnificence, the filth of its streets, the architectural grandeur of its soot-stained buildings. Hanging signs boasted everything a person could desire, from soaps and potions to textiles and rare spices. They passed pubs and taverns, coffeehouses and tea shops, millinaries and apothecaries, dry-goods and furniture stores, butcher shops and tanneries. Streets branched out at crossroads; alleyways careened crazily between tall buildings.

A soft moan drew Rogan's attention back to his sister. He saw she was awake, the motion of the carriage likely making her sick. Hopefully, he thought, she had vomited enough in the cabin, and would make it to the house before she became ill again.

He moved to sit beside her, pulled her over to him and let her head rest on his shoulder so she could see out the window, hoping the distraction would help. "Here's your London, Kieran," he said gently. "What do you think?"

"Dark," she mumbled. "Stinks."

"Aye, 'tis and does. Mum told us of that, remember?"

She nodded weakly, but her eyes were open wide as she watched the traffic of the city teem all around them.

The crowds and buildings thinned, and the roads grew wider as they left the inner city and headed west to the suburban sprawl where the courtiers and lords set up residence. They began passing large properties bordered with high stone walls, driveways shut with iron gates. The message could not have been more clear: Those who do not belong are not welcome.

Finally the carriage slowed and came to a stop, the footmen leaping down to open the gates. The carriage moved from rutted dirt to the smooth and well-maintained cobblestones of the Bradburn mansion. The carriage came to a halt in the middle of the circular driveway in front of the great home.

"Stay here a moment, while I go see to your rooms," Rogan told Kieran.

She nodded and slid back into a supine position on the seat, her head leaning on her maid's lap, unable to sit up without assistance. Glancing back at her, Rogan was moved with pity and instead picked her up, wanting the staff to see how dire their situation in hopes it would speed them along. He carried his sister, so frail she felt like a child, to the front doors, noticing the immensity of the place. The gray stones spiraled into the sky with turrets and gables, as imposing as a castle. Rather than using the iron lion-headed knocker, Rogan had to kick the door to announce their presence.

A butler answered. Rogan saw with dismay that the surprise on the man's face clearly meant they were not expected. Nonetheless, it was just as obvious the butler knew who they must be.

"My sister needs to lie down," Rogan said, after confirming their identity. "Please show me where she'll be staying."

The butler bowed stiffly, his rigid training and manners forbidding anything other than obedience. He turned without a word and led the way through the mansion.

Opulence abounded. The floors were marble and tall, granite columns bordered all the doorways and arches. Ornately-carved furniture upholstered in jewel-toned, moiré silk perched atop richly-detailed Persian rugs. Thick, heavy velvet framing the floor-to-ceiling windows was now parted to the views of manicured gardens, but could be drawn to keep out winter drafts.

Rogan followed the silent butler down a corridor that led to the wing housing the ballroom and guest suites, up a grand circular staircase, and finally to a suite of rooms for his sister.

Crossing to the bed, Rogan waited as Jane pulled down the silk coverlet and they helped Kieran lie down. He removed her slippers and her cloak and wrapped her in the comfort of the blankets. Mumbling her thanks, Kieran fell asleep within moments. Still silent, the butler directed Jane toward the tiny nook for the attending maid. Jane gratefully entered and pulled the drape, more than ready to join her mistress in much-needed rest.

Rogan indicated his readiness to see his own rooms. The butler turned on his heel with military precision and led Rogan directly across the hall, opened the double doors wide to a suite nearly identical to Kieran's, but decorated in masculine hues of green and burgundy, the chaise between the windows covered in soft, brown leather. His trunks were placed by the armoire and at the foot of his bed. Rogan waved away the servant girls, who had immediately begun unpacking his belongings.

"No need," Rogan assured them. "I'll tend to that later."

The butler inclined his head, his face impassive despite the breach in propriety. "As you wish, my lord." He gestured for the girls to take their leave.

Rogan addressed the butler once again. "I need to see my uncle. Please announce me."

The butler bowed slightly, his face schooled to inscrutable immobility. "I apologize, my lord, but His Grace is unavailable. Every day, between the hours of ten and noon and one and four, unless he sits at Parliament, His Grace attends to matters personal or public. He brooks no intrusions or interruptions of any sort." The butler gestured to the chaise first, and then swept his hand to a bookcase filled with leather-bound volumes. "Does my lord require food or drink whilst he takes his rest?"

Rogan glanced around the room, and ran a quick, frustrated hand through his hair. Clearly the servant meant to confine him to his suite. "'Tis quite urgent that I see my uncle. Surely he can spare a few moments to speak with me. It will not take long."

"I can assure my lord that His Grace will indeed refuse his audience. Such a request will be met with the highest disapproval." The dignified servant bowed low and then stood. He moved to the doorway and stood on the threshold, his spine held punishingly straight. "Please ring the bell should you find your needs have changed. Good afternoon, my lord."

The butler turned on his heel and left, closing the double doors behind himself with a nearly soundless thump.

Sorely bemused, Rogan removed his cloak and hung it in the empty armoire. He used the washbasin to rinse away the film of soot and smoke from his face and hands. Looking in the mirror, Rogan saw how disreputable he appeared. His partially untucked shirt was wrinkled from holding Kieran. Pieces of his thick black hair had fallen loose from its lacing in the back, strands of it hanging in waves around his face.

Rogan opened the larger of his trunks, withdrew a clean shirt of snowy-white linen and a jacket of thick, brushed tan cotton, a compliment to the dark green breeches he wore. He lay the garments on the bed and stripped away his soiled clothing. Noticing a comb on the washstand, he decided to make use of it, but he paused when he caught a glimpse of his body in the looking glass.

Greenish yellow, purple, and red bruises in various stages of healing mottled the skin all around his torso. A few of his ribs had been broken; they knitted improperly together, making for odd striations under his skin. Rogan turned and tried to see his back in the mirror, saw the bruises that wrapped around to the stretch of sun-darkened skin over his kidneys.

Rogan palpated the bruises and winced as he hit a particularly tender spot. Memories of the night before when he'd gotten the newest of the lot were fresh in his mind. The fight had been in the ring below decks, where the men placed bets and rum flowed as freely as the sweat and blood.

Rogan blew out a breath as he shrugged into his shirt, buttoned it, and tucked it into his breeches. He slipped into his jacket, ran the comb through his hair, and retied his lace.

He wandered his rooms, pausing as his eye fixed on a framed map of London, the squiggled lines and unfamiliar names drawing him closer, capturing his attention. He studied it for a long while, memorizing locations, roads, landmarks.

He was bored, unsettled, restless. And he couldn't stop wondering exactly what went on in a household where a guest not only was not welcomed, but was immediately confined to his rooms upon arrival.

"Brooks no intrusions," Rogan muttered. He wandered to the window and looked out on the gardens.

His room faced west, and beneath him the grounds spread out, not in the traditional English, but rather the formal French, manner. Elegant squares were bordered by rigorously tended shrubs that defined each individual garden, centering around a circular gazing pond, from which rose a massive copper sculpture of a lion, the metal aged to a burnished green patina. The lion's jaws gaped open in a silent, perpetual roar, a single paw raised as if on the prowl.

Rogan turned and faced the sumptuously decorated rooms. This mansion, along with various other properties owned by the family, had once served as his mother's home. Camille had for the most part spent her growing-up years in the country home of Beauport, alternating with this London manse. And now her son had arrived, the heir-apparent to all the wealth, prestige, titles, and lands the Bradburns owned, a heritage so weighty and a fortune so great it staggered Rogan's imagination. And yet he had been confined to his rooms by a servant.

It made him smile.

Rogan shrugged away the servant's admonitions, strode across the room, and yanked the door open. He'd tour the mansion that would belong to him and the halls his mother had once walked. If the duke would not see him until after four, so be it, he decided. He would not, however, spend hour after hour waiting on that audience.

Raised in the trade industry, Rogan possessed an experienced eye for excellence. As he paced the long halls, he saw sculptures worth thousands of pounds placed on pedestals in rarely-used guest wings where they would scarcely be seen save by the servants who dusted them. The rugs he walked upon were from Persia and Turkey. The tapestries that hung on the walls dated from medieval times, hundreds of years old and yet meticulously clean and well preserved. Likely, Rogan thought, handed down from generation to generation.

Turning the corner, Rogan found himself in a grandly appointed circular room, the marble floor inlaid with the family crest. Off the room extended four long corridors, each ending with closed double doors. Rogan realized that every single door had been shut along every hallway he had walked. Contrasted with the inviting openness of his parents' home, he thought it odd.

Just as he made to turn and leave the round room he heard the distinctive sound of a person coughing and gagging. He reversed his progress and crept down one of the long halls to where it dead-ended at the solid doors. He listened, and heard nothing more. He leaned his ear against the cool wood of the door and heard what sounded like a soft sigh come from inside, and then another cough and retch. He flinched sympathetically at the sound and waited, hoping for the words of an attending physician or maid. He heard nothing more. To save his bruised knuckles, he rapped on the door with the heel of his palm.

"Not now, I beg you. Not again," came the voice from the other side of the door, a soft, feminine voice that sounded ragged and tired.

Rogan pulled away from the door. Not again? "Who is there?"

Nothing but silence greeted him on the other side. Rogan waited for a long moment, and then thumped on the door again. "Are you ill? Shall I send for help?"

With that he heard her speak again, this time her voice coming clear and close; he could tell she now pressed against the other side of the door, though he had not heard her approach. "Who are you?"

"Rogan Mullen. Who are you?"

"Emeline." No surname or title, he noticed. Just her name, as if that were explanation enough.

"Do you need for me to send for a doctor?"

"No. 'Tis nothing. 'Tis over."

He heard the embarrassment in her tone and pressed no further about the matter.

Without giving thought, Rogan grabbed the doorknob, turned it, and found it locked. He thought about the butler trying to keep him in his rooms, and wondered how many souls in the strange, luxurious mansion were locked behind the many closed doors he'd seen.

"Are you able to open the door?"

"Do you not know who I am?" she asked, not answering his question.

"Ought I know?"

Silence again. When she spoke, she sounded resigned. "You should be on your way."

"You're locked in there, aren't you?"

"I am. What of it?"

He heard anger simmering in her tone, the snap of temper. He grinned at her acerbic manner.

"Have you committed a crime, Emeline?" He deliberately used her name and waited for her to correct him. She didn't.

He heard her sigh, long and deep. "Not really." She spoke so quietly he had to strain to hear her, her irritation completely gone. "Please give me no more thought. I did not intend to have this conversation, and I do not wish to continue it. The door is locked for reasons I do not care to discuss, and which, frankly, are none of your concern. To answer your question, I cannot open the door, and even if I could, there is nowhere I could go. If your curiosity is now sufficiently satisfied, I think 'tis best you left me alone."

Rogan pulled his timepiece from his pocket, consulted it, and saw his uncle would not be available for two hours. He leaned in to the locked doors. "If you're afraid I am going to judge you harshly, fear not. At this point, nothing you could say would surprise me."

"I fear nothing," Emeline replied, "least of all, the opinions of others. Now, please go."

Rogan grinned; the oddness of the situation was beginning to appeal to his dark sense of humor, and the tartness of her tone was most interesting. "I'll make you a deal. If your story intrigues me enough, I'll break you out of there."

A long silence followed, and Rogan wondered if Emeline still stood by the door. Just as he was about to give up and leave, he heard her voice.

"'Tis a long story."

"I have time." He tucked his watch back into his pocket. "About two hours' worth."

"I do not even know who you are."

"As I said, I am Rogan Mullen. Jeffrey Bradburn's nephew."

"Are you very much like him, then?"

"Like him? I suppose you mean in look or personality?" Rogan asked. "I don't know; I suppose 'tis possible I am."

"He will come back soon," she cautioned. "You should not be found speaking to me."

He had a sudden memory of his mother, who, as she hugged him goodbye had whispered a warning in his ear: *Watch yourself in London. Nothing is quite as it seems.* A cold prickling passed down his spine and raised the hairs on the back of his neck. Emeline sounded most worried he would be caught speaking with her.

Rogan looked down the hallway, saw they were still alone, and wondered again why his uncle would have a woman locked away. But despite his curiosity, he did not want to get the girl in trouble.

"I will come again," he assured her. "And when I return, you'll tell me what the hell is going on, aye?"

Without waiting for her to answer, he walked away, more interested than before to confront the man whose blood he shared.

Chapter 4

Rogan wandered the vast mansion, roaming into empty rooms, touching the occasional sculpture, finding great halls and grand parlors, a music room and an enormous library, all devoid of human life save the occasional silent, toiling servant. Camille had told Rogan of the great wealth of her family, but she had failed to convey just what to expect. Everywhere Rogan looked he saw murals and paintings, marble and velvet. Someday it would be his, and that knowledge filled him with a sense of dread as tangible as a stone around his neck. He knew little about English aristocracy, save the disdain his mother held for it, and he wasn't even certain what being a duke entailed.

After a while he checked the time and realized that his uncle be available soon. Rogan found his way back to his suite to wait for the butler to retrieve him.

As punctual as Rogan expected, the servant arrived at his door just as the timepiece on the mantle musically chimed four o'clock, and led the way through the vast halls. Rogan heard a male voice off the main foyer, and followed the butler to that room, an enormous parlor filled with the finest furniture, elegant artwork, and three blazing fireplaces chasing the chill.

The butler bowed as he swept his hand toward the man sitting by the center fireplace. "Your Grace, may I announce your nephew?"

Rogan stood before his uncle, taking in the man's paunchy build and his heavy brocade garments fit for a king. As their gazes met, pale eyes shimmered beneath brows so fair they disappeared against his skin. The duke ceased giving direction to the servant who attended him, dismissed her with a flick of his wrist, and kept his complete attention on Rogan. Each appraised the other openly for a long moment.

"Your sister is ill?" Jeffrey stated with no preamble.

Rogan raised a brow, and concluded that appropriate formalities had been set aside. "She is, but now that she rests in a proper bed and is away from the dampness of the ship and the rigors of travel, she'll soon be recovering."

"My physician was instructed to take her to his home until after the illness passed."

Rogan shook his head. "That butcher was not laying a finger on her, much less taking her anywhere."

"That 'butcher' is one of the finest doctors in all of England," Jeffrey said defensively. "And this is my home, not a hospital. She belongs elsewhere, where she can get the care she requires, and also where she can keep her ill vapors to herself."

Rogan reined in his temper, not wanting his first encounter with his uncle to turn ugly. He forced calmness into his demeanor. "'Tis chickenpox, nothing more. I had it as a boy, and I'm certain Kieran will recover as I did."

"Ah, the chickenpox. Yes, I had that as a boy, also." Jeffrey's posture relaxed. "Is that not an illness one catches only once?"

"Aye, I think so."

"Does she vomit?" Jeffrey asked, and then he waved a hand as if to disperse the question before Rogan could reply. "Never mind, never mind. Why don't you join me for a drink? I want you to make yourself comfortable during your stay, however long that may be. And your sister, also, once she's well, of course."

Rogan sat on one of the silk chairs and accepted a snifter of brandy from the servant who had stood by the parlor doors, still as a statue, until called into action. Jeffrey kept to his seat opposite Rogan, watching him unabashedly.

"You have the look of your mother," he judged finally. "Her eyes and hair. The Bradburn features." His eyes swept over Rogan's build, tall and broad, his well-muscled body lean, his skin dark from the sun, and his face, undeniably handsome but unlike any of their family. Jeffrey felt a wave of envy, suddenly dissatisfied with the paleness of his skin and the thickness of his stomach, paunchy and soft with middle age. "The rest of you must favor the mariner."

"Patrick Rogan Mullen. My father." Rogan allowed himself to sound stern and measured, respect be damned. He did not care how self-important his uncle felt. Duke or no, he would not speak ill of Patrick.

Jeffrey waved his hand again. "Yes, yes, of course. I meant no rudeness. 'Tis a fact, I never met the man, and had quite forgotten his first name."

"Patrick," Rogan repeated flatly.

"Right, of course. And your mother is well, I presume?"

"Your sister, Camille, is very well, and truly happy, as is my father."

Jeffrey grunted as he sipped, nodded his head. "Good, good."

Rogan turned to one of the servants who flanked the doors. "Please post a maid by my sister's rooms. I want to be informed when she wakes."

Jeffrey inclined his head, watched as the servant sprang to action. His eyes glittered with decadent amusement and something darker. "You order them as if you were already the duke and not just a vulture circling my wasting carcass."

Rogan set the brandy snifter down and stood. "I am here to see to my duty as my mother's son, and nothing more. You sent the letter to me, aye? It bears your crest."

With a booming laugh, Jeffrey downed the rest of his brandy. He stretched like a cat, dragged a footstool over with his toe, and propped his stockinged legs onto its soft top. "Ah, you do your English blood proud, ready to fight for your honor. Sit down, nephew, and relax. 'Twas a jest, and nothing more."

Rogan did not sit, but instead walked to stand in front of the fire, hoping its heat would loosen his tension. He looked toward his uncle, who had his head tilted back, still watching him, his expression making Rogan prickle with trepidation. And he wondered if perhaps duty was not enough.

"I am grieved to hear of my cousin's death." Rogan finally spoke the words he had intended to say from the beginning. "I am sorry it is such a sad event that brings us together."

"He was never well. A sickly child, a weak adult. I admit I was not surprised when he took ill and died."

"A huge loss, nonetheless, I'm sure," Rogan stated, though it was nearly a question.

"Of course. As her only child his mother doted on him and she has not rallied these long months since his passing. And I, of course, was left without an heir."

"Not entirely."

"Well, there is you, is there not?"

"Indeed." Rogan turned back to the fire.

"'Tis an awful thing, for a man to contemplate his own death," Jeffrey stated, his tone suddenly quiet and devoid of his previous heartiness. "Even worse, still, to realize that others contemplate it and, in fact, hope for it in earnest."

Rogan turned on his heel and strode away, pausing in the doorway long enough to face his uncle, meeting his eyes full on, not bothering to hide his anger. "I will leave as soon as my sister is well enough to travel. I came out of duty, but I will leave with my pride."

Jeffrey set both his hands on the arms of the chair and vaulted himself to his feet to face his nephew. "Do you dare to lie to me and say you do not want all of this?" He encompassed the room and himself with the sweep of his hand. "Riches beyond your imagining, certainly more than your father could have ever provided for you, and most definitely exceeding anything your mother could have prepared you for. My death will make you one of the richest men in all of England."

"Did you wish for the deaths of both your brothers, that it could all be yours?" Rogan countered. "How dare you question the motive that brings me to your doorstep. I came at your request, and all will pass to me whether I suffer your tutelage or no."

"I did want them dead," Jeffrey admitted freely, ignoring the rest of what Rogan had said. "What else does a third son have to long for? All that faced me was marriage to a woman too plain to catch the eye of a higher lord, and service in the military, where I was like to have my bloody head blown off. The day Eric died I dared to dream for it, and the day Niles died I did a little dance in my bedchamber." He leaned forward and enunciated his words, "And I knew them far better than you know me."

Rogan began to see with absolute clarity why his mother had chosen to leave England and its aristocracy behind without a single look back. He did the same, turning on his heel, returning to the west wing so he could check on Kieran.

Rogan leaned over his sister, his hand pressed to her forehead. He smiled at her reassuringly. "The fever feels cooler, Kieran. You are getting better."

"The damned pox are everywhere," she muttered. "Between

my toes, in my ears and mouth." She blushed beneath her red sores, but could not keep from complaining about the most indignant part of the illness. "Even in my most private of places."

"It could be worse, so try not to complain. It steals your energy for healing." Rogan turned and rinsed a small rag in the basin by the bed, handed her the wet cloth to hold to her face. He longed to discuss what was going on in the house and his exchange with Jeffrey, but she looked so ill he did not want to stress her.

She leaned back into the pillows, still exhausted from the illness but somewhat revived after a long nap and a cup of tea laced with whiskey and honey. "Thank you, Rogan, for caring for me. It can't be pleasant."

He shrugged and put another log on the fire, noticing from the mantle clock that the hour had grown late. The setting sun cast long shadows through the room. "Think nothing of it. You would do the same for me."

Rogan flexed his left hand, swollen, cut, and bruised.

"Still, it must have brought bad memories to you, and I am sorry for that," Kieran pressed, wishing her brother would talk about his pain, rather than flee every time he was faced with his memories.

"Don't, Kieran." He pulled a book from one of her trunks and held it up. "Do you want me to read to you?"

"You cannot say her name," she pressed. "Can you even bear to think it?"

He stood at the side of her bed and looked down on his little sister, leaned over and looked for a place on her face that wasn't poxed, finally settling on a tiny area on her chin. He kissed her there, gently.

"Get some more rest, Kieran," he said as he left.

Rogan closed his sister's door behind him, stood in the dark hallway, and looked down at his hands, flexing them into painful fists, trying to hold onto his emotions.

He went to his rooms, closed and locked the doors, and paced the floor, every muscle in his body tight, his breath ragged. He longed to hit someone, to punch and pummel until blood ran from jagged skin. And he wanted someone to hit him, too. To hurt him physically until he couldn't feel the ache in his heart.

Rogan moved to the window, staring down at the shadows over the gardens cast by the dropping sun, and then up to the sky, watching as it turned to the darker, bluer shades of twilight. The year past, Rogan had watched the sun set from the rail of his ship countless times, dropping behind the endless sea in a spectacle of colors so rich he could not doubt the presence of God. He'd seen it descend behind the vast blue mountains of the Americas, painting the sky with brilliant glory. And last night over the Thames of London, it was a haunting, glowing display of orange and black.

And always, always he was alone. He felt the pain in his chest grow stronger, thicker, and he suddenly didn't long for solitude anymore, but neither did he want to be with someone who knew his past. Not when those around him were wont to press for answers and try to force healing by exposing wounds that were better left under wraps.

Leaving the emptiness of his rooms behind, Rogan made his way through the labyrinthine mansion and found his way back to the hallway that led to Emeline's locked doors, his tread silent. He paused there, uncertain as to why he sought her out, second-guessing his decision to come.

He turned to go. Perhaps he would have a mount saddled, and would ride out his mood, he thought. He'd find the place his sailors had spoken about.

"Is that you, Rogan Mullen?" Emeline inquired quietly.

He stopped. Hesitated.

"Aye," he replied finally, his tone just as quiet as hers.

"Why do you come back?"

He did not answer at first but then asked, "Why do you sit by your doors?"

"I do not care for surprises. I like to be able to hear when someone approaches."

"Why are you locked away, Emeline?"

Silence greeted his question, a long stretch of nothingness that was somehow peaceful and soothing.

"I like how you say my name," she finally said, her voice still hushed. "You are not English, are you?"

"No, not exactly."

"Who, exactly, are you then?"

He leaned his face closer to the crack between the two doors so she'd be certain to hear him. "What do you suggest? A game of Tattle-Secret?"

Inside the room, Emeline laughed, a sound and feeling as unfamiliar to her as freedom. How long had it been since she'd laughed, she wondered. Years. Immediately she silenced it, but the feeling was still there, bubbling up like a warm spring through frozen earth.

"You are wicked," she asserted, her voice rich with her laughter. She could not help but enjoy it; the locked doors keeping him from her made it possible for her to relish the exchange.

"I'm not the one locked in a room," he countered. "Are you a princess, then, hidden away, a maiden whose virtue needs guarding? Tell me, Emeline. Tell me your secret."

Again she was silent, until she breathed, "You truly do not know?"

"If I did, would I continue to ask?"

"I fear you are mocking me."

"Would I mock a stranger whose face I have not even seen?"

Out in the hallway, Rogan heard the silence of her extended pause, as if she were giving deep thought to what he asked. And then she replied, the playful tone back in her voice, but this time it sounded forced. "You have guessed my secret. I am a princess."

"Ah, Princess Emeline. Are you as beautiful as your voice?"

"No, I am very plain. 'Tis quite sad, really."

He grinned, his mood lightening with their game. He decided he would rather play than press for answers. "Poor, plain Princess Emeline."

"Yes. Pity me, Rogan Mullen, for even the sun does not want to expose my pitiful countenance."

"Who needs the fickle sun? It shines on thieves and thanes alike. I prefer the light of candles that are lit with purpose. Their illumination is briefer, but at least they have intention and meaning."

"And what of the thief who basks in the sun's indifferent glory? Is he wasted in your estimation? Is the thief beyond reform?"

Rogan looked at the closed doors in the dimness of the hall, wondering at the sudden sadness in the voice of the woman on the other side of the doors, barred from the rest of the household. And he was back to wanting answers. "Why do you ask? Are you a thief? Is that why you're locked away?"

"Perhaps," she said. "Or perhaps not. I will not tell you. I will only say that I need the sun, Rogan Mullen. I need the promise of it."

"And when night falls, shall I light a candle for you, Princess Emeline?"

"Light it for yourself. I like the darkness, too, just as it is."

He closed his eyes briefly, for she'd unknowingly put words to his own truth. Darkness that cloaked, concealed.

"Why did you come here?" she asked, her voice still hushed.

He opened his eyes, leaned his forehead against the door, and this time spoke the absolute truth, every last vestige of good humor wiped away. "I did not want to be alone. There really is nothing more to it than that, Princess."

"Princess?" Jeffrey said as he turned down the hallway, a candelabra in his left hand, and a key ring dangling from his right. The flames on the candles stretched and shuddered, casting gruesome shadows over the walls. "Look at you, Nephew. A vulture, indeed, and I am not even dead yet. 'Tis not enough you lust for my wealth, but now you must circle about my new toy, as well?"

He shooed Rogan aside, inserted his key and unlocked it, but didn't open the door. He turned back to Rogan, faced him with a decadent smirk. "I will share my home, and later tonight, my dinner table. But my mistress, dear Nephew, is off limits."

Jeffrey paused as he opened the door, stood on the threshold and regarded Rogan with a gimlet gaze. "About your leaving: 'Tis unnecessary. I did request your presence, and I am happy to see that your English blood is proud enough to take offense at my words. 'Twas a test, Nephew, and you acquitted yourself well.

"Dinner is at eight, and we're having guests. I look to see you then."

And he turned and entered, the glow cast by the candles disappearing as he closed the door. Rogan heard the lock turn with a click and the sounds of muted voices as they moved farther into the bedchamber.

Rogan turned and walked briskly away, not wanting to hear any of the lovers' play.

Chapter 5

Rogan sat at the center of the dining table, alone, waiting. The enormous room held a table long enough to accommodate twenty people, with tall candelabras spaced between dangling chandeliers that hung from the high ceiling. Tall French doors leading to a parlor were closed, as were the ones leading to the prep kitchen, though the scents of the food wafted into the room and made Rogan's belly clutch with hunger, reminding him he hadn't eaten since that morning aboard the ship. He took a sip of wine and tried to catch the eye of one of the servants who flanked the doorway to the kitchens, each of them soberly dressed and standing stock still, staring straight ahead, as grave as the King's guard.

The room fairly glittered. Candlelight gleamed on every surface, the darkly polished woods of furniture and floors and moldings set against walls that glistened like buttery satin, crystal stemware and chandeliers and candelabras all shooting prismed light in wild directions, landing on the plates set at each place: creamy porcelain emblazoned with gold-painted crests in the centers, the Bradburn crest.

Rogan took in the elegant riches and tried to picture his mother seated at the table as a young woman. He had a mental image of Camille as she had looked when he said goodbye to her, her black hair streaked with silver and cropped to hang around her shoulders, the thin webbing of laugh lines around her vivid green eyes, her slender figure garbed in simple gowns that flattered but also allowed for movement.

No, he couldn't do it. He couldn't muster the image of Camille tightly corseted in jewel-encrusted silks and velvets, her black hair dressed high on her head, jewelry dripping from her ears, neck, wrists, and fingers.

And yet, that was the life Camille had been born to live.

The clock on the mantle chimed the eighth hour, and in sailed a small woman. Her tiny body was clothed in a gown of rich purple silk, trailing a fur-trimmed train that hung from her shoulders. Her thin brown hair had been lushly curled and pinned around a face that for all its plainness, possessed a certain charm as she smiled a greeting at Rogan. She held out her hand, eyes shining like brown velvet as Rogan pressed a kiss to her ringed fingers.

"I am your Aunt Anna, dear." Anna looked him over from head to heels as he bowed to her, her face lit with womanly approval. "And look at you. Handsome thing, are you not?"

She took her seat across from Rogan, and spread a napkin on her lap, nodded as a servant poured her a tiny glass of wine. "You do not mind waiting for your uncle, do you? He is likely still dressing for dinner."

Rogan kept his face neutral, wondering if his aunt knew who and what had made Jeffrey late for the evening meal. "Of course, Your Grace." He met her eyes, and though he did not want to upset her, he offered his condolences. "Your son, Your Grace. I am so sorry to hear of his passing."

He was rewarded with a melting look in her soft brown eyes, like chocolate set over a low flame.

"Thank you," she said warmly. "Kenley was a sweet boy, and the only of the three children I bore to reach adulthood.

I cannot express how difficult it was, watching him lose his fight for life. He was too ill to even make the trip to take in the waters, not that they helped much the other times we took him. Ah, my poor dear boy, I do miss his quiet company."

And then her face grew even more somber, and she held a hand to her bony chest, just beneath the enormous gold and diamond pendant suspended from a thick necklace. "I received notice last year of your own loss, Rogan, of your young bride. Your mother wrote in her letter that your wife was so lovely, and the whole family reeled from her loss. I hope you are also faring well."

"I'm fine." Rogan abruptly changed the subject, trying to suppress the urges her words resurrected, urges he grew less and less able to control or ignore. "'Tis quite a large home you have."

Anna sat back slightly in her chair and looked around as if she could not believe her good fortune. "Indeed, and is my favorite of the properties we own. I remember visiting your uncles here when they were alive and being completely overwhelmed with it. The day Jeffrey told me this would all be ours, I feared he jested in a most cruel and heartless manner."

Voices sounded in the outer rooms, and the tall doors of the dining room were opened by servants who immediately stood back to allow the guests to enter. A tall man with long gray hair pulled back into a tail strutted into the room. Dressed for dinner, his thick form was resplendently draped in gold and cream brocades, and on his arm he escorted a much younger woman. She was strikingly lovely, her dark hair richly coiled upon her head. A crimson gown was molded to her luscious figure and she caught Rogan's eyes with her own, an expressive gray beneath slashing brows, as watchful and sly as a cat's.

Anna and Rogan both stood to receive their guests, Anna making the introductions to Lord Simon Britton, and his mistress, Lora.

Rogan greeted them without raising his brows at the word "mistress," used so casually by his aunt. London was indeed a different place, he thought. Camille had understated the matter.

"Excellent to meet you," Simon said to Rogan, as he pulled out a chair for Lora. A distantly amused smile curved his full lips though his patrician face appeared bored, full of the dissipation of the very wealthy. "I suppose you're my what, third cousin, twice removed, then?"

"Something like that," Rogan replied, taking his seat.

Simon narrowed his eyes slightly, but then turned to Lora and took her hand, kissed it as he admired her breasts, bewitchingly large, soft, and round above her low décolletage.

"Dear Simon, tear yourself away for a moment and tell me, how is Madeline faring?" Anna asked.

Simon set Lora's hand high on his thigh and covered it possessively with his own, turning to his cousin-in-law. "As mad as a hatter, and no improvement. Her female hysteria has not abated one whit since I took her to Bethlem." Simon sent Rogan a manly wink. "My wife. She seemed as normal as any woman when we married, but quickly lost her mind after the first year. 'Twas a shame."

"And, no doubt, a direct result of living with you," Jeffrey quipped as he entered the great dining room, his voice hearty, his face flushed. He looked at Rogan with eyes that looked glassy and slightly wild. "Met our cousin, eh, boy?"

"Indeed, Uncle."

"Where is she? Will you not be bringing her to dine?" Simon asked Jeffrey. His tone changed, grew harder, insistent. "I would see my stepdaughter and know you do not abuse her overmuch."

"Resting." Jeffrey replied. "Fear not. She is well and happy in her new home."

Rogan listened with appalled intrigue, certain they

spoke of Emeline, and he wondered how it could be that Simon could hand his stepdaughter over to his cousin to have as a mistress. Anna's voice interrupted his thoughts, shattering any further illusions he may have had.

"Why are you not bringing her to dine, Jeffrey? I have not even welcomed her into our home, yet."

"Do not question me. She is resting," Jeffrey repeated, his manner growing impatient. But then he turned to Simon and wiggled his eyebrows. "I put the dear thing through her paces."

"Thank me, Cousin. I taught the wench well."

Rogan listened, keeping his expression as much under control as he could manage. Under the table his hands fisted on his lap, the ache in his knuckles a familiar and welcome pain.

Jeffrey leaned back in his chair, very aware of the subtle shift in Rogan's posture: a stiffening awareness, a coiled readiness. Though Rogan tried to hide it, Jeffrey could see the look of disapproval on the younger man's recklessly handsome face, the fire that burned in his green eyes, the Bradburn eyes—the Bradburn fire. And Jeffrey wished, not for the first time, that he had favored his own father's looks, so he too might possess the appearance the Bradburns were noted for. Jeffrey chose to not address his nephew directly, and turned back to Simon. Let the boy see how a duke lives, he thought. Let him see all that the title brings.

"She is an exciting bit of fluff," Jeffrey declared. "Though I do not regret the wager that gave her to me, I am appalled at your carelessness to have let her go."

Simon shrugged and draped his hand over Lora's shoulders, his fingers trailing across the delicate shape of her collarbones, dipping down lower to fondle the higher curves of her breasts. "The chit was never worth the trouble she put me through. Too much hassle for a tepid toss."

"Tepid? Bah! The girl inflames me as none other."

"Have her, then, as you like. I cannot be bothered to beg and beat her for the simplest favors any longer. My newest preference is skill and seduction. Is it not, Lora, my delicious doxy?"

Rogan stood, faster than he intended, and his chair fell over behind him. With supreme effort to control his temper, he placed both his hands on the table, his fingers splayed lest they form fists. The two men leaned back in their chairs to regard him, his uncle looking annoyed, Simon appearing amused.

"I must ask that you do not speak so casually of abusing a woman," Rogan said evenly.

"Shall we speak formally of it? Last time I fornicated with Emeline, it took her a day to recover, but I was bored within the hour," Simon quipped, and looked to Jeffrey for a laugh.

Struggling for composure, Rogan took a deep breath and met Simon's gaze full on. "Truly, Cousin," he began, biting out each word with deliberate calm, "I ask you to refrain. Need I remind you we are in the presence of ladies?"

"Ladies? Surely you ought to know of what you speak before you open your maw, boy." Simon leaned back a bit further in his chair and dipped his hand into Lora's gown so he could lift her large breast from the low décolletage of her gown. He cradled it in his palm, his thumb idly fondling her rosy red nipple. Lora remained impassive, her only expression one of detached tolerance. "Her Grace is a woman of the world, and this little tasty tidbit beside me is one of the finest and most accomplished courtesans in Londontown. They are hardly offended by me, I can assure you, though Her Grace no doubt dislikes you knocking her Chippendales about."

"Perhaps your manners could use a bit of polish." Rogan kept his temper as firmly in check as possible, even though it turned his voice hard and harsh. "Courtesan or treasured wife, duchess or woman of the world, they are ladies when they share my table."

Simon dropped Lora's breast, scarcely noticing her as she tucked it back into her bodice. Simon kept his gaze on Rogan, eyes sharp and full of nasty light, while his full lips lolled slightly open in the manner of a wolf circling, threatening, assessing this new male for strength and intent.

"You are treading on slippery ground, mate. I hardly feel I require comportment lessons from the spawn of a bogtrotter and a woman who neglected to keep her thighs together."

Needing no further provocation, Rogan grinned at him for a split second, a fast, wild smile that lit his face just before Rogan leapt forward like a panther, quick and deadly, scattering chairs as he grabbed Simon by his elegant cravat and pulled him from his seat.

"Outside, old man. I've had enough." Rogan's voice was deadly calm, and he met the cool ice of his cousin's eyes with the fire in his own.

Simon shoved back at Rogan, but couldn't succeed in prying his hands from his clothes. "I will not be called out like a common tavern rat." He swiveled his head to Jeffrey, looking for support, his outrage evident. But Jeffrey only had a brow raised, his wineglass dangling from his fingers while he watched.

"This is what happens when breeding is neglected," Simon sneered, trying to affect an indifferent mien.

Rogan shook him like a dog, marginally satisfied to see the man's head rattle and the glimmer of real fear seep into his eyes. He heard Lora gasp, but noticed that she'd gotten herself well out of the way. "You're more right than you know, aye?"

Dragging him to the front door, ignoring the protesting tugs on his arms by his aunt and the bellowed orders by his uncle to release the man, Rogan yanked open the door and bodily threw Simon out. And then stood back and watched him scrabble to get up from the granite steps. Rogan wanted nothing more than to pound Simon's patrician face, but he controlled the urge.

"I'll tell you what happens when prissy, fancy blood such as yours gets muddled up with common stock: You breed strength." Rogan said flatly, his fists clenched, ready to strike. He'd been longing for this, and though his cousin didn't provide much in the way of a challenge, he knew it would feel good, just the same.

But he wouldn't do it, not unless provoked further. His father had taught him many things, things that ran deep in his blood, control and restraint, even deeper than his compulsion. "Mind yourself to watch how you speak about my parents and the ladies who share my table, aye?"

"Mongrel. Common, ill-bred, half-breed scum," Simon spat, smoothing out his coat and retying his cravat. He gritted out the worst insult he could summon. *"Irish."*

Rogan didn't respond verbally to the epithets, instead grinned at Simon with infuriating calm. He turned on his heel and faced his aunt and uncle. "I have lost my appetite. Good night."

As Rogan left the foyer and made his way back to the west wing, he couldn't help but notice that Simon's mistress stood in the corner of the dining room, her smoky gray eyes lit with amusement. As he passed by the open door, she looked at him and put her hands together, soundlessly clapping her appreciation.

Simon ate his food without tasting it, grinding the meat to a pulp with his vicious chewing, swallowing his wine in great gulps. Nothing could soothe him; nothing brought satisfaction.

There would be no peace for him until he left the mansion behind and took his ease in his own home, surrounded by his own things, where he could vent his anger in a way that would have Lora spent when he was finished.

To be taken to the door and tossed out—humiliated—filled Simon with impotent rage, for what could he do but swallow his pride? He clearly could not fight the man and hope to win, nor could he give the mongrel the same sort of humiliation, for clearly the mutt had no embarrassment for his lack of parentage, and indeed, did he not walk through the house as if he already owned it?

Simon slammed down his empty wineglass and leveled a look at Jeffrey, who had been avoiding his eyes all through the meal. "I am finished here. I want to see my stepdaughter before I take my leave."

Anna fussed, fluttering her hands, her only relief that it hadn't been a public scene, and certainly not one that Simon would tell tale of to anyone. "Simon, dear, please stay for cigars and brandy. 'Tis a terrible thing my nephew did, but understandable if you think of how things must appear to him. He simply does not understand, but I am certain he will, in time. He is a Bradburn, after all."

"Half," Simon retorted. He turned to Jeffrey. "Emeline. I want to see her before I go."

"Fine, right. Follow me, chap." Jeffrey led the way through the maze of hallways and wings, finally stopping at the dead-end that was Emeline's suite of rooms.

Their playhouse, Jeffrey thought. What a treasure he'd won.

Simon stood over Jeffrey's shoulder as he unlocked the door, and then shoved him out of the way and entered. "I would speak with her alone, for she will not tell me the truth if you are lurking about and able to listen."

"I do not hurt the girl," Jeffrey insisted, his righteous anger ruffled.

"Still, honesty comes best with privacy." Simon closed the door in Jeffrey's face.

Emeline sat on the chaise by the windows in her reading

room, and she set the book she'd been reading aside as her stepfather entered. She showed none of the emotions that swirled inside her like a tempest: hatred, fury, and fear. Fear most of all.

"What do you want?" she asked, her voice calm and cool after years of practiced acting.

"The same thing I always want." He hurled himself on top of her, his mouth ravaging hers, his tongue pushed nearly to her throat. Simon pulled his mouth away and pressed his lips to her ear, his breath hot and stinking of wine and garlic. "Have you missed me, daughter?"

"Like the most vile illness."

"Funny girl. Pity I cannot take you home, for I do long for one of our sessions. No one pleasures me as you do, Emeline."

She cloaked herself in the indifferent demeanor that he hated, clinging to the apathy that had preserved her through the years since Simon married her mother. "Have you ever considered your own depravity, stepfather?"

"No one knows it better than you, hmm?" He pressed his nose to her neck and inhaled, a deep, decadent sniff. "Why don't you tell me the thing I do that repulses you the most?"

"You breathe," she replied calmly. "Now get your fat arse off of me."

Simon glanced to the door and then the mantle clock. He took one last nibble on her earlobe before he slid away and sat beside her on the chaise. "How is Jeffrey?"

"Slightly less revolting than you, but 'tis marginal." Emeline shifted her body, putting a few more inches of space between Simon and herself. "When are you going to tell me what I'm after?"

"In a rush to come back home?" he cooed, and picked up her hand, pressed a kiss to her palm and then licked it. "Do not fret, darling. While it has been the most difficult thing I've ever done, letting you go, Jeffrey never keeps a mistress longer than a few months. You'll be back with me soon enough."

"You know what I want, Simon."

"I do, and soon we shall both be satisfied."

"So why not tell me what I'm looking for?"

"Presently, Emeline, when the opportunity is ripe," he said with a wolfish smile. "'Tis not time yet, for you are still locked away. How will you find what I want if you cannot even leave your rooms?"

"I did not know he would lock me away."

"He is an odd duck, I agree, but a rich and powerful one. Has he indicated when he'll set you free?"

"I am afraid I shall have to convince Jeffrey to let me out. In my own special way, as you can likely imagine."

"Oh, is that so?" His expression changed, and she knew she'd hit a tender spot: his jealousy and possessiveness of her. Simon's tone turned accusatory. "You know, you always pretend you don't enjoy these things, but look how quickly you rely on them. I must conclude that you are lying at some point. Which is it, daughter? Victim or slut?"

Emeline stood up and moved away from him, wishing herself anywhere else but there. Reflexively, she clutched the ties of her robe, fisting them tight in her hands. "I am too tired for these games."

"Exhausted, no doubt." Simon stood then, also, allowed himself an appreciative look at her body, clothed in a simple robe that clung to her lush figure, and the spill of honey colored hair that fell in waves to her waist. "I must go, before Jeffrey gets his ire up at us being here, alone."

Emeline tried to avoid his grasp, but he snagged her by the hair, winding it around his fist as he pulled her into his embrace. He used his grip on her hair to yank her head back, held her still while he pressed his lips to her ear once again, whispering, "I let Jeffrey win for weeks because there is something in this house I want, daughter. It has cost me my favorite plaything, not to mention all the coin I had to lose in the process, and I will not be thwarted now, when we are so close. You are here, in this house, and when the time is right, you will get what I am looking for and you will deliver it to me. And then I will grant you the rest of our bargain, and we will both be satisfied."

He dropped her hair, turned and left, and as Emeline heard the key in the door, she knew it was over. At least for the time being.

She stood in the middle of the room, her arms wrapped around her middle in an embrace, her only other comfort the knowledge that she knew her own mind and that no man, no matter what he took from her body, could ever breach the safety of her own true self. Not as long as she refused to give it away.

She had long ago erected barriers around her heart. They were higher than castle walls, just as thick and hard as stone. They preserved her, protected her, and prevented her from invaders like Simon and Jeffrey. No one, and certainly no man, could touch her truest self.

Those walls, however, could not defend her against the things that lived within them. And so Emeline was isolated, as always, with her sadness, her solitude, and beneath it all, her shame.

Rogan strode into his bedchamber. The beast in him had been awakened. He stripped off his formal clothing, pulled on old black cotton breeches and an oft-mended, black linen shirt, worn and washed so frequently it slid soft as a breath over his hot, bruised skin. He stepped into his boots, laced them and slipped his dagger into the sheath that ran the length of his right calf, and then buckled on his sword belt. He filled a small leather purse with enough coins to see him through the night, secured it in the waistband of his breeches, and grabbed an old, black cloak. Black garments were best for hiding bloodstains.

Rogan left his rooms and navigated through the long hallways of the manse. He exited by way of the kitchens, grabbing up a few slices of bread and meat on his way out, eating as he went. The roasted chicken and hearty bread made a fine dinner for its simplicity and its lack of unwanted company. He set on the path that led to the stables and carriage house.

The air outside was cool and thick with oncoming fog, dampening Rogan's skin. He entered the stables and called for a horse to be saddled. Within a few minutes, the stable lad led out a beautiful gelding, its glossy brown coat gleaming in the light of oil lanterns hanging from iron hooks on the walls.

The stable lad watched with huge, round eyes as Rogan vaulted expertly into the saddle and whirled the horse around. Rogan paid the boy little heed but tossed him a coin for his troubles before urging the horse into motion. He gave the horse his head as they emerged from the stables, taking off at a thundering gallop down the long cobbled driveway that led to the main streets, the pace eating the miles, the noise mercifully drowning his thoughts.

He knew exactly where he was going; *Paradise* crew members who had spent time in London before had often talked of the place. The map from his rooms was emblazoned on his brain; he would find it without difficulty.

The autumn air was a chilly, damp slap on his skin as he leaned into the beast beneath him. He leaned into the beast inside him, too, gave himself over to his pursuit. The roads of London lay before him, a sinuous tangle of streets he traversed with purpose.

Rogan found Oxford Road, followed the noise of the crowd to Oxford Street. The throng could be heard from more than a mile away, a hollow rumble echoing off the low fog that rolled over the streets.

The amphitheater hunkered in the mists, lit inside and out with hundreds of lanterns. The stink of nightsoil, smoke, manure, and sour ale invaded Rogan's nostrils as he neared the squat, crude building. A low post fence spanned the front, horses tethered to it side by side, stamping and tossing their heads as Rogan led his gelding alongside and wrapped the reins around an empty post-ring. He saw an area off to the side, cordoned off with thick chains, keeping safe the carriages that bore crests of every noble rank. Raising a brow at this, Rogan tossed a coin to the men who loitered by the entrance; each sported a shotgun held casually against their shoulders and horse pistols strapped to their waists, their purpose to guard against theft and mayhem.

Up and down the street prostitutes lingered in the darkened doorways of surrounding buildings, their bodies scantily clad despite the damply cold weather. A few of the bolder women stepped out of the shadows into the pools of lantern light, their wide hips swaying provocatively, lips pressed in a seam to hide the rot on their teeth.

A surge came from inside the amphitheater, a wave of cheers crashing over the din of a ringing bell and the booming noise of fists and feet beating against the floor and walls, the crowd bloodthirsty and boiling with anticipation.

Rogan climbed the wooden steps to the entrance, his heartbeat matching the clamor of the crowds, his pulse thundering in his ears. Here he was votary to the thrill and the pain. With steady hands he paid the admission fee and joined the throng inside.

Rogan's every sense was assaulted. The press of bodies heated the stinking air, thick with the reek of unwashed skin and oily hair, the sweat of excitement and exertion, and the faint, coppery scent of blood. Hay slid beneath his boots, laid down to absorb the various fluids that would fall. A raised balcony topped the stalls that sported the boxers. Entrance to the balcony was only accessible from a set of guarded stairs, reserved solely for the peerage. Iron hooks jutted from posts and hung from the ceiling around the entire structure, each suspending crude oil lanterns of iron and puckered glass, black smoke rising in rings from flames and forming a gray cloud that hovered over the heads of the hordes of people who gathered around the center ring.

People of all ages, gender, and class gathered, from young dandies who slummed the bloodsports to take part in the betting, to the common folk who paid dearly just to watch and enjoy a few ales.

The booths beneath the balcony were occupied by fighters wearing nothing but breeches, their faces set in grim lines, their bodies shining with sweat and oil. Finding it just as the sailors had told him, Rogan knew what to do. He found an empty stall and entered it, stripping off his cloak, coat, and weapons, followed by his shirt, boots, and stockings, hung the lot of it on hooks bolted to the walls for that purpose. A small bowl sat on a crude shelf filled with lumps of soft soap, and Rogan grabbed a handful and soaped his hair, having learned onboard his ship that soaped hair was slippery, making it harder to grab and hold. He then helped himself to the little vat of goose-grease, rubbed the stinking mixture onto his skin, grimacing at the smell.

Ready for what came, Rogan leaned against the wall of the booth and assessed the ring, heedless of the two men who battled and the people who screamed their approval as one of the men dropped to his knees and then quickly regained his feet.

Constructed of wood and raised off the ground, the ring had two thick ropes spanning the perimeter. He scanned the length of it, noticing that it was twice the size of the ring they used on his ship. He estimated it to be about twenty-four feet long and wide. And inside him his blood grew hotter, as he imagined stepping over the ropes and toeing up to the center square.

"Ho! A newcomer!" shouted a red-faced man who was suddenly at Rogan's side. His garments spoke of wealth, draped over a paunchy body that swaggered as he moved. He eyed Rogan up, a thorough glance that took in everything. "Where do you hail from, mate?"

"The sea," Rogan replied, raising his voice above the din of the crowd.

"Ah, a mariner, is it?" The man hooked his thumbs in his waistcoat and assessed Rogan again before he peered up into his face. "You're strong. Big. What, fifteen stone?"

"Aye, about that. Maybe a bit more."

"You don't have the look of a salt. Not at all. You wouldn't be playing me, would you?"

"My ship is at Wapping Dock. The *Paradise*." Rogan met the man's gaze evenly. "I'm looking for a fight, aye? If I wanted to spout a bunch of pointless lies I'd be in a pub, not here, stripped to my breeches, greased and ready."

"Fair enough." The man stuck out his hand. He watched Rogan, guessing his accent, not Irish, not English, but educated, certainly. None of the other fighters spoke like that, he knew; most all were tradesmen, longshoremen, or Jews. None of the sailors spoke like him, either, and the man's curiosity grew. "I'm Cheswick Stanhope, Earl of Peterborough. I sponsor a few of the bruisers. Love the sport. Absolutely love it."

Rogan shook his hand as he inclined his head to the ring. "Do I need a sponsor to fight?"

"No, but it helps, if you want big money. Prize-fighting is technically illegal here in England, so if you're looking to line your pockets, you'd best have aristocratic patronage."

"I don't fight for money."

Cheswick raised his brows, his fever-bright face betraying even greater interest. "How's that?"

Behind the earl the crowd howled their approval as one of the fighters grabbed the other by the hair, twisted it in his fist, and dragged him to the ropes. He pinned him against them and began viciously punching him in the face and neck. The blows rained, until finally the pinned fighter fell to his knees and the match stopped. The noise escalated, those who wanted the downed man to stay down shouting for him to yield, those who had money riding on him screaming for him to get up, toe the scratch, fight again.

But the fighter swayed on his knees, finally toppling over. The bell sounded. The other boxer held his hands up high, the noise inside the amphitheater reaching a crescendo.

"Next match!" Cheswick yelled to Rogan.

The crowd cheered, whistling and calling out. Rogan heard "The Butcher," "The Knight of the Cleaver," and "The Swan" being chanted over and again, until finally Cheswick held up his hands, calling for silence.

"Who wants to see a fight?" he bellowed.

The crowd exploded, feet thumping on the floor until the whole building shook.

"We've got a newcomer," Cheswick announced, gesturing to Rogan's stall. "He's a likely bruiser; just look at the size of him."

Rogan leaned against the wooden barricade, his arms folded across his bare chest. Curious eyes traveled all over him, estimating his size, his weight, his brawn. The aristocrats had come down from the balcony and were strolling up and down the booths, looking over the fighters and deciding who would make for a good match. Finally a man was chosen and the crowd cleared a path for him as he jogged up to the ring, cheering him on and screaming his name, "The Swan."

The Swan was at least as big as Rogan, heavily muscled and glistening with oil. His brown hair hung in thick ropes to his shoulders, framing a face that bore a flat nose and scarred lips. His hands were dark brown, stained from the pickling astringent many fighters used to toughen their skin. He worked the crowd, holding up his huge fists and jumping lightly in place, his split grin revealing missing teeth. He was a favorite; the crowd loved him, their cheers spilling over the ring.

"And the newcomer!" Cheswick yelled, gesturing for Rogan to take the ring.

The crowd booed and stomped in an effort to demoralize the new bruiser. Still, they cleared a path for him, hungry for new blood even as they laid bets against him.

Rogan jogged to the ring, his blood a thick thrum in his veins, hot and ready. He ducked through the ropes and tood the scratch, meeting the eyes of The Swan.

Cheswick stood between them so Rogan would look at him. "You know the Broughton Rules?"

Rogan nodded; they were the rules they used on the ship. "No hitting below the belt, no hitting the adversary when he's down, and he's got half a minute to get up. Thirty seconds between rounds, eight seconds to come to the scratch."

"Correct." He leaned in closer to Rogan so he could speak in his ear. "You need a name."

Rogan thought quickly, and then murmured his reply in Cheswick's ear. Cheswick shrugged and turned to the crowd. "Ladies and gents, behold our new bruiser, The Duke!"

Simon and Lora careened through the dark streets in his plush carriage. Simon sat silent, fuming, his anger not the slightest bit abated. In the dim, sputtering light of the lantern swinging on its hook, he could see where his breeches had been soiled just beneath his knee, and the fine gossamer silk of one of his stockings had been gashed, revealing his pale, hairy shin.

"'Tis a lovely night, and there is a show at the Nottingham," Lora said, her tone husky, warm, soft and sweet as spun sugar. "The hour is early, my lord. Do you wish to see a play before you and I put on our own, private show?"

"No," Simon snapped. "Clearly I cannot go there with torn stockings."

She parted her cloak and cupped her breasts, her thumbs teasing the peaks until they hardened, straining like pebbles against the silk of her gown. "No one will look at your legs."

"Lora," he drew out her name with exaggerated patience. Truly, he longed for Emeline's bruised honor and inadvertent sensuality over this over-blown seductress. "Leave me be."

She blew out a little petulant sigh through pursed lips and dropped her breasts along with her coy efforts to entice, leaning back into the plush seats.

"I've no wish for theater. All simpering, whimpering players, and not a one of them able to convince me of the parts they play." Simon gripped the seat beneath him as they rounded a corner, bracing himself against the wild rocking as they hit a few bone-jarring ruts. "I say, I much prefer sport."

The carriage pulled up to the amphitheater, and Simon alighted, handing Lora down. They went up the wooden steps to the humble entrance as their carriage was driven into the lot. They entered the roaring, smoke-filled arena, the pumping excitement itching under Simon's skin, filling his need for violence, satisfying the dark roiling of his anger. Picking their way through the agitated throng, they made their way to the balcony steps, climbing the rickety stairs with care to the elevated seating for nobles.

No one paid them notice, except to raise a hand or nod absently in greeting, turning their attention back to the center ring. Simon took an empty seat on the wooden benches and leaned forward, ready to see a good blood match.

Slowly, his mouth dropped open, certain his eyes betrayed him even as he felt Lora's elbow poke his ribs. He was far too riveted by the sight to take umbrage with the undignified jab. Indeed, he welcomed it, for he realized he was not losing his mind, and that who he thought he saw climbing into the ring was real.

Rogan toed the scratch, met the eyes of the fighter before him, briefly sized him up. He was big and strong, with a glimmer of intelligence in his eyes. By experience, Rogan could gauge his movements, predict his footwork, anticipate his abilities. He noticed The Swan held his arm low across his ribs, as if protecting a weakness. He also noticed that he had a bright pink wound near his right ear, the flesh newly mending; he'd been hit there before not too long ago, hard.

But Rogan also saw through him. Around the ring the crowd screamed and cheered, the noise deafening. The air was thick and stank of sweat and smoke, unwashed bodies and the grease that covered his skin.

But he did not see any of that, could scarcely hear it, didn't smell it. In Rogan's mind he saw eyes of amber and tangles of hair, long and curly and black. He saw toffee skin and a wide, secret smile. He saw his wife.

Orianna.

Rogan held his arms in the stance, right arm cocked, left raised as well, held across his mid-chest, protecting his solar plexus. Sweat popped from his pores and broke through the grease on his body as he bounced lightly on the balls of his feet. His entire body was primed, ready, his muscles hard and taut, straining beneath his skin.

He saw her so clearly, could nearly hear the sound of her voice: *Rogan*. The final thing she'd said, one single word on a breath, nothing more than a whimper, pleading. Or maybe accusing. He would never know.

The bell rang. The fight started fast, hard, each opponent wanting to be the first to hit, the first to injure and weaken the other. Rogan struck out, a solid punch that connected with The Swan's jaw, the satisfying union of flesh and bone he craved. The Swan struck back, and Rogan anticipated his punch, tightened his belly and buckled over the fist, absorbing most of the shock.

They traded blows, and Rogan reveled in it, the mind-less satisfaction of hurting and being hurt. With every hit he saw her; with every punch he took he felt her. Only then was he truly punished for her death. And only then could he release the constant ache that festered inside him like a septic wound.

He was an instrument of pain: giving it, receiving it, needing it, deserving it.

Rogan swung his left arm around, catching The Swan by surprise as he cuffed him in the ear. His skin split under the force, blood ran and mingled with sweat and grease. Rogan hit the spot again, knuckles glancing off as they slicked through the blood, even as The Swan jabbed his ribs again and again, hitting old bruises not yet healed.

The Swan executed his signature move for which he'd been named: he took a sudden step back and flared out his arms, a giant, sweeping wingspan, and then crowded in on Rogan, fists jabbing hard against his back, solid kidney punches, unrelenting and ferocious. The masses screamed their approval, an uproar that shook the roof even as Rogan dropped to his knee.

Pain throbbed through him as The Swan backed off, jogging in place as the throng of people shouted and yelled, thumping the floor, jeering and cheering for him to get up, stand up, toe the scratch.

Rogan counted to four, took a deep breath, centered himself. In his mind he saw her as she lay across his lap, so weak she could not open her eyes. He got to his feet, and the crowd went crazy. They took their thirty second break before returning. Toeing up, Rogan breathed in short bursts, holding to the image of Orianna dying in his arms.

The Swan met his eyes, and spoke. "The Duke, is it? Fancy name fer a bruiser."

Rogan grinned at him in answer, felt the blood from a cut in his hairline trickle down his cheek, run into his mouth and over his teeth, knew it for a dreadful sight, brutally, savagely red. "Brace yourself, Birdie. This is going to hurt."

The bell rang again and Rogan sidestepped The Swan's swings, now able to anticipate him. He ducked easily as The Swan attempted to land a punch above his ear, and then swayed back as The Swan cut over with his left fist, swinging for his nose in a vicious uppercut. With a quickness, Rogan barraged The Swan on the ribs, hitting fast and hard, a ruthless rain of pain. The Swan doubled over, and still Rogan swung, his fists burying into his opponent even as his mind swam with visions of Orianna, dying, fading, a victim to the relentless fever that consumed her body and burned away her life. The Swan wobbled on his feet, and Rogan cut up to the jaw, hitting him with a forceful blow that sent The Swan toppling backwards. He hit the floor with a thud and the crowd was silent for a full five seconds, holding their breath as they realized The Swan wasn't getting back up.

And then someone called out, "All hail, The Duke!"

Fresh screaming erupted, washing over Rogan, the whole building vibrating.

But Rogan barely noticed. He stood in the center of the scratch, his body throbbing, bleeding, bruised, and battered, his demons not even close to exorcised. He could still hear the sound of her dying breath.

Chapter 6

Rogan staggered out of the amphitheater and made his way past the guards, wincing as they slapped his back in congratulations. He found his horse amongst the others tethered to the rail and hoisted himself into the saddle with the remaining dregs of his energy.

Fog had drifted over the city, blanketing it with wispy white tendrils of misty clouds. Rogan, exhausted, leaned over his horse's neck as he picked his way through the city, returning to the mansion. The hour had grown late; after the fight he'd had to endure the offers of aristocratic patronage from various earls and marquis and counts. Not one of them could understand that he did not fight for money, did not wish sponsorship.

How could he explain that he fought himself in that ring, that he fought disease and death and the cauldron of hate they left inside him, boiling like a witches' brew seasoned with his guilt?

Instead of trying to justify what he scarcely understood himself, he had pushed his way through the crowds and left.

The mansion was quiet and mostly dark as he approached. The butler let him in through the front doors with a disapproving pinch of his nostrils, obviously passing the severest judgment regarding the stench of blood, sweat, grease and soap that clung to Rogan like a shadow.

Much later, bathed and attired in fresh garments, Rogan leaned against the windowpane and stared out into the night. He flung his windows open restlessly and took deep breaths of the night air, cool, moist, and smoky, trying to capture a sense of peace.

The fog had lifted somewhat, parted like a curtain in places. Rogan looked up to the sky. The glowing moon was partially obscured; the clouds lacerated in three long, jagged stripes that ran from southeast to northwest, as if something huge had ripped the night open with its claws.

As he gazed up at the moon, her name came unbidden. *Orianna.*

Then her face swam before him, perfect in his memory, as exotic as her gypsy name. Eyes of amber, almond-shaped and lit with humor. Rogan closed his eyes against the flood of memories, the good ones that always followed a fight, a blessing for his temporary exorcism.

For a moment he was not breathing the dense air of London but was, rather, on the island, the night winds scented with jasmine and the salty tang of the sea. Orianna lay beside him as they talked in the dark, the mosquito nets draped around them like a sultan's tent.

And then, the image was gone.

The experience of living without her for the past year taught Rogan many lessons in suffering, and he knew sleep would not come for him any time soon. He left his rooms behind, peeked in on Kieran and saw her soundly sleeping, her light dinner of broth and bread still on the tray by the bed, now cold and stale. He crept back out lest he disturb her, closing the doors behind him. His body felt loose and sore, throbbing with aches he had come to welcome. A scotch sounded good, the mellow whiskey would soothe and bring sleep.

Feeling like a trespasser, he made his way through the sleeping manse. Candlelight wavered around a corner, the glow growing brighter as someone approached.

Jeffrey came into view, a long silk robe draped over his form. He held a brass candelabra, six taper candles dripping wax onto the floor, illuminating his face.

"Rogan!" Jeffrey jumped with a start as he saw him emerge from the shadows. His nephew looked different, menacing, rough and mean. In the candlelight his eyes glowed green, as bright and watchful as those of a cat. "What are you doing? Where have you been?"

"I went into the city."

The answer didn't satisfy Jeffrey, who began to feel annoyed that Rogan had interrupted his peace with his unsettling presence, looming large and radiating danger. "What for?" he snapped. His eyes roamed over Rogan, and he lifted the candelabra for a closer inspection of a glistening patch, shiny and dark in Rogan's hairline. "Are you bleeding?"

"'Tis nothing," Rogan said dismissively. He gestured to the parlor that lay beyond in the vast darkness. "I want a drink. Join me?"

"No." Jeffrey cocked his head and regarded his nephew even closer, saw bruises on his sun-darkened skin. "Were you fighting?"

"Aye. A brawl broke out in a tavern and I defended myself. 'Twas nothing."

"Irish," Jeffrey muttered. "Blood always tells."

"Indeed. Was not your father a philandering womanizer and your mother a control-obsessed harridan? So what does *your* blood tell, Your Grace?"

Surprised and delighted at the comparison to his parentage and the complete lack of respect in Rogan's tone, Jeffrey laughed. "Ah, there's plenty of your mother in you, isn't there?"

Rogan bowed slightly, his demeanor mockingly polite. "So you say, Uncle."

Jeffrey felt the silk of his robe slipping, gapping open. He clutched it, but not before Rogan saw that he was naked beneath the thin silk.

Jeffrey adjusted his ties and then his posture, sticking his chest up and out. "I will to bed now. Good night."

Rogan simply nodded, went to get his drink, poured a stiff scotch, and strolled back to his rooms. He paused in the hallway where he'd met up with his uncle, looked down the darkened corridor, and realized Jeffrey had come from Emeline's chambers.

Rogan found himself heading in that direction, drawn by the enigmatic existence of the woman locked away. He reached the lonely stretch of hallway, lit by only a single oil lamp at the other end, illuminating the path for servants and his uncle. The light barely reached the closed doors, the floor gleamed a dull black in the dimness, the runner of thick Persian wool nothing more than a dark shadow.

He approached her doors quietly and stood in the dimness, sipping his drink, tuned to her presence on the other side of the door. Did she sleep? Was she injured? Did she despise her station here as his uncle's mistress, or had she long ago come to accept it?

He wouldn't have answers, but wondering about her distracted him from his own demons. Rogan leaned against the wall, closed his eyes, and savored the burn of the scotch along with the odd company of the mysterious woman whose face he had never seen.

Emeline heard Rogan approach. She recognized his tread now, different from anyone else who approached her rooms.

The servants came with a brisk pace, to empty the chamber pot or to lay a fire or bring her food and bathing water. Jeffrey came with a certain hesitance, as if he savored the erotic walk to her rooms.

But Rogan's steps were measured and slowed as he approached, as if he came just to be and nothing more.

Emeline left the comfort of her bed, pulled on a robe, took a blanket and pillow, and padded lightly to the door. She sat on the floor and wrapped herself in the warmth of the down-filled comforter, relaxing against the wooden door, knowing he was on the other side. And for that moment, just enjoyed the feeling of being with someone who could take nothing from her but her company.

"Hello, Rogan Mullen."

He leaned closer to the doors, his voice soft and hushed. "Hello, Princess Emeline."

"Princess? Hardly that." But it had been nice talking with him before Jeffrey had come, when Rogan fancied her a lady locked away, her virtue under heavy guard. So simple and sweet and nice.

"I can think of you as I wish, aye?"

"I suppose you can," she said, closing her eyes. It had been a fatiguing, humiliating day, and if he wanted to think of her as princess rather than prostitute, she wouldn't trouble to disabuse him. "You know the truth about me now, anyway."

"I know nothing about you but your name."

"Nonsense. You know why I am here in this house, and why your uncle keeps me under lock and key."

"That tells me a great deal about my uncle, Princess. It tells me nothing about you."

Emeline's eyes flew open at his words. "You cannot possibly mean that."

A long silence stretched between them. Rogan broke it. "Why can't I?"

"Because men do not think that way," she said flatly.

His laugh startled her, and the rich warmth of it filtered to a woman's heart she sometimes forgot she possessed.

"Tell me, Emeline, what goes on in a man's mind?"

Her face burned with mortification at the myriad of thoughts his question instantly prompted. "You should know. I daresay better than I."

He grinned again. "I know what goes on in my mind, aye. But I want to know what you think occupies the thoughts of men."

Who was this man? she asked herself. This man with the deep, whiskey-smooth voice, whose accent was different from any she knew, and who asked for her truths and nothing else. He asked what she thought, who she was, why she was locked away. He launched his questions like well-aimed salvos, hitting her squarely on defenses she had thought impenetrable. Apparently, she was not immune to the powers of understanding. It was a tactic no other man had ever tried with her.

Because he looked for deeper meaning, Emeline found she wanted to give it to him, give him her truth, and at long last allow herself to say what she truly believed. "Men think about their needs, our bodies, our capitulation, their pleasure. Always their pleasure, and always at a woman's expense. They think about how to make a woman submit, how to push her beyond her limits and into theirs. In short, they think about little else but themselves."

Another long silence from Rogan's side of the door caused Emeline to wonder if he had been shocked by her crude tirade and left. But a feeling of relief and something deeper swept through her when she heard his words, heavily tinged with regret.

"You are mistaken. That is not the nature of all men. Some, aye. Too many. But not all."

Feelings she had long thought dead came back twice as strong, of hope and the fancy of childhood dreams about a man worthy of love, who would take that from her and love her in return. And even though she felt relief that she could still be capable of those emotions, she feared them more than anything else, because those sorts of ideals led to only one place: disappointment. This Emeline knew better than anything else. He confused her, muddled her mind, and she wondered how that could be, when she had never even laid eyes on him. "You should go now."

"Why? My uncle has taken to his bed for the night, and I assume he will not visit you until the morrow." His legs felt weak with fatigue and he slid to the floor, stretching them out in front of him, not willing to return to his suite. He sipped his scotch, welcomed the warm burn of it. For all the coldness and discomfort of the floor he sat upon and despite the aches and pains of his body, he felt quiet inside. "In all honesty, Princess, I feel more at peace sitting here than I have felt since I arrived in London. Go to sleep, and I will just stay a while. This hall is more restful than my rooms."

Emeline pictured him in the corridor, leaning against the door of a stranger, her presence his only comfort. And once again, feelings awoke in her, something close to a maternal rush of warmth, of giving and taking comfort, so uncomplicated and yet meaningful. She clamped down on those emotions like a dog attacking an intruder.

She was a practical girl, she reminded herself. He was just a man, like all the others, drawn to her for a reason that would be forever inexplicable. She infused her tone with mocking derision. "You will sit out there in the hallway all night? That is absurd."

"Perhaps it is," Rogan agreed. "But you could take advantage of my presence, stop listening for footsteps for once, and truly sleep."

Emeline let out a long breath, a sigh of longing for just that, mingling with the sweet realization that he knew that about her, had noticed a detail of her that had nothing to do with her physicality.

How many years had it been since she had slept the sleep of the untroubled? she wondered. How many times, deep in the middle of the night after her mother had fallen asleep, had Simon crept into bed beside her, his hand clamped over her mouth, so that she had begun to be alert even as she slept?

An alarm sounded in her mind, screaming that she would not be thinking of painful things if Rogan would only stay away. Her walls were threatened, her defenses momentarily stunned.

She desperately wanted Rogan to leave. And she desperately wanted him to stay. The confusion overwhelmed her.

"You would do that?"

"Aye. 'Twill be a long night for me whether I sit here or in my rooms. Why shouldn't at least one of us get some rest?"

She paused, thinking of his offer and the fatigue in his voice. "You are not tired?"

"I don't usually sleep until daybreak. Go to sleep, Emeline."

"And you will wait?" She had tried to keep her tone dry and acerbic, but even Emeline could hear the disbelief in her voice, as though she had asked him if he would walk on the moon.

"Aye, Princess. I will lie in wait, guarding your door like a dragon fiercely protecting his lady's slumber."

Emeline began to soften, but then realized how much he offered, and the meaning that was likely hidden behind his gentle deep voice.

"What will you want in return?"

If the question did not catch him off guard, perhaps the blunt, hard tone of her voice would, she thought. She could not afford to be swayed by seductive talk. Rogan was a man, and that was all she needed to know of him.

Emeline flinched when he responded, all vestiges of his good humor gone. "If you will ask for an exchange, so be it. Tell me the truth. Why has that pig of a stepfather done this to you?"

The bargain she made with Simon flashed into her mind, her deal with the devil. That Rogan knew her to be a whore was bad enough, but at least he thought her forced. What would he think of her if he knew she had entered into this predicament willingly?

The fact that she even wondered what any man would think of her made her aware of gaps in her armor. Still, she could not bring herself to tell him the truth. "I am his ward, and not in a position to question his motives. Simon is a complicated man, and his reasons are his own."

"Yet your voice trembles when you speak of him," Rogan observed. "Tell me, Princess, if I broke down this door and gave you your freedom, where would you go?"

"I told you before, I have nowhere to go."

"I would help you."

Emeline paused, shifted her weight on the floor. Confusion had her leaning closer to the door. Her voice came soft and wondrous, despite her efforts to the contrary. "You have not even seen me."

"Why do you point that out? You have not seen me, either, yet you keep my company."

"But my face. My body. You have not even laid eyes on me, and yet you would help me. Why? What is in it for you, Rogan?"

"In it for me?" Rogan repeated. "What an awful thing to ask."

She wrapped herself tighter in the blanket. "Why not ask it? Why not lay it out and speak of it plainly? I do not care for hidden motives, concealed meanings, and veiled lies. If it is time with my body you want in exchange for my freedom, 'tis a fair enough bargain, I suppose. But first we must establish how much time, and exactly what you will expect of me."

"I told you before, not all men are like that." His voice sounded stern to her ears; she had insulted his pride, his ethics, his honor.

She did not let that stop her from continuing.

"Nonsense," Emeline said matter-of-factly. "If you saw me, you would want to bed me. Why don't we take this opportunity to iron out the details before it gets muddied up with your lust."

"My parents taught me to never take advantage of another person, woman or man. 'Tis not who I am." And his tone was hot with suppressed heat, like coals beneath a banked fire.

Emeline dismissed the emotions Rogan had stirred in her, a few feelings she had thought lost and a few girlhood longings, all best left forgotten. She had come to that house on a mission, and she'd fulfill her bargain with Simon, get her payoff, and be done with it.

Practicality, she told herself, had preserved her thus far. She would not turn aside from it now, no matter what.

"You may not think of yourself as a person to seek his own advantage, Rogan Mullen, but 'tis precisely what I am. My interests lie in self-preservation. I am an unwilling whore, but a whore just the same, your uncle's mistress, and do not think to romanticize it with talk of princesses and dragons. 'Tis the rescue you want, not the girl. Find another way to relieve your boredom, and leave me out of it."

"You presume too much," Rogan replied. "I offered you my help and asked for nothing in return. I can do no more than that."

Emeline bit her bottom lip before she spoke. "You can go."

Rogan clearly enunciated every word. "'Tis an appalling pity that you confuse compassion with carnal desires and mistake kindness for moral weakness. It pains me to consider what you have survived that has caused you to think so little of all men. But do not worry, Princess. I shall not burden you with my offers of help again."

As Rogan walked away, Emeline pressed her ear against the cold wooden door and listened to the last of his footsteps, her hands fisted in the folds of the blanket that she held around her. She stood alone, convinced he would not return again.

But she trembled, feeling more vulnerable than she'd felt in years, like the young girl she'd once been, a girl without armor. Because his words and his voice had crept inside her gates like fog, and he had catapulted something too dangerous to contemplate over her castle walls.

Like an insidious invader, Rogan had made Emeline consider that some men might be different, at least one man: Rogan. He offered his help and asked for nothing in return. Nothing. He asked her opinions. He laughed at her sarcasm. He sought out her company time and again. He seemed to genuinely *like* her.

All without ever having seen her.

Against that, Emeline realized, she simply had no defense.

Rogan did sleep, though it was fitful and disturbed. In his mind he saw fists and wounds, battled his fears by fighting his opponent, and never truly won.

He woke as a chambermaid entered, heard her gasp, saw her freeze, her hands pressed to her lips. With bleary eyes he saw her shocked gaze and he looked down, saw her cause for concern. With arms that felt like lead, he yanked the tangled sheet out from under his hips to cover his nakedness, then buried his head back into the pillow.

"You may go," he told her, trying to sound pleasant despite a headache pounding mercilessly behind one eye. His body was stiff and achy from The Swan's punishment, and he could scarcely move without pain. "I have no needs. But please see to my sister."

The maid whirled on her heel and left, pausing for one final glance at the man in the bed who slept in his skin and nothing else, all the glory that God gifted him with on full display.

When the door closed behind the maid, Rogan roused himself from the bed, washed his face and rinsed his mouth, pulled on fresh clothes and ran a brush through his hair. He dabbed at his wounds, now crusted and scabbed, and spent a few minutes stretching, loosening his muscles. Then, dressed and ready, his head still throbbing, he made his way to Kieran's room.

The maids were busy, two helping Kieran even as the chambermaid attended to the pot. The one who had walked in on Rogan peeked up at him, her dirty face blazing with color. She smiled at him shyly, a tiny invitation, and bent low and deep so her round bottom would be best displayed as she lifted the chamber pot. Rogan shook his head as he heard the door close behind her, wondering exactly how a woman thought to appear desirable while carrying a pot of piss.

He turned his full attention to Kieran. She looked better. Her color had improved beneath the nasty pox, the dark circles under her eyes faded to little smudges. Her smoky, stormy blue eyes lit when she saw him, and she leaned forward, desperate for company. "Rogan, if you leave me alone all day I shall kill you the moment I gain the strength."

"I am going into the city, but I promise I will visit with you later tonight."

"Noooo!" she wailed, and then, drained of that sudden burst of energy, slumped back into her pillows. "I am bored and lonely and itchy," she complained crossly, "and the girl who comes to lay my fire is covered in scars from this same sort of pox, and she warns me that scratching is what caused them."

"So don't scratch," Rogan said, not caring that he spoke the obvious, and took a seat by the bed, relieved to hear his sister complaining. Since it seemed to be her favorite pastime, he knew her to be feeling better.

Kieran contented herself to pick at the pox on the backs of her knees where scars would not detract from her appearance. "Do not be a jackass, Rogan. 'Tis impossible, and I am miserable just left to lie here and die of boredom whilst I dream of scratching."

"I came to see what your needs are, Kieran, and to ask for a list of books I might get you, or anything else to bide your time." He tried to remember what his sister occupied herself with, besides her usual nonsensical talk of fashion and English court and dancing. His memory provided him with a picture of Kieran bent over fabric. "Sewing? Did you not like to stitch on cloth?"

"'Tis needlepoint, crewel, and tapestry, you bumbling buffoon, and I am an artist." Kieran pulled her blanket higher around her neck and glared at her older brother, but quickly lost her imperious demeanor and reverted to whining. "I do not have the energy to be creative."

He sighed heavily. "What of cards?"

"And whom shall I ask to play? Jane cannot read, despite my efforts to teach her, and she cannot grasp the simplest game. She is sweet, Rogan, but not much company." Kieran stuck out her bottom lip a bit, looking childish and petulant. "I am so bored, and I don't feel well."

"Is there anything you need, Kieran, besides a good whipping?"

"I need chocolate," she whimpered.

"Fine. I shall get you chocolate. Anything else?"

Kieran scratched her scalp as she thought, not from confusion, but because scars wouldn't be seen there, either. "I suppose you could get me some pretty thread, and perhaps some good woolen yarns, and I could maybe work on knitting for a time."

He pressed the heel of his hand against the pounding behind his left eye, wondering what sort of man his sister would ever convince to marry her. "As you wish. Anything else?"

"Some books would be nice, I suppose. Anything you might find with a love story. And some of that lovely lavender cream Mum gets from London. Oh, and do see an apothecary and ask what he has to stop the itching. The itching is making me insane, Rogan. And do get plenty of chocolate, not just a little. And my favorite tea, do you know the kind with the bits of vanilla bean?"

Rogan sighed again, went to the small desk and stripped a quill, dredged it in ink and wrote a list. "Is there anything else, Kieran?"

"No. I think not. But when will you return?"

"I will be back before dark." He bent down to kiss her on the tip of her nose, noting that despite how much better she seemed in mood, she still burned with a low, dry fever. "Try to rest, and I shall ask if any of the maids could be dismissed from their duties to spend time with you."

As Rogan left Kieran to her uncomfortable healing, his heart lightened, despite his throbbing headache. She would live, he was fairly certain, though he knew sometimes illnesses could take sudden bad turns. But she looked so much improved, and she longed to eat and drink again, and Rogan made a mental note to get plenty of her favorites, since the illness had wasted her and left her too thin.

As he made his way through the house, he again felt like a prowler, out of place and unwelcome. The luxury surrounding him seemed like a glittering mirage, ready to burst like a dream if he tried to reach for it. Paintings, marble, sculptures and riches graced the halls and rooms the way a queen wears jewels, easily and by right of birth. He asked himself, for the very first time, if he truly thought he had the rights to a title and such riches. He was not born to it, knew nothing about being a duke, and knew even less about England and all its many unspoken rules.

Rogan found his aunt and uncle breakfasting in the dining room, Anna at one end of the table and Jeffrey at the opposite, so far apart conversation was made impossible. Both of them set down their utensils as he entered. Pinching the spot on his brow where the pain throbbed the worst, he faced his aunt and uncle.

"What is wrong with you?" Jeffrey asked, his tone just short of an accusation.

"My head aches. 'Tis nothing. I would have a word with both of you," Rogan replied.

"Head aches? Anything else? What of your throat? Any griping in your gut?"

"Nothing; just my head. Now, about dinner—"

Jeffrey held up his hand to interrupt Rogan and leaned forward in his chair, looking Rogan over carefully for signs of paleness or sweating. "What of your skin? Oft times the fever begins with an oddness in the skin, like prickling. Other than your head, do you have anything wrong with you at all?"

"Nothing," Rogan repeated, wondering at his uncle's mood. "'Tis a headache, not the onset of plague."

"Ah, but these things start with the odd twinges. Even today my throat feels tight and my nose is running. What illness have you brought to this house, nephew?"

"I am not ill, aye? If I worsen, I'll be sure to let you know."

Jeffrey sat back, relaxed marginally. "Fine, fine, do so. But if it gets serious, keep your illness confined to your rooms. Now, what did you want to say?"

Rogan swept into a formal bow, looked at his aunt first, and then his uncle. "I cannot apologize for tossing Simon out, but I am sorry that my actions put a blemish on the evening."

To his surprise, Jeffrey laughed and then gestured to a chair, motioned for a servant to lay a place for him. "Sit down and eat."

Rogan took a seat and cocked a brow at his uncle, leaning back to allow his plate and silverware to be set in front of him. "That's it? No comments about my Irish blood showing itself?"

Jeffrey shrugged his heavily padded and draped shoulders, the morning light that streamed through the windows rippling the gilt edging on his jacket and setting his jeweled buttons to winking. He used his napkin to wipe his nose, carefully inspecting the clear mucus before tossing the napkin aside and picking up a fresh one from the stack in front of him. "Simon is an acquired taste, and quite crass if one is not accustomed to him." He lifted his teacup and sipped delicately, set it down, and added a touch more sugar. "And besides, if 'tis your wish to make enemies your first night in London with your very own cousin, it really isn't my worry, is it?"

"I do not wish to make it so, Uncle," Rogan replied stiffly, wondering if his pounding head would explode or simply fall from his shoulders and roll around at his feet. "However, truth be told, I am uncomfortable with the situation surrounding the girl, Emeline, and Simon's vulgarity drove me to the end of my tether."

"The situation is none of your concern." Jeffrey scooped up a bit of poached egg with his toast, chewing it even as he narrowed his eyes at Rogan. He spoke with his mouth full, toast and egg bits flying out as he enunciated for effect, stabbing the air with his bread. "She is *my* mistress, dear boy. Mine."

Rogan glanced down at his aunt, saw that she ate peacefully, taking in their exchange with no expression on her own face. "Your Grace," he addressed Anna, "I apologize once again. This is not an appropriate time for us to have this discussion."

Anna set down her fork and knife and smiled serenely. "Rogan, dear, please do not let my presence trouble you. I am not a jealous wife; I know all men trifle with women. Jeffrey and I prefer it this way, a nice clean mistress over the pox-ridden strumpets of Fleet Street."

"Anna, be silent." Jeffrey slapped his toast to his plate. "I will not have you explain my actions, not to him or anyone. I am the Duke of Eton. My needs and my wants are for me to indulge, and they require no explanation."

"But Jeffrey, think about it from Rogan's standpoint. It must seem odd to him, and of course he will expect me to object to the girl." Anna turned to Rogan. "I am quite fine with the arrangement as 'tis, dear. Your uncle finds solace in the arms of his mistress, and I relish the peace of not worrying about a late confinement that would certainly be the death of me."

"Late confinement," Jeffrey scoffed, and he tossed back the rest of his tea and motioned impatiently for his cup to be refilled. He took another napkin and dabbed at his nose, looked at the contents, then dropped it to the floor for a servant to pick up. "The old male dog that limps around the stables runs more a risk of bearing pups than you, wife.

"I have needs, damn it!" he burst out suddenly, slamming his fist on the table and setting the plates to rattling. "I will not be denied anything, and the girl pleases me." He motioned again to a servant and sat back in his chair, glanced over the plate of delicate pastries the servant promptly delivered, selected a few and set them on his plate.

"I will not justify my actions to anyone, much less my nephew or my wife." Jeffrey popped a cream-filled pastry into his mouth whole, chewing it as he spoke. "The girl belongs to me, and I will do with her as I wish until I grow tired of her. When she ceases to gratify me, I will find another who pleases me. And if you don't like it, dear Nephew, you may take your diseased sister and leave."

Rogan leaned across its wide, polished expanse so he could face his uncle. "Your private proclivities are the least of my concerns. I care only for the plight of Emeline."

"Well, Rogan, 'tis my bed or Simon's. I daresay the girl prefers mine. And if she does not?" Jeffrey shrugged again, and bit into another pastry, the cream oozing from his lips as he casually brushed flaky crumbs from his jacket. "'Tis in her best interest to comport herself for her time here. I shall tire of her soon enough."

"And what then? What will you do with her?"

"Send her back to Simon, of course, as she is his ward. What else would I do?"

Rogan glanced about the room, from his placid aunt to his smug uncle, and began to feel as though he were going mad. Was he the only one who saw the insanity of the situation? "She is a human being."

"Indeed. Of course. She is also a woman of relatively low birth, who possesses no dowry and no virtue. If neither Simon nor I take the girl, 'tis to the streets with her, and what will happen to her then? Some sort of sewing job or factory position for a while, until prostitution becomes the only remedy for her poverty."

Jeffrey cocked his head to the side, considered his nephew across the table. "Ranting at me will not change her situation. And for all that, Nephew, if you are so upset about the girl, I shall give her to you when I have had my fill of her."

"I am not asking for your mistress," Rogan said incredulously.

"Your interest is certainly piqued, though." Jeffrey sat back in his chair and wiped his hands on a napkin. "Yes, 'tis what I shall do with her. The poor dear hates Simon;

anyone with eyes can see that. So when I tire of her, you may take charge of the girl, though you will no doubt have Simon to contend with. Make her your mistress or your scullery maid, I care not. Only stop bringing such unpleasantness to my table. It sours my stomach."

Jeffrey set down his napkin, pushed himself away from the table and stood, flicking lint from his sleeve and then smoothing his heavy brocade clothing. "I warn you, chap. You won't get the girl anytime soon. The vixen has a grip on me."

He made to move away from the table, but then glanced once again to the plate of sweets, reached and took two more, eyed Rogan again, his manner distracted. "One more thing, Nephew."

He looked Rogan up and down, pausing on the simple linen shirt and the thick cotton breeches more suited to a ship deck than a mansion dining room, obviously at a loss for why Rogan would choose to garb himself so plainly. "You may want to put on finer garments before you begin accompanying me about town and to Parliament, and if you have none, I will send for my tailor."

Without waiting for a reply or so much as a nod to his wife or to Rogan, Jeffrey turned on his heel and exited, leaving Anna to her quiet breakfast.

Rogan, however, was unconcerned with what he wore or the prospect of meeting the most powerful men in all of England. Standing in the elegant dining room with the morning sun streaming all around him, he realized he had just been promised a person. What seemed even stranger than that, however, was that given the context of the situation, Rogan didn't find it all that strange. Perhaps he was acclimating to England better than he had thought.

Chapter 7

Rogan left the mansion through the prep kitchen and out the rear door of the house. As he went outdoors, he by habit raised his face to the sky, acertaining the weather. But all he saw was clouds and foggy smoke, the sulfurous scent of industrial fires whipped over him on gusty winds that warned of much colder weather to come.

He passed the out-kitchens where women bustled about, their work-weary faces focused on their tasks as they roasted meats and kneaded breads. The whole stone building radiated heat from the oven fires, and one solitary woman who tended a side of roasting pork lifted her head, rolled her shoulders, and wiped a tired hand over her forehead, fatigue etched in every line on a face that still possessed a worn glimmer of beauty. Rogan stood still, watching her, until she felt his gaze and turned to look back at him.

Their eyes met, locked, and then her gaze swept down his body, assessing him down to his heels. He saw a calculating glint take her expression. Her whole body shifted, and at once her figure went from exhausted to expressive, her hips swiveling toward him so he could better appreciate her generous curves through her drab homespun gown.

"May I be helpin' ye, govna?" She smiled for him, lips pressed shut to hide her teeth.

"I am going to the stables," Rogan replied.

"Off fer a ride in ter town, are ye? Care fer some company? I only charge two quid fer me services."

Rogan raised a brow, amused that she would proposition him so openly. He deliberately misinterpreted her offer. "I have no need for a guide, madam. But many thanks."

Moving away from the kitchens he heard feminine laughter, followed by the woman's voice, raised in indignation, "A score of years ago, an' he would 'ave been beggin' fer a ride on ol' Mary."

And then he heard Emeline's voice in his mind, *if you saw me, you would want to bed me*.

Rogan grasped the iron handle of the stable door, yanked it open, suddenly angry. It seemed there was nothing in London for a woman to trade upon if not her looks or her sex.

And then a hard question posed itself in his mind, unwanted and unsought: Why else does a man give a woman his protection and his money, if not for the use of her body, for sex and heirs?

He shook his head as if to fend off the thoughts, countering them with his memories. One in particular stood out, of Orianna when she'd first come to the island, laughing in the market with her mother, their long, black hair hanging in carefree curly tangles, beads and bangles around their necks and wrists and ankles. They bought and sold with abandon, their wild laughter floating around them like perfume, luring people to their side. Rogan had leaned against a table and just watched them, and he had not had a single thought of bedding either one; gypsies came and left, and he never expected anything from them. He hadn't stayed to watch that mother and daughter out of lust or anything resembling it. It was their warmth he basked in.

He saw it with his own mother, his sister; had seen it in

Orianna when she had come to live with him in his cottage after their quick wedding. In a matter of days she had transformed his place, by hanging brightly-dyed, sheer fabrics from the windows, layering the bed with richly colored spreads, and bringing in pottery pots, filling them with flowers. It had meant so much to him then, meant even more to him now.

Rogan mentally answered his own question: men build houses; women make homes.

He wandered the musty, cavernous stables, stirring up dust motes as he walked, stopping at stalls to greet the horses. They were beautiful, every one of them, not like the mangy, scruffy ones his mother preferred. The team of perfectly matched bays stood in a long row of stalls, each horse glistened even in the dim light, their coats carefully brushed to a perfect sheen. A small paint at the end of the row nosed her head over the gate of her pen and snorted at Rogan, as if to draw his attention. He moved to see her, stroked her between her eyes, down and around her nose, charmed as she nibbled his coat.

Rogan called out to a stable lad, asked him to saddle a horse for a ride into town. He waited, stroking the pretty face of the paint, sweeping his hand over the arch of her eyes, down her long nose, and back over again. The horse held still, loving the gentle attention.

The lad led a saddled stallion to Rogan, a leggy black beast with a flashy white blaze between his eyes, danger and power in every defined muscle. Rogan said goodbye to the paint and swung up into the saddle, noticing immediately how the paint seemed to turn and kick her back hooves to him, as if to curse him for choosing a larger, more powerful male over her gentle femininity.

"Give her an extra carrot," Rogan instructed the lad, gesturing to the miffed horse. "And tell her 'tis from me." And wheeling the great stallion around, he headed off to the city streets of London, ready to see it by daylight and peruse all it had to offer if it would be his home.

Emeline sat reading on the chaise in her sitting room, her ears tuned, as always, to the sounds in the hallway. The footsteps she heard were Jeffrey's, she knew, and she waited, her breath held, her belly tensed, hoping desperately that she would not hear the sound of the key being inserted into the lock.

A little whimper escaped her throat when she heard the metal on metal sound of the tumblers in the lock being turned, followed too soon by the knob. But just as fast she composed herself and arranged her expression into one of sultry anticipation.

Today she would do whatever was necessary to gain her freedom in the house, so she could find what Simon wanted and be rewarded her part in the bargain.

Jeffrey entered, wearing a dark burgundy silk robe that hung to his slippered feet, closed and locked the door, and turned to Emeline who had risen to greet him.

"My treasure," he sighed. His eyes skimmed over her tall form, lush with curves and hollows. "You are so beautiful."

"Your Grace. You are looking very well." She curved her lips in the pretense of a smile, wishing so hard it ached inside that Rogan would come, somehow make Jeffrey leave. But time and hard circumstance had taught her well: wishes are for children. So she had scorned Rogan's offer of help, insulted him, and sent him away. She had no one to rely upon but herself now, just as always.

Jeffrey preened, smoothed his hand over his robe and then his hair. "Am I?"

Emeline slowly bit her bottom lip as she looked him up and down. "Indeed."

She enticed him, her heart pounding with what she knew lay in store for her. The part of her mind that stayed rational railed against her own thoughts, that she should even think to wish for Rogan to protect her. A man saving her from a man, her thoughts jeered. As if Rogan would not just as soon deliver the same treatment as Jeffrey, as Simon.

But her face showed none of the war being waged in her mind. Emeline had learned long ago to school her face into submission, just as she learned how to look into another person's expression and see what their intentions were. Simon had taught her well in that regard, and she was so rarely wrong.

Emeline raised an elegant brow and read Jeffrey's face as easily as a page she had skimmed a thousand times; she did not need to ask what he wanted, but she did so anyway, knowing he would delight in telling her. "Does His Grace have a specific fancy?"

"I want it like last time, Eme-mine," Jeffrey whined, sounding like a spoiled child. "Last time was perfect."

"What if it were better than before?" she asked, keeping her tone neutral despite the way her throat nearly gagged on the words.

"Better, you say." Jeffrey moved closer to the bed, every nerve under his skin tingling with excitement. "How so?"

She dropped her eyelids down demurely, to soften her words with coquettish charm. "I shall not tell you until we agree to my terms."

"Terms?"

"Yes, Your Grace. You see, I am proposing an exchange."

His brows gathered into a frown. "You cannot bargain with me. I own you."

"You own me," she agreed, and shifted her body, bringing his eyes to her breasts. "But you have been treated only to crumbs and samples, Your Grace. The smallest tidbits of my concession. You have yet to experience the feast of my complete and utter willingness."

"Is that so?" In his pale eyes the flame of interest caught, flickered, and grew. "Feast, you say."

She made a small sound in her throat, a kittenish purr. "There is a wealth of pleasure you have been denied."

"Why are you withholding your favors?" he demanded.

Emeline didn't answer his question directly, but instead moved closer to him. She held his gaze with her own, and ignored the waves of nausea that gripped her belly. "I see your needs, Your Grace. I see them inside you. Desires that are dark and hidden. I will help you release them, but there is a price. If you will have the feast, I fear it must cost you."

"Anything. I can afford anything," Jeffrey breathed. His eyes bore into hers, and he wondered if he truly knew the things he wanted but never dared to experience. He nearly salivated with anticipation. "Sapphires to match your eyes, opals to glisten on your skin. Gold. As much as you can wear."

Emeline took his hand and led him to the window, thought briefly about flinging it open and launching herself to the ground, running and running away as fast as she could, but knew there was nowhere to go. She stayed put, where the sunlight would drench her hair and turn it to gold. She gestured to the outside. "I am not pleased to be jailed, as if I were prisoner rather than paramour. Let me leave these rooms and be beside you at your table." And she knew enough to ask for too much, that she might get only what she wanted. "I desire fine gowns and jewels, to be escorted to parties, to take my place in your household as your mistress."

Jeffrey paused and considered her requests, thought of his recklessly handsome nephew and how quickly Jeffrey would, quite literally, pale in comparison to Rogan's dark looks, stunning green eyes, and tall, muscled form. He would not play the fat old fool, especially not to Emeline. He shook his head. "My dear, you must understand there is pox in the house. 'Tis your welfare I seek to protect."

Despite the disappointment that threatened to overtake her mission, Emeline pressed on, knowing Simon would soon return to see if she had gained the freedom to find what he sought. "Your Grace, I am beginning to fear for my mind as I spend hour after hour locked away. Can you not confine the one who is ill and let me have a measure of freedom? Who is more important, after all? Who wants to please you more than I? Who understands you, as I do?"

"No one, my dear, 'tis true. No one understands what I need the way you say you do."

"Indeed. Now pleasure me by granting my freedom, and I in turn will pleasure you. Please, Your Grace, do this for me, and in turn, I will fulfill your darkest desires." And even as the words came from her mouth, she forced away her sickness with the knowledge that only by using her wiles would she gain her freedom.

"How dark, Emeline?" Jeffrey rested his trembling hands on the tie that held his robe closed.

"As dark as midnight, Your Grace."

Jeffrey stamped his foot and pouted. "But I do not want to share you."

"Your Grace," Emeline beseeched him, "who would dare to take what belongs to such a great man?"

"But he already comes to your door, just as a dog to a bitch in heat. How did he know you were in here?"

Emeline forced herself to step even closer to Jeffrey, ran her finger across his shoulder and down his arm. She knew he spoke of Rogan. "He must have been lost in your enormous mansion. Only you have a mansion second in size to the king's. Only you, Your Grace."

"'Tis quite big, isn't it?"

"'Tis tremendous."

Jeffrey grabbed her hand, pulled it to his sagging chest, held it over his heart. Her understanding only made him hunger for more, and with a complete loss of his usual control, Jeffrey confessed to Emeline as he never had to another soul. "I am afraid. So afraid."

Emeline inwardly sighed. She gently stroked his hair with her free hand. "What frightens you?"

"They all died. All the dukes." Jeffrey's eyes grew glassy and strange, as he looked at her with hysteria seeping into his voice, turning it frantic. "My father. My brothers. Their sons, my son. All the dukes, and their heirs. I am the only one left." His eyes began to dart from side to side. "Sickness. It is everywhere. And dangers. One never knows what may happen."

"But you are a great big man, strapping and strong," Emeline replied, keeping her voice gentle. "Nothing will happen to you. You will die a very old duke, in your bed, in your sleep, painlessly and peacefully. I know it."

"Do you think 'tis so? Truly?"

As he looked at her, his pale eyes pleading for reassurance, Emeline felt a touch of pity for him. She couldn't help but wonder what his family had been like to make him so desperate, his lust for discipline and love tangled together and disguised in the absurd roles he played. Had any of the Bradburns ever found real love? she wondered. "I do, Your Grace. Do not worry. I know 'tis true."

Jeffrey pouted again, wanting to give Emeline what she requested; she asked for so little, really, when weighed against the pleasure she brought him and the delight she promised.

Still, if he let her out, Emeline would see Rogan, and Rogan would see Emeline. Jeffrey matched them in his mind's eye, his fair mistress with his dark nephew, both so young and beautiful and fresh, their skin smelling sweetly of vigorous youth and good health. They would find the attraction for each other that no one had ever felt for him. Always alone, always unloved, forever deprived.

"I do not wish to share you," he said petulantly.

"No one will sample me. No one but you." And then Emeline spoke the truth. "I do not desire any man's touch."

"But mine, of course."

Emeline smiled and raised a brow. "As you wish it, Your Grace."

Jeffrey undid the sash and shrugged out of his robe, let it fall in a puddle around his feet. He stood before her, a ghostly pale, overweight man with thinning hair and bandy legs too thin for his thick torso.

"Done. I cannot wait any longer."

"Your word. I must have it," she pressed, her own body shaking inside, sickness churning. She swept her gaze over him, curved her lips in a smile that promised everything. A means to an end, she thought. The vilest means of them all.

"You have my word. You shall earn your freedom." Jeffrey nodded, his decision made, and held out his arms. "And I shall have my feast."

Bristol stank of the canals that ran through it, rank with rotting fish and dumped waste of every sort, human, animal, and industrial. The daylight revealed its depredation: buildings erected for trade, docks built for commerce, streets lined with tatty signs advertising the swelling ranks of shippers, brokers, dealers, wholesalers and hauliers.

Simon stepped off the barge on which he'd arrived, gingerly making his way across a dock that was as thick with sailors and traders as it was slippery with the growth of algae and also ale, spilled from a broken keg.

The man waiting for him with a carriage tipped his hat in greeting as Simon arrived, then stuck out his hand.

"I'm Graham," he said.

"Britton." Simon gestured to the carriage. "Let's go. I want to be done and back on the damned barge before too long."

If Graham bristled at the blunt order, it did not register on his thin face. With the flare of his expensive cloak, he turned and hoisted his narrow frame into the interior, took

a seat and waited patiently as Simon did the same. They
began to move the instant Simon closed the door.

Inside the confines of carriage, surrounded by rich furs
draped across the seats for warmth and comfort, Simon
leaned back and folded his arms across his chest.

"'Tis appalling I needed to come all the way to Bristol,"
Simon complained. "I should be able to conduct my business on the Thames, at the Exchange."

Graham shrugged his thin shoulders, his lips twisted into
a wry smirk. "Tell me. The bleeding Reformists, the bloody
abolitionists, that damned Sommersett case. It wasn't too
many years ago we had over 100 ships leaving our port
per year, 300 slaves per ship. We're down to nearly half as
many ships now. Nearly *half*. And damned Liverpool is
sucking us dry. Bone dry."

Simon shook his head in agreement, his disgust written
on his face. "I know, chap. What England needs is strength
and development, and instead she cripples herself with
senseless Acts of Parliament, where my voice of reason is
too often drowned by petitions for rights and sensibility.
Bah! Shore up our defenses, build, build, build, I say, ships,
militia, munitions. Keep the strongest slaves and make them
soldiers. Instead we ship them to the Americas and the
Indies, and what does that accomplish? It strengthens them
and weakens us." He spread his hands. "No one listens."

"I agree completely, but what can one do but secure one's
own fortune? I cannot waste my efforts to change other
minds. Cannot waste it."

"Right." Simon rubbed his hands together briskly, warming them against the damp chill. "So, what sort of selection
will I have? I don't want slim pickings."

"You're in luck, my lord. In luck, I say. The ship has not
sailed, and 'tis full to bursting. You'll have the choicest, I
tell you. The choicest. I have one in particular in mind.
You'll be pleased, I think. Very pleased."

"Very good. I want to be done with this business and

back in London straight away. Can't get back too soon." He wrinkled his nose at the stench of the canal they rode alongside even as he thought of the many pieces of unfinished business that awaited him. The journey from London to Bristol and back again was long and uncomfortable. But if he found what he was looking for it would be well worth the effort and expense.

They pulled up to an enormous brick building and Simon and Graham climbed from the carriage. Following the man, Simon entered, the gloomy interior blasting his face with its acrid scents of urine and sweat, instantly coating his sinuses with the stench of desperation. The voices of hundreds of men all speaking at once assaulted his ears, a din of dialects, accents, and languages.

The walls inside had once been plastered but the dampness had eaten at it like a cancer, leaving the exposed brick to gape through the holes, reddish bones rising through rotting flesh.

Bodies occupied nearly every square foot of exposed floor, a veritable human sea of black flesh, seething with motion and life. Most of the men were tall, fit, and dark as night, their only clothing scant loincloths. In the dim lighting of the warehouse, the whites of their eyes glowed eerily against the darkness of their irises and skin. Around the perimeter stood white men armed with pistols and whips, their faces grim and watchful.

"They're to be shipped tomorrow," Graham yelled above the noise and commotion. "Your timing could not be better, my lord, and 'tis a healthy bunch, too. Not even one case of cholera or typhus yet. A healthy bunch. This warehouse is all male; the women and children are kept about a mile away. Otherwise they'd all be rutting and fighting like a pack of wolves. Rutting and fighting."

"Fine. Good," Simon replied, anxious to get underway with his mission. He reached into his coat and withdrew a scented handkerchief, and made a pretense of wiping his nose to give him a momentary reprieve from the stench. "Do it."

Graham gestured to a few of the overseers. They clanged great bells, signaling silence and attention. Graham walked through the center of the masses, and Simon followed him. He kept his shoulders back and his head up, did his ultimate to not show his fear, hoped they could not smell it on him. There were so many of them. It seemed they all stared at him with an oppressive, threatening silence. Finally they reached the back of the warehouse. Simon breathed a sigh of relief as they emerged unmolested from the throng.

"Here's where he is." Graham led the way to the far corner in the rear where a few crude stalls had been erected. "We chained him because he killed one of the other males in a fight. Ordinarily we'd have put him down as an example to the others, but the fact is, 'twas a clean brawl. He was something of a tribal leader, they say, and was defending something or other. So we chained him, so they'd see that he'd been punished."

Simon paused in the opening of the stall, felt his pulse kick up. The man was huge, a black bull thick with muscle. The bones in his face were chiseled and elegant, high cheekbones and a flaring nose with a bridge as flat and straight as a knife. Like the others, he wore nothing more than a loincloth, but did so with a contemptuous dignity that garnered Simon's instant admiration and fear. The iron bands cuffing his wrists and ankles were thick and heavy, but the man lifted his hand to shoo away a fly with unfettered ease.

Simon's throat grew dry with excitement as he envisioned the black bull pitted against Rogan.

"Can he speak English?" Simon asked.

"Some. Probably more than he lets on, like the lot of them. Fact is, we try to pick up our cargo from various ports so they can't communicate, and still, they pick up the English from the overseers and sailors, combine it with their own pidgin language."

"His name," Simon rasped, sounding breathless.

"Whatever you want it to be."

Simon moved into the stall, close enough to the man that he could smell his skin, yeasty and virile. The black slave lifted his chin enough that he met Simon's gaze dead on.

"Will you fight for sport?" Simon asked him. "If you are shipped to the Americas you will toil for the rest of your days. For me, you will fight and nothing more. Do you understand?"

The slave did not reply, but curled his hands into fists and held them up. He understood.

Simon's excitement increased, a tingling in his blood that was almost sexual. "If you fight for me and win, I will set you free. Do you understand?"

Still the slave did not reply, but he nodded his head. Yes; he comprehended that as well.

Simon turned to Graham, reached into his coat and withdrew a sack of coins. "I want him. Name the price."

Jeffrey pulled his robe on and tied the belt. His body felt warm and drugged, and his mind more quiet than ever before. It was almost as if Emeline had reached inside him, dug out his desires, and then satisfied them one by one. He did not know how she knew him so intimately. And he didn't care, not when she belonged to him. With a hand that felt heavy, he reached out and caressed Emeline's jaw, pausing at her chin.

"You do please me, dear thing. And I will allow you what you request. Your stepfather will come to dinner on Friday night, and I shall have you to join us."

Knowing this to be a victory and the first step toward meeting her goal, Emeline inclined her head and smiled. Five more days locked away and then Simon would see her freedom for himself. The bargain stood one step closer to fulfillment. "Thank you, Your Grace."

He waved his hand magnanimously. "Of course, dear. Now, I shall also send a dressmaker to see you first thing in the morning, and you may choose whatever your heart desires. As many gowns as you wish, dear thing. I would have my cousin see that you are very well cared for indeed, so garb yourself accordingly."

Emeline felt the bile return, its slick waves of sickness churning in her belly. "His Grace is too generous."

"'Tis nothing, really. Am I not a wealthy duke to shower my most favored mistress with such finery?"

Emeline bowed her head, breathing deeply to settle her stomach. "You are a great duke."

Jeffrey nodded once in agreement and went to the door, ready to leave. He turned back to Emeline as he took out the key. "I will return tomorrow, and I will be looking forward to having another feast."

He left and Emeline ran to the pot in her bathing room, doubled over it as she clutched her roiling gut, and vomited until her ribs ached mercilessly. When it was over she crawled to the washstand, reached up and grabbed a cloth she had dampened and lathered before he had arrived. She scrubbed her hands and her face, her arms and her breasts with the cold soapy rag. She scoured her skin where his had touched hers until she felt as raw on the outside as she did on the inside, even though she knew that shame cannot be vomited out, nor can it be washed away.

Chapter 8

Rogan traversed the streets of London with a sense of wonder and disgust, his horse splashing through the slop-filled gullies in the streets. All around him people of all ages and classes went about their daily business. Rogan saw urchins in tattered, filthy rags brushing past ladies who shopped attired in silks and velvets and furs.

Rogan worked his way through ten shops to find the items Kieran requested, and as he did he was amazed at the oddities he saw. A particular store sold nothing but kcys, and as the toothless shopkeeper informed Rogan with whispers and backward glances, keys carried great mystical powers. Rogan could risk purchasing the key to the abyss or the key that Jesus gave Peter. A key, the shopkeeper warned, can tell a story. It is a clue. It has vast powers, the nature of which can be spiritual or magical. Buy a key, the shopkeeper dared, and see what door it opens.

Rogan thought of Emeline locked away as he held a brass key similar to those in the Bradburn manse. Its cool, smooth weight on his palm had him wondering what he would find if he opened her door. And it made him consider that perhaps he was allowing himself to become too concerned for, and too interested in, his uncle's mistress.

To the shopkeeper's dismay, Rogan left the store without purchasing anything.

Later that afternoon, Rogan traveled back through the city with full saddlebags and a much lighter purse. As he neared the western extremity of London, a throng of people clogging cross streets caught him in their midst. His horse stamped and reared. Rogan reached forward to calm him, urging the beast forward. Up ahead he saw the cause of the crowd.

The public hangings were over. The naked corpses had been piled on a cart, their clothes already purchased; what the hangman didn't want for himself got auctioned to the crowd. Stragglers milled about, on the grounds surrounding the gallows and in the grandstands. Some called out prices for the dead with teary wails, obviously the family of the condemned hoping to save their loved ones the further humiliation of dissection by surgeons. Only those slated for burial could be purchased; the murderers and thieves got sent to the public gibbet.

Rogan pulled his mount to a stop at the corner of the grandstands, glanced up and saw a crudely painted sign over the permanent wooden structure, MOTHER PROCTOR'S PEWS. A few men in the crowd began to cheer, drawing Rogan's attention back to the gallows. He watched as a lovely young woman, barely twenty years of age and dressed in the modest homespun of a servant, climbed the ladder to the hanging platform and presented herself to the hangman.

Rogan called out to a man who walked by. "What is she doing?"

"Gettin' the death sweat," the man replied, and he grinned up to Rogan with a mouth full of rotted teeth and gaping holes. "Aye, the crowd got its blood, and now titties ter boot. A foin day at Tyburn."

The young woman, pale and trembling in the executioner's arms, pulled down the bodice of her gown and exposed her breasts. Her cheeks flushed red as the men in the audience began to cheer. But she held to her resolve. The hangman picked up a limp arm from the cart of corpses and placed the lifeless hand on her naked, wobbling breasts for a moment. When the woman nodded her satisfaction, the executioner took away the hand as the woman smiled up at him and covered herself.

"Why?" Rogan asked the man beside him. The men in the crowd were hooting and cheering for the woman to have her bum touched, as well, and the man beside Rogan was no exception. Rogan ignored the frown of annoyance the man shot him. "Why would she do such a thing?"

"The death sweats got the power."

"What power?"

"Ter 'eal 'er. She's like to 'ave the fevers or the pox. Maybe the morbid sore throat's been at 'er 'ouse." The man shifted his weight and considered Rogan. His expression changed from aggravation to one of interest. "'Oo don't know about the magic o' the executed? Ye ain't English, is ye?"

"Not exactly," Rogan replied.

The stranger peered up at Rogan. His eyes darted quickly, assessing the richness of Rogan's clothes and mount. "Ye got a few shillins fer a bloke down on 'is luck, govna?"

Rogan dipped into his purse and flipped the man a coin. The man moved on and Rogan remained, his attention back on the gallows. A queue of parents and their babies had formed in front of the pile of the hanged. Each in turn held up their children to be stroked by the dead. Once satisfied, they tossed a few quid to the hangman for his trouble and carried their offspring away, their place immediately taken by the next parent and child.

Rogan had seen enough. He wheeled his stallion around and rode back to the mansion, deep in thought.

Rogan sat in the dark. He had long since snuffed the candles, the heavy scents of pooling wax and wood smoke from his dying fire mingled with the night air that breathed through his open window. He'd pulled a chair over and sat looking out at the sky. A halo rimmed the partially obscured moon, a perfect companion for his distant and restive mood as it could offer no solace, no answers, and no absolution.

The nights hit the hardest since Orianna died.

Rogan stood and braced his hands on either side of the window frame, pressed his hands flat and pushed against the solid wood, his muscles bunched, his mind focused. A war waged inside him, a battle of his will and his suffering.

The timepiece on the mantle chimed midnight. Rogan lifted a small bundle and left his rooms, grateful for the temporary reprieve.

He would not fight tonight. He would see to a different matter: Emeline.

With a silent tread he traversed the still, gloomy mansion. The only light came from the occasional low-burning oil lamps and the silvery moonlight that filtered in through parted drapes.

Emeline heard him come. Moved by curiosity, she withdrew from her bed and approached the door. Against the paleness of the wall the wood looked like a gleaming black hole gaping like an open portal. For a moment she fancied she could step through and be transported to another place, a distant land. She shook off the thought; such notions were for dreams. She set her hand on the wood. And as she felt the reality of its cool, smooth, solid surface beneath her fingertips, she knew Rogan to be on the other side. He was just as real, and for a moment she wondered what he would feel like. She immediately dismissed the thought and returned to the practicality she depended upon.

"Why did you come back?"

"To allow you to apologize," Rogan replied.

She laughed ruefully. His answer did not surprise her; she already knew him to be a man more perceptive than most. He saw things in her, intuited her truths. She didn't know how he managed it, but he must have ferreted them from her heart somehow, for he had never even seen her face. "You know what I meant to do."

"Aye, and it nearly worked, Princess. 'Twas quite a send-off you gave me. I admit, I was not going to return."

"Where did I go wrong?"

"I rode past the gallows today." He paused, and Emeline did not have to wonder what he'd seen; she'd attended hangings. As if reading her thoughts, Rogan continued. "We only know what we are taught, Princess. Your life has taught you much about men, and judging from what you've said, all bad, aye? I came back because I think maybe I can teach you something different."

Emeline's breath snagged in her throat, held there by a huge lump that gathered at the sound of his voice, so deep, resonant, and gentle. Again he threatened her defenses, but she was powerless to tell him to leave. "What would you teach me?"

"My father, Patrick, met my mother in England. He was common, a sea merchant, and she an aristocrat, a Bradburn. But they did not see each other as what they were born to be, or who others thought they were. They saw the person inside, and nothing else mattered. I was not raised to believe that a person's station in life is a definition of their worth, and after I went out into the world and saw a bit of it for myself, I knew that my parents were right."

Emeline kept silent, allowing him to continue. On her side of the door she clutched her hands to her mouth, her breaths shallow and fast.

"I would like to have the opportunity to know you, Emeline, with all of our labels set aside. Thus far, you are the only person I can call a friend in all of England."

A long silence fell as Emeline struggled to grasp what he genuinely seemed to offer. If he truly wanted to teach her something different, he was certainly doing a fine job. When she could finally respond, her tone was incredulous. "You want to be my friend?"

"Aye, but first you must apologize. Friends do not insult their friends' honor."

Regret shot an arrow through her heart. What had Rogan done to her, but offer his kindness? He had not tried to woo his way into her rooms and press his advances on her, as some men might. For that she could have called him a blackguard, and known him to be a man ruled by his lust. Nor had he broken down her doors to release her, which in fact would simply have been for him, so he could play the valiant knight in his own mind. For that she could have called him a brute, and thought of him as just another man who would force his will upon her.

Instead he offered friendship and asked for nothing in return but the same.

"I am sorry, Rogan Mullen," she finally said. "In fact, it weighed heavily on my heart all day."

"'Tis forgotten," Rogan replied, and Emeline understood that Rogan had instinctively known that she had needed to say it more than he needed to hear it. She wondered how it could be that this man, to whom she was nothing more than a stranger, his uncle's mistress, and a marked, fallen woman, could show her such kindness.

"A token of my friendship," he added, and she heard the rustle of paper.

Rogan slipped a small, thin package under the door. It shone whitely against the dark wood of the floor. Emeline hesitated a moment before lifting it. She unwrapped the waxed paper and out wafted a scent straight from her childhood. "Chocolate," she said on a breath. "You brought me chocolate?"

"Aye. You care for it, I hope?"

"My father used to bring me chocolate, when I was a little girl." She held the candy to her face and inhaled deeply, its rich fragrance bringing back memories of her father, his easy smile, his kind touch on her hair, bedtime stories and the brush of his whiskers on her cheek. For a few seconds, the memory of him was so strong and so clear, it almost felt like she had him back. "I have not had it since he died."

"I hope it does not bring too many bad memories."

"I do not have a single hurtful memory of him. He was a great man. Thank you, Rogan."

On Rogan's side of the door he heard her voice, so soft and wondrous it made him smile. He was suddenly very glad he'd gotten the idea to bring her the candy.

So strange, this situation, he mused. And even odder that he should find himself so drawn to Emeline, that it would please him so to bring that tone to her voice.

"Tell me about him, Princess."

As Emeline leaned against the door, very aware that Rogan did the same, she imagined she could feel his heat through the wood. She took a little nibble of the chocolate, reveled in the sweet, velvety melt of it, and smiled at the memories it brought. It was a warm, safe feeling, to have Rogan with her, to taste the candy, and remember her father. "His name was Charlie. He was very tall, and very thin, and he loved us, my mother and me.

"They married for love, though my mother came to him with a house and money of her own, left to her by her own parents when they died. Plenty of men courted my mum; she was fair and lovely, and they all fancied the idea of possessing the woman, and her holdings as well. But my father did not care about her money. He didn't care for anything but my mother, and by God it showed." Emeline took another tiny nibble, and sighed. "He brought her a flower the sixteenth day of every month, to mark the day they met. They were married nine years and seven months. That is one hundred fifteen flowers, and she pressed every single one of them."

Emeline closed her eyes and leaned her head back, lost in wistful emotions and distant memories. "They were so happy."

"And so were you."

"Yes, though I did not know it then. I did not understand my own happiness until after it was gone. But I remember it well."

"I know of what you speak."

Emeline held the wrapped chocolate to her breast, and tried to gather her defenses, but failed. Lost in the welter of the memories of long ago, she allowed the gaps in her armor to remain open, and for a little light to spill into darkened rooms in her heart. "No one has brought me such a gift in a very long time. I feel awful, Rogan, because I have nothing for you."

"Nonsense. Did I not just tell you that you are my only friend?"

"Yes."

"Good. And I have one final thing for you, Emeline. You're listening?"

"I am."

"Your freedom. My offer stands, to release you and to help you, but I will not force it on you. You've been forced too many times, aye?"

Feelings shuddered through her, relief and hope and fear, but at the top, shame. He knew, both in reality and instinctively, just how she had been coerced.

She would not need to ask for help, because she had gone and furthered her own cause. Her gorge rose again, the pressure of it against the back of her throat, and she nibbled the chocolate to try to cling to the memory of her father, and all she had been as a little girl, innocent and fearless and free.

With the chocolate melting in her mouth, Emeline wondered again how one man who had never even seen her could offer her so much and ask for nothing in return.

Memories flashed in her brain, imprinted forever. Jeffrey, naked. Her seduction. His needs. Her bargain.

"I cannot ask for it, Rogan. There is a reason, something I must do."

"Tell me what it is, Princess. I would help you."

Her humiliation grew, burning her face and neck with it. "I cannot tell you. I am sorry."

"Why not choose to be free instead of sorry? 'Tis easier, aye?"

But Rogan did not know the thing Simon dangled in front of Emeline like a baited hook. Simon knew better than anyone what could make her resort to the lowest depths of depravity: her mother.

Simon had her mother locked away in Bethlem Royal Hospital, or Bedlam, as the Londoners called it, a place worse than any of the vilest pits of hell, and Emeline would do whatever was necessary to free her. Whatever Simon wanted in that mansion, she would find it, steal it, and deliver it. And in exchange she would have her mother set free.

Nothing would stand in the way of that. Nothing, and no one.

Emeline held fast to that, when she degraded herself with Jeffrey and when she vomited afterwards, alone and afraid, sweating and retching. She thought of her mother, locked away in an asylum, chained to a wall while people who wanted a cheap thrill paid admission to walk through and taunt the inmates by poking them with sticks and tossing spoiled fruit at them as if they were less than human.

Her mother, who long ago had rocked Emeline to sleep when she cried for her daddy, even though her own heart had been ripped apart and she wept for her only love. Her mother, who had endured Simon's fists to try to protect Emeline from his advances.

"Nothing is easy," Emeline asserted, "least of all my situation."

"Maybe no, but it can be made simple, I think. You tell me what you need to do. I will set you free; I could help you do it. Not easy, aye, but simple enough." And, Rogan added in his mind, it would be a fine distraction from his own worries, to help Emeline with hers.

"I will take care of myself, as I have always done. The only thing you can do for me is to see beyond the station my life has forced me into, to be my friend, as you've offered. I've actually never had one before." Her voice grew very quiet and small, and Emeline struggled with her need to say the words and the pride it cost her to do so. It felt so much easier to bare her feelings with the door between them, the reality of its barrier enabling her not to rely so heavily on the ones she had so painstakingly erected over the years. "I hate what I have had to become and have been happy to be alone in this world, so that no one witnesses my shame."

"Only you. Isn't that enough?"

The feelings that had surfaced began to swirl into a

messy clog in her chest, making it hard to breathe. How could he see so much? It was if he had stripped her naked, flayed her skin, and seen her bones. And he had never even seen her face.

"I am very tired now, Rogan. Thank you for the chocolate."

"No, 'tis not that easy. Answer it for yourself if you won't answer to me. Isn't it enough that *you* see it, Emeline?"

A memory came back to her, startling in its clarity, of her mother on her father's lap, he nuzzling her ear and whispering something that made her cheeks flush and her eyes shine. She'd turned her head then, and seen her daughter in the doorway to the room. Her mother, still pink with laughter, raised her hand and reached out to Emeline, and pulled her onto her daddy's lap with her, the two of them cuddling her close, bathing her in their warmth and love. *My two favorite girls*, he'd said, and mother squeezed Emeline, spoke very softly in her ear, *marry for love*.

The memory hurt and healed at the same time, bittersweet, for having her father back in memory only meant she had to lose him again. And that meant losing the child she had been, as well. "I cannot tell you, Rogan Mullen, because I do not know. I only get through each day, doing what I can to endure, and hope that it will be enough to see me through to the next day. And then the next."

Again silence fell over them, companionable this time, each lost in their own thoughts for a time. After a little while Rogan leaned his head back against the door, his eyes closed. "Does Jeffrey hurt you, Emeline?"

"Not visibly."

Her answer, so plain and honest, told him she had thought about it before, those internal scars we gather that no one ever sees. Rogan understood completely; nothing more needed to be said.

"Tell me more about your father." Rogan shifted his

weight and got more comfortable, content to listen to the husky softness of her voice, the melodious lilt of her accent. With his eyes closed he got lost in her childhood, came to know her parents, saw the city streets of London through her eyes.

Sitting there, long into the night, the hours passed quickly for them. Before they realized it, the first streaks of dawn began to lighten the sky outside of Emeline's windows.

She sighed and stretched. Her body ached from sitting on the cold, hard floor, and her throat was sore from being sick and talking for hours, but she felt more at peace than she had in years, too many to remember.

"You should go," she said, with regret. "Daylight comes."

"Do you wish me to return?" Rogan asked as he got to his feet.

She glanced again at the lightening sky, the first rays of dawn bathing her room in lavender shadows tipped with rose and gold, full of the promise of a new day. "Tonight?"

Rogan decided to come after his fight, remembering the peace of conversation and whiskey that had soothed his battered body and mind. "Aye, tonight. Late."

"I shall look forward to it."

Rogan gathered up the bit of fabric he'd wrapped the chocolate in and stuffed it in his jacket pocket. "Someday we will meet, Princess, and when that day comes do you suppose we will long for a door to speak through?"

Emeline held to her secret; she would meet him in a few days, and longed for the first few seconds of his honest response to her as a woman, not as a disgraced mistress and stepdaughter to Simon.

She imagined meeting him, had thought of it from the moment Jeffrey agreed that he would grant her the freedom she requested. She had come to trust Rogan, to view him as different, even though she knew the danger. Hadn't her mother trusted Simon at one time? Emeline wondered how exposed she would feel before Rogan, the only man besides her father who had never tried to hurt her, who did not seem to want anything from her. Now she realized that Rogan thought about it, too. "Perhaps I will hang a veil over my face, so we can keep the barrier between us."

Rogan laughed lightly at the image. "I am not afraid of that meeting, Emeline. I think maybe we should save our veils and barriers for those who do not care to meet the real person. You don't need to hide yourself from me, *anamchara.*"

She smiled despite herself, for it seemed he read her mind, and yet that did not frighten her. She had longed for understanding more than she'd realized, and the more he gave to her, the more her defenses crumbled away, castle walls being demolished, stone by stone. "Your little game will get turned around, Rogan Mullen. Tonight you give me your truth. I want to know why you walk the halls at night, why you don't sleep."

Rogan's grin faded away and he leaned against the wall, stared at the floor, suddenly very tired. "I have nothing much to share, I'm afraid." And in his mind his conscience filled in the gap. *I have nothing much to share because I'm afraid.* The hated voice was enough to make him yearn for the ring, where the physical pain squelched the mental, if only for a short while.

"I wasn't looking for this either, but you pressed your point hard enough. Come again, Rogan, but only if this friendship will go in both directions."

Rogan felt as if his being had been drained to a husk, the fatigue of night after night of fighting, fitful sleep, and disturbing dreams finally caught up to him in a rush. "You fight dirty."

"'Tis the only kind of fighting," she replied, keeping her tone light, "when one wants to win."

Gathering his strength, Rogan pushed himself upright, grinned despite himself at her words. She was more right than she knew. "Very well. I will come back." He turned to leave but remembered something he wanted to tell her. "If you want to keep the old man away, try feigning illness."

"Illness?"

"Aye, he gets very upset by it. It might be enough to keep him from coming to your rooms."

Emeline thought about that afternoon when he came to her, his paranoia and fears of getting sick and dying. She calculated the days until Friday, and decided that pretending to be sick would not interfere with her freedom if she claimed to be well again by Thursday. She glanced over to the chamber pot. It was covered with a scented cloth, but had not been emptied since she'd vomited earlier. "I will try it."

He turned to leave again, but her voice stopped him, hesitant and shy.

"Rogan? Before, what you said. Was that Gaelic?"

"Oh, aye," Rogan replied. "*Anamchara*. It means soulfriend." He felt a sudden wave of embarrassment, and tapped on the door a bit, signaling that he was ready to leave. "Goodbye, Princess."

Chapter 9

The day did not pass quickly enough. Rogan longed for the night.

The night was oppression; the night was liberation.

Its demand for sleep had long since become a burden on Rogan: the pressure of trying to lie abed, alone and sleepless, guilt and regret as his only companions.

And its darkness was a cloak, concealing his flight from the house, freeing him. The call to fight was hot in his blood.

Rogan flew on horseback, galloping through London's dark, tangled streets, the black stallion beneath him a beast like himself, both driven, both running.

The screams from the amphitheater were carried to him on gusty winds. It stoked the fire in his veins and numbed the voice in his head. Tonight there would be release and pain.

He entered and a few recognized him. Soon they called for him, their newest, untamed favorite. The Duke.

They escorted him to an empty booth, cheering and calling his name. A few women brushed by him, their hands trailing over his body, making offers of companionship as they cupped his buttocks and caressed his shoulders.

Standing on the balcony, Simon watched as Rogan entered. The cheering of the fickle crowd turned his stomach. When Rogan entered the stall beneath the platform on which he stood, Simon leaned over the rail and hailed the attention of a man below. He raised his left hand and gave the signal.

Simon sat back down and caught Lora's eye, smirking as he arranged the drape of his garments over the rough wooden bench. "So much for The Duke, eh? Soon enough they'll be calling him The Sitting Duck."

He laughed at his own humor, but it died as Lora smiled in response, her lips curved in her professional smile. The smile that gave nothing and meant even less. Again he longed for Emeline, for the daring truth of her contempt.

The lords trolling the booths already knew who would be fighting the next match. Bets were laid on Rogan and the slave, who Simon had dubbed The Bull.

Rogan, stripped to his breeches and greased once again, walked to the ring, carried along by the screaming of the crowd and the cries in his mind, soft sobs as Orianna lay dying in his arms.

The smoky air was even thicker than the last time Rogan fought, the stench even stronger. The amphitheater was full to bursting, word had spread quickly of the black slave who would fight that night. Londoners loved their curiosities, paid handsomely to see everything from madmen to midgets, and whatever else fell in between. The gossip that went from tavern to coffeehouse to brothel spoke of the size of the slave, growing larger with every telling. Just as Simon had known it would.

But still, Rogan was already a favorite, cutting a dashing, handsome figure unusual to the ring. And so the crowd exploded as he climbed through the ropes.

Rogan watched the crowd part to make way for his opponent, and felt the rush of excitement when he saw him emerge from the sea of whites, a huge black man. A worthy contender.

The Bull moved with purpose towards the ring, his face immobile and completely blank. He did not look around at the crowd, or even at Rogan, but simply put one foot in front of the next, kept moving. Climbing up the wooden steps, he ducked between the ropes and toed the scratch, meeting Rogan's gaze for the first time.

Behind the resolve that glimmered in the black irises, Rogan thought The Bull looked confused.

But there was no time to explore it as Cheswick Stanhope hollered for the crowd's approval, and pandered to the excitement by raising both Rogan's and The Bull's arms, comparing their size.

Dropping their arms, Cheswick faced them both. "Broughton's Rules. Wait for the bell."

Again The Bull seemed hesitant, sweat breaking through the grease on his skin. Rogan took a step back, away from the scratch. The throng of onlookers booed and stomped, not wanting their newest bruiser to be a coward. Cheswick rushed to Rogan's side.

"What the hell, mate? Toe up!"

"Does he speak English?" Rogan demanded.

"What difference is it to you? He's here to fight."

Rogan met The Bull's eyes once again. Raising his voice to be heard over the agitated, screaming crowd, he asked The Bull directly. "What are you fighting for?"

Behind Rogan, up in the dark, smoky balcony, Simon leaned forward and cursed a low stream of vicious oaths. "Fight him," he urged through gritted teeth. "Fight him."

The Bull faced Rogan. "Myself," he said, his voice as deep and low as a foghorn.

"Satisfied?" Cheswick asked, the delight apparent in his tone even as he yelled the question.

"Aye," Rogan answered, and he toed the scratch.

It was madness, and Rogan thrilled to it. To want to be hit, pounded, hurt until his skin ran with blood and was marred with bruises. It was utter insanity, and he wanted it like breath.

And he wanted to win, too. To defeat his opponent the way he could not conquer himself.

As he sized up The Bull, Rogan let the memories come, the ones that drove him to the edge and held him there, like a man who walks the plank and stares into the roiling void of oblivion.

The bell rang, and Rogan dove into the fight.

The Bull didn't shy away; here was where he could relieve his frustration, too. He'd been captured by his enemies, a neighboring tribe, and sold at the block as if he were less than human. And then he'd been taken aboard ships, too many to count, sold and resold, traded and worked, before finally landing in England, ready for transport to America.

His English was good; better than most, thanks to many months at sea and in warehouses. He understood nearly everything they said, though he was careful to not reveal how much. He'd learned quickly that the white men killed the slaves who dared to show signs of intelligence.

What he did not understand was why he'd been bought once again, taken to this place and told to fight a white man. The Bull knew what would happen if he killed him. Knew he'd be dangling from a rope before the sun rose a second time.

An uppercut to his jaw rang in his brain like a gong, and The Bull staggered back, fell to his knee. The man he fought threw punches like a warrior, a hard, fast rain of brutal blows as if he battled more than a man.

But The Bull fought for something, too.

A quick glance to the balcony had The Bull rising back to his feet.

Many rounds later Rogan staggered to the edge of the ring and slumped over the ropes, The Bull lay on his back, knocked out from a rabbit punch to the neck. The crowd was screaming so loudly the building shook, the floor vibrated. A few fights broke out in the crowd, chairs tossed about like flotsam on a raging sea. He gasped for air, panting heavily from exertion, sweat running from his skin, mingling with his blood.

And as if completely alone, Rogan closed his eyes and waited for the good memories to come, the ones bestowed like a benediction following a fight.

Again the night cloaked him as he rode back to the mansion. Bruised and battered, he slumped in the saddle, leaning over the horse's neck, the reins tangled in his swollen fists.

When he entered the mansion, the butler bowed stiffly. "Will my lord require another bath?"

"Aye," Rogan mumbled, too tired to be amused by the disapproval of the servant's expression.

In a matter of half an hour he was sinking into hot water, letting it ease the pain. The light in his bathing alcove was steamy above the candles, and loneliness lurked in every shadowy corner.

How long? How many fights and how many months would it take until he could rest again? How much penance would he have to endure?

As always he received no answers, because there are none for people who choose to suffer alone. This he knew from far too many nights just like this one.

After his bath he wrapped a towel around his middle, and with the light of candles and oil lamps, surveyed the damage to his face and body.

The Bull had split his lip, and it swelled around the cut. Blue bruises welled fresh beneath yellow ones around his right eye, and his left was swelling. But fortunately, The Bull wasn't otherwise much for hitting above the shoulders. Rogan's body had taken most of the punishment, his entire torso mottled, cut, and abraded. And his hands. He looked down at the swollen, split knuckles and knew he would not be able to fight for at least a few days.

He glanced over to the made bed, the turned-down covers a silent taunt. After dressing, he left the empty room and again prowled the dimly lit halls in search of scotch and company. He hoped he did not see his uncle emerging from Emeline's rooms once again.

It had begun to truly sicken him, the fact that she was caged like a criminal, their deeds a mocking mystery in Rogan's imagination. And why should he care what play they engaged in? Was it any business of his?

Imprisoned. Locked away behind closed doors. The thought of the madness he would suffer at that treatment had Rogan shuddering.

His uncle was truly demented.

And yet, Rogan could go to her, and she would be there. Perhaps that is why Jeffrey locked her inside those rooms, he thought. Like a bird in a cage, who sings a private song.

And like his uncle, Rogan was drawn to her.

Rogan did not understand fully why Emeline's company soothed him, but it did. She was by turns acerbic and kind, playful and guarded, cagey and generous. He'd called her *anamchara*. Soul-friend.

Aye, he thought, she is that. A friend whose face he had never seen. And so, being unable to see her with his eyes, he was forced to listen with his heart.

He poured himself a stiff drink from a cart in the parlor and wound his way back through the dimly lit halls, coming to Emeline's door quietly, not wishing to wake her if she slept.

"Rogan," she stated. "You've returned again."

She had heard him, just as always.

He smiled, then winced as he felt the new scab on his lip break open. "Good evening."

"You sound tired. Are you unwell?"

"Only a fair bit drained." The day had been long. He'd worked alongside his uncle, learning what land holdings the family owned, the rents that were collected every month, the duties that would be expected of him. He'd also endured the ministrations of a tailor, being measured and fitted for a brace of suits that his uncle assured him would be needed at Parliament.

And after that, he'd fought until he could barely stand. Yet, sleep would still not come. He rested his head against the door, glad for its barrier and the darkness that cloaked the corridor. He sighed heavily, breathing in the scents of wool rugs, waxed wooden floors, and the faint odor of burning oil that wafted from the lamp at the end of the hall.

Every part of his body ached.

"You should go to sleep, then," Emeline said.

"No." Rogan lifted his glass, with an arm that could have been weighted with lead, and sipped his scotch again, wondering why the fight, the bath, and the booze weren't doing their usual trick.

"What troubles you, Rogan? You can tell me."

He hesitated. It seemed his resolve had been beaten out of him, left him nothing but a shell that could only feel pain, emotional, physical, mental. "There are things of which I never speak. Not to anyone."

"I understand," Emeline said. "There are things that run too deep for mere words."

Rogan could hear the sounds of Orianna's crying in his memory, the weak sobs, her final breaths. And it angered him, because after every other fight he'd been able to enjoy a few good memories.

Before he knew it, the words slipped out, buffered as they were by the barricade of the door, easier in coming because no one could see the pain on his face. "I was married."

And the shuttered, barely repressed agony in his voice was enough to tell her that his wife no longer lived. Compassion welled inside of Emeline for this man who had obviously loved so deeply, and lost so much.

"You loved her."

"More than life." He cleared his throat, shifted his weight. "More than anything."

"How long has it been?"

"A year."

She had formed a mental image of Rogan, and she sought to pair it with the woman who had captured his heart. "She must have been very beautiful."

"She was."

"And you still grieve for her."

Rogan did not answer, couldn't. He tossed down a large gulp of whiskey to soothe the fist squeezing at his throat.

"Of course you do," Emeline said quietly, humiliated. "Forgive my vulgarity."

"Do not apologize. I took no offense." And in Rogan's mind, he finished the thought. *I do not have the right to grieve.*

"That is why you do not sleep."

"Aye. The nights are long."

Emeline pressed her hand against the cool wood of the door. If its barrier had not been there, she would have wanted to touch him, to lay a hand of comfort on his shoulder. Perhaps even his face, cupping his cheek. And with a start she realized that she did not find the thought of touching him to be revolting. A man, her touch, and not of lust, but kindness, and given with a willing heart. She never would have thought it could be true.

"She was very fortunate," Emeline observed. "So few women are loved and cherished."

"Aye," he repeated, and cleared his throat.

And she closed her eyes as she leaned against Rogan through the door, imagined the heat of him filtering through to her, and she wondered if any man could ever love her the way Rogan loved his wife and her father had loved her mother, see into her and know who she really was inside.

"Can we speak of something else?" he asked, his voice ragged beyond his ability to control it.

"Of course, Rogan."

"Do you know what puzzles me?"

"What?"

"Why does my uncle lock your doors when he has you housed on the first floor? Are there no windows in your rooms?"

"You do not understand his mind," she answered. "He does not lock me away to prevent my escape. He knows there is nowhere for me to go." Her voice shook. "He locks my doors to display his control over me and also to keep me for himself."

"I could come to your window."

"Why would you do that?"

"So we could finally meet, face to face."

"No. Do not come."

"You don't wish to see me?"

"No."

Her tone was so flat that Rogan was taken aback. "Why not?"

Emeline thought of Friday night, the release she had debased herself for, when she would show Simon that she was free to find what he wanted her to obtain. But that night she hoped to also meet Rogan, and for a few short moments to be greeted as a stranger before they were introduced. Emeline wanted those moments, longed for them, to be seen as a woman and nothing less.

"There will come a time for that, but for now, I like things as they are. Once you see me, everything will change."

"Ah, back to that, are we? I will see you and I will want to bed you, correct? So much for the poor plain Princess Emeline."

"I am comely," she replied, without the slightest bit of pride. "But there are women just as lovely, many far lovelier. 'Tis not my looks alone that brings on the response of the men around me."

"What is it, then?"

"I do not know what they see that I do not."

"Perhaps I will come to your window, take a good long look, and let you in on the secret."

The offer did have its appeal, she thought, because if it were something she could change about herself, she could perhaps make men no longer want her.

But she wanted to wait, to hold out for her stolen moments on Friday, when for a few brief ticks of the timepiece, she could pretend herself to be a maiden greeting a potential suitor. To most people those kinds of longings might seem too fleeting to be worthwhile, but Simon had stolen her innocence before she was even a woman, and any tiny moments of normalcy were precious and meant to be savored. She thought of her new gowns, and what she would wear when she would meet Rogan.

"What is your favorite color?" she asked.

He grinned at her change of subject, but decided to play along. "Blue. What's yours?"

"Green, like grass and growing things." She pulled her lap blanket higher and shifted her weight so she was more comfortable on the floor. "When I was a little girl, I would transplant grass into pots when autumn threatened, and keep it alive on a windowsill so that all winter long I could touch and smell the grass, picture summer days and pretty wildflowers."

Rogan closed his eyes and imagined a little girl growing grass, smiled at the fancy of it. "Tell me more about Little Emeline."

"I did all the talking last night, Rogan. 'Tis your turn. Tell me about your family and your home. Tell me about your parents. Didn't you say that your mother is English and your father Irish?"

And so Rogan spoke about Patrick and Camille, hardships of his mother's life before she met Patrick, the love they had found in England, the bravery with which Camille had left it all behind, the new life they built in Barbados.

He told her about swinging from bearded fig trees as a boy, swimming with colorful fish in crystal waters. The stories were funny, and he told them the way his father had always done, taking his time, giving plenty of detail, until the island seemed alive around them.

Patrick and Camille were with them, and Emeline pressed with more and more questions about his mother, Camille, intrigued by this woman who was English like herself, but unlike any other woman she had ever met. Strong and independent, willing to take risks and to love deeper than most can dare to imagine.

When the streaks of dawn painted the sky, Emeline sighed with regret. "We talked the night away again."

"Do you want me to return?"

"Yes," she replied, too quickly. Had she actually sounded breathless? she wondered. *For a man*, her conscience jeered. But not any man, she answered herself. Only one man. "If you wish."

Rogan stretched in the hall, his entire body one enormous ache. He would not be able to fight for a few nights, he knew. The Bull had definitely punished him to the point of needing time to heal.

"I will come back, Princess. I do enjoy your company."

He did return to her doors, every night that week, and they spent the hours talking until Thursday came, and Emeline had to tell Rogan not to return that night.

As much as she hated it, she knew the reprieve from Jeffrey's attentions had to end. If she would be free for Friday, she would have to send word to Jeffrey that she was well enough to see him once again.

Chapter 10

Rogan gritted his teeth in frustration as he attempted to tie his cravat for the fifteenth time, his thick fingers unable to force the flimsy fabric into submission. Finally, he tore it from around his neck and unbuttoned the top two buttons of his shirt, leaving him free to breathe without constriction. The clothes his uncle had ordered for him might be the latest in London fashion, but he determined they would be worn without the foolish adornment of a frilly noose.

Still, he had agreed to the need for new garments and did think the cut of the fine camel breeches paired with a dark green velvet jacket suited him, the bright white cotton shirt a stark contrast to his black hair and his dark skin. Since he had not owned anything that could not be worn on a ship deck or horseback, he did appreciate that his new position in the succession for an impressive dukedom required more formal attire.

He had time before dinner. Rogan strolled into Kieran's room, ducking just in time as a novel went sailing past his head and hit the wall with a loud *thunk*.

"Let me out of this prison, damn you!"

He grinned at his sister and picked up the dodged book. "Not until you're completely recovered."

"I feel fine," Kieran snapped. "Scarcely a pox left on me, no fever, and no aches. I am well, Rogan. Well enough to kill you if you do not let me out of this bed."

"Da and Mum put you under my care."

Rogan deftly sidestepped a hurled pillow, moved closer to his sister, and sat on the side of her bed. He took her chin in his palm and tilted up her head, considering her carefully. She did look almost completely healed, but a few pox still oozed by her right ear, and most of the others still bore scabs. Her coloring was still pale, and dark smudges underscored her decidedly furious eyes.

"I am so bored I shall soon go mad. Mad, I say, Rogan. Do you hear me?"

"I daresay everyone in the entire mansion hears you, Kieran." He looked directly into her eyes. "I won't risk a relapse. You'll lie abed until completely healed, aye?"

"I must get out of this room!" she screamed into his face, her frustration and boredom ballooning to cataclysmic proportions. "I cannot endure another day of this!"

Completely unaffected by her tantrum, Rogan stood up and went to the table where a crewel project was half finished, a tranquil scene framed by wisteria, the design complex and unique, the color palate entirely appealing. Rogan's eye appreciated the quality and precision, and he knew that a finished piece of that caliber would bring a fair price. "This is excellent work. If you want, I will take it to the Exchange when you're finished with it."

"Why would I want you to do that?" Kieran snapped.

"Because I can easily get ten pounds for it, maybe more."

"Ten pounds? For that?"

He leaned against the table and grinned at his sister, glad

to see the gleam of greed in her eyes replace the lust for blood and mayhem. "Easily. It really is very good."

"I have more of them already completed, some much larger."

"Do you want me to sell them for you?"

"Of course I do. What else would I do with them, once they're finished?"

"You've never sold them before, aye?"

"Well, I never knew they were worth that kind of money."

As Kieran's temper passed, she noticed bruises on her brother's face, purple and yellow blotches under his tanned skin, along with a few cuts in various stages of healing. His hands were cut and bruised as well. "Have you been fighting, Rogan?"

He shrugged casually. "A tavern brawl, nothing more."

"What happened?"

Rogan's grin widened. "I won."

"I meant why did you have to fight?" She was fast losing patience. She was confined to a sickbed and her brother was out and about in London, fighting in taverns and no doubt enjoying himself. The least he could do was tell her the story.

"I did not *have* to fight, Kieran. I could have walked away."

Could you, really? he asked himself. *Could you stop?*

"Did he insult you?"

A memory flashed in his mind of The Bull, fighting like a gladiator. "No, indeed he did not."

"Tell me what happened, Rogan," she demanded impatiently.

"You're awfully bloodthirsty this evening." He picked up the fabric and brushed his fingers over the embroidery, ready to change the subject. "Do you design these yourself, Kieran?"

"Yes."

"Well done. You are indeed an artist."

Kieran's mood softened at his praise, and because she could tell that he would not speak anymore on the subject of fighting, she allowed him to distract her. "Thank you."

"Do you love to do it?"

"Yes, very much."

"Good." Rogan took the piece over to his sister, along with the large box of threads and needles. "Work on this, and try not to focus on your boredom. I know 'tis difficult, but dying seems worse, aye?"

"I will not die if I join you for dinner."

"Maybe no, but general wisdom says you remain abed until completely well. I think we should err on the side of caution. And besides, Aunt Anna says she's never had the chickenpox before. We don't want to make her sick." He leaned down and kissed his little sister on the head, and then looked into her eyes, the same color as their father's: dark and stormy blue. "Sew. Stitch. Get well. And when you're all better, you'll have a hefty purse for your first sojourn through London."

Kieran spread the fabric across her lap, mollified enough by his praise and the promise of earning her own coin to keep her demeanor civil. "A few more days, Rogan. No more."

"You won't leave this bed until I agree that you're completely well. No matter how many days it takes. Swear it."

"No. I will not."

"Swear it, Kieran, or I will have every last stitch of clothing removed from your rooms to assure myself you cannot leave."

"Fine," she snarled. "I swear it." She gritted her teeth and shoved the needle into the linen as he left her rooms.

Rogan walked in the direction of the parlor, thirsty for a cocktail of some sort, maybe a nice scotch or a mellow

Irish whiskey. His sister exasperated him, but her lack of fever and her insistence on getting out of bed assured that she was indeed getting well, regaining her strength.

Voices filtered from the sitting room, male and female. Rogan entered with a ready smile of greeting, which rapidly faded away when he saw Simon sitting between two beautiful women on a long sofa. One of the women Rogan remembered as Simon's mistress, the other was a stranger to him. Jeffrey and Anna were not yet in attendance.

A fire burned in each of the three hearths, chasing the chill of the approaching evening. Outside a strong wind blew, causing the glass in the windows to rattle and the flames of the candles to bend and stretch, the heavy velvet drapes that framed the huge windows to sway. Still, despite the damp, raw weather and the gusts that buffeted the great mansion, the room was warmly inviting.

Rogan bowed to the two women without really looking at them. "Cousin," he addressed Simon, keeping his tone neutral. "You have returned, I see."

Simon's posture grew more rigid, his patrician features hardening around hazel eyes that glittered with annoyance. He draped his arms around both women and pulled them closer. "Indeed. I am far more familiar to this house than you, chap. You would do well to remember it. I belong, whereas you are simply a pretender."

"If that is what you tell yourself, Cousin, I will not trouble to disabuse you." Rogan raised a brow and allowed his tone to drip with meaning. "At least, not until I am duke."

The dart hit its mark, and Simon's face took on a ruddy tone. "Are those bruises I see on your face and hands, chap? Been fighting?"

"An altercation in a tavern. Nothing more."

Ah, so you will lie about it, Simon thought victoriously. *Even more interesting.* "Truly? A brawl, you say."

Rogan did not deign to reply, but turned his back on Simon and strolled over to the serving cart, poured himself a short glass of fine scotch, took a sip and savored the peaty flavor, the familiar burn. He sat across from the women and raised his glass to Lora. "You are looking well."

Lora's lips curved upward, her eyes glowed as she looked Rogan over, methodically taking in every interesting detail. "And you as well, my lord. Have you been occupying yourself in a satisfactory manner these days past?"

"Oh, aye. I've been all over the city." Rogan winked and inclined his head to Simon. "And here at home I've been pulling my own weight, removing the trash when need be."

Lora hid her laugh behind a sip of wine. Simon ignored them, chose instead to rise and finger the keys of the clavichord in the corner idly with one hand, his own glass of gin dangling from his fingers.

Rogan inclined his head to the other woman in order to introduce himself. The greeting died on his lips as he met her eyes. She sat completely unmoving, watching Rogan the way an artist scrutinizes a subject.

And he felt his heart pick up its beat, hard and fast in his chest. High cheekbones and dramatic arching brows framed eyes the shade of Prussian blue, a color that made him think of sapphires and clear midnight skies. She watched him evenly, not faltering or glancing coyly away as he openly studied her, and she observed him in return.

It seemed as if the others in the room faded away, and there was only the two of them, the connection instant and undeniable. Just as Rogan wondered if she felt it also, she raised a single brow and her full lips curved at the corners, as if to answer him, to tell him that she read the thoughts in his mind.

Emeline.

He knew who she was without a trace of uncertainty. Rogan pulled his gaze from her eyes, took in the honey color of her hair that framed her face, held up with combs and left to stream in waves down her back. She wore a blue gown of watered silk, bereft of adornment save the deep V of lace set in the square-cut bodice and frothing from her bell sleeves. She was lovely. Magnificent. Alluring. He tore his eyes away from the full, soft curves of her breasts and the tight nip of her waist, and brought them back to her eyes. His skin grew hot with remorse and a deeper, more visceral need.

He did want to bed her.

Just as she had predicted and he had not believed possible, he saw her, and he wanted her. Until this moment, he had regarded Emeline as his friend, but now it was different, changed the instant he looked into her eyes.

Against his own wishes Rogan longed for her, wanted to trace the outline of her delicate ears with his tongue, to test those full lips with his teeth, unlace that gown and see every inch of her creamy skin, know the scent between her thighs, touch all her secret places, bury himself inside of her.

The desire was potent, the temptation of her powerful, and Rogan fought it, tried to tamp it down like a dangerous fire that threatens to burn out of control. He had not wanted any woman since Orianna. He did not *want* to want any other women. He tried to conjure Orianna's face in his memory, but saw eyes of blue and not of amber.

"Emeline," he whispered.

"Rogan, you are earlier than expected," Jeffrey fussed, making a beeline for Emeline's side, taking a seat beside her, his hand possessively resting on her upper thigh.

Rogan could not stand to watch his uncle touch her. He stood and went to the far window, fixing his attention on the bare, gnarled trees, the windswept lawns, the dormant rosebushes.

Jeffrey stayed firmly in place beside Emeline and Anna called for savory pastries to be brought out, the drinks refreshed for their guests, water heated for tea for herself.

Simon approached Rogan and invaded his thoughts, stood so close to him that they felt the heat of each other. Simon pressed even closer, his jaw over Rogan's shoulder so he could speak into his ear.

"You understand her, chap. I see it."

"Go away." Rogan did not move, but his body was tense and ready to defend himself, whether against Simon's words or his actions he knew not. But he was prepared, just the same.

"She is extraordinary, isn't she. Look at her now, sitting there with him. I say, look at her!"

"There is no need," Rogan replied, fighting his feelings with rational thought. No one, he told himself, could have that strong a reaction to another person just from seeing them. No one could exude that much information, give and take without speaking even a word.

"There are *your* needs," Simon urged, "and mine, and Jeffrey's, and every man who looks at her."

Against his own will, Rogan turned his head and saw Emeline beside Jeffrey, like a golden goddess beside a mere pasty white mortal. She turned her head at that moment and met his eyes again, and as before his heart hammered, fast and hard. The structure of her face reminded him of legendary women who wore armor and fought alongside their men, the long, elegant length of her body suggesting she could lie against a man, his hard and ready parts thrusting into her soft and warm and wet ones, a perfect fit.

But at the same time her fragility matched her strength, something in her eyes and her posture radiating a wounded allure, like a bruised creature that still radiates danger, making Rogan long to secret her away, to pull her underneath his body, keep her from all others and only for himself. He wanted to ravage and save her at the same time. He wanted to possess her.

Simon kept standing close to Rogan, speaking into his ear, his words for Rogan only. "Strength and vulnerability. Sensuality and elegance. But that's not the only thing about her, is it, chap? 'Tis the way she looks in your eyes. The knowing in her own. She reads a man."

Rogan felt disgust well up inside of him, but he was compelled, just the same. "Shut up, old man."

"I saw it on her when I met her mother, and I wanted it. Married the woman just to get to the girl, though I knew 'twas a sin that will cost me my eternal salvation. But I could not resist her, what she radiates. 'Tis a sensual aptitude, what I call it. She knows what a man needs, what he wants, can smell it on him."

"You are vile."

"And you are intrigued." Simon dared to place his hand on Rogan's shoulder, his breath a hot wind on Rogan's ear. And when Rogan did not pull away, Simon's features tightened, grew fervid. "They say the blind hear as well as a dog, and that there are those who can intuit things other cannot. There are sixth senses, boy, and the girl has one for men. Make no mistake, she was made to be a man's whore."

"Say nothing more," Rogan commanded, and he pulled his shoulder away from Simon, wanting to move away.

But Simon pressed on with his words, his thick body caging Rogan against the window, the silks and brocades of his clothing redolent of musk and tobacco smoke. "Do you know why she is so potent? It took me years to figure it out, but I will tell you now, maybe save you from trying to ferret out her secrets yourself."

He leaned in even closer. His humid breath stank of gin.

"She does not know," he said, so quietly no one else in the room could hear him. "'Tis completely unconscious, unmeditated, unaffected. And for that very reason, she is absolutely irresistible."

Jeffrey seemed to grow annoyed at the two men watching Emeline, and he stood and moved so his body shielded her from their view. Reaching out, he stroked Emeline's long hair with proprietary fingers. "Do you wish a drink, dear thing?"

"Some wine, please, Your Grace," Emeline replied, and Jeffrey motioned to a servant to see to the request.

Rogan felt his knees grow weak at the sound of her voice, as his friend behind the door became the woman who sat before his uncle. He cleared his throat, took another deep sip of scotch, and decided he needed a refill. He pushed away from Simon and made his way to the liquor cart, poured another tall drink. As he did he overheard Anna speaking to Emeline.

"Are your comforts seen to, dear? Is there anything you might require?"

"No thank you, Your Grace. His Grace has been most generous."

"Excellent, dear. I see you have outfitted yourself in a lovely gown."

Rogan turned and saw that Emeline watched him furtively from the corners of her eyes, even as she accepted her wine from a servant. He lifted his glass to her in a silent toast and sipped deeply. She turned her head then, met his gaze full on, and the look in her eyes had him lowering his glass, standing frozen in place.

If they had been completely alone, her look could not have been more intimate. It was as if she communicated longing and desire, secrets and hidden needs.

Jeffrey saw the exchange and wrapped his arm around Emeline's waist, pulled her close enough that he could press kisses along her neck, and watched Rogan as he did so. He tucked his hand inside her bodice and squeezed her breast as he again kissed her, this time slobbering his way along her neck.

Emeline closed her eyes, wishing herself anywhere but there at that moment, hating the humiliation that swamped over her at her own submission, the degrading touch on her breast that was meant to brand her as the whore she had been forced to become. But her freedom from her rooms meant more than her pride, she reminded herself. Her mission could not be met otherwise.

Rogan set his glass down on the cart and strode across the room. He knocked Jeffrey's hand away from Emeline's breast with a quick, hard slap. "I know she's yours, Uncle."

Jeffrey leaped to his feet. He faced his nephew, hating that Rogan stood taller than him so he had to tilt his head up to meet his gaze, hating even more the snapping green of Rogan's Bradburn eyes.

"You overstep your bounds. You are in *my* parlor. I touch whom I want, when I want, and how I want."

"You have not seen me overstep. Touch her like that in my presence again, and I'll overstep my way to having you at the end of my blade."

Jeffrey's hands curled into fists. "You dare to threaten me? I am the Duke!"

"You are a perverted old man," Rogan spat, "who degrades his wife *and* his mistress in an effort to prove his virility."

Jeffrey puffed up, began to sweat, and just as he readied himself to take a swing at his taller, younger, stronger nephew, he felt a gentle touch on his arm.

Emeline stood beside him, pressing her hand against the thick brocade of his jacket. Her eyes were moist, her lips parted and trembling. Jeffrey had never seen her look lovelier, and he felt his anger begin to dissipate, turning rapidly to lust.

"Your Grace," she murmured. "Perhaps your nephew does not realize that I crave your touch and your kisses."

Jeffrey relaxed even further, took Emeline's hand and pressed a kiss to her palm. He felt at that moment like the Duke of Eton, as powerful as a god, as rich as the king, as desirable as a man half his age. "Tell him, then, Eme-mine. Tell him yourself."

Emeline swallowed heavily, faced Rogan, her skin hot with shame, her stomach a leaden ball in her gut. She cast her eyes downward in a display of feminine meekness, desperate to keep up the farce that would allow her to achieve her goal. Behind them Simon watched the entire incident with amused patience. It galled Emeline to know he watched her debase herself, for she knew nothing pleased him more.

She addressed Rogan. "Sir, you do me a grave injustice. His Grace favors me with his attentions."

Rogan glanced from Simon to Jeffrey, then to Lora and Anna, both of whom appeared unaffected by the entire situation, and then back to Jeffrey and his smug expression. Rogan took a deep breath and braced himself. And then he did the exact opposite of what he longed to do.

"My apologies to the lovers." He picked up his glass of scotch and turned back to the window to resume his study of the windy evening, watching dispassionately as the gusts swirled and blew fallen leaves, scattering them as far as the eye could see.

Emeline ate her dinner without tasting it, the rarebit and bread pudding that she would ordinarily have enjoyed as tasteless as paste. As she dined, she struggled to seem as though she did not notice that Rogan avoided even the most casual glance her way, as if he wished that she did not share his table. But she had seen the fire in his eyes when he had looked at her in the parlor. The longing, the desire, the heat of a man who wanted what all men inexplicably wanted. Her. In their bed.

Emeline watched him furtively, helpless to do otherwise. Rogan did not look as she had imagined. His voice was deep, whiskey-smooth, his accent a charming mix of English, Irish, and something beyond her knowing. His gentle treatment of her and his restraint had her visualizing him shorter, fairer, plainer, perhaps some tweedy, bookish sort who hailed from a country estate.

She could not have been more wrong.

He burned with life, seethed with it in every inch of his powerfully muscled frame. His fine clothes molded to his body, a tailor's dream to fit, no doubt; no padding was required to fill the shoulders and certainly no cincher needed to narrow his middle. Black hair framed his face, that for all its Celtic beauty, possessed the danger of a devil. And his eyes. Emeline could not stop stealing glances to see the green beauty of his eyes, framed by long, black lashes beneath thick, slashing black brows.

A bite of bread lodged in her throat in a doughy lump, and she lifted her wine glass, took a deep drink to wash it down. She had hoped he would be different, that their initial friendship would be enough that he could see beyond her station and her lure, that he could see her as Emeline. Just simply Emeline.

She did realize, however, that it was not entirely fair, because she did not see him as just Rogan, a friend who visited her, brought her chocolate, and told her stories.

When he had entered the room she had felt her blood heat, her skin tingle, and though she had not thought it possible, she longed for his touch, for his hands on her body. After all the years with Simon, Emeline thought it impossible that she could want a man, could trust a man enough to see him as something more than an animal with constant sexual needs and endless demands.

But Rogan did not seem that way to her. He exuded maleness without the dissolute edge she was accustomed to, his obvious physical power tempered with control. He was the man who offered sleep to a woman who listened for footsteps, who gave her comfort when he could take none of his own.

His collar was open. Her gaze was drawn to the thickness of his neck, the masculine, square line of his collarbones, a bruise that bloomed beneath the dusting of black hair that curled from his parted shirt.

And the stirrings of real attraction awakened in Emeline.

Simon had taken a seat between Lora and Emeline. Emeline struggled not to show any indication that Simon was using the toe of his shoe to lift her skirt and rub her ankle. She scooted her feet farther and farther to the other side, until she nearly sat sideways in her chair.

Simon leaned over until his shoulder brushed against hers. He offered her a morsel of his roll, gravy dripping from the bread unheeded onto the rug below. "Take a bite, fair Emeline. You are a bit too thin."

She turned her head to face him, and did not bother to conceal her hatred. "If I am too thin, 'tis from years of vomiting after your touch."

Simon's face grew red, especially as Jeffrey laughed loud and long. Pulling back his hand, he ate the bread and wiped his fingers on his napkin.

At the sound of Emeline's voice, Rogan pushed his chair away and stood. He bowed slightly to all those around the table, keeping his eyes averted from Emeline.

"I am going to retire for the evening. Good night, all."

Jeffrey looked up from his hawkish watch over Emeline. "You are ailing, Nephew?"

"No, Uncle. I am fatigued." Rogan bowed slightly to his

aunt, and as he turned to leave he saw Emeline. His eyes caught on hers and held.

Emeline held her breath. She was an expert at reading people, and Rogan was no different. But it wasn't just that she could read him. Him she could *feel*. He radiated emotions barely contained, sexual awareness, lust, and hot, potent needs so dark and compelling they burned like pain.

A shiver ran through him, barely visible. But she saw it, indeed, felt it herself, a quivering of his muscles beneath skin: tension and restraint. He arched a brow and bowed slightly, a self-deprecating look that she barely had time to register before he turned on his heel and left at a fast clip, leaving them all behind.

Emeline watched him leave, kept her eyes on the dark green velvet stretched across his broad shoulders until he disappeared from sight. She knew he left because of her, and it made a pain grow in her chest, a thick messy clog of emotion that snagged her breath.

She had wanted the evening to be very different. Had envisioned him entering the parlor and seeing her as a woman, had even dared to hope he would not recognize her voice long enough that they could exchange some pleasant banter before her ruse was exposed.

That was the foolish longing of a young girl, she knew, but she could not help but to have wanted it. Instead, Rogan had seen her beside Simon, looked at her and known her for who and what she was. She rankled him as much as she compelled him. She saw the battle of it on his face, as clearly as if the words were written there for her to read.

With nothing to do but endure the evening, Emeline fiddled with her food, eating no more until the dinner finally ended and they made to retire to the parlor. But Jeffrey, wanting to show Emeline his generosity, clapped his hands twice and then folded them just under his breastbone, held them clasped there as he rocked back on his feet, one eyebrow raised.

"I have arranged for music. Please join me in the ballroom."

"Music? For just the five of us?" Anna asked.

"Indeed, indeed. I want to dance," Jeffrey insisted. He knew that for a man of his age he had remarkable grace and agility and he could perform any of the dances. That Rogan had seen fit to leave their company only sweetened the evening, for he would not be shown up by Simon, Jeffrey was certain.

The women followed the men through the mansion, and for one brief moment when no one would see them, Lora reached out and took Emeline's hand, clasped it and squeezed before letting go. And Emeline felt the thickness in her chest lessen, ever so slightly.

As they entered the ballroom, Emeline stopped and looked around, awed by the soaring, painted ceilings, the frescoes on the walls, windows as tall as the room itself. Groupings of sofas and chairs bordered the huge room, and one side was composed of alcoves with dark red velvet drapes that could be drawn for privacy. Above the alcoves she saw the small orchestra on the balcony. The whole room seemed to glow gold and cream, lit by hundreds of candles held by gilt chandeliers, sconces, and candelabras. It seemed a waste to Emeline, to go to so much expense to light the room for only five people, but Jeffrey strutted into the room with his chest puffed out, the proud peacock displaying his magnificence.

Jeffrey waved his hand in the air, and the music filled the room, strings and clavichord and winds, a brisk piece by Handel. He swept into a low bow over Emeline's hand, and then pulled her into his arms and out onto the center of the floor, whirling her around in a dance Emeline did not know and could scarcely keep up with until finally it ended and she pulled away, pleading exhaustion.

The night wore on as they alternately danced and sat, drank wine and listened to the weeping sounds of a bittersweet violin solo.

Finally, Simon figured he had waited long enough. He grasped Emeline's hand and pulled her to her feet.

"You must dance with me at least once, stepdaughter." Simon turned and held up his fingers, snapped at Lora who leapt to her feet as quickly as a well-trained dog and offered herself to Jeffrey for a dance.

Emeline did not demur. She had been waiting all evening for the moment when Simon would find a moment of privacy to tell her what her quarry would be, perhaps a painting, a sculpture, a piece of jewelry. He had told her there was something in the mansion of incredible value, and that he wanted her to obtain it for him. And with visions of her mother in chains in Bedlam, Emeline willingly allowed herself to be led to the dance floor, knowing there would be nothing she would not steal, no risk she would not take.

Gesturing to the orchestra for a pavane, he pulled Emeline to him and held her tightly, leaned his head down and put his lips against her ear. "Well done, daughter. Now that you have won your freedom, 'tis time for us to talk."

Chapter 11

Emeline endured the feel of Simon's arms around her, the scents of his body odors and his breath, his heat and the thick feel of his chest pressed against her own. It seemed he suffocated her with his presence, making her feel small and powerless, like the young girl she had been when he first began to touch her.

She was not a child anymore, she reminded herself, but a woman, grown and with a mind all her own. She would play his game and free her mother, and when Emeline had her safely out of Bedlam, she would see to their escape from Simon's clutches. No matter what she had to do to achieve it.

"What do you want?" Emeline asked him. "I see wealth and paintings everywhere I look, and nothing you could not steal yourself. What am I to get for you?"

Simon held her tighter, his whole body aflame with the feel of her in his arms, once again. She had a spell cast over him, and he admitted to himself that the jealousy of having Jeffrey touch her was nearly eating him alive. But he would never say the words, never tell anyone that a mere woman had managed to get under his skin. Still, he had her now for the space of a pavane, and he wanted to make the music they danced to last forever.

"Are you certain you're up to the challenge, dear daughter of mine? Perhaps you will shy away from the danger inherent in the task."

Emeline pulled her head back so she could look directly into his eyes. "I want my mother released."

"Ah, yes, though have you considered how distressed she shall be when she retires to her lonely room while you warm my bed? I mean, remember my dear, how she was driven insane when she found us thus entwined. Do you think it was my mouth between her daughter's thighs that finally drove her to the end of her tether, or was it the moans of delight coming from your lips?"

"They were cries of pain, not of pleasure." Emeline could still see the look of horror on her mother's face, and could still feel the the cords wrapped around her wrists and ankles, binding her, rendering her helpless.

"That line is so blurry, isn't it?" Simon continued. "Pain and pleasure, pleasure and pain. 'Tis so difficult to know where one begins and the other ends."

"There is nothing indistinct in how you have tortured me, Simon. Nothing so clear as the suffering you have put me through." Emeline spoke the words as plain fact, no sadness in her tone at all. They swept and spun through the steps of the dance, the music swirling around them in the creamy gold room.

"You did not always suffer, stepdaughter. I can recall a time or two that your body responded to my touch."

"Never!" she hissed. Emeline's reaction was if he had held a hot poker to her gut, and she tried to wrench away, pull from his grasp. He was too quick, yanking her back into his arms, this time holding her even tighter, his fingers digging into her waist.

"Ah, you do not want to recall that you liked it, do you?"

Simon taunted. "For then you cannot call yourself prey, but prostitute."

"If there are words for your depravity, I do not know them."

He inclined his head meaningfully in the direction of the alcoves. "I would teach you."

"Find another student," Emeline replied, her voice once again dry and flat. She had recovered herself only with sheer will, for inside boiled a heedless, wild cauldron of emotion, pent-up and seething for release. But she would not give him the satisfaction of seeing her loss of composure, and she would not lose sight of her goal. Her mother was chained in a living hell, and Emeline would ransom herself to Simon if that is what it would take to gain her freedom.

She pressed him for answers. "Surely your fat arse will soon require a soft cushion, and I see His Grace glancing our way, growing impatient for you to take your disgusting hands from me. So why not get to it, and tell me what I'm after in this house. The music is nearly over."

Simon glanced over and saw Jeffrey leading Lora through the steps of the pavane, his pale eyes never leaving Emeline as he swirled through the paces. Frustration welled in Simon again, mingling with the pure covetousness he felt whenever he pictured Jeffrey's pale, plump fingers touching his golden Emeline. He dug his own fingers even tighter into the curve of her waist, pulling her so he could feel the resistance in her body. She inflamed him as no other.

The orchestra moved into final stanza of the piece, making him grit his teeth, and he let out his breath in an impatient burst from his nose. "Very well. Here 'tis. And remember, my dear, to keep your face schooled to indifference. Anna is no doubt curiously studying the woman who shares her husband's bed, and the husband in question cannot keep his eyes from you."

"Simply tell me what you want, Simon. Your theatrics are wasted on me."

He pulled back to a more seemly distance from her, the proper distance between a stepfather and his daughter, so he could watch her reaction and make certain she did not reveal anything as he spoke. "I want the dukedom."

The slightest frown shadowed her arching brows. "Pardon?"

"Steal the dukedom for me and I will return your mother."

"'Tis you who belongs in the asylum."

"You are too short-sighted. Think, Emeline, of who stands between Jeffrey and me."

Emeline did not know very much about the laws of succession and the aristocracy, but she did not need to understand primogeniture to figure out what Simon wanted from that house.

He wanted Rogan.

"I cannot."

"You will."

"'Tis impossible."

"No, my dear. 'Tis inevitable." Simon swept Emeline into a twirl, and as she spun away from him he reached into his pocket with his free hand, extracted a small vial and then brought her back into his embrace, discreetly pressed it to her palm and held it there with his own.

"Poison. Deadly and quick. You will get close to him, ask for wine, dissolve this in his glass. Or you will put it in his food, his water, his scotch. I care not, Emeline, but you will give it to him."

"No," she breathed, careful to keep the horror from her expression.

"You will." Simon leaned closer, his hot breath against

her ear as he hissed out his intentions in a rush, wanting to say everything before the music ended. "Listen to me. That puppy is a pretender, an outsider, half-common, only half English, and worse, he is half *Irish*. I will not abide to see him take what is due to me when Jeffrey is dead and gone. He must be dealt with now, and I can be nowhere near the deed when it is done, lest I come under suspicion.

"You will give him the poison. I saw his attraction to you; he will let you get close to him. Indeed, he would likely do anything you asked of him." Jealousy was a fast, rolling boil in his chest. "Don't we all want you, my dear?"

But the music would soon end. Simon forced himself to focus on the matter at hand. He pressed his hand tighter against hers, squeezing the vial between their clasped palms. "I paid a small fortune for this poison, and another to silence the one who prepared it. 'Tis a blend of herbs designed to bring on illness that resembles the pox. First the fever will take him, then spots and flushed skin. Before a full day passes, he will expire."

The music seemed to grow far away in Emeline's ears, tiny black spots danced before her eyes. Rogan. Kill Rogan. The vial was the only real thing that existed, pressed hard into the flesh of her palm. The music grew even farther away, as if it came to her from a tunnel, echoing, fading.

Simon shook her, hard. "Stay with me. Listen."

Emeline took a deep, shaking breath, trying to stay conscious even though she craved the sheer black drop that promised to engulf her. "I will not do it."

"You will," Simon insisted, his tone still a hard, fast hiss. "You have a fortnight, and if he is not dead, I will kill your mother. I swear I will."

She tried to cling to rational thought, but over and over she kept thinking of Rogan, of Jeffrey, of Simon, and her mother, imprisoned in a hell to which Simon held the key, her only crime trying to protect her daughter.

Emeline had felt trapped for many years, but never so neatly as now.

"I thought you wanted me to steal for you," she said, her voice a toneless breath. "I agreed to come here, to steal something from the house."

"Thieves dangle alongside murderers on the public gibbet, dear daughter. The stakes are the same. Only the game has changed." Simon drew her closer again as they whirled around the gleaming parquet floor, and he couldn't help but notice how her skirts fanned out as they danced, how her skin glowed as if lit from within, how her scent invaded his nostrils and stoked the flame of his need for her. "A fortnight, Emeline. If I do not hear that an unfortunate illness has struck the puppy by then, you will hear of your own grievous loss."

He drew her in so he could speak in an undertone into her ear, finishing his warning as the final strains of the music ended. "And do not think to use your wiles to gain freedom or help from Jeffrey or Rogan. 'Twill only seal your mother's fate, dear thing. You see, you shall have blood on your hands either way, and rest assured, if you do not succeed in your task I will only be forced to hire some thug to do the deed for me in a London alleyway. Rogan will be dealt with, for I will not play second to a half-Irish mutt. 'Tis for you to decide if your mother needs to die as part of the bargain."

The dance ended and Emeline stood stock still as Simon pressed the vial into her hand, and she held it into the silk of her skirt, hidden like the sin it was intended to be. She stepped away from him, then, and turned to Jeffrey, her empty hand pressed to her mouth.

"I am unwell again, Your Grace," she said, unable to keep her voice from trembling, hysteria tugging at her throat.

Jeffrey froze, torn between wanting to rush to her side and his fear of contagion. As always, his fears won out. "What is wrong with you now?"

"My stomach, 'tis bad. Perhaps I emerged from my sickbed too soon."

Jeffrey glanced around the room, not wanting Simon nor Anna to escort Emeline to her rooms, for he would have to share his table with them. He did not want a servant who would tend to him later, either. Jeffrey's gaze latched on Lora, Simon's mistress. He could send her; he would not be seeing her again anytime soon.

"Take her to her rooms," he commanded. "See to it she is brought whatever she requires."

Lora nodded briefly, and without glancing at Simon for permission, she went to Emeline's side, took her elbow and led her away, out of the ballroom.

The two women went in silence at first, until they were farther away, enough that they were certain none could hear them.

"The house is not the same since you left, Emeline."

"Do you know what he wants?"

"Of course. He has spoken of nothing else since the day Jeffrey's son died and he found out that Jeffrey intended to bring Rogan to England."

Emeline felt her joints grow looser, and as they reached her rooms she sank to the floor, close to where she would sit when Rogan would come and visit her in the night. But he wouldn't be coming again, she knew. She recognized revulsion in a man's eyes clearly enough.

"What am I going to do?" Emeline asked.

Lora rested her hand for a moment on Emeline's shoulder, and then went to the washstand, poured her a glass of water and brought it to her. "You'll do as you must."

"Which is?"

"Kill him," Lora said simply, as if the answer was to the simplest arithmetic problem. "Or else you kill your mother."

Emeline looked up to her stepfather's mistress, the woman he'd brought into the house so he would have someone to take to balls and dinners and events, not wishing the fact that he had made his stepdaughter into his whore to be common knowledge. Lora's eyes were a soft gray that betrayed the canny instincts that had thus preserved her in a town that publicly reviled professional courtesans. Emeline knew Lora to be wise in the ways of self-preservation.

"What would you do, Lora?"

Lora's left brow raised high, a single elegant arch. She smiled a courtesan's smile, knowing and shrewd. "I'd bed him before I killed him, that's for certain. He's quite something to look at, obviously. But did you see his hands?" She shivered a bit, and her smile deepened until dimples flirted with the corners of her lips. "Hands to make a woman beg, I swear it."

"You would not truly kill him, would you? Could you bear to do it?"

Lora lifted her shoulders in a little shrug and seated herself on the chaise. "I would not doubt Simon."

"I know. I do not." Although Emeline did not welcome the knowledge, she knew Simon very well. He had never been a man to make idle threats.

"My mother—"

"Your mum is as good as dead if you refuse Simon," Lora interjected into Emeline's argument. "You know what he will do, and what he is capable of. Think of the alternative if you fail." Lora spread her hands as if to say the matter had no other resolution. "If you do not do it, your mum will die and Rogan will get his throat slit in an alleyway."

"Why me?" Emeline wondered aloud. "Why is Simon doing this?"

"Think, Emeline. You are a smart girl, I know it."

Emeline fell quiet. She did know why. She will have committed a murder for Simon; information that he could use against her for the rest of her life. He would truly own her, more so than he already did. "Two birds with one stone," she said finally.

"Indeed." Lora shrugged almost imperceptibly. "I am sorry."

"Rogan is my friend," Emeline confessed on a breath, the tiniest slice of her voice breaking the air. Still, it felt satisfying to say aloud, made it more real.

Lora was quick to laugh, a short, ugly sound. "A man as a friend. 'Tis a good jest, Emeline."

"In truth, I think he is unlike most other men."

Lora waved her hand in a dismissive gesture. "A dog, a pig, a man. One animal is scarcely different from the other, and all the males are ruled by their cocks."

Emeline looked down in her palm at the small vial of powder, imagined Rogan poisoned and dying, his parents, Camille and Patrick, who had become so real to her through Rogan's stories, grieving over the loss of their only son. And then her own mother, brought so low, likely spending each day praying for escape, wishing for her daughter to come and rescue her.

The answer came to her in a flash of clarity.

Emeline lifted her head, held out the vial. "You could do it. You could give this to Simon, and end the whole problem for all of us. Rogan would live, and I could find another way to save my mother. Do it, Lora. Please. He is an evil man, you know it. It could not be a sin to kill such an evil man."

Lora stood and walked to the door, her beautifully cold face touched with a rare expression of sympathy. She paused, her hand on the knob, looked down on Emeline, who sat on the floor in a heap of blue silk skirts.

"You are an agreeable girl, Emeline, and I have always been fond of you. But if you think I would risk stretching my neck at Tyburn to save a man's life, no matter how handsome he is to look upon, you do not know me at all. As I said, one cock is like another, and for now I ride Simon's to pay my way."

She turned with a flare of her skirts and left, closing the door on Emeline's plea.

Emeline sat in the dim room, all alone with her problem. She slid over to the door, leaned against the cold wood and wished Rogan would return. Wished she could tell him of the danger he was in, of the threat Simon posed, of her growing feelings for him, the awakening of desires she never thought she could feel. That she did not fear him, that she even began to dream of his touch. That she wanted so much to share everything she was inside with him, only without the barriers between them.

It seemed her walls had disintegrated to rubble, and her once carefully constructed armor had been cast aside. There was no defense to the only man who contradicted everything she knew of all other men.

She wished he could know that about her.

But all she could see in her mind's eye was the look on Rogan's face as he had watched her, compulsion and revulsion combined, and she knew that to Rogan she would become what she'd been to Simon, what she was to Jeffrey. Apparently, what she was meant to be to all men: a dirty secret.

A daydream came back to her, a fantasy from long ago, of a little thatched cottage on a hill, wildflowers and sunny skies. The vegetable garden was just as she had left it from her last dream there, the beans and cucumbers sprouting new growth, the sunflowers so tall they were nearly as high as the highest peak of the roof. Somewhere in the distance children laughed, the happiest sound Emeline could imagine, free and careless. She saw the floors of the cottage, waxed and shiny from her own toil, knew the pride and pleasure of making the house their home. She stood in the doorway of the cottage, wiped flour from her hands as she looked to the hills for her children, her eyes resting briefly on the back of the man who was always in the garden, tending to the plants.

This time the man stood and turned, and he had Rogan's face, his eyes as green as the grass that covered the rolling hills around them. He grinned at her, a restless, wild smile that held a promise of love, of respect, of a future.

It was a child's dream, she told herself. A dream for a young maiden with a dowry and innocence. A dream for someone else.

Emeline held the vial up and peered at it in the dim light, the only illumination coming from the moonlight that filtered in through the windows. She considered taking the poison herself, but forced herself to go beyond that simple, easy answer and think of the consequences to that action.

Simon would still see to it that Rogan was removed as a threat to the dukedom, would let her mother languish and die in Bedlam. The only person her suicide would benefit would be Emeline herself, for she would not have to live with the guilt of allowing the death of two people without even attempting to protect them.

No, she thought, she would not take the coward's way out.

She held the vial between her palms and lightly rubbed it back and forth, like the genie's lantern, as if she could make answers magically appear.

The only thing she knew for certain was that someone would die as a result of Simon's plan. And Emeline had a good idea of who she intended it to be.

Rogan did not want to fight; he needed to.

A body should not have to endure such punishment, but his would have to withstand it.

Even as he had the stable lad saddle a mount for him, he thrummed with the need, a darker, deeper urgency than he'd ever felt before. The stables were dimly lit, redolent of horses, tack, and hay, but all Rogan could smell was blood and grease and sweat.

Why should he care if Emeline debased herself with Jeffrey, his conscience demanded. She was Jeffrey's mistress, and Emeline chose that over the freedom Rogan had offered her.

What did it matter that Rogan's body responded to the look of her? A man lusting for a woman is oftentimes uncontrollable and, after a year of celibacy, was to be expected.

But the thoughts did nothing to assuage his guilt, that he should sink so low in his own estimation and also in Emeline's. Hadn't he told her he was different? Hadn't he earned her trust and friendship?

If you see me, you will want to bed me.

Her words taunted him with their accuracy.

"Milord," a small voice spoke, and Rogan turned to see the stable lad handing up the reins to him, his blue eyes huge and round in his pointed face.

Rogan had seen the boy look at him like that before, always when he returned from a fight, bloody and battered, stinking and exhausted. The look was the same as now, his eyes reflecting fear, curiosity, and respect in equal measure.

Rogan took the reins and swung up into the saddle, reached into his purse and handed the boy a coin.

"Thank ye, milord." The lad bobbed his head and backed away.

Rogan considered the boy for a moment, grateful for the momentary distraction. The boy was always in the stables, grooming horses or saddling them, and Rogan had yet to

see him with man or woman who seemed a parent to him.
"What age are you?"

"Twelve, milord."

"What is your name?"

"George."

"Do you live here, George?"

George's chest swelled, with pride or defiance, Rogan
did not know, but he respected both.

"I'm a man, milord, an' I work for my keep. On me own
since eight, an' never a day without honest work. I got me
a little cot in the loft, an' the duke never waits for his tack."

"Is that so?" Rogan mused, hiding his smile behind a
scowl. "You wonder where I go, don't you, George?"

"Aye." The boy answered with no hesitation or apology.

Rogan's respect redoubled, and this time he did grin. He
held out his gloved hand to the boy. "I could use an attendant. If you're through with your duties here, I'll pay you
a pound for your services. But I warn you, the bargain
comes with a stipulation. You must give me your word . . .
as a man, of course . . . that where I go remains a secret."

George didn't hesitate, but accepted the proffered hand
of the man who wore all black and rode into the night, and
allowed himself to be hoisted onto the rump of the stallion.

Rogan steered the horse through the stables to the outside, where the night air slapped at their faces. He urged
his mount to pick up speed, and the two of them thundered
off into the night.

Simon, long since bored with Jeffrey and Anna's company, sent for his carriage to be brought around. As they
stood in the foyer exchanging mundane pleasantries, the
sound of hoofbeats caught their attention. Simon leaned
out the open door in time to see the dark figure of a

cloaked man on horseback riding away from the property, a small form clutched to his back.

Keeping his expression indifferent, he turned to Jeffrey. "Where do you think our dear boy is off to?"

Jeffrey shrugged. "Why should I care where he spends his time?"

"Do you not notice his bruises? He is cut up and his hands looked swollen."

"He had cause to defend himself. Something of a tavern brawl," Jeffrey said, his manner bored and distracted ever since Emeline had returned to her rooms. "Young men, full of piss and vinegar."

"I say, the bruises looked fresh to my eye."

"Will you kiss them and make them well?" Jeffrey asked with asperity.

Simon pulled Lora to his side and gave her his elbow as their carriage pulled up. "I shall do far better than that, Cousin." Simon gave Anna and Jeffrey a smile and a nod before leading Lora down the granite steps.

Once settled with a lap robe and warming pan, Lora folded her arms across her chest, swaying with the motion of the carriage as Simon lighted and rapped on the roof with the head of his cane. She waited for him to inquire as to why she appeared upset.

When he did not respond to her pout, she raised her voice above the din of rumbling wheels clattering on cobblestones. "Drop me home, Simon. I do not wish to accompany you to that vile place again."

"You're going."

"It stinks in there; the people are rough and uncouth, the filthy floor soils the hem of my gown, and the privy is a nightmare. I shall wait in the carriage."

"You're coming inside. And remember who bought your gown. 'Tis mine to have soiled if I wish it." He rubbed his hands together, his eyes glittering in the lamplight. "I want you there with me. 'Tis not enjoyable to go alone."

Lora rolled her eyes, and without thinking first, she spoke. The lapse marked a rare occasion and, in her profession, a dangerous one. "'Tis because you cannot fight him yourself, isn't it?"

Simon's face drew into hard lines, and across the bouncing carriage he suddenly seemed larger, more threatening. Lora found herself suddenly reminded that while he could not fight Rogan and win, he could most certainly beat her.

His voice was cruel and nasty, and she could not restrain a flinch.

"Shut your mouth, Lora, unless it is opening for my cock. I do not pay you to talk."

Lora turned her head and stared at the leather shade, watching the shadows and light from the swaying lantern roam across the surface. Tears bit and stung at the corners of her eyes, but she held them in check, willing them away as she fantasized that she had taken the poison when Emeline offered it. Pictured standing above Simon while he took his dying breaths.

Silence reigned until they reached the amphitheater.

As they walked through the crowded lot and approached the stairs, Simon reached out and took her hand, placed it on his elbow, raising his voice to be heard over the screams and cheers washing over them as they grew close to the door. "Drop your anger, Lora."

"I spoke out of turn. I apologize." But her tone was stiffly formal and ice cold.

He paused and faced her, ready to be finished with the matter. "You were correct in what you said; I cannot fight him myself. He is younger and stronger, and it galls me to admit it."

Simon cleared his throat. Speaking to her about these things galled him as well, but he would not have his evening spoiled by her sulking. He used the weapon of choice in his arsenal of diffusing an angry woman; he revealed his emotions. Simon went so far as to infuse a hurt tone into his voice. "He tossed me out, Lora. Tossed me from the home that will one day be mine. I am only human; I can't help but want to watch as the puppy is beaten senseless and humiliated. However, I did not design the situation. Why should I not exploit it, though? 'Tis not my doing that he steps into that ring; I don't lure him there. Indeed, he seeks it like opium. That much you've seen for yourself."

Simon reached out and tilted her chin up so her eyes met his. "Come, Lora, and let's both not pout. All is forgiven. Let's go in and enjoy the show.

"I had my man bring the slave every night this past week, and the time is now. Who knows how soon my step-daughter will gather her courage? Perhaps as soon as tonight, or on the morrow. This may be my final opportunity to see the finest blood match ever." His eyes shone with excitement and expectation, and again he rubbed his hands together. "This should prove to be a most pleasant diversion whilst I wait for Emeline to kill him."

When it came to be his turn, Rogan climbed through the ropes. He took his place in one of the corners, jogging in place to warm his muscles, oblivious to the thunderous noise around him and the small presence of George behind his corner, ready with a cup of water and a towel. The crowds that filled the amphitheater screamed and stomped, an undulating mass of people all demanding their share of titillation.

Inside Rogan, churning with their own chaos, his desires and his guilt clamored for their share of satisfaction.

The Bull emerged as the crowd parted like the Red Sea,

and he met Rogan's eyes as he took his corner, his placid stillness a contrast to Rogan's light bouncing. Cheswick climbed into the ring as well, and held up his hands in an effort to silence the crowd.

"We've a special treat tonight, ladies and gents! The esteemed Father of Pugilism, the one, the only, Jack Broughton is here with us!"

Cheswick gestured to the balcony, and as the throng cheered for Broughton, Simon ducked down lest he be seen, scrambling to the floor as if he'd dropped something. Broughton stood and bowed to the crowd, a still-fit man of seventy-one years whose bald head shone in the yellow light of hundreds of tallow candles and oil lanterns.

After Broughton had taken his seat again, Cheswick gestured to each corner of the ring. "Our champ, The Duke, returns! He will once again be facing the very worthy adversary, The Bull!"

They toed the scratch, faced each other and waited as Cheswick finished working the crowd. Rogan sized him up again, though he felt he knew him. There were ways a fighter knew his opponent that others would not, deep truths shared while blows are traded. And Rogan knew the man before him fought for far more than simply himself; he could see it in his eyes.

"Who is your sponsor?" Rogan called out to him, though they stood only three feet apart.

The slave did not understand the question.

"What do you really fight for?" Rogan saw the recognition flare this time, and the slave's shoulders pulled back ever so slightly as he raised his chin.

"Freedom."

Rogan nodded. That, he could tell, was the truth.

The bell rang as Cheswick scrambled from the ring and Rogan dove in with a series of quick, hard knocks to The

Bull's face until they were blocked, and he took a few jabs to his ribs.

The fight wore on, and sweat and blood rained to the wooden floor of the ring as the two men battled like beasts, each fighting for reasons that ran deeper than wanting victory.

Rogan fought until he could no longer hear Orianna's voice or see her face, his guilt in her death pummeled into temporary submission. He pressed on, reaching for endurance, The Bull's blows more punishing than before. He took a blow to the gut; it seemed to go through him like a cannon ball to his spine. And he saw Emeline, the look of her, the lure of her, and he thrashed back at The Bull with all he had. Sweat burned his eyes until he could barely see, but his arms still swung out, thrusting quick blows that numbed his swollen hands.

The Bull landed a slow, slogging punch to Rogan's gut, and they both heard the crack of a bone breaking in The Bull's hand, but still they fought on.

All around them the crowd screamed and called encouragement, the air heavy with smoke and thick with urgency. The fight was longer than most, and they loved every moment of watching the battered men relentlessly brawling.

Slipping on the floor, Rogan grabbed onto The Bull before he fell, and the two of them locked arms, both feeble with exhaustion but unwilling to concede. They were both stumbling, sliding, their feet scrambling for purchase on the slick surface as they held each other up. Rogan felt The Bull going down, and he blinked rapidly, trying to clear his eyes as the whole room was a blur of burning sweat and The Bull's black, glistening skin.

His vision momentarily cleared, then clouded again, and The Bull was falling to his knees, dragging Rogan with him. He blinked and his sight cleared, just long enough for Rogan to catch a glimpse of Simon in the balcony.

Simon was on his feet, arms draped over the rail, leaning down as if his whole life were in the ring, watching Rogan with a flushed face and an odd expression of eager bloodlust and pure happiness.

Chapter 12

In the space of an instant, the crowd turned into a mob. Chairs flew and the cheers turned to screams as people were trampled beneath the feet of the churning throng that charged the ring. On the platform, slipping through the mix of sweat and blood, Cheswick struggled to take the center of the ring, while various lords followed suit.

The Duke and The Bull lay gasping for air on the floor. All around them the chaos intensified as those who had money riding on the fight tried to argue over who had won, whose knee had hit first.

A rickety wooden chair was tossed into the ring and shattered when it hit, pieces of wooden shrapnel flying into the air, a few of them scratching Rogan as they rained down. He was too exhausted to care.

A tiny tugging at his hand had him opening his eyes a crack, and in the smoky yellow light he saw George's face, pinched with worry and fear.

"We's got to go, milord. Can ye get up at all?"

Rogan didn't answer, couldn't move his mouth.

George glanced around at the insane mass of heaving bodies. "If we stay here, milord, I think we'll be killed."

"I don't care," Rogan mumbled. He closed his eyes again.

"Damn ye, milord," George yelled. "I do. Now get up!"

Slowly, excruciatingly, Rogan rolled to his side, and then his belly, pushed his legs and hands under him and managed to get to all fours, swaying with pain and effort. He stayed in that position until the room stopped spinning, and with George tugging on his arm, he struggled to get to his feet, slipping and falling back down until a hand clamped down on his upper arm and hauled him up.

Rogan opened an eye and saw the face of Jack Broughton. Too beaten and punished to be surprised, Rogan let Broughton wrap his arms around his waist and help him from the ring and out of the amphitheater. The crowds parted, allowing them to pass even as the noise grew louder, screams for payment colliding with cheers for Rogan and Broughton.

As they emerged from the amphitheater, George led the way to Rogan's mount, and with Broughton's instruction to the guards, the three men heaved Rogan into the saddle. Broughton took the reins and wound them around Rogan's wrists, knowing he'd never be able to hold them in his battered hands.

"Have you no second, other than this lad?" Broughton asked Rogan, after the guards had returned to their posts. "You're a fine bruiser, as good as I've seen, but you need more than a boy to look after you when you've been fighting."

Rogan managed to speak through his split lips. "I've never been beaten like this before."

"Aye. I have, only once, and it was the last time I fought. It'll be two days at least until you're out of your bed."

Broughton handed George up onto the rump of the stallion with an ease that belied his years. In the light of lanterns and the moon, he met Rogan's eyes, his own full of the wisdom of a man who had lived a complete life. "Take my advice: Stop fighting. Pugilism is a great sport for those who treat it as such. But you're fighting for something beyond sport, and it won't be found in that ring, son. It just won't."

The pain was so great Rogan thought he would be sick, his entire body hurting to the point of near unconsciousness, and yet still, he knew he would get back into the ring the moment his body would allow it. That knowledge had his heart feeling swollen, leaden, a useless lump of crippled matter. Would he never be free of the compulsion?

"I can't." Rogan confessed to the stranger what he could not admit to anyone else. "I can't stop."

"I know it feels that way," Broughton replied, his voice low and rough. "But you're going to kill someone fighting like that, and it won't likely be yourself. Take my word for it, son. I know what it's like to beat a man to death, and I know what it's like to live with guilt. Stop fighting, and start living."

With a slap to the stallion's rump to get them moving, Broughton turned and walked away.

Emeline waited five days and four nights, unable to execute her plan until her menses abated. At least, that's what she told herself when the truth of the matter ridiculed her: she waited for Rogan.

He did not come. Rogan did not return to her door any of those nights. Time ticked by on Simon's demand; now only nine days remained until her mother would be in danger from Simon's henchmen.

When it became obvious that Rogan did not intend to return to her doors, she knew she would have to press the matter. Her menses had passed; her excuses were gone; the time had come.

Emeline had a plan. She packed her bag with the finest

gowns Jeffrey had provided, and stuffed the vial of poison in the center where it would not be in danger of breaking.

Ready but for one thing, Emeline sat at the small desk and penned a note, setting it aside for later.

She opened her window, and a rush of cold autumn air swirled in, ruffling her hair and bringing with it scents of burning coal and wood, food cooking in the out-kitchens, and the fertile smells of damp earth and rotting leaves. Emeline leaned out into the wind, let the surge of it take her into its wild embrace, as if it could lift her and carry her away on a gust, and deposit her in a far-away place.

Mentally pushing aside the fantasy, she lowered her bag down the side of the building and let it drop. It fell behind a large bush, and she hoped it wouldn't rain.

Emeline sat on the side of her bed and waited, the clock on her mantle ticking away seconds, the monotonous, incessant sound driving her near to insanity.

The chambermaid came at precisely nine o'clock to empty her chamber pot and give her fresh water, bank the fire and see to her final needs before retiring.

"Ye're all set, then, miss?"

"Almost," Emeline replied. She came to stand by the maid and gave her her best smile, hoping she appeared friendly. "What is your name?"

The maid narrowed her eyes, took a step back. All the servants in the manse knew the master of the house doted on this woman, and Molly had made certain to be timely and efficient when servicing her rooms. "Molly."

Emeline sought to alleviate her suspicions. "I am very happy with your attentions here, Molly. Please do not distress yourself."

"Wot else will ye be needin', then?"

"A favor."

Molly dropped her suspicions and relaxed, this territory far more comfortable. "Oh, is ye? Wot, then?"

Emeline picked up one of the gowns Jeffrey had allowed her to have made, held it out so the maid could admire the ivory satin and lace, the bodice crusted with beads. "Are you aware how much this is worth on Monmouth Street?"

"Aye," Molly breathed, practically salivating over the gown, valued at more than she would earn in many years of service. "An I'm like ter get accused o' stealin' it."

"Not if I do not report it stolen. The Duke does not even know how many gowns he has purchased me. You would not get caught." She held it up so the beading would best be displayed, letting it catch and reflect the fire and candlelight until it sparkled like a dream. "Take it to Daniel Jones's on Monmouth or to Godfrey Gimbart's on Long Lane. Or take it to both, and then tell them so. They would likely try to outbid the other."

Molly took a few steps so she could get close enough to reach a finger out to touch the satin. She ran a grubby finger across the bodice. Her face mirrored a myriad of questions, from the wonder of what it would feel like to wear it, to the calculation of its worth, and finally the suspicion and mistrust Emeline had expected.

Emeline held the gown in the crook of her arm, went to the desk, picked up a folded piece of paper. "Do you know of His Grace's nephew? The one called Rogan?"

Molly's cheeks flushed. "Aye, I ken 'im. The one wit the green eyes."

"Yes, that's him," Emeline confirmed, and she handed the note to the servant. "Take this to him and tell no one. I will leave the gown between the mattresses of the bed for you to take when you are ready."

Molly narrowed her eyes once again. "That's it, is it?"

"That is it. But you must see to it that he alone receives the note. And you must tell no one. If you tell my secret,

Molly, I shall have to report the gown missing. But if you keep your silence, I will keep mine."

"Done." With that one word Molly accepted the paper and the terms. She stuffed it into her bodice and returned to the chamber pot, lifted it and left.

Jack Broughton's estimate had been accurate. Rogan had been unable to rise from his bed for two days. On the third day he was able to hobble around, his entire being having been rendered one giant, aching bruise. By the fourth day he could breathe without pain, and by the fifth he was able to dress and make his way to take his meals in the dining room, though Jeffrey and Anna had asked too many questions about the marks and cuts on his face and hands. This time Rogan told them he had been waylaid and robbed in an alley.

He doubted they believed him, but did not much care anymore. Let Simon tell them the truth, if he wished to, Rogan thought as he made his way back to his rooms after dinner.

He entered his sitting room and lowered himself onto the chaise. He did not possess the energy to remove his clothes or to make it to the bed. The Bull had beaten him worse than any other man he'd ever fought. Usually Rogan was able to recover rather quickly; his body was hard and fit, well accustomed to the rigors of hard work and a good fight. But not so with The Bull.

Rogan had nearly fallen asleep when a discreet knock sounded at his door.

Emeline.

The first thought that came to his mind was quickly dismissed with a surge of disappointment. It was he, not she, who prowled the halls in search of company.

"Enter."

The chamber maid slithered into his rooms, her face pink and expectant beneath the thin film of dirt on her skin. She scuttled over to his side. Her gaze slid over his body before darting to the bed. When she met his eyes again, she blushed furiously.

"I've somethin' fer ye," Molly said timidly. She extended her hand.

As Rogan reached for the paper she offered, Molly gave his fingers a quick caress as she passed it to him.

"What is it?" Rogan asked.

Molly lowered her voice. "A note."

"I daresay," Rogan remarked dryly, and he dipped into his purse for a coin, handed it to the maid so she would feel free to take her leave. "My thanks."

She accepted the coin with a little bob of appreciation, but she did not return to her duties. Molly stayed put, stood in front of Rogan with her hands dangling at the sides of her simple gown of dyed homespun.

Rogan waited for her to say or do something, and when she did not, he prompted her. "Is there something else?"

"She's sad." Molly screwed up her face in annoyance.

"Pardon?"

"Her eyes." Molly shrugged her shoulders and then used a grimy finger to scratch the side of her nose, staring at Rogan all the while. "Like yers."

She turned to leave, her hips swaying provocatively as she walked. She paused at the door before exiting. "I've worked 'ere a long while, and learnt plenty. I 'ear plenty, too, ye ken?"

"Aye, Molly, I ken fine," he assured her. Servants who were caught gossiping were dismissed without references. "Go ahead and speak freely. It will go no further, you've my word on that."

Finally Molly seemed to decide on the safe route, leaving with only a single warning. "Watch yerself. Ye seem too good a man fer this place, an likely as not, too good a man fer her.'"

She escaped through the door and closed it before Rogan could ask her another question.

Rogan got to his feet and went to the window, leaned his hip on the sill and opened the note, the moonlight bright enough that he did not require a candle to read it. He noticed that Emeline's handwriting was beautiful, her lettering displaying an advanced education. Who was this woman underneath all the layers? he wondered.

And then just as quickly he reminded himself that he did not need to know. Did not want to know. The instant longing he had felt for Emeline far too closely resembled what he had felt for Orianna, and he did not want or need to open himself to that kind of pain again, much less for a woman who belonged to his uncle.

Still, he read the note, his brows rising at the content.

> *Rogan,*
> *I would see you again. Will you meet me at midnight tonight in the carriage house? Please say yes.*
> *Your friend, Emeline*

He smiled and shook his head a little. *Your friend*, she wrote, to remind him of what they had shared before their meeting. It served as an effective enough reminder, he thought, because it made him feel sufficiently obliged to grant her simple request. He glanced at the timepiece on the mantle, saw the hour approached ten.

Rogan went to check on Kieran, found her sleeping, a novel open on her chest and the candles still burning. He tenderly took the book and set it aside, pressed his hand on his little sister's cheek for a moment before blowing out the candles.

He returned to his rooms, made use of the washstand

to freshen up, changed his clothes from the fancy velvet he had been wearing for dinner into his plain cotton breeches, a clean linen shirt, and a brushed cotton jacket. He filled a purse with money, enough to buy Emeline passage on a ship or a fortnight at an inn, tucked it away so he could offer it to her, and set out his cloak.

Sad eyes, like yours. The maid's words had unsettled him, enough that he regarded himself in the mirror, meeting his own eyes.

He leaned in closer to his reflection, the oil lamps that burned in sconces on either side of the looking glass illuminating his face. Sad eyes? The eyes that gazed back at him looked the same as always, bright green, framed by long, thick black lashes and the mottling of healing bruises. The Bradburn eyes. His mother's eyes. He saw his father there, too, in the lines of his face, the cut of his jaw, the shape of his mouth, the arch of his brows.

And Rogan could not help but think of the strength of both his parents, and he knew it coursed through him, as well.

He would go see Emeline in the carriage house, and he would dig deep inside of himself. Not be like the other men who saw her in a mercenary, predatory way, but as a woman, a human, a friend.

He could do it, Rogan assured himself. He had strength of character. He was his parent's son, Bradburn and Mullen combined.

Rogan looked deep into his own eyes again. "It is all inside me," he told his own reflection. "I decide who I am. What I will be."

The moon hung fat and full in the unusually clear night sky, the moonlight so intense that it cast long, vague shadows over the property. Rogan kept close to the cover of the naked trees, the gnarled, knotty limbs stretching over his head like supplicating fingers reaching for the sky.

Beneath his feet the earth felt spongy and cold, gripping the bottom of his boots and releasing them with little sucking sounds as he walked.

His heart pounded. He tried to think of its cause as friendly concern, and not anticipation.

The carriage house was tucked alongside the stables, a pretty little structure that mimicked the lines of the mansion but lacked the monstrous Gothic intimidation. He approached with care, skirting the side of the building, noticing that all the windows were dark. Had she come, he wondered, or had she changed her mind?

The question was almost instantly answered when he saw something move by the door, a flash of ivory flesh not covered by the long cloak and hood she wore. A hand, ghostly white in the darkness, and a finger, crooked and beckoning.

He followed, feeling as though in a dream. The gravel crunching under the soles of his boots sounded far away and surreal, the cold gusts of wind and dampness seeming illusory despite the chilly droplets condensing on his skin.

But there was nothing imaginary about the way his heartbeat increased at the sight of her form, shadowy though it seemed in the moonlight. He had but to see her and he felt an immediate punch of agitation, the thudding of his heart coming harder and faster, the rush of blood in his veins an unsettling tingle.

The iron handle stung Rogan's bare hand, so cold it hurt to grab it and pull the door shut. Around him the carriages looked like huge, black boulders in the darkness. The thick, trapped air smelled of leather, oiled metal, and the underlying whiff of horses, manure and hay. Beneath his feet the floor was gritty with dirt and tracked-in gravel on the hardwood. He reached out his hands to feel his way, seeing in the distance the light of a single lantern.

As he grew closer he saw that the lantern hung inside

one of the largest carriages. He approached the open door and stopped when he saw her.

Emeline sat on one of the long bench seats, the hood of her cloak pushed back so it fell down onto her shoulders, revealing her hair, gleaming burnished gold. She sat and watched him, her sapphire eyes even on his, her face inscrutable, the only sign of her anxiety the rapid beating of the pulse in her neck.

"You came," she whispered.

"Aye." And he was grateful for the darkness that she could not see the way his hands shook.

"Come in."

He climbed inside and she reached to pull the door closed behind him. Inside the carriage she had the leather shades drawn tight so the light would not disturb the darkness of the carriage house and thus not betray their presence in case anyone would by chance enter. Rogan sat on the opposite seat, noticing the rich velvet, the drapes that surrounded the little windows, the lap rugs neatly folded and ready for use. Looked at anything but her.

Emeline let herself stare at him, long and hard, wanting to memorize the shape of his face, the exact green of his eyes, the way his hair hung in waves to his shoulders. He had bruises on his face, and again she felt the urge to reach out and touch him, to soothe his pain. She took in his every detail. She would not see him again after this night, and she wanted to remember her only friend, the only man who had ever wanted to know her for who she was inside, even if that had ended the first time he saw her. It had been a gift.

Even still, his presence unnerved her. The sight of him so close, the undeniably rugged male power he exuded served to make her aware that she had designed to make herself very alone, and very vulnerable, to a man who clearly could overpower her if he chose to do so.

She cleared her throat and unconsciously wrapped her fists around the opening of her cloak. "I am grateful you came, Rogan Mullen."

He shifted uncomfortably on the seat, his heart hammering away. His attraction to her had not changed, and lust spiked in his belly, hot and almost painful. Best to find out what she needed and be on his way. "How much money do you need?"

"Why do you ask me that?"

"I offered you my help, and 'tis obvious you do not need me to aid your escape from the rooms where Jeffrey locked you, aye? So I assume you need money?"

Emeline did not reply at first, but simply watched him, trying to read his expression in the golden light of the lantern. He spoke bluntly, as if in a rush, and yet as he did his eyes lingered on her lips, her throat, her hair.

"Shall I hang a veil between us, Rogan?"

He relaxed slightly, the slightest hint of a grin tugging at his lips. "I don't know if it would help at this point."

"Can we speak plainly? Please? The way we once did."

He shrugged and slipped out of his cloak, finding the air too warm despite the chilly grip of the damp autumn night. "I don't know what to say."

"I missed our talks. I missed your company."

Looking at her beauty, hearing her voice, feeling his own lust, Rogan felt like Orianna had never been farther from him since the day she died. And it made him ashamed that he did not even want to leave Emeline's presence, despite how disloyal it was to his wife's memory. Instead he wanted to take her, right there on the floor of the carriage, pull her underneath his body and thrust himself into her.

But he would not be like the other men, like Simon and Jeffrey. He tore his gaze from hers. "It was as you predicted it would be. 'Tis partly why I did not come back to your door."

"I know."

"I do not want it to be so."

"Because you do not wish to want me, or because of your wife?"

"Both."

She nodded, had figured as much.

"Have you ever been to the theater?" she asked.

Her sudden change of topic caught him off guard. "Of course."

"I have been, also," she said, remembering. "My mum used to take me, long ago when I was small. I saw many plays, and would fancy someday becoming a player. It was a foolish dream, of course, and yet I would wish to be on the stage, playing a part. My mum told me only the lowest of women did so, and I never mentioned it to her again."

Emeline looked down at her twined fingers gripping the folds of her cloak, wanting his understanding. "And I got my wish, in a twisted way. That is me, Rogan, as if on a stage. I am like the players, the actors. That is me, Rogan, when I am with Jeffrey, with Simon. The other night, in the parlor, I played a part. The part of mistress. For years, I have been playing parts, so much so that I began to think I did not know who I truly was anymore. And my mum, she was right, wasn't she? Only the lowest of women. . . ."

Rogan opened his mouth to speak, but Emeline held up her hand. "Please listen. 'Tis difficult, and I would say these things before I lose my nerve."

Rogan nodded, gestured for her to continue.

Emeline gathered her thoughts and began again. "I played the part with them, Rogan. It was the only way I could get by. Survive it all. Do you see? I cut myself off from myself. Played the parts, acted the scenes, and tried, desperately, not to feel anything.

"But not with you. Never with you. The girl I once was, so long ago I scarcely remember her, wasn't truly cut off at all, but was only sleeping somewhere inside of me. She woke the day you knocked at my door. I have been myself with you, from behind the safety of the barriers between us. 'Tis for that reason that I asked you to come here tonight."

He watched her as she spoke. She was scandalously beautiful, everything about her soft and alluring, from her hair to her lips to her breasts, a man's most erotic fantasy sprung to life. She was pure and defiled; innocent and sensual. There was promise in her eyes, tempered with bruised naïveté. Hers was a look that ignited a man's lust even as it pleaded for his honor.

And yet there was more: quiet strength. Bold honesty. He forced himself to try to look beyond her appearance, to be the man he'd promised her he was.

"You woke me, Rogan," she whispered again. "I wanted to thank you for that. You have opened my eyes, unlocked my doors, brought down my barriers. In a way, given me back my self."

"I did nothing." Rogan pushed away the praise that was unwarranted as he sat before her simmering with lust.

"You did everything." She smiled at him, then, and tilted her chin down, looking at once incredibly sad and infinitely wise. "You would have fought him, that night in the parlor, wouldn't you?"

"Jeffrey?"

"Yes. You were willing to fight for my honor, even when you know I have none."

He shrugged away her words. "'Tis what any decent man would do."

"Decent man," she whispered. "No, Rogan, it goes beyond decency, though that is rare enough. You are an uncommon man amongst multitudes of ordinary men, Rogan. I see that in you. I see the struggles in you, your pain. And I see your goodness."

Rogan felt a tightening in his chest. "You do not know me, Emeline."

"I know enough." She leaned forward, an encouragement for him to once again look deep in her eyes. "And I wanted you to know me, too."

She paused, her heart pounding so hard she thought it might burst. Her defenses were down, and she felt like a butterfly newly emerged from the barrier of its cocoon, naked, exposed, soft and vulnerable. But she had come this far, and would see the rest out.

He wanted her, she could see it in his eyes. But he controlled himself, and she saw that, too. Underneath it all, it was his control that drew her. She had never known a man to show restraint; she had never felt safe with a man.

He had done what he promised. He'd taught her something different. She did not fear him.

Sitting still and silent, Rogan watched her, his eyes burning. He smoldered with his leashed passions, and the combination of his proximity and his self-discipline made something tremble inside her, a wobbling, tremulous emergence of her own unlocked feelings and desires and needs.

"I can only imagine how deeply your wife loved you, Rogan."

He felt a burning in his throat, his eyes, his chest. Still, he said nothing.

"'Tis so beautiful to me."

"What is?" he asked, and he hated the sound of his voice, rough and thick.

"How deeply you love. I see it in your eyes, and it is the most beautiful thing I have ever seen." She smiled, a fanciful curve of lips that was too young, too sweetly girlish for the devastatingly sexual look of her. "I never knew a man could love that way."

She averted her eyes and pulled her hood over her head, fastened her cloak. It was time to go.

She moved closer to the door of the carriage, but paused in front of him, brought her eyes to his once again. Slowly, as if of its own volition, her hand reached out and touched his face, her fingertips the barest caress on his cheek.

It was the very first time Emeline had ever touched a man because she'd wanted to, and the newness of it stole her breath.

His skin was warm, soft on the plane of his cheekbone and then rough with the bristle of his emerging beard beginning just at the hollow of his cheek. With a small motion she did as she'd longed to do before, and she tenderly brushed her fingertips over one of his bruises, wanting to soothe him. She hoped she always remembered the heat of his skin against hers, the scent of him so close to her, faintly spicy, undeniably male. Her fingers began to tremble. She dropped her hand away. "Goodbye, Rogan."

Chapter 13

Rogan's hand flew out and grabbed Emeline's before she could reach for the door to the carriage.

"Wait."

She let him gently pull her back until she sat beside him. With his eyes boring into hers, he reached out, pushed her hood down, and unfastened her cloak with two deft twists of the frogs. He pushed it from her shoulders until it fell away, revealing her blue silk gown, the same one she had been wearing when he had seen her in the parlor. He saw the pulse in her neck pick up its pace once again, a fast throb in the elegant column of her slim neck. And he felt the same pounding in his own chest.

"I am only a man, Emeline. I cannot look at you and not desire you."

Emeline's lips parted and trembled, but she held her silence.

He reached out, cupped her chin and tilted it up so he could look into her eyes. And he tried to see beyond her allure, past her appearance. He looked for the woman inside, the hidden person of her heart.

The way she approached him, fearlessly, openly, despite all that had been done to her made him aware of just how strong she was, how able she was to separate one man from another, her own pain from someone else's. He saw doubts in her eyes, hopes, secrets, understanding, and so much more.

He saw Emeline, the person, the woman behind the barrier of her own beauty.

It touched him deeply, made him want to be the man she hoped he could be, to show her that at least one man could see beyond her seductiveness and find the woman within.

With gentle hands he swept her hair back from her shoulders, then let his hands touch the skin of her neck, his fingertips tracing the graceful lines up to her jaw. He cupped her face and leaned in close, let his breath mingle with hers, savoring the scent of her, like honeysuckle and warm summer nights.

"You know you are beautiful to look upon," he observed quietly, "and you know you are desirable. But you are more than that. I see more. Your soul's beauty beggars that of your flesh."

She trembled beneath his touch, his words, did not move or blink, afraid to break the spell. His words should have been dangerous and insidious. Even a week before they would have been dismissed as the words of a man who wanted something in return, and would have bounced off her walls like wayward arrows. But it was too late to attempt to raise the drawbridge against Rogan. He was inside her castle gates, and Emeline did not want him ever to leave.

And so his words were a nostrum, healing and wondrously invigorating. She was truly awakened; every feeling she'd ever painstakingly numbed now lay open, raw and exposed, prickling with awareness.

"Rogan," she breathed, but did not give voice to the words that welled up, wanting release: know me; understand me. She wouldn't ask for what she didn't deserve.

"What do you want, Emeline?"

"Touch me."

"I am touching you. My hands are in your hair."

No, she thought, they are around my heart. But she couldn't say that, either. His face was close, so close. She wanted him to kiss her, to touch her, to teach her what the feelings in her body meant. Never before had she felt this way; she hadn't known herself capable. And yet, here she was in a carriage after midnight with Rogan Mullen's hands buried in her hair, cradling her scalp, his long fingers moving in slow circles as his breath mingled with her own. She felt drenched with desire, saturated with sensation. The slightest stroke of his fingertips across her skin made her tremble.

"You do not have to desire me," she said at last. Her voice was breathless, but she was beyond caring. "You may have me."

Rogan struggled against his baser instincts. She was so close and tempting, her breath a humid caress on his skin, her mouth slightly open so all he could think of was entering it with his tongue.

But it was the way she looked at him that had him holding back. In her eyes glistened pure admiration. She looked at him as if he were a hero, a Prince Charming of fairy tales that ended in "happily ever after."

Rogan knew what he really was, though. He was a beast, a man, a hero, and a scoundrel, all in one. He wanted to lift her up and carry her away from Jeffrey and Simon, be her knight, her savior. He also wanted to ravage her, keep her, and plumb every silken depth of her body.

He wanted to do these things even while knowing he could give her nothing of himself in return, because unlike fairy tales, Rogan had learned painful lessons about real life. In real life, people became ill and died long before their time, and happily ever after got burned away by a morbid fever. In real life, people did horrific, awful things for which there is never enough punishment, never enough suffering.

Rogan thought of the amphitheater and wished he were well enough to return. Five nights were too many, and his demons were not even close to satisfied.

And here was the most beautiful, desirable woman he'd ever seen, his uncle's mistress, no less, offering herself up for a release that Rogan hadn't allowed himself since Orianna died. A release his body wholeheartedly desired. His penis was thick, full, as hard as stone, and his balls ached worse than a wound.

"No, Emeline." Rogan spoke more harshly than he intended. He pulled his hands from her hair. He would not be like Jeffrey and Simon. He would not take from Emeline what he could not return in full, his baser nature be damned.

"I understand," she said, even though she clearly did not. She tilted her head down in that way of wisdom and sadness combined. "I suppose there isn't anything left to say."

She pulled her cloak around her shoulders once again, fastened it with fingers that shook. Raising the hood, she lifted her chin. When she reached for the handle of the carriage, his hand stopped her once again.

Emeline froze, looking down at his hand circling her wrist. His hands were large, square, and strong, the rough skin dark and abraded and scabbed. In his grip her arm looked pale and slim, velvet-smooth, as fragile as a flower's stem, easily snapped.

"I cannot seem to let you go," he said softly.

Emeline brought her eyes to meet his. His eyes burned like nothing she'd ever seen, a brilliant green blaze of emerald fire. With his dangerously handsome face and waves of black hair, he could have been a fabled pirate. As if reading her mind, he sardonically raised a brow, his mouth curling up on one side in an ironic grin, making him look all the more like an infamous buccaneer.

"So what shall we do, Princess Emeline?" He tilted his head and let his eyes roam over her, from the top of her golden head to the bit of cleavage her gaping cloak revealed. She was so lovely, so sensual, and yet, somehow innocent. It didn't seem possible until a thought occurred to him. "Has anyone ever pleasured you, Emeline?"

"Pleasured," she repeated the word as if in a trance. She couldn't stop looking at his mouth, the shape of his lips.

"Come here."

She moved closer, helpless to do otherwise. Slowly, he pulled her onto his lap so she lay across him on the bench seat. The carriage bounced slightly in time to their movements, the lantern light swaying and casting shadows over them as he cradled her closely.

"Have you ever been kissed?" he asked.

"Of course. Many times."

"Did you like it?"

"No," she said firmly. "Never."

"Do you want me to kiss you?"

Emeline did not answer, couldn't. She nodded.

"Do you think you will like it?"

"Yes," she breathed. "I think I shall."

He watched her for a long moment, and finally he lowered his mouth to hers, lightly traced her lips with his tongue. She tasted honey-sweet, as he knew she would. He pulled back and looked into her eyes again. They were dark with hunger, curiosity, and arousal.

"They say that Sleeping Beauty was awakened with a kiss."

"No, Rogan." Emeline slid her hands behind his neck, pulled his head so his lips touched hers. "She was awakened with your words."

Emeline's whole body felt heavy, drugged, her senses overwhelmed with sensation. And strangely, there was no fear at all, no reservations, no sense of danger. Only a curious heat that curled through her, from her belly to her thighs, and she knew it to be real desire. She lifted her head a bit, wanting to deepen the kiss, but Rogan held back, smiled a reckless grin, so darkly male it stoked her heat.

He spoke only two words, but they inflamed her as nothing else. "Not yet."

Restraint was not something Emeline knew men to display. Rogan was in control of himself, and knowing that made her all the more comfortable to allow him to lead her.

Rogan shook with his control, nearly overwhelmed with the beauty of her, her scent, her wicked purity, the heady mix she exuded, temptress and wounded innocent combined. She stared up at him with trust and hunger, her body like Venus draped across him. The light of the lantern turned her skin to creamy gold, her hair gleamed like pale amber around her lovely face, her full lips were parted and still moist from his tongue.

He had not touched another woman since Orianna, and the year of celibacy hit him like a rogue wave, crashing over him and threatening to sweep him under and away.

But he held to his discipline. He remembered one of his first conversations with Emeline, what she had told him she believed: *Men think about their needs, our bodies, our capitulation, their pleasure. Always their pleasure, and always at a woman's expense.* He would teach her something different, no matter how hard the lust hammered his resolve.

"Don't be afraid."

"I do not fear you."

"You shall never have cause to. I swear it."

Rogan lowered his mouth to hers again, inhaled her breath as if he inhaled the scent of a flower. He dipped down, and as she reached for his mouth with hers, he feinted left and instead kissed the delicate line of her jaw, the tender skin of her neck. He kissed the hollow beneath her ear until she moaned, soft, raspy sounds of pleasure that came from the back of her throat. The sounds lured him to find the place of their origin, and Rogan did, nibbled his way to the vibrations until his lips pressed against them.

And then there was no more teasing. Her lips were parted when he took her mouth, and his tongue entered, touched hers in sensual battle.

Emeline's head spun as if from too much wine. She was falling, falling, but no, his arms had her, strong and tight, clasped to his warm, hard chest so close she could feel his heartbeat, as fast as her own. His mouth was magic, his lips soft but firm, the scent of his skin intoxicating, the stubble on his face an erotic brush against her chin.

Rogan's hand wandered over her back. He could feel the stiff fabric of her stays, the boning, and beneath it, the warmth of her body. Her gown was silk, but he longed to feel the warm velvet of her skin, knew it would be plush and supple. His fingers found her laces and began to pluck them open. He wanted her. Oh, he wanted her naked and writhing. In his mind's eye he saw her spread out, the tip of his cock shining as he pressed between her silken folds.

Her fingers were on his, helping him open her gown.

"I would do what you need. What you desire. I would give you that." Emeline spoke against his mouth, her breath mingling with his. And in her mind there was only one thought: yes. Oh God, yes, this is what it is really about. Giving without reservation to the one you desire. The same flesh but your own choice. It should not be allowed to be called the same act.

But then Rogan's hands moved away, and he set her from him. "No," he said. And then again, firmer. "No."

"Rogan, what are you doing?"

"Nothing. We're not doing this."

Confusion shadowed her brow. "You want me."

"I—" he seemed to cut off his own words before he said too much. "You wanted me to kiss you, and I did." He heard his own words, realized how offensive they sounded and wished he could take them back, hating the way she looked, sad and soft and vulnerable. "Jesus, Emeline. I can't be more than this to you. I can't offer you more. I won't take what I can't give. Do you understand?"

Hurt welled up in her chest, unlike any other injury she had ever felt. Hating Simon as she did, he could not hurt her, and her mixture of disgust and pity for Jeffrey did the same; they insulated her from them.

None of that applied to the way she felt for Rogan. He had come to her from behind closed doors, and by doing so had seen more than anyone else. She opened herself to him then, and now, and there could be no going back.

Emeline had lived through too much to shy away from something that held such promise.

"It is you who does not understand." Emeline smiled at him. "I could love you, Rogan." She quickly placed her fingers against his mouth before he could reply. "Wait, before you speak, let me say this: I know you do not feel that way for me, that you never would. I do not expect you to. I know what I am, what you likely think of me."

She smiled, her eyes dark in the dim light, far away and full of fancy. "I have imagined your life. Imagined your wife. She must have been very special to be worthy of you, to win your love. And you love her still, I know, and it makes it all the more beautiful, to know that love can last beyond death.

"But you reached out to me despite everything. You

looked beyond what you know I am. You made me know that I could love a man. You maybe cannot imagine what a relief that is, to know I could. I am still capable, despite everything.

"Again, I do not tell you this to burden you with it in any way, but to thank you for that and to tell you before—" she paused, not wanting to reveal her plans lest he try to stop her. "Because it is the truth," she finished simply.

He took her hand and kissed it a bit too fiercely, held it tight like the gift she'd just given him. "What can I say, Emeline? I do not want to hurt you."

"You haven't. You have shown me more than you could ever know. Given me back pieces of myself I thought dead. Given me strength."

What she did not share was that strength would be directed at Simon. She would kill him herself before he could murder her mother and Rogan. Emeline had been many things in her life, a daughter, a stepdaughter, a whore, a thief, a player, and a pawn. Now she would sink even lower, become a murderer, risk dangling on the gallows rather than see hurt those she cared for. And if she succeeded and escaped without being caught, she would steal everything of value, sell it all, find her mother and release her, buy them passage on a ship sailing into an unknown future, anywhere, it did not matter.

If she did not succeed? Well, better to die at the hands of the hangman than to live with the blood of her mother and Rogan staining her hands. For that matter, it was better to die on the gallows than live the rest of her life as Simon's ward.

Emeline slid from his lap and retied her laces. She adjusted her cloak and covered her hair once again. From deep in the cowl of her hood, she looked at him one last time, committing everything about him to her memory. Her lips were swollen from his kisses, her chin burned from the rasp of his incipient beard. And inside her mouth she could still taste him.

Once again she moved to the door of the carriage, and this time they both knew he'd let her go. She paused, turned and looked at him one last time, unable to keep her eyes from him. "I think I maybe do love you, Rogan, as strange as that may seem to you. How could I not, when you have gone to such lengths to make it possible." A feeling of shyness had her cheeks burning. "Goodbye."

She ducked out and took off at a run, her mission still ahead of her.

"Emeline. Wait, please." Rogan reached out to grab her once again. But her cloak slid through his fingers and she disappeared into the darkness of the building as if swallowed by the night.

He sat for a minute, the scent of her lingering around him, her warmth gone. The unreality of the night still lingered, as if it had been a dream. Had she really sent for him, lain across his lap and offered herself until he thought he would go mad with need and desire?

Rogan played it out in his mind, wishing he had said different things. Thought about what she had told him about herself. And the things she had shown him: Her strength, her ability to extend what could not be returned, her utter boldness.

Just then he remembered something, a certain look in her eyes, a hesitation. A reticence. The way she watched him as if painting a mental picture. He realized then what had been nagging at him, a subtle perception about her that had been eclipsed by her offers of sex and the nearly mindless punches of pure lust that he'd had to fight against. She was not a woman who simply wanted to share a moment. She was a woman saying goodbye.

In an instant Rogan extinguished the lantern and leapt from the carriage. He took off after her. She had not taken his money; he could not imagine how she thought she would escape, where she thought she would go.

Clouds had rolled in, obscuring the moonlight that had shone brightly only an hour ago. Rogan glanced to the sky, mentally cursing the English weather that so rarely cooperated.

He searched the grounds for her, his eyes straining through the darkness. He did not dare to call out. He glanced around, getting his bearings, afraid to skirt the long driveway in case she had taken off into the woods that began in the rear of the property. His body ached, fatigued and battered, but he pushed away the pain as he walked.

Rogan saw something moving in his peripheral vision, turned and spied a shadowy form in the distance, just beyond where the driveway met the road. He spied what could have been a cloaked woman moving between the two huge pillars that dominated the entrance.

Rogan followed in a soundless jog, not moving too fast lest he slip on the wet, slick patches under the naked trees, where only moss and lichen grew beneath the fallen leaves. The night air sighed all around him, damp and cold, scented with pine and smoke.

Foolish woman, he silently raged. Likely too proud to ask him for money or help. Did she care nothing for her own safety?

He made it out to the road, glanced up and down the street both ways for a glimpse of her, saw nothing. Stealing into the shadows of an ancient oak, he crouched down and waited. Finally he saw her, moving among the shadows in the direction of the city. Her figure appeared hunched, and, for a moment, he wondered if it was Emeline he followed after all. Still he kept up his pursuit, unsure until the cloud cover parted enough, for once fortuitous, and he saw it was, in fact, she. She carried a bag, so bulky and stuffed it tilted her to one side, its weight obviously slowing her progress.

He swore under his breath, a stream of wicked Gaelic curses best kept to a ship's deck. How dare she endanger herself this way? He wanted to grab her, shake sense into her. She could not have made herself more of a target if she'd dressed as a prostitute and strutted down the Strand.

Still, he wondered what mission had brought her to this conclusion, what she was after, and the curiosity kept him at bay. He would follow her, he decided, and see where she went, regretting that his only weapon was the dagger in his boot.

Rogan drew as close to Emeline as he dared but kept to the shadows, watching over her like an archangel.

Chapter 14

Emeline paused under a tree, leaned against its trunk and set her heavy bag down on the ground, panting from the strain of carrying it. She gave the bag a peevish kick, annoyed with herself for bringing so much. Still, she knew that the gowns she carried would bring a hefty price, and she would need as much money as she could raise if she would buy her mother's freedom and escape England before she was caught for murder.

Murder. The word sounded so hideous for what she intended to do. It sounded more like what one does in an alleyway with a knife, fast and quick, to steal a hefty purse.

It did not sound to Emeline to be the correct word for killing Simon. An image of him welled in her mind like a nightmare, his patrician features twisted into a mask of ecstasy as he forced her to her knees in front of him. And of the pain of that night, the pain of rape and also of defeat; she had fought with him until she had nothing left. Always he tried to take the elusive essence of her, the only thing that cannot be taken by force: her heart and soul.

She pushed the images and thoughts away and reassured herself that Simon would never hurt her again.

And she thought of Rogan, his breath against her ear as

he said, *Don't be afraid*. I do not fear, she answered him in her mind. Not anymore.

What is there to fear, when there is nothing left?

Simon had taken her mother away, stolen her innocence, her girlhood, her virtue. He had turned her into a whore, his own, Jeffrey's. He had made her sink so low.

Emeline clung to what she knew, what was real in a world where her existence did not seem to matter. She thought of Camille, Rogan's mother, an Englishwoman like herself who had dared to want more, dared to think she could decide her own future and worth. Camille, Rogan had told her, had risked everything.

And so shall I, Emeline assured herself.

She would risk anything, even her neck on the gallows, to save the only two people left in this world who mattered to her. She bent and hefted the bag, slinging it on her left shoulder to give her right a break from the weight. Down the lane she pressed, stepping around an uncollected pile of night soil.

The tangle of city streets lay a few miles ahead. She glanced around, wondering if she were still on Bradburn property or if she had passed that point. She felt her legs tremble, from the weight of her bag and her mission, combined.

Murder.

The word screamed in her mind again, piercing all other thought, as cold and ruthless as a blade.

She pressed farther on, mile after mile, as the sun began to light the sky. She'd been walking for hours, and hoped to find her way to Monmouth Street by noon so she could unload the gowns, gain enough coin to buy a meal, and then hire a livery to take her the rest of the way to the brownstone that Simon most frequently inhabited.

The stink of the city grew stronger, a combination of animal droppings and human waste, sulfuric industrial smoke and coal fires. As she approached the denser clog of streets, off to every side there seemed to be an alley or passage, the cobbled streets veering off haphazardly, pitted with deep holes and gullies. The traffic picked up, even in the pre-dawn hour. Liveries and carriages rumbled past her, splashing through the streets and sending sheets of dark, filthy water spraying into the air.

Emeline kept the handles of her bag slung over her shoulder and cradled the bundle to her chest. She had grown up in the city, knew well the dangers inherent in walking alone. She also knew that the dangers intensified when one carried anything of value.

A few street urchins ran by, jostling her, kicking up dirty water from puddles as they streaked past her. Emeline gasped a bit as some of the liquid flew into her face, temporarily blinding her eyes. She used her cloak to wipe it away, but as she did she let go of her bag enough that another guttersnipe came flying out of nowhere, swooping in to grab it. He wrenched it from her grasp and took off running.

Emeline screamed for him to stop, ran after him, but the corset around her waist had her gasping, unable to breathe after a quick sprint. She slowed her pace, her hand clenched to the sharp pain that gathered like a fist in her side, and knew to give up the chase. A woman in skirts and stays was no match to children who lived on the street and ran to stay alive.

"Noooo," she wailed. Her hands were hot, balled fists, and rage at her own impotence had her stomping her foot. Her whole future had been in that bag. Tears of fear and anger sparked in her eyes, and she gulped to keep from sobbing. She'd risked everything, and had lost it all at the very first turn.

A blur went by her, and she did not bother to look up as she struggled against the tide of hopelessness that threatened to engulf her. What did it matter? Everything she owned had been in that bag, even the poison meant for Simon. Everything.

She leaned against a brick building, its rough exterior pulling at her woolen cloak. Her legs threatened to buckle. What now, she wondered. Where could she possibly go? She put her hands over her face, and gave in to her despair, just for a moment.

Traffic grew heavier, the noise of the clatter of carriages, horses, wagons, and all manner of conveyances filling the air, mingling with the vendors who hawked their products, selling everything from fruit to the latest political pamphlet.

And all Emeline could do was sob into her hands, slumped, exhausted, and starving, without a single thing to sell to gain even a shilling to buy an apple.

She pushed herself away from the wall so she could stand on her own power, to glance around the busy street and try to force her mind to form a plan. Her legs wanted to give out from sheer exhaustion; she'd been walking for hours and miles, had been awake all night.

Emeline made herself reckon with the truth: She was alone in the city. Rogan and the Bradburns were behind her, even as Simon hunted them as surely as a falcon hovers over an unsuspecting rabbit, silent and unexpected.

She needed a new plan. The time had come to salvage what remained of her mother's life, and by God, her own.

Emeline saw a few people staring at her, and supposed she made a fine sight, with her hair dank and dirty from the water that had been flung in her face, the hem of her gown and cloak stained dark with mud, wet with dirty water and blotched with grass stains. The noise on the street intensified, the vendors' voices shouted above the rumbling racket, and a few passersby bumped into Emeline as she tried to make her way down the street on wobbling legs.

Rogan emerged out of the chaos. He registered the look of astonishment on Emeline's face and he grinned. His hands were full; in his right he carried the bag that had been snatched, in his left he had the scruff of the lad who had stolen it.

He stopped in front of Emeline and set the bag at her feet, then dangled the boy before her, both of them breathing heavily from exertion. The urchin could not have been more than ten, but it was difficult to tell his age when he looked so undernourished. The boy hung from the back of his jacket as Rogan held him up, his feet off the ground. The boy said nothing, just met Emeline's gaze with an insolent look on his dirty, heart-shaped face.

"Apologize to the lady," Rogan ordered.

At first the lad held his tongue, until a shake from Rogan prompted a response. "Sorry," the boy muttered dutifully.

Rogan turned the boy around so to face him, and took a stern, fatherly tone. "Go down to Wapping Dock, find the ship called *Paradise*. Ask for the captain, and tell him Rogan said to put you to work. You'll get three meals a day, your own bunk, and wages with it." He appraised the boy as he grinned in reluctant admiration. "If you can climb as you can run, you'll be a boon in the rigging."

A glint of interest gleamed in the lad's eyes and overtook his truculence. Rogan set the boy down. The urchin hit the ground running and disappeared into the crowds. Rogan shook his head as he turned back to Emeline, picked her bag back up, slung it over his shoulder, and took her by the hand. "Come with me. We'll get you something to eat, and then you're going to tell me what is so important that you'd walk all the long night for it."

Emeline yanked her hand away from him with as much energy as she could muster, annoyed with herself for the relief she felt. "You are serious?"

"Of course."

"You followed me."

"I did."

"Why did you do that?"

Rogan shrugged, and to her increasing annoyance, managed to look amused. "I had no other plans for the remainder of the evening."

"Don't be brazen, Rogan."

"I would tell you not to be foolish," he remarked, glancing around at the busy street and then down to the bag in his hand, now sodden and dirty from being repeatedly splashed. "But it's a bit late for that, aye?"

She scrubbed her face with her hands, exhaustion making everything feel fuzzy and distant. "How did you know?" she asked.

He paused, cocked his head. His eyes gleamed with something beyond understanding. "Let's just say I'm looking deeper."

Emeline swayed a little, and Rogan slipped his arm around her waist, pulled her to him and gave her no more room for argument. In a state of complete fatigue, she let him take her where he would, the trust she had in him making it easy to lean against his strength, his warmth, and to know that wherever he took her she would be safe.

Pulling her along, Rogan spotted a tidy tavern, its front walk meticulously swept, the hanging board on the outside claiming the cleanest rooms in London. He took Emeline inside, made arrangements for a room and food, and waited as the staff readied one and gathered the key.

In the interior darkness, a trio of lonely men sat grouped together at the bar, as if to deny that they were truly alone. Despite the early hour, each had a pint of ale sitting by his food. One glanced over to Rogan and then back to his companions. He murmured something. Soon enough, all three men lifted their pints and saluted the brawny, younger man.

"The Duke," one cried. And then together, in a drunken slur, "All hail The Duke!"

Just then the goodwife returned, an iron key ring dangling from her hands. Rogan ignored Emeline's surprised expression, merely shrugged his shoulders and took her around the waist once again. He tugged her along, up three narrow flights of stairs until they reached the top floor. The room the goodwife showed them to was a charming nook, the bed tucked under the eaves between gable windows that overlooked the street.

The hanging board was accurate, Rogan noted. The floor had been scrubbed clean, a round rag rug in the center. The quilts on the bed had a mended, patched look to them, but smelled of washing soap and appeared unlikely to be crawling with lice and vermin. Though sparsely appointed, the room had the amenities they would require, a small table with two chairs, candles in pewter sticks, a stand with a basin and a pitcher of clean water, folded linens and flannels on the bottom shelf.

Rogan thanked the goodwife and shut the door as she left, then turned and faced Emeline, aware that they were alone behind closed doors. And he knew he had passed beyond her barriers as well, and reminded himself to be careful with her.

Emeline had collapsed on the side of the bed, and Rogan went to her. He looked down on her bedraggled appearance and shook his head. Why had she put herself through so much? He stooped down in front of her and tugged off her wet, filthy shoes. She had smudges of pure weariness under her eyes, and he wondered if she had slept at all in days past, and how she had found the strength to walk all through the night.

He sighed heavily, his own body tired and incredibly

sore. Heaving himself up to his feet, he went to the ewer and pitcher that sat in front of one of the windows and poured fresh water. After wetting a square of flannel, he returned to Emeline, and very gently began to wash the muck from her face and hands.

"Why did they call you The Duke?" she asked, leaning into his ministrations.

"Drunk, no doubt."

"They could not know you as Jeffrey's nephew."

"They do not know me at all."

"Tell me, Rogan," she urged gently. "Does it have to do with the bruises on your face?"

His head snapped up; his hands dropped away. "Why would you ask that?"

"When they spoke to you, you touched the bruise on your jaw, as if in memory."

He did not reply.

She reached out and pushed open the gap of his shirt, revealed the mottling of more bruises there. "Are you fighting out of anger or for atonement?"

Rogan held his breath. Her fingertips traced the line of his clavicle, and he could feel her hand tremble, like his heart, his resolve. It seemed she peered into him and pried open his darkest secrets. Yet there was nothing in her eyes but compassion.

"Both," he whispered.

"What have you done? Why do you beat yourself?" she asked, her voice just as hushed. Her finger dipped down into the vulnerable hollow between his collarbones. "You can tell me. I know I will understand."

Her words raised his guard; no one could understand the depth of what he had done. Murder allowed neither understanding nor forgiveness. Not from himself, and certainly not from anyone else.

Rogan broke the tension by looking away. He dabbed

at the dark patches of dirty water that stained her hair. He lightened his tone, chided her as if the entire exchange had not happened. "You should understand the gravity of what you did, running off into the night. You could have been raped, you know." He returned to the basin and rinsed the cloth. "Raped or murdered or taken by a highwayman, where not even I would have been like to find you. And if I hadn't been following you after you'd been robbed? What then? You, alone in the city without a coin to your name."

Emeline did not reply, could not, for the tender way he took care of her had her heart lodged in her throat. His gentleness was completely at odds with his size and strength. She wanted to know everything about his fighting, but opted not to press for the time being. Now they were both tired. She let the matter rest, content to watch him as he gently ministered to her.

He met her eyes and his hands fell to their sides. He glanced at the door, and then back to her.

"What you said," he began, but then paused, looking down at his hands as if they were huge and clumsy. He brought his gaze back to her. "In the carriage."

She shrugged, embarrassed now of the way she had offered him everything: her body, her heart. "I never meant to see you again."

The spell was broken by the sound of approaching footsteps along with the creaking wheels of a wrought-iron serving cart in the hallway. Rogan left Emeline's side and opened the door, accepted with thanks a tray of food from the goodwife. The steaming tea filled the room with its fragrance, mingling with the homey scents of warm breads, cold meats, soft cheeses, and thick porridge. He carried the tray to the tiny table in the corner of the room and set it down.

"Come eat," Rogan invited.

Emeline stood on weak legs, made her way to the table

and sank onto the hard wooden chair. Her belly clenched with hunger. Rogan poured the tea and handed her a cup, and she blew across the steaming liquid, keeping her eyes focused on the tiny wakes caused by her breath rather than on his face, his eyes, the way he moved. But soon enough her regard was pulled back to him.

Rogan had awakened her; her senses were alive. She watched him unabashedly as he fixed her a plate, studied his large hands, long, square fingers placing breads alongside meats, piling on the food. Emeline wanted to touch him, smell him, taste and feel him. He was everything real to her, solid, alive. Until that day when he had knocked on her door, she had been paper-thin, a vague, nebulous concept, her truest self smothered into unconsciousness.

Not now, though, she thought. Now she was wide awake, and there would be no going back.

Rogan set the full plate in front of her and handed her a fork. Still he did not look at her. "Eat, Princess."

Together in stilted, eloquent silence, they ate.

Emeline lifted her cup of tea and sipped again, cupping the porcelain in her palms to warm her hands. She spoke offhandedly. "Are you going to tell me, then?"

He met her gaze. "Tell you what?"

She noted the heat in his eyes, the attraction, the conflict. She tried to ignore the harsh reminder in her mind: he could never love her. "You said you would tell me, after you saw me."

"So I did," he murmured. He tried to think of the words for it, to explain the sexual danger she exuded, the way her lips trembled and her eyes promised.

But he would not see her only that way. She was more than that. And, he assured himself, he was more than those who did not see beyond it.

"What you said," he began again, "in the carriage."

She shook her head. "'Twas nothing. Forget it, Rogan. I was saying goodbye, is all."

"No, listen. You said you know what you are. What I must think of you." He picked up his teacup and sipped deeply, wishing for something stronger. He set it down with a rattle. "You do not know."

"Tell me, then."

"'Tis nothing so simple."

She sighed and pushed her plate aside. She rubbed her eyes. "But this does not have to be so complicated. I know what I am. You know. There is nothing between us but truth."

"There is more than that, Emeline." He sighed, still staring into her eyes, Prussian blue backing tiny flecks of light, like stars in a midnight sky. She looked at him with such open, soul-searching sincerity it moved him. "There is more between us, but 'tis not because of what has been done to you. I do not judge you so harshly, and I would not have you do so, either."

Emeline swayed on her seat, and Rogan knew she was too fatigued for any further conversation. He reached out his hand to her. Without hesitation, Emeline put her hand in Rogan's.

The feel of her hand in his shouldn't have been erotic, but he couldn't deny it: It was. It was dewy soft and rose-petal smooth, he thought, and then he jeered at himself in his mind: comparisons of women and flowers, as if he were some untried schoolboy swooning over his first unrequited flame.

Her hand was a trusting weight in his. And yes, he added, it was beautifully made, just like the rest of her, long, slim, elegant bones beneath creamy, golden skin. He could admire her and protect her, he assured himself. He could desire her and yet still respect her.

Rogan led Emeline to the bed and helped her loosen her gown. He turned his back as she lifted it over her head, the shushing of the silk as the rushing of his blood, knowing she unclothed herself. It was a painfully lewd awareness, and he no longer felt the least bit poetic. Gone were the thoughts of flowers, replaced by visceral need: he craved her.

There was the sound of her climbing onto the bed, the rustle of her sliding between the quilts. Rogan turned back to her and pulled them to her chin, tucked her in like a child, and without otherwise considering it, pressed a kiss to her forehead.

"Sleep." He smoothed her hair. It was soft and warm. "We'll talk later."

She reached out her hand, patted the other side of the bed. "Won't you sleep, too?"

Rogan nodded, weariness hitting him hard. He took the tray and piled on the empty plates, set it in the hallway where it could be collected later, shut and locked their door. He closed the curtains on the windows, softening the sunlight that streamed into the room into a diffused pink. He removed his boots and his jacket, loosened his breeches, and untucked his shirt, unbuttoned it down to the middle of his chest, and then eased onto the bed, careful to not touch her.

She rolled over to face him, her eyes drooping shut. "I am ever so grateful that you followed me."

He kept his own counsel and closed his eyes. His blood was a hot torrent of raging lust with her so close beside him.

She shimmied a tiny bit closer, presumably to get warmer. A wry grin twisted his lips. Warmer indeed. He was hot, a veritable furnace; the heat must be pumping from him.

He kept his eyes closed, tried to relax his body despite the tension that had him almost vibrating as he felt her supple body moving on the bed, remembering all too well how she had felt in his arms.

She has offered you her trust, her truth, her body and

heart, Rogan counseled himself. Don't take anything beyond what can be offered in return.

He tried to think of Orianna, struggled for a vision of her face, her hair, wishing he could recall the exact sound of her voice. He remembered her slim, brown hands, always gesturing as she spoke, the cadence of her speech, accented from her gypsy upbringing. But he could not call back the precise sound of her voice.

He heard the sound of Emeline's breathing grow slower, more regular. As sleep took her, she sighed, and he could not help but roll to his opposite side and study her face in the diffused light. In repose she looked innocent, all vestiges of the temptress gone. Her lashes lay against her cheek, dark and thick, fluttering now and then as she entered and moved through her dreams. Rogan wanted to touch her, to run a fingertip over those high cheekbones, across the arch of her brow, down the nose that could have been carved from marble. Her lips were slightly feline in their fullness, provocatively plump. And he knew them to be moist and sweet and yielding.

In her sleep Emeline moved yet closer, curled against his warmth. His breath hissed between his teeth as he felt her curves press against him. Every inch of his body was hard and suffused with blood.

Rogan took a deep breath, and then another. He ruled his lust like he ruled his pain, with disciplined control. He allowed himself only one indulgence, surely it wasn't wrong. Slowly, ever so slowly, he reached out his hand and stroked her hair, let it sift through his fingers like strands of silk, lifted it and watched the way the light turned it from gold to honey to amber. She sighed in her sleep again, the warm caress of her breath stirring the hair on his chest.

He watched her sleep until his own dreams took him. The last thing he saw before succumbing was her face.

Chapter 15

Emeline awoke slowly, coming to consciousness as if from a long journey. For a few moments she wondered where she was, glancing around in the darkness for a familiar sight to ground her in reality. Her whole body felt warm, weighted to the bed. As she grew more awake, she realized it was Rogan's arm holding her down, draped across her. Memory came flooding back. His slow, even breathing stirred her hair, and his body lay curled around hers, like husband and wife. His heat permeated her whole being, the warmth of flesh and blood that cannot compare to fire or wool.

Emeline held perfectly still and lay in Rogan's embrace, eyes closed, savoring it for as long as it would last.

Too soon she felt him move, the sounds of his breathing deepen. He rolled slightly away, pulled out of the embrace.

"What time do you think it is?" she asked.

"We slept the day away. It must be after eight."

He withdrew from the bed, moved to the window and pushed open the curtain to peer out the wavy glass. From her perspective she could see it was dark, the only light visible that of candles and oil lamps lighting windows. The glass sparkled, sprinkled with droplets of water.

"'Tis raining. Again."

Rogan sounded annoyed, frustrated. She smiled, though he could not see her for the darkness. "Fine English weather," she murmured, remembering her mother speaking those words many a time.

Rogan grunted, began feeling his way around the room, hunting for a candle and flint. "We will have to stay the rest of the night. We'll leave in the morning."

Emeline stayed buried under the covers, her belly fluttering with the nervousness of not knowing what would come next. Would he take her back to Jeffrey? she wondered. Would he come to the bed and decide to accept the offer of her body? He seemed so large to her, as if he filled the room with his presence, and she could not help but be very aware of his every movement.

She heard the scraping of flint, saw the flash of light grab the candlewick and begin to burn, illuminating Rogan in its golden glow.

"You look like a rogue," she said, referring to his undone, rumpled shirt, his unfastened breeches, his bruised skin and tousled hair. He also looked like a man just risen from a lover's bed, but she did not say that.

Rogan gestured to the chamber pot in the corner, raised a brow in question. At her reticent nod, he left the candle on the table and opened the door, went out in the hallway, and waited until she'd finished her ablutions. Emeline grabbed her cloak and wrapped it around her body, the wool still damp and cold, chilling her skin as she changed places with him, waiting in the lonely dark hallway while Rogan saw to his own needs.

"Come back in," he murmured quietly, opening the door again.

"Thank you." Feeling unaccountably shy, she hung the cloak back up and climbed back into the bed where the quilts still held their warmth. She wrapped them around her. And she waited, her belly turning.

The room had no fireplace, yet Rogan did not seem cold. He placed the candle on the bedside table and pulled a chair over by the side of the bed. His message was clear: he was not getting back into bed with her. When he spoke, his tone was severe and blunt. "Why did you run away?"

In the wavering candlelight, she saw the hardness in his eyes, the set of his jaw. He meant to have his answers. A wave of fear washed over her, and she thought it would have been much easier if he'd only wanted her body.

For a few moments she tried to decide what she would say. She cleared her throat, picked at the quilt where a few strands of thread unraveled from a red, triangle-shaped patch. "I am quite thirsty."

"You're quite fine, Emeline. Tell me why."

"Is it not obvious why I would leave Jeffrey's house?"

He cocked his head to the side, his expression clearly asking if she thought he was an imbecile.

She did not reply but rather kept picking the threads loose, twining the longer ones around her slim fingers.

He grabbed the quilt, pulled it away from her and took her by the shoulders in order to capture her full attention. In the light cast by the single candle, he met her eyes, nose to nose. And she saw he was growing angry. "You'll listen to me, aye? You told me yourself you've nowhere to go outside that house, and that there's something you must accomplish. It seemed important enough that you'd submit to my uncle's attentions. And now it has you running off into the night, penniless and unarmed. You'll tell me what you're about, or I swear I'll take you back to the mansion, and this time I'm sure Jeffrey will lock you away where there will be no more chance for escape."

She measured his expression. "You would do that?"

"Without hesitation," he answered flatly.

"But you offered to help me escape. Now I am away from there, and you threaten to take me back?"

"I am not threatening you, Emeline. 'Tis a promise, plain and simple. Tell me what you're after."

Emeline hesitated, her fingers twisted together in her lap. If she told him, would he go after Simon? Emeline shivered at the thought. A little voice urged her to tell everything and let him help her. She was so afraid to handle it herself, afraid she would fail the only people she cared for.

He saw in her eyes the desire to unburden herself, and took his advantage.

"Tell me. I will help you," he urged. He leaned forward, touched his lips to hers, as soft as a breath. Ever so lightly he traced her lips with his tongue, until a low sound came from her throat and she leaned in to deepen the kiss. Then he pulled away, but kept his face close to hers. "What are men capable of, Emeline? You know, better than most. I do not need to tell you I am stronger than you, bigger than you. I could hurt you, if I chose to. I could kill you, too, if murder was my motive."

"Why are you saying this?"

"I could do those things, Emeline, and more. You are at my mercy in this room." He took her hand and placed it on his arm, on the large bulge of his muscle. "Feel my strength. Feel it. Do you think I will hurt you?"

She shook her head. "No. You are not a cruel man."

"Look at me." Rogan moved her hand, this time pressed it to his chest. She felt the hard strength of him and the beating of his heart beneath her palm. His voice was strong and sure. "Trust what you know about me. You know I won't hurt you. You know it."

He overwhelmed her, with his size, his proximity, his strength, and his words. His body made her feel vulnerable and his words made her feel strong. The duality of the two emotions had her aroused and alive in ways she never felt before.

"See my eyes," he entreated, still boring into her, invading her mind and her very soul. "Do you see hatred there? Do you see rage?"

"No," she said on a breath.

"What do you see?" It was a command, enjoining her trust, her truth.

"I see a man like no other." Emeline did not say that she saw much, much more: sadness, festering guilt, and demons he did not dare to release.

"Trust what you see. I will help you."

And he stared deep into her eyes, the light of the candle throwing shadows and light onto his face in equal measure. He kept his gaze locked on hers. His warm breath touched her skin and he took her hands, held them tight in his own.

"You'll remember I told you about my mother?" he asked.

"Camille," she affirmed, thinking of the stories Rogan told her, of her strength and her courage, and how deeply Emeline wished for the kind of love that had made any risk seem worthwhile.

"Aye." Rogan kept his voice quiet, his eyes boring into Emeline's. He saw the flicker of warmth as she spoke of his mother, and it touched his heart. "She had faith in my father. She trusted him, even after an entire lifetime of being taught such things were impossible."

"They loved."

"They did. But they trusted first."

Her breath broke in her throat, her heart swelled so huge it felt it would burst. Still, she pushed away the hope that his words gave her, beat it back into submission with what she knew about him, what she saw in his eyes. He feared love. She could read that truth in him as easily as the written word. "You cannot love me, Rogan. No matter how much I trust you."

"No," he agreed, not wanting to hurt her, but unwilling to lie. "And I'm sorry for it, for you, for me. For my wife, too. It would have made her sad to know it." His eyes betrayed his surprise. He had not expected to say that. "But I can believe in you. And you can rely on me. We're friends, aye?"

He admitted that he could never love her with such ease of manner. Stripped of her defenses, she couldn't help but feel the pain of that rejection, no matter that he did not intend to hurt her. At least she did not have to feel the hope again, she told herself, reaching for that comfort. There was honesty between them, friendship and caring. It was more than she ever thought she would have, and she tried to feel grateful for it.

Love, the kind of love she dared not long for, was reserved for untainted virgins who came to a man with a dowry and dignity, she reminded herself. Not for women like her, who knew exactly what men wanted, and it was not her love.

Rogan looked into her eyes with patient intensity. He would have his answers, but he would not use physical force to get them. He was a man of honor, a man of his word.

Emeline pulled herself to the now, to what he wanted, what he offered. She had endured the years with Simon by being practical, and that same practicality is what she would rely on to see her through this. Rogan had followed her, and he was not going anywhere. Telling him the whole truth was really her only option. She had only one caveat.

"I will tell you everything, hold nothing back." Emeline held her breath for a moment, but then plunged on. "But I want something in return. You want me to lean on you, trust you, let you help me. I shall, but only if you will lean on me, as well. We will be friends, Rogan, or we will be nothing at all."

He turned away from her, stared at the candle, the flame stretched up high and thin, wax dripping down in clear beads, gathering, cooling, and hardening to form an opaque patch on the wood. Memories of the day he had killed his wife came in snatches, flashing through his mind in rapid-fire, in full color and hideous detail. And always, the sound of her sobs, growing thinner, weakening until she had no strength to weep.

"You don't know what you ask for," he said, his voice as sharp as the spears of guilt stabbing his chest.

"I am not asking, Rogan."

His lips twitched at the corners at the firmness of her tone. "You're not?"

She shook her head and leaned forward so she could touch his face. She turned him to look at her. "No. I am not. You must tell me about my friend. Tell me his wife's name."

"Orianna." He spoke her name on a breath, and realized he had not once uttered her name aloud since the day he buried her. "Orianna Zigana Mahala Jafit." He grinned wryly then, and added, "Mullen."

"What sort of name is that?" Emeline asked.

"Gypsy. Romany." He saw a shadow cross her face. Typical English, he thought, uncomfortable with anyone who did not spring from English soil. "Not what you expected?"

"No. I pictured a different kind of woman, I suppose." Emeline did not tell him that when she imagined Rogan's love, she thought of a woman with honey-colored hair and eyes of dark blue, a better version of herself.

"I do not care for English snobbery and its insular view of the world," Rogan said. "'Tis in part why my mother left England. They would have kept her from my father simply because he is common and Irish. The English hate the Irish as they hate the Scots as they hate the French, and they reserve a particular kind of disdain for anyone who is dark-skinned or has slanted eyes. The English hate any who aren't English, and for that, I hate them."

She noticed how easily he slid into his fury, and compassion overtook her curiosity. Emeline reached out and took his hand, twining her fingers with his. "'Tis so much simpler to be angry. To rage over what is and what is not, rather than confront the pain and sadness."

Rogan tightened his grip on Emeline's hand. "She was wonderful. Colorful. And very funny." Unanticipated relief seeped into his body. He hadn't realized that it would feel so good to say her name, to speak about her.

He suddenly had a memory of Orianna in a high rage, pieces of pottery in shards at her feet from the bowls she had thrown to the floor. He remembered her temper well, when she would get angry and curse him in that strange tongue, her words wild and fast as she threw whatever she could lay her hands on at the walls. Nipping at that memory's heels came the awareness that he also had not recalled any of their fights until just then. He liked it better this way, the whole woman instead of the pieces he kept to fuel his pain and feed his addiction. He would think about that later. For now, though, he was ready to move away from the subject.

"That's enough, Princess. I want you to tell me what drove you to risk your neck."

It was almost as if Emeline could feel Simon's hot breath on her neck and ear, warning her to do as he instructed. And so Emeline did just the opposite, believed in the man who had earned her respect over the man who took trust and raped it.

"You did. My mother, too. But 'twas your mother, Camille, most of all."

"My mum?"

"Yes, she risked everything for love. She is the bravest

woman I have ever heard of." Emeline began from the start, when Simon had first taken her mother, Madeline, to Bethlem because she had dared to try to kill to Simon in his sleep. Emeline recounted that night, when Simon had grabbed Madeline by the throat, lifted her off the floor and shaken her until she dropped the fireplace poker, her mouth opening and closing like a fish out of water, both of them covered in blood from the gash on Simon's head. He'd bundled her up and taken her away, and even as he dragged her out, Madeline struggled with him, meeting Emeline's gaze with all the intensity of a woman making a last attempt to help her daughter in any way, continuously mouthing the same words to her again and again, *I love you; protect yourself.*

After that, Emeline became Simon's ward, and his abuse of her escalated without Madeline's interference. And always, Simon had Madeline to use as leverage to threaten Emeline.

Just when Emeline had been considering suicide as her only option for escape, Jeffrey's son died and Simon found out that Jeffrey would send for Rogan as his successor. And a plan had been born, using Emeline as bait, pawn, and executioner. But Emeline had formed a different plan. She told Rogan how she planned to sell the gowns, to find Simon and kill him, save her mother and buy their freedom.

"That's it?" Rogan surprised Emeline by chuckling. "That's what had you running off into the night?"

She did not hide her offense at his glib attitude. "'Tis serious, Rogan. My mother languishes in an unimaginable hell, and now her very life is at stake as is yours." She tossed back the quilts and leapt from the bed, stalked over to her bag, opened it and extracted the vial of poison. She held it to him and shook it. "Does this seem like something to mock?" she demanded.

Rogan tried not to notice how her body looked in the

filmy shift she wore, curvy and begging for a man's touch, or the way the light of the single candle illuminated her lustrous skin. He tried not to imagine how it would feel to run his fingers through the mass of honey-colored hair that streamed to her waist, and what it would feel like to have her pressed naked against him. With every bit of self-control he possessed, he fought the memory of her response to his kiss, and the recollection of the exact feel of her mouth and the taste of her tongue.

"I am not afraid of Simon." He wished his voice did not betray him, husky and tight.

"Well, you ought to be," she snapped. "My mother is in danger, as are you, and if you do not care for her life, perhaps you should care for your own."

Rogan shrugged away her concerns. "Simon deserves my contempt, not my fear. Sending a woman to do his dirty work. 'Tis pathetic."

"I do not appreciate how you are trivializing this matter. Perhaps if it were your mother jailed in a madhouse, you would not take this so lightly."

The images Emeline's own words conjured crashed into her mind. Madeline starved and in chains, her once beautiful hair as dirty as a hag's, her face twisted with humiliation and suffering until she truly looked mad.

Emeline tried to cling to her composure, but it was slipping away rapidly. Her breath hitched and caught, and she fought the tears with all she had. But she did not fight the confession. She needed it too much.

"My mother. My mum. She has suffered so greatly, and it has been all my fault. I did everything to fight him, make him not want me. I stopped bathing, would not wash my hair, my clothes. But he would not stop coming back. And she saw it. Saw too much. She wanted to protect me." A few sobs caught her breath, but she pressed on. "But I endured everything to get to this point. I see it now. To be able to save her, save you, maybe even save myself. And now . . ." The tears came, unstoppable now, rolling down her cheeks.

Rogan went to her and pulled her into his embrace, wrapping his arms around her as she sobbed. "Shhh," he soothed. "I will take care of her. And you, too. All will be well."

"You are not listening. He will come for you. You won't know who or where, but he will see it done. And me," she said, breathless. "He will own me forever."

"No."

"How, Rogan? How can you say no? I am his ward. He can do whatever he wants to me, and no one will stop him."

She trembled in his embrace, her skin covered in goose-flesh, and her hand still clenched around the bottle of poison. He pried the vial from her and opened it, dumped the contents into the dirty chamber pot along with the vial. He went back to her and drew her to the bed. "Listen, aye? Can you calm yourself enough to listen?"

She sobbed heedlessly now, her emotions completely out of control. She hiccuped, gasped, hiccuped again. "I will kill myself. I can't go back to him. I can't. I won't. I will kill myself."

"You're not killing anyone, least of all yourself."

"I will do it. I will. I have wanted to, but I was afraid. 'Tis a sin to do it. Probably a sin to want it." A sob caught in her throat and she stared up at Rogan, her eyes wild, her face wet with tears and sweat and snot. She knew she babbled, but she could not stop. "I am not afraid of sin anymore. The God I love would not want me in Simon's bed. And if He does not care either way, I do not care either way. He can forget about me. I will not care. I will be too dead to care."

Rogan saw there would be no reasoning. So he stroked

the hair away from her face, gentling her as he would an agitated mare, sweeping his hand over her forehead and back, his touch light and slow. After a while her sobs came slower, and he rose from the side of the bed to wet a clean flannel with cold water and then returned to her, wiped her face, cooled her brow.

Slowly she came back to herself, her breath hitching as she calmed. The damp, cold flannel swept across her skin, chasing away the heat of her worries.

And once again his tenderness touched her deeply, reached into all her dark places and filled them with light, opened doors she had thought closed forever. With a hand that did not tremble in the slightest, she reached up and cupped the back of his head, pulled him down so she could press her lips to his.

"Make me forget," she said against his mouth. "Make it all go away."

"You are not saying goodbye to me this time, Princess." He resisted, though he did not pull away entirely. "Do you understand? 'Tis your mother's neck at risk, and my own is threatened as well."

She shook her head, tried to pull him down to her again, wanting him to kiss her until the room spun, the walls fell away, London disappeared. She wanted the oblivion of feeling that she sensed Rogan would release in her.

"Listen, Emeline. Open your eyes and look at me."

She did, reluctantly. Saw the intention in his expression.

"When I say you're not saying goodbye, I mean it both ways. First, you are not alone in this anymore, aye? I'm involved, and I'll see it through. Second, you don't run off again."

She nodded, willing to agree. Willing to admit that his taking over made her feel relieved and protected, sheltered in a way she never had anticipated.

"And finally, there's one final matter that needs to be addressed." He lowered his head and kissed her chin, her jaw, and then brought his mouth to hers, to once again trace the outline of the lips he wanted to taste every time he saw them. He pulled back again and looked deep into her eyes. "This."

Chapter 16

Emeline's head spun, the way she had wanted it to, rational thought drifting away. She tried to reach for it, knowing she needed to think. "I do not understand it," she confessed. "I have never felt anything like this. Nothing has prepared me for the feelings you awaken in me, Rogan."

"You wanted me to tell you what it is about you, Emeline. What attracts men so when they look at you."

"Yes." Like frigid water thrown in the face, his words snapped her to reality. "Tell me, and I will do whatever I must to change it."

"Your understanding, your compassion," he answered, finally coming to the realization himself. "You look into a person and see their needs, their fears, their limitations. You look and you see what others ignore or feign blindness to. And you are not afraid of it." He needed to resist the desire to sink into her eyes, to let her compassion touch places in his heart that he'd secreted away from everyone, even himself. "Do not change it, Emeline. 'Tis lovely, and it transcends even your beautiful face."

Rogan pulled away from her, moved to the side of the bed and blew out the candle before lying down, not feeling the least bit tired, but knowing that only sleep could solve his dilemma of being locked in a room with a woman he found intensely desirable. And she was more than just that. He knew her heart to be as deep as he could fathom, and her bravery to be as great as any man's. The way she had endured such humiliation and loss, and yet remained strong, merciful even, and still able to give. She humbled him.

She threatened his heart, and he knew it. The heart he would not risk again.

In that moment, his longing to step into the ring and fight was never stronger. He wanted another fifteen minutes with The Bull, where the pain would drown his thoughts and erase his temptations.

"Rogan?" she said, her voice tentative in the darkness. "Do you want me to sleep on the floor?"

"Why would you ask that?" Rogan responded, wishing his voice did not betray the needs he so barely restrained.

"I can feel your tension. 'Tis my presence beside you, and I am sorry for it."

"I am not a beast to lie warmly abed while a woman sleeps on the cold floor."

"I know. I only meant to give you some peace."

"'Tis fine, Princess. I am at peace." And he knew he would likely never voice a more boldfaced lie.

She turned on her side to face him, unable to make out any of his features in the complete darkness that engulfed them. She wanted reach out, to touch him, to offer some solace or reprieve from his pain. She could see the conflict in him, could feel the tension in his body radiating from him as heat from a fire. He was heartsick, still, and again it moved her to see a man who could love so deeply, even beyond the grave.

But she was part of his problem, and she knew it. She

decided to ask him the question that nagged at her, hoping that it would also steer the conversation to safer ground.

"What will you do to Simon?"

"I will not do anything," came his answer, his voice seeming even deeper because she could not see him. "I told you, I'm not afraid of him, aye?"

"But he will have you killed, Rogan."

"He is like to try."

Memories flashed through Emeline's mind, reminding her exactly what Simon could be capable of doing, the lengths he would go. "I think you should approach the situation with far more caution."

"Is that right? And is that what you were doing? Approaching it with caution by running off alone in the night?"

Shame stained her cheeks as she recalled the urchin grabbing her bag and running off. A man could have grabbed her, just as easily, and she would have been almost defenseless. "I was trying to protect you and my mother. If that makes me a fool, I care not."

"I did not call you a fool."

"You insinuate it."

He shifted on the bed to face her, even though they could not see her each other through the veil of darkness. "I do not mean to sound insulting. 'Tis only the folly of your actions that astounds me. Why would you not have told me and allowed me to handle the matter rather than risk your life?"

"I did not want to ask you to commit a murder."

"But you would have committed one yourself?"

"Yes," she replied flatly. "And I would still do it, if you had not dumped the poison. God reviles me already, as a whore and a thief. I will add murderer to that rather than see you or my mother hurt."

He heard the defiance in her tone again, returning once more when she spoke of how the Lord saw her.

"God does not revile you, Emeline," Rogan said, his tone turning gentle. "Nor does He blame you for wanting to kill the man who has spent years torturing you. I don't claim to know the mind of the Lord, but He is just and merciful, aye?"

Visions flashed into Emeline's mind, of how she had debased herself in ways that sickened her to think about. "You say that, but you do not know the things I have done."

"And I'm not caring, either." His hand reached out and cupped her face. Although he could not make out her features in the darkness, he wanted to make certain she truly listened. "You call yourself whore, and you speak as to how I think of you. Do you want me to tell you what I really think?"

Rogan pulled Emeline to him then, because he could feel tears rolling over his hand, though she did not make a sound. He held her to his chest. "I think you judge yourself too harshly. You're a woman who managed to stay merciful when others showed no mercy. Who kept sane when insanity raged around her, who can show compassion when others have treated her with ruthlessness. And who has enough bravery to face down the man who tortured her. You've the courage of a warrior, but the heart of a woman."

He kissed the top of her head and murmured low sounds as he held her, her silent sobs wrenching at his heart more than any wailing ever could. "No more calling yourself names. I'll not listen to you speaking about my friend like that, aye?"

She lifted her face to his, her lips finding his without error. She pressed a single kiss against his mouth, and he tasted her salty tears along with her sweetness.

He went perfectly still, his control slipping with the feel of her body against him and the touch of her lips on his.

"'Tis the second time tonight you kissed me through your tears."

"Will you resist me again?"

He hesitated, but merely for a second.

"I am only human," he replied, and this time he took her whole mouth in a savage, searing kiss, all his pent-up needs combined together in an assault that blistered and ravaged, ignited their bodies.

He crushed her against him, her long body matched against his in a way that intoxicated him, her soft curves pressed to his hard angles. With one hand he gripped the small of her back, kept her held to him as he buried the other hand in the softness of her hair, cupping her scalp. He trailed his kisses down her neck, pressed his lips against her throat, felt the vibration of her moan.

He dragged his mouth from her neck, returned to her lips. And he dipped deep, fed by the way her kisses matched his own in intensity. She kissed him as a starving woman eats: with total abandon. Her fingers dug into his back, her nails pressing into his flesh through his shirt.

And so he pulled away long enough to rip the shirt over his head, pulled her back against his chest, grinned darkly at the feel of her hands on his back again, this time flesh against flesh, her nails like tiny talons gripping him. His reserve slipped a little further before he reined it in, tried to exert his control over the lust that gripped him with a velvet fist.

"Not again, Emeline. We cannot continue this." He tried to pull back and shuddered as that caused her nails to dig deeper into his flesh, sending sizzling bolts of pleasure directly to his groin.

"Rogan, I desire you, and I have never desired any

man," she said back, her voice husky. "What spell are you casting over me?"

He sank his hands back into her hair and pulled her mouth to his once again, their tongues meeting. He pulled back, held her so their breath could mingle, feeling the humid promise of her mouth so close, so open to him. "This time I will make sure you know your own desire," he promised.

His mouth took hers again, a savage mating of lips and teeth and tongue as she matched his ardor with her own. Against his chest he could feel the press of her breasts, the quick pace of her heartbeat, the heat of her body. He stroked her body as he had in the carriage, but this time his hands were not gentle.

Emeline pulled back from his mouth, her head thrown back as she gasped for breath. His callused hands were everywhere, cupping her breasts, teasing her nipples, stroking her back and her legs.

She could feel his hand sweeping down her body, the hem of her shift being raised, and he was caressing her legs, up and down, his touch so light it made her squirm against him, wanting his hand to reach higher until it touched her where she burned so hot it almost hurt.

And then he did. His fingers traced the shape of her womanhood, and then drifted away to stroke her thighs again, and she had to pull away from his mouth, throw her head back just to breathe. He kissed the long arch of her neck, nibbling, licking, and his hand came back to touch her again, right at the center of the wet heat, and then back again to her thighs, and then back to her center, over and again until she could only gasp when he his fingers brushed the swollen, sensitive flesh.

Then his fingers did not leave. They stroked, lightly at first, exploring her hot, wet flesh until she shook as if from extreme cold, her whole body taut and trembling.

He put his mouth against her ear, his tongue tracing her shape, sucking her earlobe, and then he whispered, his warm breath sending hot shivers through her whole body. "Let go."

Before she could gather her senses enough to ask what he meant, his finger returned to the center of her heat, tiny fast circles that made rational thought disappear like smoke from a flame.

Sensations she had never felt before assaulted her, an urgent need that grew inside her, for what, she did not know, until it reached the summit and her whole body convulsed, again and again and again, wave after wave engulfing her.

He held her after it was over, cradled against him, slowly smoothing back her hair. Inside of Rogan there was a storm of heat and desire, his arousal so full and complete he throbbed with every beat of his heart, straining his breeches until he ached. But he would not turn this interlude into a release of his own needs. He would show her that a man could give and not take. He would show himself what kind of man he chose to be.

Trying to cool his own blood, he reached for the edges of the quilts, pulled them to cover her.

Emeline shifted, slipped her hand to grasp the center of his heat.

The feel of her touching him was too much. He pushed her hand aside. "No."

She shifted her body, tried to pull him on top of her, but Rogan resisted.

"You must. I know you must."

"No," Rogan asserted, and he pulled away. It would be so good, he thought, feel so good to slide into her. Her whole body was ready, hot, wet, and he knew she would be tight and perfect.

He held back, though, his blood pounding through his

veins, his heart beating rapidly, his groin on fire for her, desperate for the release her body would bring. He felt her tugging at him, offering herself, and he nearly gave in, until she spoke.

"It does not matter, Rogan. You would hardly be taking my virtue."

Some things run deeper than lust. Things like honor and the conviction to do right by another, no matter the cost. Her words proved what he suspected.

"No," he said again.

With every last vestige of restraint he possessed, Rogan pulled away and rose from the bed, fumbled in the darkness to find the flint, lit the candle, and made his way to the washstand. He poured a glass of water, briefly considered pouring it straight onto his loins, but then drank it down, moved to stand by the window and leaned his head on the cool glass, took deep breaths, and waited for his body to settle.

After a long while he poured another glass and went back to Emeline's side, handed it to her so she could drink. She sat up, looking like a rumpled golden goddess in the light of the single candle, hair tousled, lips swollen, eyes heavy. But she also had an expression of pure confusion on her face.

"I want you to understand, 'tis not because I do not desire you. I do. Intensely," he added. He could feel the warmth of her body, and it took everything he had to keep from grabbing her and pulling her close once again. "But I won't use your body because others have. I will not be another man who uses you, simply because he can."

He cupped her chin, tilted her face and looked into the depths of Prussian blue. "In my eyes you are a lady."

With that, he grabbed a pillow and a quilt and lay on the cold, hard floor, wishing for a pallet or a fireplace or even better, another room far, far away from the temptress in the bed. He blew out the candle, but not before he saw the look on her face, full of wonder. And it made all of his discomfort suddenly seem worthwhile.

The blush of dawn filtered into the room, turning the whitewashed walls a pale blue. Rogan turned over on the hard floor, then forced himself to a seated position, rubbed his eyes, ran a hand through his hair. His body hurt from the cold floor, its abuse adding to the aches and pains of his healing bruises. But beyond that, he felt strange. Something was missing, he thought, an odd quiet hung in the air.

Emeline was gone. He leapt to his feet in an instant, grabbed his boot off the floor and pulled out his dagger, foul Gaelic curses muttered under his breath as he strode to the door and yanked it open. She'd promised not to run off again, he raged in his mind, his imagination supplying him with graphic visions of her lying in a pool of blood.

He ran down the long hallway, took the stairs two at a time until he reached the bottom floor, surprising a few of the guests who sipped their tea in the main dining hall.

There was Emeline, dressed neatly in her gown, her hair raked into a tidy braid that hung down her back. She carried a tray laden with breakfast, steaming tea, marmalade, scones and cakes. At first she looked surprised, but then a smile curved her lips. A look of wicked amusement stole across her face as her eyes swept over Rogan, head to heels.

"My lord, I sought to bring you your morning meal," she murmured, as demurely as a submissive wife to her husband.

Rogan knew he made a ignominious sight with his wrinkled clothing askew and unfastened, his hair practically sticking straight in the air, his legs and feet bare, the blade of his dagger out-thrust from his hand. Still, he bowed slightly to the guests and then swept low before Emeline.

"My lady, I woke to find you gone. I feared for your welfare," he replied, his tone courtly. He bowed low again to her, as a knight before a princess, and then stood straight and took the tray from her, balanced it on one hand as he formally offered his other arm. Emeline sank into a deep curtsy before placing her hand on his and allowing him to escort her back upstairs.

As they entered their room a giggle overtook Emeline, and she dissolved into laughter, collapsing onto her back on the bed, gasping for air.

"Are you quite finished?" Rogan asked, kicking the door closed behind him. He placed the tray on the table, set his dagger aside and poured himself a cup of tea, stood sipping it while he watched Emeline roll around, giggling like a girl.

"No," she wheezed. "Not even close."

"Fine, then. Have at it." He shrugged his shoulders and took a seat at the table, stretched his long legs out and crossed them at the ankles, sipping his tea until Emeline regained herself.

She came to the table wiping happy tears from her eyes, poured herself some tea while little giggles shook her shoulders; she tasted it, and winced as she found it too hot. "I am sorry," she said, but her voice still held the richness of her mirth.

"Aye, and you sound it," he replied dryly.

"It's just you looked so frantic. And your hair, your feet." She bit her lip to keep from succumbing again.

"Aye, 'tis extremely entertaining to see someone sick with worry. I cannot fathom why 'tis not portrayed more frequently on stage. You're right to laugh, Emeline." But then he grinned, recalling the startled expressions on a few of the ladies' faces.

After she had fully recovered, Emeline found herself completely famished. She sat with Rogan and selected a scone, nibbled it while intermittently sipping her tea. The dry, crumbly sweetness of the treat tasted just right with the strong tea. Sunlight filled the room, and down below in the street vendors bellowed their telltale street cries while liveries rattled by. Emeline thought how deliciously intimate it felt to share breakfast with Rogan while the early morning light shifted from blue to pink to gold, streaming into the room through the gabled windows and bathing them in the promise of a new day. It made it almost easy to ignore all the threats that loomed over them, to not worry about when Jeffrey would notice she was gone and what he would do about it. She was perfectly content to watch Rogan as he ate, aware of his smallest details.

"So when you're finished eating, I suppose I will send for fresh bathing water and we'll get set to be on our way," Rogan said, his manner conversational as if he, too, were absorbed in the domesticity of their current situation.

"That sounds quite fine," Emeline replied, hoping to sound like a proper lady.

"And then I shall send for a livery to take us to a cleric so we can be married, and then we'll be off to Bethlem to fetch your mum."

Emeline very slowly finished chewing her bit of scone and set down her teacup with extreme concentration and care before looking, meeting Rogan's face to see if he mocked her in some way.

He sat sprawled in the chair casually, his legs still stretched out, but he lifted a brow as if to inquire whether she had heard him properly.

"I gave it quite a bit of thought last night," he began, his tone still conversational, as if discussing the weather. "I had plenty of time to think. The floor was cold and hard, I was not the least bit tired, and you were warm and willing in the bed. Thinking about Simon and Jeffrey and your mum made for a fine distraction, aye?"

She kept quiet, only nodded once, slowly, waiting for him to continue.

"Simon poses a threat to you. No matter what else becomes of the situation, you are his ward in the eyes of English law. If I marry you, you will then belong to me, and he cannot control you any longer."

"Yes, however—"

He held up a hand to silence her. "You'll hear me out first. I will not abide seeing you treated as less than a lady anymore. You will not return to Jeffrey or Simon." He leaned forward then, his eyes like emeralds, hard and cold. "Do you hear me, Emeline? It ends today. It ends with me."

"But I am—"

"No," he commanded. "You'll listen. I cannot give you my protection unless I marry you. I have thought about it every way, and 'tis the only answer. Any other option provides Simon with the legal right to take you back and lock you away forever. If you think that is something that I would ever allow, then you do not know me at all."

He sat back, grinned in his wild, restless way, his manner once again casual and calm. "Now you may argue."

Emeline sat stock still, silent and aghast. It was as if a strong wind scattered her wits like diary pages and she struggled to collect them even as they swirled and blew about.

"You do not love me, Rogan," she said finally.

"It does not matter how I feel. I shall never marry for love again." He cleared his throat, shrugged his shoulders. "'Tis a fact that love is not required for marriage."

She twisted her hands in her lap, but she met his eyes, dead even. "I am not an innocent, young virgin girl who has been bred for this, and I am not a fool to think myself worthy of your offer. You deserve a better wife, someone who can be mother to your children, a lady with proper breeding and training who can one day make a proper duchess. I am not the kind of woman a man takes to wife, let alone one who is bestowed with privilege and titles."

She forced her hands to be still. And then tried to explain herself, as best she could. "I am broken, Rogan. I have been defiled in ways you do not understand." She dropped her eyes then, unable to meet his gaze as she continued with what needed to be said, her voice breaking, halting, as she forced out the words. "And that is not the only problem. 'Tis a fact that Simon . . . had intercourse with me. Many times. And I never . . . have been . . . made . . . pregnant," she finished on a breath, her cheeks burning with shame.

"Emeline—" he began.

"No, 'tis your turn to listen. I am broken. Not whole. Not complete. Perhaps you cannot fathom it. What I am saying. Listen," she repeated, stumbling over the rocky road of her emotions to try to find the elusive words that would make him understand. "For years he controlled me. Simon. With my mother. You see, he would say . . . I must do . . . things. Sexual things. Or he would send a man . . . to hurt my mum. I did not believe. I did not do what he demanded. And, you see, he did it. He took me to see her. Once. After. She still bled."

Emeline closed her eyes tightly, wishing she could block out the memory of Madeline in a dirty bed crawling with lice, amidst the madness and chaos of Bedlam, a chain running from her ankle to an iron pin embedded in the wall. Bruised, swollen, and defeated.

"After that, he owned me, Rogan. Do you see? He owned me. Everything I did, I did for her. To protect her from being hurt again. It was . . . the only way."

"Stop, Emeline. Look at me."

She took a deep breath, struggled for composure. She opened her eyes and forced herself to meet his again, prepared for his revulsion. But instead she saw understanding. Compassion and sorrow and sympathy, without a trace of disgust. It eased the pain in her heart, lessened her shame, ever so slightly.

"Never again. He will not hurt you again."

"Rogan, I—"

"Stop. 'Tis enough. I will near no more of it." He took her hand, held it so tight her fingers ached, a pain that felt good. Solid, real. "You're with me now."

Rogan's words felt like rain following a drought, trickling into her heart, making hope grow. But still, doubt plagued Emeline. He offered out of pity and duty. He deserved so much more.

She looked into Rogan's impossibly beautiful eyes; he was transfixing: handsome, certainly. But it was more than the arrangement of his features. He possessed a certain nobility of qualities, honor and courage, that in and of themselves were compelling. But they coupled with such primal savagery, as if he were prince and pirate combined. He engendered confidence in Emeline, galvanized her with it. He was a man who meant what he said and would follow through. Yet, she felt very small for wanting to let him take care of her.

"If I accepted your offer, it would make me lesser in my own estimation than I already am." The words were bitter on Emeline's tongue.

"You do not see." He was still squeezing her hand. "We are both broken. 'Tis not you alone who bears scars from the past. We're both broken, Emeline, 'tis true." He leaned forward then, and met her gaze intensely. "But maybe we're stronger together than broken alone."

Stronger together than broken alone. His words flooded

through all the doorways he had opened in her heart, filled them with the light of hope. She'd been in isolation for so long in all her suffering. Alone, lonely, numbed and tired, never able to sleep deeply for listening for footsteps, never safe, never at ease.

Rogan offered peace and help, his strength, his protection. *Stronger together than broken alone.* She thought of the bruises she'd seen on his body and thought that perhaps he needed healing just as much as she did, that maybe she could help him.

Emeline decided she would work at being worthy rather than sink down into the darkness that Simon designed for her, to reach out for what might be.

She placed her other hand on top of Rogan's, felt the warmth of him, the solidness, the promise. He might not love her, she told herself, but she would try to see to it that he could respect her.

"I will do it, Rogan. I will be your wife."

Inside Rogan waged a war of right and wrong, of duty and honor versus memories as powerful as a day only just gone by, of vows he had spoken a little more than a year ago, vows to forsake all others.

Until death parted them.

And now he found himself in a new land, with a new future, and he would have a new wife. Love and dizzy passion were not for him any longer, dead with the wife of his youth and his heart. But he could find friendship with this woman, Emeline.

But there was more than that, he admitted to himself, as he looked at her. The look in her eyes, hunted prey and sexual predator combined. He felt the now familiar lust, the urge to slide inside of her, to possess her, to make her belong to him and no other. He wanted to protect and to plunder her, to dominate and surrender. To kiss those lips, feel them tremble beneath his own, taste her, inhale her scent, bury himself where there was no pain, no loss, and no fighting, where there was no world outside of the heat and wetness of her body.

He would make her burn, and burn only for him, the way he wanted to from the first moment he saw her. She would belong to him, and no other. He would save her from Simon and Jeffrey, true; it was the honorable thing to do. But in doing so, he would keep her for himself.

Rogan had been raised to do the right thing, and so he would. He would do that right thing, even if it wasn't for all the right reasons.

Chapter 17

Jeffrey loomed over Kieran as she lay in her bed. He held a silk kerchief pressed over his mouth and nose to prevent inhaling her foul vapors, but she could clearly see his eyes, glassy, wild, and full of rage.

"I will ask only once more, where is Rogan?" Jeffrey demanded once again, furious with this sickly girl who would not cooperate.

"I tell you again, Uncle, I know not."

"Why would he leave and not inform anyone of his intentions? He did not even take a horse."

"I am certain the errand that takes my brother from this house is one of great importance," Kieran said. "He is not a man to take matters lightly."

Jeffrey glared down at his niece, so disgusted by her illness he could not even appreciate her beauty. Her skin seemed clear enough, but there was something nagging at him. Though her immaculately coifed auburn hair was clean and she was elegantly garbed in *dishabille*, he was still fairly certain he could detect the underlying whiff of sickness lingering around her. His thoughts then turned worrisome; what if scenting illness meant the foul vapors had passed through the silk barrier he held over his nose and mouth? He risked much by entering the sickroom, but Emeline and Rogan were gone.

"Perhaps you do not comprehend the gravity," Jeffrey continued, struggling to remain reasonable. "My mistress is missing, and I believe 'tis your brother who has aided in her flight."

Kieran shrugged her shoulders and swept a hand around the room, indicating her solitude. "I am sorry, Uncle. As you are aware, I have been confined to my bed. I know nothing of the goings on in the household."

"Very well," Jeffrey snapped, his patience at an end. "Good day to you."

He whirled on his heel and stomped from the rooms, slammed the door behind him. Not only had he left with no answers, but he had also braved the sickroom for naught. The pointlessness of it inflamed his already bubbling temper, and as he stormed through the house he checked his timepiece. He had duties that required his attention, matters with his estates, an appointment with his solicitor, papers that needed signing, letters to be written to his landlords, and what seemed like a mountain of documents sent from Parliament, awaiting his review.

And all he could think about was his golden Emeline in the clutches of his darkly handsome nephew, no doubt writhing beneath him, their firm bodies locked together in a passionate tangle that celebrated their youth and vigor, their beautiful faces contorted with mutual ecstasy.

His gut churned with resentment and jealousy of Rogan, along with sheer annoyance with himself that he had allowed the girl to captivate him so completely. She was just a woman, he told himself over and over, and could be replaced at his whim. He was the Duke of Eton. He could have any woman he desired.

The only trouble was, Jeffrey fumed as he entered his

office and faced the endless work that awaited him, he only wanted Emeline.

Rogan helped Emeline alight from the carriage, pleased with the trouble she had taken with her appearance. After they had finished breakfast, Emeline had waited as Rogan washed and dressed, and then sent him downstairs to wait for her while she readied herself to be wed.

She had emerged some time later, causing a hush to fall over the entire room as she entered wearing a gown of dusky rose satin, the bodice tight across her nipped waist and full breasts, the neckline square, low, and embroidered with gold thread. She had pulled her hair away from her face, fastened it with combs and allowed the curls and waves to fall in a cascade of honeyed gold to her waist. The gown showed a few folds and creases from having been stuffed with all the others in her bag, and a number of small blotches marred the fabric where it had gotten damp, but still she glowed, radiant, her skin as luminous as crushed pearls, her eyes like a moonlit, sapphire sky.

Rogan had bowed low, taken her hand and pressed a kiss to it, breathed in her complexly warm, sweet scent, and asked in a low voice if she were ready to become his wife.

Now they alighted in front of a cleric's office, where the goodwife assured them the marriages were legal and binding. Rogan bade the hired livery to wait. They entered the building, a simple brownstone that boasted little adornment save a single, ornate railing in black iron. Emeline gripped it as she climbed the stone steps and paused as Rogan opened the door for her. She entered with her heart beating a rapid tattoo, and wondered if Rogan felt as nervous as she.

The room they entered was spare and simple, the wooden floors bare, the only furniture a bench and a desk, which held a pot of ink and a pewter cup stuffed with a dozen quills, a few stubby candles, and a stack of documents neatly arranged into a pile. For all the room's sparseness, it held a hushed quiet, a reverent silence.

Rogan stood beside Emeline, holding her hand. As he glanced down at her, he saw her face was pale, her lips rimmed with white, beads of sweat glistening on her upper lip.

"You're nervous?"

"So much so I feel ill," she replied.

"You're wanting to change your mind?"

"No. Are you?"

"No."

She took a little, shaky breath. "It feels wrong to do this now, when my mum is still captive."

"Aye, I know. But 'tis important to get it done, lest anything happen to me. Once you are my wife, even if I die, you are safe from Simon."

She squeezed his hand and looked up, deep into his eyes. "Please don't let anything happen to you."

He grinned down at her, then lowered his mouth to her ear so he could murmur, "And risk not consummating our nuptials? I think not, Princess."

Heat gathered in her belly, tightened her nipples, made her conscious of warmth and wetness between her thighs. It burned away her nervous chill, replaced the flutter of butterflies in her belly with a hot twist of arousal. How could it be that she could anticipate sex, could desire it, could even name it love-making in her mind? Rogan made all things possible, it seemed to her. She glanced around briefly to see if anyone witnessed their exchange. "You are audacious."

"I am a man who is anxious to bed his wife after the vows are spoken," Rogan replied, still against her ear where he could inhale her scent and savor the way his words made her shiver. "If you think of what I can do to you with my fingers, imagine what it will be like with my tongue and my—"

"Hello and welcome," hailed the cleric as he entered the room. He wore a simple black robe and cap, his angular face as pale as skimmed milk. "You're to be wed, then?"

"Aye." Rogan stood straight, but kept Emeline's hand pressed tight in his own, and tried not to think of the vows he had exchanged once before, on a sandy beach, with a beautiful gypsy girl who wore flowers in her hair. He remembered Camille had wept tears of joy as she leaned against Patrick while Rogan and Orianna exchanged their vows. His mother had married his father on a beach, in front of the ocean and under the eyes of God, she reminded him later, and it had been just as lovely.

"Right. And you've witnesses?" the cleric asked.

"No, 'tis just us."

"Right, excellent, not to worry. I'll send for my wife and daughter, then." The cleric went to the door and stuck his head through, called out, and then returned. He stripped a quill and dredged it in ink, then began filling out the appropriate forms, asking them questions, scratching their names and paternal information onto the parchment. His wife and daughter arrived, both as impossibly white as the cleric. They bobbed their heads in unison to Rogan and Emeline, then took their positions as witnesses.

The cleric instructed Rogan and Emeline to face each other and clasp hands. In his reedy, high voice he had them repeat promises and vows as unfamiliar to Emeline as they were painfully reminiscent to Rogan. Just that easy, Emeline realized, and the ceremony was over and a new life began.

The cleric moved aside and handed Rogan the quill. He and Emeline signed their names in ink, a covenant binding until death.

"Kiss your bride, then," the cleric bubbled happily, tossing a handful of sand onto the parchment to set the ink. "'Tis legal now, and none can stop you." He winked broadly at Rogan, one knowing male to another. "Not even her father."

At those words, ignorant as they were on the cleric's part, Rogan did not hesitate but pulled Emeline to him, wrapped his arms around her, lowered his head and pressed a kiss on her parted lips. He pulled back slightly, quiet words intended for only her ears, "'Tis your turn, my lady. You spoke the vows, as well. Do you kiss your groom to seal them?"

"I will," she replied, and reached up to bury her hands in his unbound black hair, felt the warmth of his skin, the solid curve of his skull beneath her fingers, and pulled his head down, placing her lips on his, moving hers against his as she spoke, "I marry you this day, and give you all I am."

The cleric's daughter let out a little sigh as she watched, but scampered out as her mother shooed her into the back rooms.

Rogan paid the cleric and tipped him, took his copy of the marriage contract, folded it, and tucked it into his jacket. He turned back to Emeline, his golden bride gowned in pink satin, a beauty to stir any man's heart. She stood there in the starkly bare room, a look of apprehension and confusion on her face, clearly at odds with what to do next. With her hands clasped in front of her, she twisted her fingers together as if she wanted to wring her hands but kept them still by sheer self-control. Looking up at Rogan, her lips parted and shook, the pulse in her neck a rapid throb.

"Am I to call you my lord?" she asked in a small voice, thinking that she had never seen a man look so dangerously handsome, tall, strong, and tough.

And yet, she did not fear him.

"If you desire."

She cast her eyes to the floor, her whole body trembling. "I have not been trained as a wife, my lord, but I shall endeavor to please you."

He cupped her chin and turned her face up to meet his eyes. "What is wrong, Princess? The ink is scarcely dry and you are already different."

"I am striving to be wifely in manner."

He grinned at her, a flash as fast and bright as lightning. "Please, don't."

"No?"

"No. I beg you." He leaned down and kissed the tip of her nose. "Be Emeline."

"I want you to be proud of me. I do not want you to regret doing this." A shadow crossed over her face, and for a moment she looked very young and extremely vulnerable. "I never truly thought I would be a wife."

"And I had not ever considered that I would be a duke, but some things aren't anticipated, aye?"

She nodded hesitantly, bit her bottom lip.

"Let's go fetch your mum."

He took her by the elbow and escorted her outside, the unpredictable autumn weather dappling them with sunlight, setting Emeline's honeyed hair to gleaming, glistening gold. Around them the city teemed with people, animals, and traffic of every sort of conveyance. Rogan opened the door to the waiting livery and directed the driver to take them to Bethlem Hospital, doing his best to ignore the way the driver gawked at Emeline.

Inside the carriage he sat opposite her, but he forced himself to watch out the window of the livery, his thoughts tangled around his feelings. He lusted for Emeline; he missed Orianna. He cared for Emeline; he feared the pain of loss.

It was done, he told himself. Emeline and he were wed,

and nothing but death would put it asunder. He only had to protect his heart.

A few miles from where they rode, on Oxford Road, was the amphitheater where he could relieve it all. The screaming crowd roared in his brain, and as if in memory, his body ached. He could not fight until Emeline was safe, he told himself, pushing the urge down into his gut. No matter how much he longed for it, he would have to control his compulsion.

He looked at Emeline then, met her eyes across the carriage.

Emeline observed him with the same unabashed attention as she had in the parlor when they first met face to face, and then again in the carriage house, and also in the room they had rented. Rogan thought to himself that he had never before been gazed upon with such a searching, penetrating stare.

"What are you looking for?" Rogan asked.

She smiled then, a trembling little curve of lips that revealed her embarrassment. "I am sorry to ogle."

But still, she did not look away.

"What are you thinking?" he asked.

"I do not grow tired of watching you," she replied.

Once again Rogan was impressed with her utter boldness, her open way of speaking her mind. It struck a deep chord with him, for he had long despised the coy flirtation that many women used as a device to attract men. To Rogan, those sorts of efforts smacked of manipulation.

"You have little crinkles around your eyes," she observed. "And your grin, 'tis untamed."

"'Tis Irish."

"You are beautiful to me," Emeline said.

Rogan glanced away, then brought his attention back to Emeline. The carriage jostled them around in its humble interior, and though it hardly seemed the right time to broach the subject that nagged at him, he felt it best to be as honest as possible. She'd said she loved him, but he knew that was a mixture of gratitude and newness. He wanted to warn her, to protect her from what could hurt her further.

"Do not fall in love with me, Emeline."

Emeline shrugged her shoulders. "I shall love you if I like, and there is naught you can do about it. You are my husband, and though you are correct that love is not required for marriage, 'tis not forbidden in it, either."

She moved her hand to brush a stray curl that tumbled across her eyes, tucked it behind her ear. But she kept her gaze on his face, her demeanor unapologetic and matter-of-fact. "For years I felt nothing, save fear and my hatred and my shame. You changed that. You awakened me, opened my eyes, and I have not blinked since that day."

"I do not want to hurt you."

"Nonsense," Emeline declared flatly. "'Tis your own heart you seek to protect, not mine. You may lie to yourself, Rogan, but I see through it."

They rode in silence.

"You shame me," Rogan admitted after a long while. He was determined to be as boldly honest as she. "You reveal my cowardice."

Emeline's tone grew more gentle, but it remained factual. "You are not the first man to lose his beloved wife. You will not be the last, either. Trite as it may sound, time will indeed dull your pain. Time takes everything away, if given long enough. Someday your heart will heal, Rogan, and you will fall in love again." A shy smile curved her lips. "I dare to hope it will be with me."

If she had taken a razor and flayed him bloody, she could not have wounded him more. She exposed his hurts, his fears, and she did it with the same boldness with which she exposed her own. He had thought himself honest with her, but he realized she had lessons to teach him in what it was to be truthful. Before he could respond, Emeline continued speaking.

"Simon took everything from me. My hopes, my dreams, my innocence." Her voice was so quiet it seemed to disappear in the rattling noise of the livery, the hoof-beats of the horses, the signature street-cries from the patterers, milk-maids, flower-girls, and merchants who clogged the streets alongside the heavy traffic that clattered up and down the cobblestones.

And yet, he heard her perfectly.

"Look at me now: Your wife. And I will love you as I desire, and I want him to see my love for you. I want him to know he did not break that in me," she continued, and a vicious gleam came into her eyes. "I wished Simon dead for so long. Day after day I dreamed of killing him myself. But now I want him to live to be old and feeble, shattered and alone. I want him to live long enough to see me become the Duchess of Eton. I want him to see *me* live the life he tried to steal. I want to rub his face in the wealth and privilege he craved enough to try to force me to murder for it. I want to see him seethe with envy."

Rogan raised a brow, both amused and surprised by her words and sudden vehemence. "Is that so?"

"Yes."

"I shall be ever vigilant to stay in your good graces, Lady Emeline."

The title snapped the gleam from her eyes, replaced it with a look of confusion. "Do not call me that, Rogan."

"Why not?" He mentally went over the information Kieran had been certain and gleeful to tell him, wished he'd paid more attention. "It appears I am currently the Marquis of something. I don't recall precisely all the titles I am currently wearing—carrying? Holding?" He waved his hand, dismissing the question. "But I do remember that if I were to marry, my wife would be a lady, up until I become duke, which of course will in turn make you my duchess, and therefore allow you to—what was it? Rub Simon's face in it?"

Emeline flushed a dark pink. "'Tis your turn to shame me."

"No, indeed I do not. I respect your truth far more than you know, Princess. Relish your titles, speak your mind, and love me as your husband if that is your desire, as deeply as you dare. I will not ask you to be a player ever again." He swept his eyes over his enigmatic wife, whose audacity and honesty humbled him. "And carry your grudges, for as long as they please you. Lord knows you deserve them."

Bethlem Hospital stood atop a hill, its stone facade dark and imposing, as if sending a warning to any who approached, about what sort of pandemonium it housed. A long, circular driveway paved with cobblestones wound its way in front of the monstrous building, and as they approached, Rogan and Emeline saw it was congested with traffic of all sorts: carriages and conveyances, men on horseback, women walking with their stiff parasols resting on their shoulders.

The driver stopped the livery at the foot of the hill and jumped down, then came around to the side of the coach and opened the door. "Ye'll git 'ere faster ifn ye walk up."

"Fine," Rogan said as he hopped down, reached up and helped Emeline alight. "Wait for us here, then."

The driver nodded his assent with a quick bob of his head, climbed back aboard and clucked to the horses, driving the livery over to the grass where the horses could stand and graze beside a huge oak tree.

Rogan held Emeline's elbow as they walked the long

driveway, approaching the hospital. He felt her body tighten beside him.

"How long has it been since you last saw your mother?" he asked.

"One year, four months, and six days." Emeline swallowed heavily, trying to subdue the lump in her throat. "That was when Simon brought me to see her, after. . . . Before that, it had been seven months and fifteen days."

Her words pained his heart, for Rogan knew exactly what it was to count days as they passed. He tightened his hold of her elbow, and said nothing more as they grew nearer, making their way through the crowd of conveyances and people. Horses snorted and stamped, restless amidst the chattering and commotion, and Rogan reached to pull Emeline even closer to him, shielding her the best he could. All around them people mingled as if at a social party, laughter rising above the group they passed as Rogan heard them talking about one of the inmates on the upper level, how he finger-painted with his own feces on the wall above his head.

"A veritable John Crome," one man quipped, causing his companions to dissolve in high-pitched laughter.

Emeline glanced up to Rogan, her expression pained and embarrassed. "Londoners love their freaks."

Rogan tightened his hold of her reassuringly. "We'll get her out, Princess."

She nodded, took a deep breath, swallowed hard against the stink that began to seep into her nostrils as they climbed the granite steps and neared the main entrance. The thick, oak door hung ajar as people entered and left.

They stepped over the threshold and into the dim foyer. Two staircases led to the upper level, and off the foyer stretched long hallways, two to a side. Ahead of them sat a small table with a woman seated behind it, ledgers in front of her, and a look of boredom on her face. She took money from visitors, which she stowed in a leather purse that she had strapped to her waist. She directed people in the monotone of one who spoke the same words day after day, and answered the same questions year after year. Behind her stood a man who loomed like a Goliath, his ruddy face impassive, his eyes vacant, his hands resting on huge pistols holstered to a thick leather belt around his trunk-like waist.

Rogan and Emeline queued up behind a pair of skinny, giggling young swains, both of whom stank of liquor, body odor, and raw silk dampened with cologne. They each wore the foppish clothes of *nouveaux riches* nabobs who spent the majority of their time playing cards, wasting time, and wooing women.

After the dandies had paid their admission and were on their way, Rogan stepped up to the scarred table. A sheet of parchment, faded with age and stained with various spillage, had been nailed to the table, the prices spelled out in large print. He scanned the paper and saw that full admission to the entire facility cost two shillings per person, partial admission to the lower half of the hospital, one shilling per person.

Rogan glanced once at Goliath, and then met the gaze of the woman behind the table. "Madam, I am looking for a particular woman who has been here for two years. She is called Madeline Britton. Do you know of her?"

"The inmates're nameless ta the public, sir," she droned. She held out her hand for the admission fee. "Two shillin's, if yer wantin' ta tour up-n-down."

Rogan placed his hands on either side of the table, and leaned forward. "Madam, I beseech you to use your heart. This lady, my wife, is looking for her mother."

"The inmates're nameless ta the public, sir."

Goliath took a step forward, glared down at Rogan and made a sound closely resembling a growling dog. Rogan sighed, giving in to the inevitable, and pulled four shillings from his purse. He handed it to the woman, took Emeline by the elbow, escorted her to the nearest corridor, and paused.

The hallway stretched in front of them, long and dank, paint peeling from the plaster walls, the baseboards rotting and stained with wetness. The air was thick with the reek of unwashed bodies, illness, and excrement, and the noise of the inmates echoed in the halls, wailing and moaning, mingled with the laughter and shouts from the visitors who toured the building.

"This will not be pleasant, Princess. Why don't you tell me where your mum was held last you saw her, and then go wait in the coach? I'll take a look around, ask about, and see if I can't find her."

Thick emotions had balled into a confusing clog in Emeline's chest and throat, and the way Rogan treated her as if she were a delicate vessel of womanhood nearly had her slipping into hysteria. Did he not realize that she had been nothing more than a receptacle for Simon to vent his lusts for years? Nothing more than a lowly slattern with Jeffrey as well, she thought. And now Rogan treated her like a lady, whose eyes should be shielded from unpleasantness.

And as much as Emeline thought it should make her feel honored or even honorable, she instead felt the exact opposite, as if she were taking something that did not belong to her. On the heels of those feelings came familiar ones, the humiliation and the anger, along with a nasty voice that taunted her, reminding her that she would never, ever be truly free of Simon and what he had been able to make her submit to.

"No. Let me go and leave me be." She didn't care that her tone was nasty and cutting. "I am quite capable of finding my own mother."

Emeline twisted her arm from Rogan's, walked away, leaving him free to remain or follow in her wake.

She gasped as he grabbed her arm and spun her around to face him. Rogan brought his face down to hers, his eyes a snapping, angry green.

"Don't you walk away from me. Ever."

Chaos raged around them, people milling up and down the corridors, in and out of rooms. Somewhere nearby an inmate howled, long and frighteningly loud, eliciting screams of laughter from the visitors and cries of fear from other inmates.

But Emeline and Rogan never moved an inch, both of them suddenly in a rage, but neither one completely certain as to why.

"You do not order me," Emeline hissed. She slapped his hand but he did not remove it from her arm, his grip iron hard and biting into her flesh. But it was a welcome pain, the kind that feeds anger when other emotions are best left unfelt. "Do you hear me? I will not take orders from any man, ever again."

"You will take them from me. You are my wife now."

"You married very poorly," she taunted, and the truth of her words made her eyes sting. "A duchess whore. It is laughable."

He shook her, hard. "Enough, Emeline. Shut your mouth. I have done nothing to deserve your contempt."

Across the hallway a visitor stumbled from a room, puking on the floor as he walked. He leaned against the wall, gagging, recovering himself. He wiped a hand across his face and gagged again. "Damned filthy animal!" he screamed into the open doorway, and was rewarded by the inmate throwing a mound of feces at him. The man retched, puked once more, and took off running down the corridor.

Still Rogan and Emeline did not move.

Then, as slowly as a fire dying, Emeline took a breath, then another, and closed her eyes so she could not see the anger in his. "You are kind to me, Rogan. It breaks me as nothing else."

He sighed heavily and released his grip on her arm. "Let's go find her so we can be out of here. This place has us acting like we've gone mad as well."

Emeline nodded her agreement, and gestured to the stairs. "Last I came she was held up there, the third cell down the second corridor, on the left."

They made their way through the hospital, Emeline holding her skirts up lest they trail on the filthy floor or be soiled from one of the noisome puddles that intermittently blotched the floor. On the upper level the noise lessened, as fewer visitors paid two extra shillings to see the entire hospital, and therefore the inmates spent less time being poked and harassed. Also, those who needed to be sedated were caged on the second level, as they made for far less entertainment.

Rogan and Emeline found the room where she had been taken to see Madeline before. As when Emeline had been there, the room contained four beds, two to each wall, and a single window barred with iron shafts. There were only women in this room, chained to the walls with lengths of iron links that allowed them to move from their bed to a chamber pot. Rogan glanced around, taking in the filth and the nasty stench, and he wondered how long it would take a sane prisoner to truly be driven out of her mind.

"She is gone." Emeline looked around, searching the women's unfamiliar faces, hating the way the crones in their beds peered at them. Hating them for reminding her of what Madeline had become.

Rogan's eyes met one of the women's as she watched them from her perch on the side of her lumpy mattress. She had long, greasy gray hair and a nose as thin and sharp as a razor. She wore a dirty dressing gown that hung from painfully thin shoulders, and she had a blanket clutched around her like a cloak. With a wiggle of her thick, bushy brows, she grinned at Rogan, exposing rotten gums and a single black tooth.

"Look at you," she drawled, her voice thick with a Scottish accent. "Like a fair bonny prince. Come here, laddie, an let auld Magda take a closer keek."

Rogan squeezed Emeline's hand once, a signal to wait where she stood, and he addressed the woman.

"Magda, is it?" Rogan asked, and he went over to her, knelt down in front of her bony knees. He looked her over, and then lifted her hand and pressed a kiss to it, as gallant as a knight to a lady. "You don't look daft to my eyes, and I've eyes like a hawk."

Her grin went wider, and she reached out to finger his hair. "Black Irish, are ye? I've a *cúpla focal*, I do. Ye dinna sound quite right, though, but you've got the face of *Cú Chulainn* himself. Where're ye from, laddie?"

"All around, and not England, aye?" He winked at her, and she grinned in delight. "I've come with my wife; she's looking for her mum. Are you knowing the woman called Madeline Britton? She was in this room a bit more than a year ago."

"Maddie?" Magda's brows shot up. She addressed Emeline for the first time. "Maddie's girl, are ye?"

Emeline nodded, took a few steps forward. "Do you know my mother?"

"Aye, I kent her weel. I've been locked in this room for nigh these many years, aye? I've seen plenty come and go." Magda stared hard at Emeline. She swept her hand to encompass the room, the upper floor, the hospital, and the injustice. Deep in her throat she made a sound of derision. "They group the wives together."

"Where is she? I've come to take her home."

"Home?" Magda looked at Rogan, as if to see if Emeline had lost her mind. And then it sank in, memories of the things Madeline had spoken about, her daughter and her husband. She looked back at Emeline, her face now contorted in sympathy. "*Och, ochón.* She's passed, lass."

"Passed?" Emeline's eyes glazed over. The room was spinning. "Passed?"

"Aye." Magda pushed herself from the bed with effort and hobbled to the wall, dragging her chain with her. She consulted her calendar, a series of scratches and marks made with a piece of her bed frame pried free years before, a tiny fragment of iron that saved her sanity. With the tip of her finger she counted, mumbling all the while, until she found what she looked for, and turned back to Emeline. "Fourteen months ago."

Chapter 18

"Mum," Emeline whispered. Images of Madeline flashed through her mind; her mother dressed in her Sunday finest, thin, lace gloves on her slender hands; as lovely as a portrait sitting at the dinner table, her face serene as Emeline's father gave the blessing; eyes ravaged and circled with bruises, her lips swollen but contorted in a curse as she came at Simon again and again; the final time Emeline saw her in the hospital, the way Madeline had lain in the bed, immobile, violated, how she turned her head to look at her daughter, and managed to smile for her as if to say, *don't worry for me, love*.

And that expression had served one purpose: to make Emeline completely at Simon's mercy, willing to do whatever she must do to keep her mother from being injured ever again.

Love. The word felt like the bitterest acid, burning, burning, eating away at Emeline's gut. Love had been beneath it all, an ugly tool that Simon used to twist Emeline into submission. *Do it, daughter of mine, or the next man I send for your mother will use orifices not intended for entry*. And Emeline had done what he wanted. She had even pretended to like it, making the sounds Simon liked best, moaning and groaning so loud her throat would be on fire.

Love. Emeline did it all for the love of her mother, to save her, to protect her, to see to it she would not be raped again, not if Emeline only had to bend over like a dog, crawl on the floor in front of Simon, take Simon into her mouth. It was all worth it, if it meant that Madeline was not injured further. Enduring the humiliation was infinitely easier herself, a far cry better than knowing that resistance would cost Madeline even more than she'd already paid.

But Madeline had been dead. Dead all those long months of debasement. Gone forever, far beyond Simon's reach, and Emeline had been crawling and submitting for nothing. Nothing but love. And Madeline had suffered in a horrible hell, been chained and raped and left behind as if she were meaningless, nameless, forgotten. Without a single soul to hold her hand and say goodbye as she passed away.

From a million miles away she heard a voice, Rogan's, asking her to come with him, to leave the hospital. But she was too far away, could not answer, could not tell him that she wanted to lie down on Madeline's filthy bed and die. *Madeline, mum, mother, I loved you so much. I did it all for you.*

Emeline felt Rogan's hands on hers, tugging her along. Her feet did not move, though. She remained rooted in the repulsive room, smelling the stench that had surrounded her lovely mother. *Mummy, I remember your skin, your beautiful fine skin.*

And then came Rogan's arms, wrapping Emeline up, lifting her, holding her to his chest as he carried her out of the room where Madeline died alone.

Emeline could not fight him, lacked the strength to push away, to demand to be left there to die, even though that was what she wanted, what she deserved. *I'm sorry, sorry, sorry, so sorry. Forgive me, mother. Forgive me.*

But who did she ask? she wondered numbly. Who could forgive her?

Rogan took the stairs at a fast clip, and then strode through the foyer, pushing his way past the people milling about, and then kicked the door wide open, and carried her out into the sunlight. He glanced down at her again, saw her frozen face, pale and stricken, her eyes empty. He picked up his pace, jogged down the long driveway to where the carriage waited. He motioned to the driver to just wait as he yanked open the door and climbed inside. He gently placed Emeline on the seat, took off his jacket, and wrapped it around her shoulders. He knelt in front of her.

"Emeline, do you hear me?" He peered closer, saw that she did not respond at all, not even a flicker in her empty eyes. He cupped her cheek, his thumb a simple, soft caress against her cheekbone. "Try to come back, *anamchara.*"

But there was nothing around her but the thickest fog, so dense she could scarcely draw breath as she drowned in the grayness, submerged in it, completely outside her body in a place removed from reality.

And the fog stank of Simon.

Flashing through the clouds came staccato bursts of Madeline, pictures frozen in Emeline's memory. And Simon. Always Simon. His scent saturated her nostrils, as real as if it were he who knelt in front of her now, and Emeline felt as though all the doors Rogan had opened were closed again.

She was cold, lost once more in the lonely, darkened corridors where no one knew her or cared for her beyond the prize of the genitals between her thighs. Her womanhood had been her currency, and she had been willing to pay any price for her mother.

For nothing. It had all been for nothing. She had protected no one, stopped nothing. Like a fool, she'd believed Simon, given everything, paid, paid, and paid some more, and it was all for nothing. The fog swirled, grew denser, the stink of Simon growing thicker. Sickness churned in her gut, made her skin clammy and cold, filled her mouth with a vile taste.

Rogan watched her grow even whiter still, her color faded to nothingness, her eyes huge dark circles of empty blue. Worry gripped him; the shock she'd received seemed to be making her body shut down. He left her there for a moment, and hung out the door. The driver swiveled around in the high seat, his brows lifted high in question under his cap.

"Is yer leidy all right?"

"She is not. Do you know of an inn nearby, where I can get her settled and abed?"

"Aye, the Plough's not too far from 'ere."

"Fine," Rogan said. "Take us there."

The driver nodded and lifted the reins, slapped them against the backs of his team as Rogan pulled back into the coach and shut the door. With a lurch the livery swung into action, and Rogan seated himself beside Emeline and pulled her to him so he could hold her steady as they rattled down the uneven roads.

"Can you speak to me, Princess? Please?"

Emeline tried, opened her mouth, but no words came. It was as if all her perception of reality had crumbled under the weight of her shame and guilt. She had not protected Madeline. Simon's fog shrouded her, gray and devoid of feeling, where she was shut away from her own sense of self. But Rogan reached for her, feeling his way through her daze, his voice sanity, when nothing else seemed real.

She turned her head, met his eyes. Looked into the vivid green, vital, like life and growing things, and then lay back against him, let him hold her against him like an anchor, the only solid thing in her world that kept her from dissipating completely away.

The carriage pulled up in front of the Plough, and Rogan hurried to pay the driver and thank him, and cradled Emeline in his arms like a child, her bag hooked on the crook of his arm. He sent the driver on his way and carried Emeline into the building, noting that the downstairs main room looked clean enough, save a few dirty dishes that lingered on tables, waiting for the goodwife's attention.

As he waited to be helped, he held Emeline close, still wrapped in his coat. The goodwife bustled into the room, gowned in a simple, faded dress and apron, her silky blond hair falling from the bun at the nape of her neck. She saw Rogan holding Emeline, set down the bucket she carried and hurried over to the desk in the corner that held the register, tucking her hair behind her ears.

"Sorry, sir. Ye weren't waitin' long, I 'ope?"

"No, not to worry," Rogan replied, and he shifted Emeline in his arms. Though she was not a heavily rounded woman, she was taller than most, and she hung so listlessly that his arms burned with the strain of holding her and the bag of gowns. "I'm needing a room for the day and the night, and I'll also need tea and food brought up as soon as possible."

The goodwife bobbed her head in understanding, took down his information, and reached into her pocket for the keys to a room recently cleaned and readied for new guests. She gestured to Emeline, then, a worried frown creasing her brow. "Yer not bringin' the catarrh 'ere, are ye? What's got her ailing? I can't 'ave pox or plague 'ere."

Rogan hated having to say aloud the thing that pained Emeline so deeply. "My wife just found out her mother passed away. She's had a bad shock."

Sympathy touched the woman's face, and she reached

out to press her hand on Emeline's shoulder. "God bless ye, miss." She turned her attention back to Rogan. "Follow me, an I'll see to it yer settled."

Rogan fell into step behind the woman and waited as she unlocked the door and stood back so he could enter. He crossed the space quickly and laid Emeline out on the huge tester bed that dominated the room as the goodwife knelt before the cavernous fireplace and set about lighting a fire. Rogan dipped into his purse and withdrew five pounds, turned to the woman and pressed the money into her hand. He gave instructions that had the woman bobbing her head in agreement, ready to do anything for the man who obviously wanted his wife cared for in the very best manner, and was willing to pay generously to see it done.

"Aye, sir. I'll see to it all meself," she replied, and went briskly from the room, the door closing behind her with a little thud.

Rogan draped a cover over Emeline and saw that her expression had not changed. She lay completely still, her skin as white as death, her eyes empty and unfocused as she stared up at the ceiling. He touched her face; she did not move or flinch. Slowly, gently, he ran his finger down her cheek where tears should be falling, but did not.

He knew something about not being able to comprehend the loss of a loved one, knew dark and painful truths about sadness so great it seemed there could not possibly be recovery.

"Do not worry, *anamchara*," he said tenderly. "We'll see it through together."

He sat on the edge of the bed beside her, held her hand even though it was limp and cold. "You'll remember I told you about my mum, Camille?"

She was still silent, but her fingers tightened around his hand.

"Aye, she is a fine woman. Strong and proud, so much so that she told me about her upbringing, her life, her losses, her trials. She came through all of it, and built a life despite it. She endured much in London, Emeline. I think she would not mind if I told you of them, now. I know my mother well, and if she were here, I think she would tell you about it, to help you draw strength."

And so Rogan told Emeline about Camille, a story about beatings and degradation, manipulation and a struggle for power over her life. He told her about his father, Patrick, and how he was like a light in her darkness, and how it made her reach for more, until Patrick was taken away and Camille believed the worst of lies, that he had left her behind.

But there was a child, Rogan told Emeline, and Camille wanted the baby, a miracle that sprang from Patrick's and her love. But the control hung over Camille in the form of her mother, Amelia, who would go to any lengths to see to it that her daughter knew who owned her. And the rape, that took Camille's ability to believe in anything, and even worse, took the life of their child, who even to this day was not forgotten and was still missed.

And the final indignity of all of it, that Camille believed that it had been all her fault: that through her actions, she had brought pain and suffering to her own baby. She'd felt dirty and shamed from the rape, and thought that Patrick would never be able to love her after all that had happened.

"You see, Emeline, she thought she carried the burden alone, and the weight of it was so great she wanted to die." He leaned over her so that his eyes were in her line of vision. He forced her to see him. "She did not die, though. And she was able to accept that it was not all her fault. Do you see? Do you understand what I am trying to tell you?"

She did not move, but the look in her eyes changed. Softened. Asked for answers when she had none.

He tried to give them to her, even as he floundered for the right words. Rogan smoothed Emeline's hair, his heart twisting as she looked into his eyes with such steadfast soul-searching. It was as if she were a child who would believe anything he said, so trusting was her expression. It made him want to be worthy of her belief. "It wasn't your doing." He probed her eyes with his, looking for her acceptance of what he told her and wished for better words. But it really was simple, and he kept it that way. "It is not your fault."

Emeline took a deep, shaky breath. When she spoke, her voice was tiny and timid. "Camille was raped?"

"Aye," Rogan said flatly, and he tried to quell the rage it made him feel to say it, to know someone hurt his mother that way, killed his brother or sister. And it made the compassion he felt for Emeline grow even deeper, for she had endured it many times over, and his respect for her became deeper still, for she had goodness in her heart despite everything she suffered.

The rage remained in his chest, a white-hot ball of revenge that demanded release, and he promised himself he would find Simon and kill him. He would see to it that Simon died slowly, his death taking long enough that Simon would have plenty of time to beg for mercy. Mercy that would not be shown. Rogan's fist curled, clenched, his body tight and ready. Rogan wanted to beat him to death, could already feel the flesh splitting and running red as he reached bone.

A small knock sounded at the door and Rogan gave Emeline a pat on the hand before leaving her side, giving her time to think about all he'd told her as he saw to their basic needs.

He opened the door and saw the goodwife in the hallway, her reddened face beaming with pride and exertion. Behind her stood an army of servants, some wearing the clothes of stable hands, kitchen help, and scullery maids. Rogan grinned down at her, knowing she'd gone above and beyond to see to it that his wishes were carried out. He moved back to allow them to enter and returned to his purse to draw out a few more coins, to see to it the goodwife was well compensated for all her efforts.

The staff wrestled in a huge tub of wood and brass and set it in the corner. They laid out towels and soaps while buckets of steaming water were carried in by still more servants, the vapor rising and fogging the windows of the room as they poured the hot water, filling the tub three-quarters full. At Rogan's request they left a full bucket by the fire. The goodwife wheeled in a cart laden with steaming plates of food and a pot of fragrant tea. She showed Rogan each dish. After his final nod of approval she handed him a bottle of spirits.

"You did very well. I thank you." Rogan waited as the staff left them alone.

He closed the door and bolted it, added a few logs to the fire, and then went to Emeline's side. He stood over her as she lay on the bed, all too aware of her vulnerability to his strength and his size. How could he lust for her so completely and yet despise any man who felt the same? Looking at her made him want to shed every vestige of his humanity and give himself over to the animal within. And yet she also made him want to be her champion, her savior.

He forced himself to speak. "'Tis time for your bath, my lady."

A long sigh slid from her lips. She closed her eyes. "I asked you not to call me that."

"You've yet to give me a reason not to."

"I am not a lady, Rogan. 'Tis a mockery and all will know it. How long before people find out what I have been to Simon, to Jeffrey. What will they say? I am disgraced, and no titles can make it not so."

It seemed the protector was now in full charge. Rogan lifted a golden curl and rubbed it between his fingers. "Accustom yourself, Princess. You're my wife now. Everyone will treat you accordingly, or they'll answer to me."

"You cannot change how people think."

"No, and neither can you. So get up, take off your clothes and get in the water. Worry if you must, but you might as well do it in the bath."

Emeline pushed up from the bed, surprised to find that she had the strength. It came from Camille, she realized, the knowledge that other women had suffered and had survived. Knowing she was not alone, and that others could and would understand, it amazed Emeline just how much that mattered and helped.

She cast a sidelong glance at Rogan, who watched her every movement. He was easy enough to read: He was a man who walked the narrow line between light and darkness, his savage nature thinly concealed beneath his sense of honor. He'd picked her up when she could not walk. Given her his absolution when he could not take solace in his own. And yet, he wanted to toss her on her back and take her, she knew. She could see it. But he would not do it; she knew that, too. Emeline said a mental blessing to Camille, that she could have raised a man so well.

Emeline was drawn to the side of the tub and trailed her fingers in the hot water. The steam rose up, scented with spicy oils that made her think of far-away, exotic lands. The mist gathered in tiny, shivering droplets on her skin, and she dipped her hand farther into the heat, wanting to strip her clothes and sink in, soak away her troubles, cleanse her skin and hair. What a luxury, she marveled, a bath brought to her room as if she were indeed a princess.

Emeline could feel him watching her: a palpable

awareness. She turned and saw that Rogan stood by the fire, watching her as he leaned casually against the mantle, his thumbs hooked in his waistband. The look in his eyes was anything but casual, however. He burned for her; it was written in every line of his body and in the intensity of his gaze. Their eyes met and held.

He looked dangerous, disreputable, wild, his hair as black as a pirate's, unbound and disheveled. His suntanned skin made his eyes sparkle, bright green and burning with the power of life itself. His wrinkled clothes and healing bruises added to his rakish appearance, his shirt unfastened, askew, revealing the broad planes of his chest and the black hair that dusted his sun-darkened skin. And Emeline knew that chest to be warm and hard. Knew the beating of his heart beneath his muscles, had felt it throb beneath her palm, her cheek, her own breast.

She wanted him to kiss her, to hold her, and dear God, yes, she wanted him to enter her, to possess her. Yes, she craved his possession: His passion. But the desire that burned in her did not spring from his appearance. He had become far more to her than simply a handsome man. He was Rogan Mullen, a man like no other.

Rogan, who came to her out of the darkness and spoke to her through all her many barriers, until only the door remained between them. Rogan, who pushed Jeffrey's hand from her breast and wanted to fight for her honor. Rogan, who treated her as if she had virtue, who married her to protect her, to give her his name, to keep her safe. Rogan, who took her to save her mother, and then carried her out when she had no strength to stand. Rogan, who made her believe all things were possible.

"My mother would have approved of you," Emeline said softly.

He grinned at that, and came to stand by her side, turned

her and began loosening the laces of her gown. "Camille will embrace you, as well."

Emeline held her breath as he undid the stays that bound her ribs and waist. She pictured Rogan's mother, with his black hair and green eyes, her gentle soul and her strong will. And Patrick, a man like Rogan. A family. A place to be welcomed. Emeline craved it deeply, so much so it became an actual, physical ache. "Do you really think so?" she asked shyly.

"I know it."

That, however, was the crux of Emeline's problem. She had abused Rogan's honor too much, had allowed him to insert her into his life in ways she did not deserve and could not reciprocate.

Emeline had long since overcome her fear of the act of sex, indeed, had learned how to use it to her best advantage. Which was precisely her worry now, as she experienced her first feelings of sexual want. Did she want to have sex with Rogan to repay him?

One thing was for sure: Emeline would never again trade sex for anything. When she finally did make love with Rogan, it would be for herself and for him. Nothing more; never again.

Rogan pushed her gown from her shoulders and took it from her as she stepped out of the folds of the skirts, and then waited as she unwrapped her corset. She handed it to him and he accepted it, gripping the stiff panels. And though he held to his control, he allowed his gaze to sweep down the full length of her as he stood behind her. Her gauzy shift hid nothing from him. He saw how beautifully made her body was, appreciated the lean length of her legs, the full roundness of her hips, the tiny nip of her waist and the narrowness of her back that could be easily spanned with his hand. From where he stood he could see the side of her breasts, full and round, and he wanted to reach around and cup them, bend her over the tub and slide into her snug sheath. And he knew it would be tight and hot, the pleasure of her exquisite.

But Emeline had offered herself to him twice, and both times it had been to ease his lust. Rogan wanted her to come to him out of her own desire, to welcome him into her body, to demand it, to crave it, to need it. He wanted her desires unveiled and raw; as bold as his own.

Emeline glanced shyly over her shoulder, and Rogan knew she could likely feel the heat that pumped from him, as hot as the fire in the hearth. "Will you attend my bath, my lord?"

"No." His voice was husky and tight, and his hands itched for want of the feel of her skin, the texture of her hair. "Get in the water, Princess. It cools as my blood heats."

Rogan moved away, as far as he could get from her, to the window. He wiped away the condensation on the glass and watched outside as London seethed around them, people going about their day-to-day lives. Trapped inside the room, Rogan tried to ignore the reality of his wife, even as he heard the sound of her shift being dropped to the floor, the slosh of the water as she stepped into the tub, the little sigh of pleasure as she slid down into the hot, scented water.

And he burned for her there at the window. He kept his back to her so he could not see the way the water curved around her breasts, the way her skin flushed from the heat, the way she leaned her head back and melted. And yes, he admitted it to himself: He envied the water for its fluid embrace of her.

Rogan clamped his control down on his lust. Emeline would come to him. She would want him. She would beg for him to slide inside her. He would have it no other way. He would not be another man who took his ease with her body.

In the tub, Emeline lathered her flannel, washed her skin, dipped deep under the water and wet her hair, washed it, and slid under again, her hair fanning out as she rinsed. She delighted in the bath, washed way the dirt and grime of traveling and of Bedlam. She scrubbed her skin again until she shone pink and clean, and then leaned back and soaked until the water turned cold.

Emeline rose up from the water feeling like Venus, the water running in rivulets from her skin. The room was warm from the blazing fire, and she reached lazily for a towel. She patted dry and wrapped a towel on her hair and then another around her body. She rummaged through her bag for a clean dressing gown and slipped into it. "You may turn around, my lord," she said, reaching for a comb.

Rogan did, and he was apparently careless of his obvious arousal. Her attention was riveted as he picked up his bucket of water, took it to the side of the tub, and began to undress. Emeline's brows shot up and her face grew hot. How could she have been so selfish, so thoughtless? "My lord, I did not realize you would want to bathe. I would have left you warm water."

"I am fine." Rogan glanced over to her as he dropped his shirt to the floor. "I'll ask for what I want, Emeline."

Rogan stripped naked and dipped a flannel in the water, lathered it and began to wash, seemingly unconcerned that Emeline stood and watched him.

Emeline stared at him in fascination. Far from Jeffrey's pale, paunchy build or Simon's barrel-chested frame, Rogan could have been sculpted by Jezebel herself, his muscular male body beautiful to look upon. His long limbs were defined, his belly flat and rippled with definition, his chest tight and wide. Every inch of his body was hard and firm, most especially his manhood: It thrust away from his body as tightly drawn as a sword.

His cock held her fascination, rigid and darkly suffused with blood, helmet-tipped and smooth. She knew if he were a different man it could be dangerous, a weapon. But because it was Rogan's, she found the sight of it curiously beautiful, an extension of the man himself.

When he had cleansed himself from head to toe, he dipped his head in the clean bucket, then held his dripping hair over the tub of used water as he lathered. He stepped into the tub and lifted the bucket, upended it and rinsed his hair and his body.

Rogan wiped the water from his eyes as he reached for a towel, but then stopped in mid-motion. Emeline was close, so close that he could feel her body heat. She held out a towel for him.

It was a simple gesture, but it touched him, wifely in manner and thoughtful. Emeline's eyes were wide, glistening in the firelight. She had never looked more alluring to him. She was still damp from the bath; her skin was still moist, flushed with warmth. But that was not what aroused him further. It was not the way the light illuminated her either, though it did; he could see the shadowy outline of her body through the thin cotton. No, he realized, it was not the intimacy of the setting or the erotic glimpses of her curves. It went beyond the physical. Her face registered every emotion he felt himself: desire, uncertainty, bruised honor, and nervousness. Seeing his feelings mirrored in her made his balls tighten, his cock throb.

"Your towel."

He nodded his thanks and took it. He dried his hair as he watched her gaze slide down his body, from his face to his shoulders, chest, belly, and penis. She dragged her gaze back to his.

"You want me."

"I do."

She seemed flustered, confused. He stepped from the tub and finished drying off, then stood straight, let her be near him, feel his heat and see the evidence of his hunger.

"There is nothing of this earth that would make me press you for your favors, Emeline." Rogan saw her take another peek down at his erection, and he knew she heard the thickness of his voice, heavy and taut with desires he kept leashed and held at bay. "Aye. Look at how much I desire you. Do I force you?"

She shook her head.

"Aye. And I will not. Ever." Rogan reached out and took her hand, placed it on his arm where his muscles bulged, solid and powerful. "Feel my strength and know I will never use it against you. See my cock, hard and ready and hot for you, and know that I can control my body and my lusts."

"You are . . ." Emeline hesitated. Her eyes dropped back to his erection and her fingers dug into his arm. "Overwhelming."

Rogan closed his eyes, unable to continue watching her look at his erection. She was too close, too beautiful, and too naked beneath the dressing gown she wore. All of that, and the expression on her face was driving him over the edge of logic. "Do you want to touch me?"

"May I?"

"As you desire, my lady."

"But can you . . . and not?"

"I can restrain myself." Rogan reached out as he spoke, unwound the towel from her hair and let it cascade down to her waist, ropy, wet, and tangled. He picked up a heavy lock of it, brought it to his lips and pressed a kiss to her tresses. "There is no force. No seduction. No manipulation. Only me and you, our bodies as they are, and not a single lie between us. Touch me if you want to, or just walk away. I will not think differently of you no matter which you choose."

Emeline took her hand from his arm, wrung it together with her other. His tone was raspy and rough, his body huge and hard. She wanted to touch him, yes, because she had never touched a man when compelled by her own choice. Emeline stopped hesitating. She reached out, gripped him, and trembled as a myriad of sensations ran through her. He was hard as stone, true, but also silky soft. He quivered in her grip, leapt in her hand.

Yet, Rogan did not move. His breathing was labored; his eyes were closed. His body was tight, veins bulging with the effort of his restraint. Still, he made no sound. No movement. He let her explore his flesh, from base to tip.

Emeline let go. Her hand felt as hot as if she still held him. Rogan opened his eyes and met her gaze.

"Go wait by the fire," Rogan told her.

She nodded then, uncomfortable with the effect she had on his body, even as she felt a surge of feminine power. To cover her confusion she knelt before the fire and began combing out her hair.

Rogan slipped into his breeches, went to the window, opened it, and stood in the draft of the cold, damp air.

A long while later, Rogan's movement caught Emeline's attention as he moved to the cart and lifted the plates of food. He brought them to her and sat beside her in front of the fire.

"I am not hungry, my lord." She did not look up but stared into the fire, methodically combing her hair. She hoped she appeared calm, for inside her was a battle of desire versus dignity, along with grief for Madeline that she could not spend, could not reconcile, and guilt she was not certain she would ever be free of.

"You will eat anyway. You need your strength."

Emeline sighed and nodded, set down her comb and

began nibbling at the fare of meats and cheeses and breads until she felt that he would be satisfied by how much she'd consumed. Rogan ate as well, and when they were finished he set aside the plates and reached for the bottle of whiskey and two glasses, opened it and poured them each a splash.

"You'll have heard of a wake?" he asked, pressing a glass in her hand.

At her nod, he held up his whiskey. "To Madeline. A fine woman." He tossed back the whiskey and then grinned. He cleared his throat, filled his glass, and nodded to Emeline. "'Tis your turn, Princess. We're going to get good and pissed, and you'll be better for it. Now there's rules to a wake, aye? No ill talk, no regrets, no weeping. Just a fine homage to an admirable woman, and of the many good memories you'll carry forever. 'Tis the best way to remember the ones you love. No crying for their death, but giving tribute to their life."

Emeline held the glass of amber liquid, swirled it and watched how the firelight made it glow from within. Sadness nipped at her, threatened her with its fog, and she decided against its grip. She held up her glass. "To my mum, Madeline Elizabeth Spencer Wolfe, who loved to laugh and loved to sing. She loved me, too, and I her, more than words can say."

Emeline tossed back the whiskey, gasped as its searing heat scalded her throat and lungs and gut. Her eyes watered and she wiped away the tears. She held out her glass to Rogan for a refill.

Rogan poured them each another drink and then held up his glass. "To Madeline Elizabeth Spencer Wolfe, a woman who raised a woman, and did a superb job of it."

Sorrow shadowed Emeline's expression, but Rogan held up his glass and shook his head, tossed back the drink with a neat twist of his wrist. "Mind the rules, Princess. Your turn."

She took a deep breath, pushed away her sadness, and searched her memory. Finally she was able to look at Rogan and smile, even though her lips quivered and her voice shook. "To my mum, who made the best roast and the worst gravy, who until Simon, never had a negative thing to say about anyone, even the king, and who tried to look her finest each day." She put the glass to her lips, hesitated, and then knocked it back in a single gulp.

"Aye, good." Rogan refilled her glass, held up his own. The whisky was threading through him, warming and loosening his body, easing his aches. He held his glass high and did what he hadn't done when he'd needed it most. But some things really are better late than never. "To my first wife, Orianna, who could dance the dance of the seven veils, and did so, whenever I asked her to." He caught Emeline's expression of surprise, grinned, winked, gulped down his whiskey and poured another.

Emeline's body was hot, inside and out, heated from the warm bath and the blazing fire, the whiskey, and the wake. She held up her glass again. This time when she spoke of Madeline her voice was strong and sure. "To my mum, who despised ignorance, and who taught me my letters and penmanship, and then spent a portion of her inheritance seeing to it that I was tutored." She drank down the whiskey, wheezing and gasping as it hit her gut, and then set down the glass. The room tilted and then spun around her. "Oh. I need a break."

"Fine. We've all night, aye?" Rogan held up his glass. "I'll continue on, if you don't mind. To your mum, Madeline, and my wife, Orianna. Two women, both deeply loved and sorely missed, who made the world a finer place for the time they spent in it and who live on in our hearts and memories. Gone, but never forgotten."

Emeline decided she needed to drink to that and lifted her glass, held it out for a refill, and then knocked it back again. They continued on for a long while, hours passing, the fire dying down until only embers remained and the whiskey bottle lay on its side, empty in front of the warm hearth. Emeline tried to stand, but found the floor to be a much safer place. She curled up in front of the fire and closed her eyes.

Rogan staggered to his feet, lay a few logs on the fire and waited as they caught. He turned and looked down on Emeline as she lay in front of him, the curves of her body alluring beneath her cotton nightgown. Light and shadows roamed over her as the flames stretched towards the chimney, caught in the updraft. And tenderly, Rogan reached down and lifted her into his arms, cradling her for a long moment as she slept. He then took her to the bed, lay her down, and covered her.

"'Tis our wedding night, *anamchara*." He heard his own slight slur. "And forgive me, but I am still saying goodbye to my wife."

He reached out to smooth her hair back from her face, his vision wavering as the whiskey did its work, but still he noticed the perfect shape of her lips, the high curve of her cheekbones, the striking slash of her arching brows.

"I cannot love you." It was easier to confess to her while she slept under the whiskey's influence and while he himself was caught in its warm, soothing clutch. He climbed into the bed beside her, lay on his back, feeling the spin of the bed and the buzz that dulled any real feeling. "I cannot," he repeated, and then again, "I cannot love you."

And as the whiskey took him into its fragmented visions, he saw Orianna dancing the dance of the seven veils. The brightly colored scarves streamed from her jeweled belt to her slim brown feet, parting and shifting with the swaying of her hips. They offered him tantalizing glimpses of her legs and the dark triangle patch between them before closing again, only to part once more, flashing him a just a peek, so fast it made him wonder if he'd seen her prize at all.

She gyrated before him, arms outstretched, her wide mouth curved in a smile as she drew closer and closer, so near he thought he could smell her scent. Orianna leaned forward, her pert, naked breasts swinging in front of him like cherry-tipped, ripened fruit. And then her lips moved, her voice audible in Rogan's mind, husky and accented with her Romany tongue as she spoke: *You cannot keep her safe from death by withholding your love.*

And then the deep, rough voice of Jack Broughton: *Stop fighting, and start living.*

Rogan gripped the bed as it spun beneath him, and for once let the feelings take him on a journey that did not end with punches and pain, blood and fury.

The place they took him was one of a different agony, of guilt never assuaged, of faith misplaced. Rogan felt the wave coming and this time there was no fight to distract him. No bruiser to punish him.

The wave engulfed him. In his drunken state Rogan whimpered from its onslaught. He relived that night. He saw her dying. Her blood was all over him, on his clothes, his skin, covering his hands. He held them up, closed one eye to focus against the double vision, saw the dripping blood, red, so crimson red. It stained his skin, stained his soul.

"To Orianna." The dream clutched him in a vise-like grip, and he was powerless to stop it. She was everywhere, in his mind, his heart, and most of all, on his conscience. "Who trusted me enough to let me kill her."

Chapter 19

Rogan woke to blazing morning sun streaming into the room, torturing him with its brightness. His head throbbed mercilessly. He rolled away from Emeline, staggered from the bed, made use of the chamber pot and then went over to the cart. He filled his empty whiskey glass with cold tea from the night before and gulped it down, feeling slightly more human as he set down his glass.

The day before had brought surprises, but the one ahead of them loomed with reality. Rogan meant to deal with it, head on.

He lit a new fire and sat in front of it deep in thought. The disturbing dreams plagued his mind. He worried for Kieran, as well, and though he knew she was safe and tended to at the mansion, he hoped she did not fret too much at his sudden disappearance.

His thoughts were disturbed as Emeline woke, stirring in the bed before sitting up. Her honey hair streamed all around her, tangled and tousled, her eyes bleary and puffy with sleep, the side of her cheek sporting the impression of the wrinkled pillowcase. For all that, she was beautiful. She met his gaze and a slow smile curved her lips.

"I dreamed of you. You and my mum. 'Twas a happy

dream." She placed her hand on her forehead and then lay back down. "Oh, my head."

Rogan brought her a glass of cold tea, made her sit up and drink it. When she'd finished he took the glass, set it aside, and sat beside her on the bed.

"Listen, Princess. Time is limited. How long until Simon realizes you've gone from the mansion? We need a plan to deal with him."

"No. A plan is not necessary. I will kill him for what he did to my mother." The look of sleepy goddess faded from her face, and in its place there was nothing but the cold hardness of a mercenary. Rogan watched the transformation, fascinated to see how she spoke of murder without apology, as savage as any warrior who desired justice and longed to deliver it personally.

"'Tis understandable, but Simon's not worth hanging for. If we're to get rid of him, we'll need to be smart about it."

She did not keep the accusation from her tone. "You dumped the poison."

"Right, well. 'Twas before all this, and you were in a fair state. Keeping poison around seemed like borrowing trouble."

"I need a gun." Emeline pursed her lips in contemplation. "Or a knife. A knife would be better to kill him."

Rogan took her hand and held it in his own, gripped it hard to get her attention. "Listen, Emeline. Think. I need to know where Simon lives, what his routine is, what his weaknesses are."

"You will murder him, won't you?"

"Aye, I'll avenge your honor and your mother's life. It makes me sick, knowing what he put you and her through." He squeezed her hand a bit more, making certain she understood he was deadly serious. "And you'll stay out of my way, and let me do my work. I don't send women to do what must be done."

Emeline's breath caught in her throat and her body grew warm, the slick dampness of desire heated her loins. As perverse as she knew it to be, it was the most romantic, sensual thing she could imagine: Rogan, her valorous knight, finding Simon under the cloak of darkness, slitting his thick neck as Rogan cursed Simon for his many sins.

As thrilling as that image was, Emeline also wanted to watch Simon die herself, deal the blow with her own weapon, to look in his eyes at the moment of his death and see the knowledge that he died at her hand.

Emeline shivered sensuously at the images, reveled in the decadence of her own murderous desires. She leaned forward and pressed her lips against Rogan's, her knight, her savior, her husband and friend. Gone were any reservations about sex with Rogan, along with the worries about remuneration and honor. It was suddenly all so simple: She wanted Rogan; he wanted her.

Again she thought about Rogan killing Simon, and her blood grew even hotter. And as their mouths met, she slid her tongue into his, her whole body on fire. A moan escaped her control.

Rogan pulled back, assessed her. "'Tis bloodlust I see in your eyes."

"It is. I am hot with lusts of every sort. Come inside and burn with me."

In the fireplace, a log split in half with a loud *crack*. Sparks shot out of the center in a shower of glowing red.

"I am only human, Emeline. A man. I can't withhold myself from you again."

"I want your sex in me, Rogan."

"There can't be any stopping. Be certain." His hands curled into fists as if he held himself physically at bay.

Emeline's lips curved in a seductive smile. "No more treating me like some wounded angel. You do not have to protect me. I am not afraid, and I know what I am doing."

Her finger twined in Rogan's hair and tugged. "The devil in me is in full charge. I will not stop you, my lord. Indeed, I may beg you for that cock you let me touch. 'Tis magnificent, you know."

A long breath hissed between Rogan's teeth. "Do what you desire."

Emeline did. She pressed her hand against his chest, felt the thrill of his hot, hard body, slid her hand down over his taut belly, and then lower. She traced the outline of his manhood through his breeches, cupped him through the fabric and felt him pulse against her palm, the heat pouring from his body. Emeline's smile deepened, and like Eve she rose from the bed, lifted her nightgown up and over her head. She dangled it out to her side and let it drop at Rogan's feet. Emeline stood before him, completely bare.

"Look at me, my lord," she invited him. "I am your wife, and 'tis your right."

Rogan's eyes moved over her with such intensity she could nearly feel it like a hot caress. He fed on the sight of her feminine glory, tangled tresses cascading over full, rosy-tipped breasts, and down a narrow, flat belly.

"You are . . ." Rogan's voice drifted off into a hiss as she placed both hands on his shoulders and pushed him onto his back. As he lay on the bed she unlaced his breeches, her touch bold and sure.

"And I would see you as well." Emeline freed his manhood, hooked her thumbs in his loosened waistband, eased them from his hips, and pulled them from his legs until he was as naked as she. She dropped his garments carelessly to the floor as her gaze roamed over him freely, from face to feet, and then back again, settling on his erection. She reached out and stroked the length of his cock with her finger, tip to base, drawing seething curses and a single drop of his seed as his control slipped a fraction.

"My lord," she said in awe, "you are beautifully made."

She climbed onto the bed in a fluid motion, straddled him with her knees beside his hips. And again she felt her power surge through her in an exciting rush as he muttered a few soft Gaelic words from between his clenched teeth, his voice thick and tortured.

"Yes, Rogan. Burn with me," she urged him, and she lifted her hair high, let it fall over her body as she knelt above him. Everything was sensation. "I feel your strength, I see your desire, and I crave it as I have never wanted anything before."

She looked down on him, reveled in the sight of his eyes, bright, focused, intent on her, his attention so complete that her feeling of power expanded even more, became mythic in its proportion. He was so handsome, strong and urgent, and yet he was vulnerable beneath her, his needs as unguarded as her own. He was at her mercy, and she felt as powerful as Jezebel, Eve, Aphrodite and Cleopatra in one.

"Take what you want," Rogan urged her.

His was a restrained passion, his discipline so complete he had yet to even touch her. He lay still; Emeline held the reins. And she did it with giddy delight. She could feel the pulse of his blood beneath his skin, his heart pounding when she touched his chest. Emeline was on fire with it, and she unveiled her desires before him, one by one, his control as erotic as the most intimate touch: it allowed her to burn, wild and free.

Emeline wanted to do it all, wanted to cradle him and kiss him, thank him for all he had given her. She wanted to caress his body and give him pleasure beyond his imagining. She wanted to slide down on his hard cock and be joined with him, once and for all time, consummating the vow she would hold sacred until death. She wanted every piece of him, all at once, but also wanted to savor each taste and sensation.

She lay her hands on his chest. She was wet and ready, and did not want to wait any longer. "You have touched me in every way, my heart, my soul. You have touched me in every way but this." She rose up over him, pressed down on the sword that begged to be sheathed, let him penetrate her just a bit.

His breath hissed again, his hands grabbed fistfuls of the linen sheets as he held completely still.

Emeline's eyes went wide, her breath held. She realized that there was no horror, no degradation, no submission. Nothing but the joy of controlling her own passion, and his as well. Only a hunger for him to be deeper, sheathed to the hilt, her body clenched around him, reveling in the sensual delight of giving and receiving. No longer a whore, but a wife.

Slowly Emeline slid down on him, taking him inside of her inch by inch, gasping at the hot pressure, the fullness, the pleasure.

Only then did Rogan grip her hips. His fingers dug into her supple flesh. "Ride me, Emeline. Take what you will."

She leaned forward, her heels digging into his thighs, breasts pressed against his chest. And she did as he commanded: She rode him.

Emeline's breath hitched and caught, and then again. They were lifted together in the moment, both of them giving themselves to it as one. It swept them up and away until there was no bed beneath them, no room around them, no London, no England, no earth, no sky. Only she and Rogan locked together in that one shared moment.

Emeline's body arched; her head fell back. She shuddered, trembled, her breath snagged in her throat. Hesitated. Couldn't quite let go; the feelings were so intense, too intense. They threatened to engulf her. "Rogan?"

Rogan released his hold on her hips. He fisted his hands

on the sheets again and gritted his teeth. "You can stop if you need to."

That was all it took to push her over the edge. A soft moan escaped her throat as she fell; willingly though helplessly, she descended.

His ragged breathing stirred her hair as she collapsed on his chest. He wrapped his arms around her and held her tight against him, rolled over and pressed her into the mattress as he kissed her, long and deep.

Pulling back a bit, Rogan looked down at her. God, she was beautiful, especially now, all flushed with passion. Her skin was as dewy pink as a rose petal, a blushing bride. He found himself comparing her to flowers again, but this time dismissed the requisite jeer. Yes, she was like a rose: slowly blooming and velvety soft in her fragility. But she was also dangerously seductive in her defenses, a veritable bramble of thorny doubts that spoke to the valor in a man: Slay the beast, hack through the thorns, save the girl.

Rogan was still hard, still buried deep inside her body, and she looked into him searchingly. He could see the questions in her eyes as plainly as if she spoke them aloud. When she did not seem to find the answers she sought, a new look came into her eyes. She did not speak. Only met his gaze as if to warn him that he'd met his match.

"You make love as you live," he said admiringly. "You are intrepid."

She laughed a little, a nervous sound. "Do not think to put me too high."

"I'll be hard-pressed to have you anywhere but at my side." Rogan nuzzled against the lissome, graceful length of her neck. "I'm thinking of keeping Simon alive just so I can talk to you about killing him."

The sheer wickedness of his words and the lust it

inspired in Emeline had a naughty giggle bubbling in her throat. It was salacious talk, obscene even, but it was delicious in its wanton indecency. Emeline surrendered to it, laughing out loud even as her body was impaled on Rogan's erection. Her giggles shook her; the movement sent hot shafts of sinful delight from her loins to her belly.

It spiked fresh need. And that need was greedy, hot, and earnest. Emeline wrapped her legs around his waist, held him close and rocked against his pelvis. "Give it to me," she said insistently. "I need it."

Rogan arched his back and thrust deep, hard, and then again, and again, short strokes that filled her beyond her imagining. Emeline came undone in a rush, this climax shorter but more intense. And she was dizzy, caught in the throes of pure pleasure, her body clenched on him like a silken fist, contracting until she laughed and cried. She was gasping, gone from her own body it seemed; the only hold she had on the real world was the feel of Rogan moving inside her and the hard muscles of his back beneath her fingers.

When it was over she lay still, panting, little giggles and sobs mingling with her gasps until she calmed.

Rogan had to pull out of her, so treacherous was his heart. Damn her for her vulnerability, her wickedness, her contradictions. He could not lose himself too completely.

He forced a chuckle and stood up, rolled Emeline to her side and slapped her rear-end playfully. "Get out of bed and get dressed. We've a man to hunt."

"Rogan, honestly." She pushed herself to a sitting position, looking a trifle dizzy and half-dazed from expending so much passion while suffering a hangover. Still, her eyes gleamed with mischief. She pressed a hand to her bare breast and fluttered her lashes. "I am only a woman, and can scarcely bear such excitement."

He laughed easily and tossed her shift to her. "You're

nothing less than a warrior, *anamchara*, and far too naked for sane conversation. Clothe yourself before I plan Simon's murder and have you ravaging me again, aye?"

Emeline's gaze dipped down to his manhood. His penis hung long and thick from its nest of black hair, still shiny from their sex. She brought her eyes back to his, and blushed at the look of confident male pride on his face, a sensual smirk of utter satisfaction.

Shyness and boldness waged their usual war in her, rendering Emeline at once painfully aware and embarrassed of her show of passion, but also making her want to take it further, be even more daring. Rogan awakened feelings of security, but the shame still existed inside her, all twined together like a braid.

Relying on her female power to mask her uncertainty, Emeline shifted her body so he could appreciate her form, and thrust her breasts forward. She gave him a smoldering look of her own arrogance, gratified when she saw his member stiffening.

"You may not love me, Rogan. You may never love me." She stood and moved so she was in front of him, close enough that her nipples brushed his chest, rose on her tiptoes and brushed a soft, lingering kiss on his lips before moving quickly away. She curtseyed deeply, letting her nudity distract him from anything else he might read in her eyes. "But you will not be sorry you brought this whore into your bed."

Rogan's arm shot out in a flash caught her just under her armpit and pulled her roughly up. She gasped as he dragged her to him and grabbed her head, crushed his lips onto hers in a kiss that blistered and plundered. When she had no breath left, he let her go. "Do not taunt me, Princess. You'll get more than you bargained for."

She snatched her arm away, surprised when he let go

without a struggle. In an instant her anger came to the surface. "I'll not pretend to be a virgin in your bed."

"Good. Don't feign slut, either."

"Perhaps you will never know when I am a player," she mocked him, and hated how her voice trembled.

He ignored her, went to her bag and pulled out a gown, handed it to her without a word, his green eyes hot and full of nasty things he chose not to say. She accepted the garment and watched him as he strode over to the tub, wet a cloth and washed away the evidence of their sex from his body.

Between her legs, Emeline felt the slick, slippery feel of his seed, and she wondered if she would ever carry a child.

The thought came from nowhere, completely irrelevant to the moment, but still, Madeline had only been able to carry one baby to term, and she had told Emeline that it had been a pregnancy filled with periodic bleeding and cramping.

Emeline shoved the thoughts away from her mind, pulled her shift over her head and wiggled into it before walking on unsteady legs to the tub. She stood beside Rogan and took a cloth, lathered it and washed between her thighs, keeping her attention on the water in the tub before her. As she rinsed her rag she watched as the soap bubbles gathered into timorous, trembling clusters, shining in beautiful iridescent spheres before popping and disappearing forever.

"Simon owns properties that straddle four counties, but spends the majority of his time at Devonshire. I can write down the exact locations of his homes for you." Emeline's voice was a monotone. "His main occupation is overseeing the development of his London land-holdings. I will also write down the locations of those sites. As for his weaknesses—as far as I know, his only one is me."

Rogan said nothing, but strode naked across the room,

picked up his clothes and began to dress. Emeline did the same, pulling on her gown and lacing it up the side, her hair draped over her opposite shoulder. She then made quick use of the comb, untangling the snarls and knots until she could plait it into a long braid that hung down her back in a single, thick twist. After fastening it with a scrap of ribbon, she tidied the room and packed her belongings, then stood waiting for Rogan to speak to her. And wished desperately that she had not spoiled the morning.

She watched as Rogan combed his thick hair, left it to hang around his shoulders as he tucked in his wrinkled shirt and pulled on his jacket. With his black brows drawn into a frown over eyes that gleamed green and bright, his jaw darkened with stubble and the simple, elegant cut of his clothes, he looked like a dangerous, disreputable lord.

She couldn't help but match the sight of him now with the image of only minutes before. He had been completely naked beneath her on the bed, his whole body hard and hot, his face contorted with passion, desire, and a pleasure so intense that thinking of it stabbed Emeline with fresh want so powerful that it abashed her even as it aroused her.

And it filled her with remorse, for she had risen from bed and immediately reminded him of why he should not want her.

"I am sorry," she said.

Rogan turned to her, and she held her breath at the expression on his face, so ruggedly wild it stopped her heart. In an instant he crossed the room and grabbed her, pulled her to the long length of his body and pressed her hips to his as his mouth took hers once again, a brutal, untamed kiss that had her weak and ready and willing, wanting him sheathed once again inside her.

"Your passion is ready, isn't it? Right there at the surface." Rogan pulled back and cradled the her skull in his large hands, tilted her head back and held his mouth to her ear, his breath hot, his words an assault on her senses. "Hear me well, Princess. Feel free to use me in bed anyway you please, but don't look to me to shame you when the deed is done."

Tears stung her eyes, but she did not let them fall. He saw her begin to crumble and his expression softened. Rogan loosened his grip on her, cupping her head gently, and dipped his head to brush a soft kiss on her lips, her nose, and then her cheeks and forehead. "You told me you're broken, remember?"

She nodded slowly, a fist of razors gripping her heart as he licked a single tear with the tip of his tongue, and kissed where it made her skin glisten. "I can't put you back together, *anamchara*."

He pulled back, met her gaze, and looked straight into her eyes, beyond her tears and her pain and all her barriers, the way only he could. "Sometimes, I think you want me to hurt you, and other times you want me to mend you. I won't do either, Emeline. I can't do for you what I cannot even manage for myself."

She took a deep, shuddering breath. "I don't know how to do it, Rogan. What is expected of me. I don't know how to be a proper married woman."

"It doesn't matter."

"It does. It matters to me." Emeline asked him again, "What do you expect of me?"

He shrugged and his lips twitched as his fingers rubbed tiny circles on her scalp in a way that sent relaxation spiraling to her toes.

"If I'd wanted a prim, pure wife who would lie still in bed while thinking of her religious duty, I wouldn't have married Orianna or you. Prudish virgins are for men who fear a woman's passion." His expression softened, grew contemplative. "I only expect your honesty, be it in bed or by my side."

Emeline brought her hands up to cup his face. He had awoken her with his friendship, provoked her with his patience, aroused her dormant desires. He had given her hope, his name, a future. "You do fix me, Rogan, piece by piece." Inside her the butterfly so newly emerged spread its wings and tried to fly. "Please don't let me push you away."

They each searched the other for a long, quiet moment, the only sounds in the room that of the timepiece on the mantle and the creaking, muffled noises of the inn coming to life around them. As the last of their anger faded and only peace remained between them, Rogan nodded, once, as if to say he was satisfied.

He let go of her, picked up her bag, and hoisted it over his shoulder. Rogan took Emeline by the hand, and his grip on her was strong and sure. "Let's go."

London fairly boiled with activity, the streets alive as the city's denizens bustled with their daily lives. Above them all the sky loomed dark with fumes and smoke, the sun a feeble halo burning weakly behind a gray cloud of mist and soot.

Rogan hailed an empty livery, tossed the bag inside and gave the driver the address of the Bradburn mansion. They lurched into motion, Emeline gripping the wooden base of the plain bench seat and bracing herself against the jarring as they bounced down the rough, pitted streets.

Rogan saw that Emeline grew pale, and he knew she feared returning to the manse.

"I need to check on my sister, and I also need a change of clothes. I need my money and my weapons. I cannot continue on without them," Rogan explained.

"'Tis only the prospect of confronting Jeffrey that has

me worried." Her jaw chattered from the bone-shaking bouncing; the livery rattled like a child's toy.

Rogan shrugged. "He said I could have you when he tired of you, anyway. I only took early what would eventually belong to me. He'll find another woman, I'm sure."

"What did you say?" Her grip on the bench tightened, but it had nothing to do with the motion of the carriage.

"I asked him what he would do with you when he no longer desired you. He said he would return you to Simon." Rogan's brows drew low over his eyes, and again he looked like a savage pirate, his handsome face darkened from the sun, stubble, and his mood. His tone was mocking. "Should I have allowed that, Princess?"

"Your intentions for me, what were they? To have me in your bed instead of Jeffrey's?"

"'Twas before I'd even seen you," he snapped. "I planned on giving you your freedom, aye? Shipping you off with some money and maybe a position as a governess."

Her defensive expression melted, leaving only wonder. She stared at him; with his dangerous looks and his hard, powerful body, he could easily have given in to the seductive powers of seducing women, like so many of the rakes in London. It had her thinking again of what his mother and father must be like to have raised such a man. "Now I must apologize again, Rogan."

Rogan did not answer to avoid giving voice to the whole truth. He had indeed intended to give her freedom, until that moment in the parlor when he had laid eyes on her. In that instant he had been transformed into a man who would never again marry for love, but who would indeed marry for lust and ownership of a woman.

Rogan stared out the window of the carriage, feeling the weight of her scrutiny as they neared the center of London. All around the streets people thronged as the city teemed with commerce of all kinds: prostitutes peddling sex and priests selling salvation amidst the street vendors, street-criers, street-urchins, and ballad-mongers. The air hummed with activity and noise and was densely fragrant with unwashed bodies, horse manure and night soil, freshly baked bread and coal smoke, and the heavy stink of tanning and tallow, dyes and butcher shops.

Their carriage slowed as the horses were forced to pick their way through the clogged streets, and Rogan peered out of the small window and saw that they neared the houses of Parliament, the gothic gold, grandly appointed facade spearing the sky with its many spires. They came to a complete stop, the carriage bouncing as the driver leapt down and ran to the door. He yanked it open and pointed ahead.

"'Ere's a wheel break on the livery up aways."

"We'll wait, thank you." But before Rogan could settle back onto the bench seat, he saw the now familiar gold crest of the Bradburns, emblazoned on a black shiny carriage just in front of the entrance to the House of Lords. The footman held the door politely open, his eyes downcast as Jeffrey alighted. His Grace, Jeffrey William Henry Bradburn, the twelfth Duke of Eton, walked with a stiff gait, jaw held at a dignified angle. His paunchy frame was draped in regal brocades and furs; a gentlemanly jeweled sword swung at his side. He wore the powdered, curled wig of a sitting lord, and Rogan watched his uncle enter Parliament amidst other lords who arrived, noted their silent nods of greeting and their solemn manner.

Someday that will be me, Rogan thought. The concept made his blood turn cold. It occurred to him the extent of Jeffrey's power, and the authority that would one day belong to him, Rogan, as well. Power came in many forms, Rogan knew. But the kind that came backed with the blind acceptance of a powerful government was among the most dangerous.

Rogan turned to Emeline, grabbed her by the hand and hoisted her bag, leaping out of the carriage as he dragged her out into the crowded street. He tossed the fare to the surprised driver without a backward glance, and began pulling Emeline in his wake as he barreled through the throngs of people, animals, and children congesting the pitted road.

"Rogan." Emeline tried to pull her hand from his vise-grip. "What are you doing?"

Rogan spied a tavern across the street and yanked her in that direction, neatly dodging an oncoming livery that careened wildly down the road, the horses' eyes rolling whitely as they clopped past them. Rogan and Emeline entered the warm tavern. The air was redolent of frying ham and spilled, stale ale, and it bustled with maids whose breasts bobbled over their low bodices as they fetched food and drink. One of the maids caught a glimpse of Rogan and Emeline, and a knowing look overtook her expression as she wended her way through the clog of tables and chairs to approach them. "Yer needin' a room, aye?"

"Aye," Rogan answered. He caught a few leering glances sent Emeline's way from some of the more seedy looking patrons at the bar, and added, "One with a stout bar on the door."

"Two quid per 'our."

"Fine, fine." Rogan was already reaching for his coin.

The maid nodded and led the way to the back of the establishment, took them up a narrow flight of stairs that spanned the back wall. She threw open the door and stood back to allow them to enter. Rogan pulled Emeline into the room, looked around and noted that the door did indeed possess a sturdy oak bar that could be passed through iron links that had been bolted into the frame, and that the single window had been hung with solid oak shutters and a thick wooden bar of its own, ready to be dropped into place. Rogan nodded his approval, paid for the room, and shooed the maid out the door. He turned to Emeline and pulled his dagger from his boot. He handed it to her hilt first and met her eyes, dead even. She hesitantly accepted the knife, worry casting a shadow across her face.

"You'll stay put here. Bolt the window and door after I've gone and don't open them for anyone, not even God."

"You're going to leave me here? Where are you going?"

"Aye," he said, in answer to her first question. "To Parliament," he said, to the second. "I've a need to speak to my uncle."

Chapter 20

Simon climbed the steps to the Bradburn mansion and entered as the butler opened the door for him. The old servant bowed, and gestured to the right wing of the great house.

"Her Grace is taking her mid-morning lie-down in her chambers, but generally takes her tea in the solarium in about an hour's time," the butler informed him.

"I'll wait for her audience."

"Shall I show you in, my lord?"

"No, no thank you, chap. I'll see to my own needs."

"As you wish." The butler bowed once again before he left.

Alone in the two-story, grandly appointed foyer, Simon inhaled strongly through his nose and rocked back on his heels as he surveyed the interior, taking note of what would one day belong to him. One day very soon, if his mission was carried out to plan. Before him two staircases wound opposite curves to the second floor, wings and rooms extended from the main entranceway. The richness favored by the former duchess, Amelia Bradburn, still reigned supreme: everything was gold and bejeweled and well-crafted. Art, in all its many forms, adorned each room so it seemed that all of Europe and beyond had been ransacked to satiate the desire for things gracious and beautiful.

Simon headed in the direction of Emeline's suite of rooms, knowing that Jeffrey was safely at Parliament for the entirety of the day. He would have plenty of time to spend with her, and even as he thought about it, his loins tingled and his blood sang.

As he walked through the familiar rooms and halls, he took note of the value of the sculptures, paintings, tapestries and rugs. He shook his head, disgusted that so much coin would be squandered on simple adornments, when there were far greater ways to use it, such as the many building projects he invested in. Urban growth, he mused, was where the real opportunity lay for amassing a fortune larger than one dared to imagine.

Simon fingered a wall hanging as he passed by, noticing the intricate details of the tapestry. He recalled Jeffrey once mentioning that it dated from the ten-hundreds, salvaged from a medieval castle shortly after Normandy invaded Saxony. A priceless treasure, Simon noted, and he wondered how much gold it would bring him when he sold the moldering fabric at the Royal Exchange.

He turned the corner to stride down the long hallway that ended with Emeline's double doors. As he did so he jingled his jeweled belt, blood coursing in anticipation, his whole being alive with the knowledge that his stepdaughter lay just behind those doors. He could picture her in his mind as clearly as if he gazed upon her portrait, his memory providing him with her every detail, from her fair hair and sapphire eyes to the precise texture of her skin, weight of her breasts, length of her feet, shape of her toes. No part of her had not been catalogued by Simon, with his fingers, lips, tongue, teeth.

He knew her in every way, biblical and earthly. She

belonged to him as the stars to the sky or water upon the earth, intermingled and conjoined.

Simon rested his hand on the knob, pausing to savor the tingle that coursed under his skin. Finally unable to withstand the torture of being away from Emeline, he turned the knob and barged into her rooms.

"Daddy's home," he crooned.

He paused when he did not hear a sigh or groan, no familiar sound of her dismay at his arrival. Silence reigned, a complete and total stillness hung in the air. Glancing wildly around, he saw the perfectly made bed, the cleanliness of the rooms that had not a single item out of place. He knew instantly that she was gone.

Rogan strode into Parliament, ignoring the outraged stares of the bewigged men who gathered in clusters, their conversations stopped mid-word as they openly gaped at the disgraceful sight.

With his hair unwigged, unpowdered, and even uncombed, Rogan swaggered into the elegant halls of the House of Lords with his wrinkled clothes and wild waves of black hair streaming around his face. He did not care that he was unshaven and unkempt, did not mind the difference between himself and the men who stared at him with disapproval. All the men looked like Jeffrey, Rogan noted as he searched for his uncle's pale face. They were all robed in satin and velvets, furs and brocades, robust in the gut and chest, long since fat on the spoils of the countrymen whose interests they so regularly ignored in favor of protecting their own.

They certainly minded Rogan's presence, however, and finally a man broke from the safety of numbers and approached Rogan. He pulled his jewel-encrusted gentleman's sword and thrust it outward to block Rogan's path.

"Sir, you intrude where you have no rights," he declared, his deep baritone ringing with authority. "I insist you leave now."

Rogan cocked a brow as he met the man's gaze. He ignored the outstretched blade. "I'll see my uncle, Jeffrey Bradburn. Where is he?"

The earl bristled, held his sword out farther. "Uncle, is it?" His eyes swept down Rogan's rumpled clothing.

Rogan grinned then, knowing that his unfastened shirt revealed an undignified amount of his chest; that his unbuttoned coat hung grossly open; that his stockings, stained with grass and various other soils were indecently inexpensive; and the shoes he wore, unpolished and certainly no cleaner than his stockings, did not even sport a buckle or adornment of any type.

The earl smirked, obviously quite assured of his superior bearing, and made a display of sheathing his sword, indicating it would not be needed. "And 'tis a complete wonder that he has never boasted of the existence of a nephew."

Rogan's grin deepened until a few dimples flirted at the corners of his lips, and he rubbed his bristly chin in mock contemplation. "If you've a mind to tell me where I can find my uncle, I'll conduct my business and go. Otherwise I'll be forced to withstand the threat of your," he paused and glanced doubtfully at the jeweled sheath, "*blade*, and conduct a thorough search."

The earl huffed, opened his mouth to rejoin just as Jeffrey strode over and interrupted.

"What have you done with her?" Jeffrey demanded. He shoved himself between the earl and his nephew, not bothering with preamble.

Rogan glanced around at the men who now openly listened, their ears as pricked and as ready for gossip as a gaggle of scullery maids. "Do you really want to do this here?"

Jeffrey saw the cause for Rogan's concern and momentarily relented. "No. Follow me."

Jeffrey turned on his heel and strode the halls. Rogan followed in his wake, taking in the incredible interior. Carved paneling lined the walls all the way to the soaring ceiling, beneath his feet polished parquet stretched as far as his eye could see. The air smelled of wealth and privilege, the scents of cigar smoke, whiskey, leather, and heavily polished wood mingling together with the reek of money as ancient as the aristocracy itself. Off to the sides of the main hall, Rogan saw rooms bigger than ballrooms, with red velvet-cushioned chairs arranged in rows that undulated like waves from the center dais. The men who filled the rooms were all bewigged and bejeweled, garbed in the heavy robes that displayed the advantage of their birth.

Jeffrey turned on his heel and entered a small antechamber to one of the great halls that was not currently in use. Rogan pulled the door closed behind him and they were alone. Jeffrey glanced around, as if at a loss as to what to do with hands that lacked a cigar or a drink or even a stack of papers to hold. He finally clasped them together just under his breastbone and lifted his chin. He tilted his head back so he could regard his nephew down the bridge of his nose, rocked on his heels, and exhaled heavily through his nostrils.

"Emeline."

"Aye, Uncle. I am sorry for taking her without your permission."

Jeffrey waited for a few moments. When Rogan did not say anything further, he exploded. "You steal my favored mistress and that is all the explanation you give? Where is she? Damn you, Rogan, you will return her to me today, or I shall bring all of England down upon your head!"

"She is mine, now."

"What?" Jeffrey gaped at him, obviously at odds with the younger man's appalling nerve.

"Aye." Rogan swallowed heavily, and then jumped into the truth like a frigid lake, feet first. "I married her yesterday."

"My Emeline?" Jeffrey croaked, and as he spoke he felt his head throb with a sudden rush of blood. Fearing an onset of apoplexy, Jeffrey took a few deep, steadying breaths, even as the many implications of what Rogan had done flashed through his mind in a succession of horrors. "She is common, a tramp, a slattern. She is not a duchess!"

Rogan crossed the small room in two steps to stand toe to toe with Jeffrey. Rogan's eyes hardened, like his features, his muscles, and a brutal violence crossed his face. It was controlled, though, like his cold voice. "Say no more. 'Tis done, and she is mine now."

A sudden vision of his mother, Amelia, came into Jeffrey's mind. The thought of what she would have done if she knew what would become of the family heritage she so jealousy guarded made Jeffrey's head ache even more. "I cannot abide to see that common hussy reign in my mother's and my wife's place. I will personally see to it that Parliament grant an act sanctioning your divorce."

"You will not see her take their place, Uncle. When Emeline is duchess, 'twill be because you are dead, aye?"

Jeffrey involuntarily took two steps backward before he regained himself and stood what remained of his ground. "Do you threaten me?"

"I state the obvious."

"Do not speak of my death, Rogan. You exceed your bounds."

"I speak the truth, and now I will tell you the rest: Simon arranged to have Emeline kill me. He planted her in your house when he found I was summoned to England, and the night he danced with her he gave her a vial of poison intended to cause my demise." Rogan then told

Jeffrey the remainder of the story, from Emeline's escape to save her mother, the hurried wedding to protect Emeline's interests, and the trip to Bedlam that proved futile. "You see, Uncle, 'tis only a matter of time until Simon grows impatient for your wealth and strikes to seize it. How long before his greed prompts him to remove you, as well? I came here to warn you of two things: Watch your back, and keep away from my wife."

Jeffrey paled even as beads of sweat pearled from his pores, beading along his upper lip and under his arms until he felt the trickling down his sides. The way Simon freely came and left the mansion had him in mortal fear, wondering if poison had already been slipped into his foodstuffs. He would hire a food taster immediately, he decided, and someone to try on his clothes before he put them on. Hadn't he heard about poisoned pins hidden in garments? And his gin, it too could be contaminated. And guards. He would hire an army of sharpshooters to guard him.

Illness. The word sprang up in his fevered mind: a threat that one could not see coming. What if Simon arranged for persons suffering the mortal sore throat to be brought to his home? Recollections of history books rushed into his mind, of medieval warriors launching plague-ridden bodies over the castle walls, decimating entire villages.

Not safe, not safe anywhere. The room began to spin underneath Jeffrey's feet, the walls pitching to and fro. Staggering to a chair, he gripped the back, his fingers digging into the velvet cushion. "I am doomed," he moaned. "Condemned. Who can protect me?"

"Uncle, compose yourself," Rogan commanded. "Simon has yet to make a strike at you personally. Now, send word to everyone, the House of Lords, the House of Commons, the magistrates and judges. Tell them all a threat has been made against you and me, and make it known that 'tis Simon who thirsts for your power."

"Yes," Jeffrey agreed, a semblance of sanity returning. "This will work. I will do as you say."

"Good."

Rogan nodded once and turned to leave. But he paused as his uncle spoke.

"I will give you twenty thousand pounds to kill Simon."

Jeffrey watched Rogan with a predatory stare. And felt the spurt of conquest when his nephew turned to face him, changed in that instant from guardian to mercenary.

Simon pushed aside Anna's maid. With both his hands he threw open the double doors to Anna's suites, eliciting more gasps from the attending maids who sat doing needlework by the fire and the harpist who had been plucking the early baroque tune preferred by the duchess for her morning nap.

Anna sat bolt upright in bed at the commotion. With the drapes pulled tightly closed to the morning light, she peered through the semi-darkness, trying to identify the intruder. Her pointed, plain face was frozen with fear, her hand pressed to her throat.

"Simon! By all that is holy, what are you about?"

"My stepdaughter. Where is she?"

"Emeline?" Anna's hands fluttered around her neck, her flushed cheeks. "I have no idea."

Simon pulled puffs of breath through his clenched teeth, struggling to maintain a semblance of control lest he begin tearing at the drapes, the wall hangings, the women, destroying everything in his path.

"No idea," he finally managed to grit out.

"Why, no. I did notice she did not join us at dinner these nights past, but that does not necessarily mean anything. Are you telling me the dear thing has escaped?" Anna leaned forward a bit, and a vicious smile turned her rather plain countenance ugly. "How sad for Jeffrey, to have frightened away a plaything so soon. 'Tis no wonder he has been insufferable of late."

"How many nights?"

"Well, I have not seen her since the evening you and Lora joined us for dinner and dancing."

Simon closed his eyes, reached into the depths of his being for self-control as Anna began chirping and chattering like an insipid bird, apparently indifferent to his concerns.

"Why, we all know how intolerable Jeffrey can be with his constant needs and demands, and 'tis only a matter of time until his mistresses take flight or are dismissed for laughing at his illicit desires. Why, you may or may *not* know how Jeffrey was taken with the last mistress so much so that he did not even attend his own son's death. Now, between his rutting on that poor girl and his fears of illness, my own son died without the simplest touch from his father, not even a visit. Think about that, Simon, the poor lad. Why, even now it makes me want to weep—"

Simon bowed low before Anna, cutting off the flow of her conversation before she began caterwauling. As he did, he thought he saw a sparkle of malice in Anna's eyes, suggesting she intentionally babbled to chase Simon from her rooms. No, Simon corrected himself, the woman was not that clever. So few were. He addressed her with as much charm as he could muster. "Your Grace, I humbly beg your forgiveness for my indiscreet intrusion. 'Twas only a fear for my daughter's safety that prompted such an ungentlemanly display. I swear it will never happen again."

"Of course you are forgiven." Anna demurely sank back into the lavender-scented, linen comfort of her pillows. With the flick of her wrist she gestured for her harpist to begin again. An ancient, moody melody filled the room. Simon withdrew his presence, nodded his apology to the woman he'd knocked down, and heard the click of the door being discreetly locked as he moved to the top of the staircase.

His heart thundered in his chest. His palms glistened with cold sweat; he rubbed them together. The folly of sending Emeline to Jeffrey had his gut churning.

Emeline.

The creature of his dreams, the woman who embodied everything he'd ever longed for. He could never replace her. No other woman captivated him as she did.

If Jeffrey had been boorish to Anna, it seemed to Simon that Emeline's whereabouts must be unknown. For Jeffrey would have paid any amount of money for her return, would have gone to any lengths to have her found. She had quite likely been frightened by Simon's ultimatum and run off into the night.

The prospect of her alone and unprotected wrenched Simon's heart with genuine fear.

Emeline.

A sob formed at the back of Simon's throat, tore itself free and escaped, a low keening cry of terror and sorrow. His plan, so delicately constructed, had fallen apart. Never, ever, had Simon considered that Emeline would run. He'd thought the bribe was too motivating; it had worked on Emeline too many times in the past for him to consider it would fail him this time. His plan had been elegantly simple: Bait the hook, set the lure, cast the girl, and wait.

But always, always, in the end, Simon counted on getting Emeline back.

Now she was gone. His mind screamed the word: *Gone!*

In a blur of heavy garments, Simon rushed down the stairs and tore through the mansion, ready to take all of London apart piece by piece, desperate to find her.

The butler heard him approaching and hurried to the door to open it. The men's eyes met, and as they did Simon thought of the grapevine of servant gossip, a method of communication superior to most others. Simon dug in his purse for a few coins, pressed them into the hand of the man whose training was too entrenched for him to show any signs of greed.

"The mistress, Emeline. Do you have any information of where she went? Anything at all."

The butler's expression remained completely impassive. He bowed stiffly and handed back the coins. "I am sorry, sir."

With the fingers of hysteria tickling the back of his throat, Simon thrust the money back at him and added a few more coins. "Anything," he repeated.

The butler's fingers clenched around the money. The weightier sum apparently prompted his memory. "His Grace has been most distressed to find both his mistress and his nephew missing, and hopes they are safe and well."

With that said, the butler bowed again, turned on his heel and left Simon's presence.

Simon stood red-faced and alone in the empty foyer. Rage sickened him like poison, swelled his heart until it felt like it exploded, his blood a pounding roar through his veins.

"It will work," Jeffrey urged Rogan to see the beauty of his plan, his voice a raspy hiss in the antechamber. "I will tell everyone of Simon's intention to have you and me both removed. When you kill him, 'twill seem like nothing more than self-defense."

Rogan turned and faced his uncle, saw the glimmer of fear and hope in his pale eyes. Twenty thousand pounds. The sum staggered Rogan; it was a fortune.

"Done," Rogan stated. "But you must give me your word that Emeline is safe from you. You will treat her as my wife, accord her the proper respect, and never, ever again will you touch her."

"Done."

Jeffrey relaxed marginally, his gaze sweeping over his untamed nephew as he looked upon his taut, muscled frame with relief. What once had inspired his jealousy now provided him with security. Surely Simon was no match for the rugged Rogan, whose own father was nothing more than a common seaman. Jeffrey knew them to be a sturdy bunch, well accustomed to the arts of warfare and survival. Rogan would eliminate Simon, and for that Jeffrey would gladly part with a chunk of his fortune and the captivating Emeline.

Jeffrey clapped his hand on Rogan's back, his demeanor suddenly jovial as he led him out of the antechamber and into the main corridors of the House of Lords. Their footsteps echoed in the halls, blending with the sounds of muted conversations from clusters of men and the dignified assemblies that gathered, the combination sounding much like the humming of hornets.

"'Twill be yours one day, Nephew." Jeffrey swept his hand to encompass all of Parliament and beyond. London itself sat at their feet. "Look around you."

He moved to a set of double doors and opened them in order to show Rogan the interior, the grandeur of the room comprising its own rarefied world. "Look on, Rogan. See the lords. They are you and me, men privileged by birth and titles. They are the men who passed the necessary acts restraining the Americas, who shut down the entire port of Boston, stopped town meetings, put an end to civil disturbances, opened Quebec's provinces, and saw to it that not a single colonist can refuse to give quarter to our royal soldiers. Parliamentary supremacy, boy. 'Tis the lifeblood of England, and the heart-blood of the lords. Soon you shall be part of it."

Rogan frowned as he looked upon the overfed fat cats who feasted on the suffering of the poor of England and the labors of the colonists who struggled for survival on a wild continent.

Jeffrey continued speaking as he led Rogan from the guarded halls of Parliament out into the open air of the street. He gestured to the ducal crest emblazoned on the side of his carriage. "Remember, dear boy, that Emeline, as intriguing as she is, is just a woman like so many others, her parts interchangeable with any wife or whore."

Jeffrey felt Rogan stiffen beside him, and he kept speaking, willing his nephew to learn from the wisdom of his greater experience. "Women are nothing to be considered when power and money are at stake. Think, Rogan. Think with your head and not your prick.

"Look around you, boy. There is no end to what we can attain. Think clearly of what matters: land, titles, ascendancy. You will secure it all, for me, for yourself, for the sons you will bring forth. Kill him," Jeffrey spoke furtively in Rogan's ear, leaning against him in the crowded street. "'Tis the only way to protect our interests."

Around them the streets swarmed with the city's people, shopkeepers and butchers, tradesmen and weavers, merchants, millers, and maids. The traffic of the streets made for a terrific racket, and smoke from a nearby coal fire burned Rogan's eyes and nostrils.

"Look, Rogan. Look around us. The city belongs to the lords. 'Twill belong to you. Do not allow Simon to take what will be yours."

Rogan glanced down at his uncle, whose face was flushed and expectant, wisps of his pale hair escaping his wig and sticking to his damp cheeks.

As certain as Rogan had been earlier that killing Simon was the necessary thing to do, he could not help but be reminded of the biblical account where Satan showed

Jesus the kingdoms of the earth, promising them all to him if he would only do one act of obeisance.

Rogan turned on his heel and left his uncle behind, striding through the streets. He ignored Jeffrey's calls to come back and listen, the cries of the vendors, the rattle of the carriages that rumbled by. For in that instant, nothing seemed as urgent as returning to Emeline.

Simon stepped outside the mansion, stood on the granite steps and looked up to the gray autumn skies, noticing how the clouds were rimmed with light as if the sun struggled to burn them away. The air smelled thin, the bitter threat of winter in the slight gusts of wind that blew across his face, pinching his skin with damp, icy fingers. Birds chirped as they flitted from naked branches to the earth to rustle in the fallen leaves before returning to the shelter of the trees, the flutter of their wings mingling with their songs. Somewhere a meadowlark answered them, its own cry as thin as the wind itself. He lowered his gaze to the steps beneath his feet, watched the progress of a tiny beetle as it made its way to the garden of sculptured evergreens that bordered the grand entrance to the mansion behind him.

There, on the steps that led to everything he deserved, Simon struggled for control. In Emeline's absence he felt an emptiness that could only be filled with fury.

Rogan. The name made Simon's blood boil. The image of his cousin rose mockingly in his mind: tall, well-muscled, black hair framing a face as handsome as a maiden's fanciful dream. In Simon's imagination, Rogan grinned ironically at him while he pleasured Emeline with deep thrusts, making her shriek with unfeigned pleasure.

A growl erupted in Simon's thick chest, even as he

clamped control and logic upon his own furor. He needed to be calm. He needed to be reasonable.

Rogan had taken what belonged to him, Simon reasoned. And so, he would see to it that Rogan received a dose of his own treatment.

A new image replaced the old, of Rogan tattered and frantic, tearing through dark London streets with an expression of pure fear twisting his handsome face.

The thoughts calmed Simon. He turned and entered the mansion, once again a dignified lord. He took the steps to Kieran's rooms with a sense of purpose and a lightness of foot. At her call of admittance he stepped over the threshold and bowed gallantly, first to Kieran and then to the attending maid. The well-trained maid set down her needlework and moved discreetly to the next room where she could act as a chaperone but still lend privacy.

"Dear Cousin, I hear you are finally well enough to receive visitors. Upon this happy news I rushed to meet you." Simon lifted Kieran's hand and bowed low over it, pressing a chaste, familial kiss upon it. "I am your cousin Simon, dear Kieran, and 'tis most pleasant to finally have the privilege of making your acquaintance."

Kieran gestured to the chair her maid had recently vacated, where she had been learning the art of needlework while keeping Kieran company. This new guest was courtly and oh, so *English*. Kieran readily accepted his company. She was relieved that she was garbed appropriately, in the style of French *dishabille*. She wore an elegant dressing gown of pale blue silk cut low enough that it displayed a tiny bit of her embroidered, beribboned corset, over which she had donned a matching robe of deep blue velvet. She inclined her head in a regal manner, aware of the pleasant weight of her elegantly coifed hair.

"Please sit, Cousin Simon. 'Tis a relief such as you

cannot imagine, to finally have an opportunity to indulge in pleasant conversation."

"I admit, I have been fair deprived of the company of beautiful women, and did not expect that I would find you looking so well."

"You flatter me."

"Not without cause. Now tell me, Cousin, of this beautiful island from which you come. I hear 'tis a veritable paradise."

Kieran happily acquiesced, regaling him with vivid descriptions of Barbados, the flora and fauna, the blinding white sands, the water the shade of turquoise that must be seen to be believed.

While she spoke, Simon took in her every detail. She possessed elegant, fine features, a delicately full mouth that put him in mind of porcelain dolls, and incredible eyes the shade of a stormy ocean, under arched brows. Her shiny dark auburn hair, its color a striking contrast to her fair, luminous skin, was prettily curled and fixed with brilliant-tipped pins, little ringlets dropping to rest on her collarbones and the higher curves of her breasts. Simon had known Kieran's mother, Camille Bradburn, when she was a young woman, and he saw her uncommon beauty in Kieran.

No, Simon thought with satisfaction, it would not trouble him at all to take her. She had asked him something and waited for his response, but he could scarcely focus on anything but the poetic justice he would deal Rogan.

"I am sorry, dear Kieran. I fear I only just now remembered that I have an appointment with my solicitor later this day, and I quite forgot to bring along the papers he will need. I am going to have to go to my home and get them." Simon picked up Kieran's hand once again and bent over it. "I knew your mother long ago, when we were children, and I see her comeliness has been passed on. 'Twas quite a pleasure meeting you."

Kieran could not hide her disappointment. She had only just begun to enjoy herself, and he was leaving. Worry nagged at her. Had she spoken too much? Been a bore?

"Of course, of course," she said, forcing cheer into her tone. "'Twas lovely to have met you as well. I hope you visit again soon."

"You'll not be abed much longer, will you?"

"No, as you see I am quite well. I only await my brother's permission," she nearly gagged on the word, "as I did give a promise to remain abed until he declares me fit. You see, his dear wife died not too long ago, and he worries for my health."

Simon's brow creased at first in pity, and then raised as if he had been struck by a brilliant idea. He glanced around and leaned forward, his tone conspiratorial. "I know for a fact that Rogan is busy in town and will not return today. Why not get dressed and come with me for a ride in my carriage? I will fetch my papers and return you forthwith, before anyone knows you have even gone. 'Twill allow you to see a bit of London and gain some fresh air. Surely 'twill do no harm, and your brother will be none the wiser."

Kieran hesitated, biting her bottom lip as she contemplated his offer. A ride in the city sounded like heaven itself, and she visualized the sights and sounds and excitement. True, she didn't know Simon at all, but he was family and quite obviously welcome in their home.

Her promise to Rogan had been made days before, she reasoned, and he was not there to see that she was completely well, the last of her pox totally cleared from her skin. He had not even visited her in days, and just left her there to languish in bed. Her young body was fit and strong again, humming with eagerness to be out and about, busy once more. The thought of Rogan's anger made her pause, but she dismissed the worry.

He is my brother, not my father, she thought rebelliously. I owe him no extra consideration; I am fully grown and know myself to be completely healed. Lying abed is simply foolishness.

"I would love to go for a ride with you," Kieran said. "But I will need to take my maid, of course."

"Of course." Simon swept into another formal bow. "I will wait for you both in the main parlor. Please take your time preparing yourself, Cousin, though clearly yours is a beauty that needs no adornment."

As he stepped from the rooms and closed the doors, Kieran leapt from the bed as if she had been released from prison, dashed to the armoire and yanked out a gown of dark green velvet and a matching cloak lined with ermine, lest she get chilled. She dropped her dressing gown to the floor and trod over it with a little dance of delight. She would be free, finally.

Kieran called for her maid's rapid attention and bade her fetch their outerwear. A few moments later Kieran was nothing short of resplendent, clad in a fashionable traveling gown as she descended the stairs as regally as a queen. Her maid followed her with both of their cloaks draped over her arm.

As Kieran sailed through the mansion, she decided that the riches surrounding her felt as natural as breathing, a legacy of her birth. And when Simon rose as she entered the parlor, her heart trembled with pleasure, for here was a lord attending her as a lady, his patrician features courtly and refined, his manner charming. She delicately rested her fingertips on his proffered arm and swept through the manse, out into the open air that had been denied her for far too long.

The carriage was elegantly appointed, and she sank into

the soft seat with a sigh of delight, flattered and appeased when the footman offered her the warming pan and a lap robe, along with a tiny flagon of sherry.

The maid tucked herself beside her, and Simon took the opposite seat. He rapped on the roof with the head of his cane, and the carriage lurched into motion.

Kieran had finally arrived in London.

Chapter 21

Rogan thundered up the back steps of the tavern, thumped on the thick oaken door where he prayed Emeline still resided, unharmed and unmolested.

"Princess. Open up, 'tis me."

He heard the scraping of the bar being slid from its iron cuffs and then the screech of the rusty lock being turned from within.

Emeline opened the door. She was framed by shadows and light. The window was shuttered and barred, and only firelight and rush candles lighted the room. They lit her form with golden halo, as if she were a fairy sprung from the depths of night. The expression on her face was somber and quiet, her eyes downcast, and she stood back and let him enter without a word.

"Are you ready to go?" Rogan was impatient, but he tried to soften his words with an explanation. "I've a need to check on Kieran, and I feel naked without my pistol and sword."

"As you wish." She moved to gather up the few belongings she had pulled from her bag.

Her movements were efficient, her demeanor affable.

But there was something deeply troubling about the way she did not once meet his eyes.

Rogan took his dagger from the table where Emeline had laid it and slid it into his boot. He approached her hesitantly, stood close to her back, close enough that he could hear the soft sound of her breath as she inhaled and exhaled. He could smell her, too, the scent of spicy bath water clinging to her skin. The awareness of her had his body responding despite his concern for her well-being, but he ignored his baser urges and laid a gentle hand on her shoulder.

"Are you unwell, *anamchara*?"

"I feel fit, my lord, thank you." She closed her bag and fastened the leather toggles.

He took her by the shoulders and gently turned her to face him, tilted her face up so he could look directly into the dark indigo of her eyes. They were lovely, inky blue and kohl-lashed. And filled with a deep sadness, that despite being devoid of tears, had Rogan's heart clenching in response.

"Are you thinking of Madeline?" he asked.

"No. Yes." She sighed and shrugged her shoulders. "Thinking about everything, I suppose."

"Tell me what troubles you."

Emeline opened her mouth as if to speak but then closed it, clearly confused. A frown creased her brow, and she pulled away from him and moved to stand in front of the fire, stood staring into the leaping flames that greedily devoured the wood.

Willing to wait for her reply, Rogan sat on the hard chair by the fire. From his angle all he could see was her silhouette, the shifting yellow light that bathed her in reddish gold.

"Talking to you has been my problem, Rogan," she said finally, her voice as hushed as the rush of flame in front of her. "'Tis what has opened all my doors, raided my defenses, torn down and destroyed my barriers. I have nothing left with which to protect myself. All I can do is *feel*."

She turned to face him, then, her eyes dark pools of shimmering sadness in her oval face. "Do you not see? I was the daughter of a merchant's daughter, and I was raised to do as my mother did, to make a nice match with a decent man, to go to his bed a virgin with a dowry, raise my own respectable family. I had hoped to marry a farmer, because I have always wanted to plant things and watch them grow."

She held her hands out in front of her, palms faced up, as if to indicate their emptiness. "What can I do, Rogan? I buried those dreams deep, and now they've been returned to me. Gifts from you, but curses as well, for now I have hopes of being more than what Simon tried to convince me I was."

Slowly, with excruciating composure, she began unfastening her gown as she stared at Rogan in the firelight. As she plucked the laces loose, she spoke. "I need to know what it is safe to hope for. I want to know how much of you I can hope for."

Her gown unlaced, she pulled it from her shoulders and let it drop to the floor, stepped out of the puddle of wrinkled silk as she unfastened her corset and let that drop as well, along with her shift. With her foot she pushed the garments to the side and stood before him, stripped completely bare.

"I am beautiful, my lord. Lovely in the ways of Venus and of Cleopatra. Men think they want me, but they could not be more wrong. 'Tis not me they want, but this." She gestured to her body as if it were something she wished she could escape. "But all other men are not my concern. The only one who matters to me is you. What you think of me matters, now, because you have worked so hard to make it impossible for me to shield myself from the weight of your opinion.

"Look at me. Can you see more than my beauty? Can you want more than my sex?" Her voice trembled, like her body, her composure crumbling. "I see the hunger in your eyes, my lord. And yet, I want so much more than your desire. I am naked to you in every way. I told you before that I will love you as I like, and so I do. But why is it so hard to know you will never love me? It should not be so; I know I needn't expect it. But it hurts me so deeply, and I want my defenses back, Rogan. I want them back, and I can't have them and you."

She began to sag, her knees growing weak with her trembling, her belly and breasts quivering with it. Rogan rose from his chair and gathered her in his arms, pulled her close to his chest.

Emeline tried to resist his embrace, but failed and sank into his arms, the safest place she could imagine. She spoke into the warmth of his shirt as she buried her face against him, enveloped by his heat and strength. "You warned me, I know. I must seem so foolish to you."

Rogan's hands slid down the elegant length of her spine to touch the two dimples at the small of her back, and then lower, to cup her perfectly formed buttocks. She unveiled everything to him, hid nothing, exposed her heart and laid it bare, set it at his feet like an offering.

Her honesty moved him beyond his own lust. It made him want to be stronger, to return her truth and bravery with his own. Rogan lowered his mouth so he could speak in her ear. "I think of her less and less," he confessed. "And that frightens me, Emeline. How can I love her and love you too? And if I let myself love you, and you die . . ."

His voice caught in his throat and tears stung his eyes, from emotion or smoke from the fire, maybe both. "I am weak. I was weak, and that is what killed her."

His muscles tightened. His hands curled into fists behind Emeline's back. Restless desires sang in his blood.

He wanted the feel of flesh and bone giving way, he longed for searing spasms that drowned rational thought. But this time there was no opponent to hit, no physical pain to mask his truth. There was only grief. A gaping wound that had festered too long.

Emeline reached up and cupped his face. "No, don't say that. You didn't hurt her. You loved her."

"I did. I did it." His voice broke, but he couldn't control it, couldn't stop confessing. "I held her down and helped the doctor cut her. I promised her she was going to be well, and she let me do it because she trusted me. And I killed her. What kind of man kills his wife? What kind of man kills his wife?"

He could see Orianna's slim brown arm draped over the shallow bowl, bleeding life. And his hands. Holding her down.

A sob took him, a hot swirl at the center of a storm. Without the release of fighting and in the face of Emeline's mix of compassionate courage, Rogan finally let it come.

She held him as he wept, harsh animal sounds of grief and guilt. His tears fell and ran down her naked body, wet tracks that glistened in the firelight.

"It's all right." She stroked his hair, his back. "You didn't know she would die."

He told her what he had told no one, not a single soul, not even his parents. "I did know. I'd seen it before." He fought for control but there was none to be found. "I knew. I didn't want to do it. But she was so sick, so weak, burning with the fever, and the doctor insisted we must, that she would most certainly die if we did not. Let out the bad blood. And she was fighting it. Didn't want to be cut. Pushing him away. And I held her down. I held her down and helped him do it. She trusted me and I killed her."

The blood on his clothes that night, staining his skin, his hands. Rogan's hands were behind Emeline but he knew they dripped with blood. He could still see it. He could always see it.

"I wanted to climb inside her and make her breathe. I wanted to pour my blood into her veins. I wanted to fight it for her. I wanted to make her live. To stay with me." Rogan then forced out the shame that had haunted him since that day. "'Twas the first time she was not safe in my arms."

He squeezed Emeline tightly, as if to demonstrate how hard he could hold on. His hands bruised her where he gripped her flesh, but she did not mind the hurt. No, she reveled in it, knowing it was his pain he was letting her feel. Rogan looked deep into her eyes, sharing with her what Emeline knew he had held from everyone else.

"I held her for hours after she died." He pressed on though his voice was now nothing more than ragged breath. "I held her and I cursed God. How dare He ignore my prayers for her to be spared? I cursed myself, again and again, so stupid, so weak. And I cursed her for leaving me. And then I cursed her some more, for not coming back."

"Of course you did."

"I was helpless," he admitted finally, and then he glanced away, ashamed.

Rogan realized how hard he gripped Emeline and he relaxed his hold. He brought his gaze back to her, at first questioningly to see if he'd hurt her, but the look of complete and total understanding in her eyes had him staring down at her for a long time, both of them suspended in a place where nothing else existed but the feel of each other, pressed together as the fire warmed them.

"That is when you began the fights?" It wasn't really a question; she knew.

Rogan nodded, once. No more evasions or excuses. All the fights had been the same, fights with no victor since he fought against himself.

Emeline's heart ached for him, a man who had tried to

save his wife and failed, driven to battle his demons in a boxing ring, trying desperately to drown his pain and exorcise his guilt. She pulled him close to her again. The rise and fall of his chest beneath her cheek was her whole world. He was her everything. She no longer wanted her barriers back, not if being exposed also meant being able to have this moment.

It felt right somehow, to hold and nurture him, a slim woman clutching a broad, strong man, lending him strength. Yet, she could not give him absolution. Emeline knew better than most that such a gift comes from within, from the inner voice that is the harshest of judges. Still, because words can be so powerful, she gave him the ones he needed to hear. "You don't have to punish yourself anymore. Your sentence is over. You can stop."

And she heard his breath exhale, like relief.

They stood entwined, Emeline's head nestled in the curve of his shoulder, his cheek resting on her head as the two of them stared into the fire.

After a long time, Rogan reluctantly released his hold of her and bent down, picked up her shift and gown and handed them to her. He suddenly felt foolish for weeping. His lip curled up on one side in self-deprecating derision.

"I'm sorry," Rogan said.

"Please don't be. I want your truth."

"But to go on like that. To cry." He shrugged his shoulders, looked at the floor between them. "There is no dignity in weakness."

"The dignity is in the recovery," Emeline said softly, gently.

That brought his head up. Something that looked like a challenge glimmered in her eyes, like the implication of defiance in the shadows that roamed across her face. She humbled him again and again.

"You know something of being powerless, aye?"

"I do." Emeline took her shift from his hand and pulled it over her head. She brought her eyes back to his. "I know what Simon taught me. And now, as promised, you're teaching me something different. I am powerless to my feelings for you, Rogan. And 'tis frightening, but also wonderful."

He reached out and cupped her cheek. With his hard thumb he stroked the softness of her skin, felt the solid bone beneath. It was Emeline herself, he thought, silk over steel. She had asked him how much of him she could hope for.

"Hope for all of me, *anamchara*," Rogan said. "And so will I."

Rogan and Emeline entered the mansion together. The butler showed no emotion as he closed the door and informed them that Her Grace was taking tea in the parlor, and that His Grace was at Parliament. Rogan thanked him for his help and hurried through the corridors as he pulled Emeline along with him, anxious to check on Kieran.

He burst into her rooms with a grin on his face, prepared for her look of shock when he informed her he had gotten married.

But the bed was made, the room tidied and empty. He glanced around and saw no signs that Kieran occupied the rooms, save a basket of embroidery and a stack of novels on the nightstand beside the bed.

"Perhaps she is well enough that she is taking a walk in the gardens," Emeline said, venturing an explanation to what had Rogan looking extremely upset. The grip of his hand on hers had grown harder, as savage as the grip on a sword.

"She gave her word she would stay abed."

"But we were gone days."

"Nevertheless. She was raised to abide by her word."

Rogan dropped Emeline's hand and began to search the room. He threw open her armoire but was not familiar enough with her garments to know if she had dressed and left. The copper tub in the bathing alcove was completely dry, the towels by the washstand only slightly damp. He could detect the faint scent of perfume lingering in the air, and found a few scattered pins in a small porcelain dish on the dressing table. There was not a single clue to her whereabouts.

"Stay here," he instructed Emeline. "Do not leave these rooms."

He turned on his heel and left, searching the mansion until he found a maid who swept a fireplace in one of the sitting rooms, meticulously wiping away the last traces of cinders from the hearth.

"My sister, Kieran. Do you know her whereabouts?"

Nearly jumping from her skin, the maid narrowly avoided dumping her bucket of ashes as she skittered around to face the duke's nephew.

"No, milord," she stammered, clearly frightened by the man who loomed over her, demanding answers.

"She's gone," said a voice behind Rogan.

Anna had entered the room behind him. Her hair was meticulously curled around her homely face, and she balanced a teacup on a saucer in her right hand. She wore an elaborately beaded gown of brown silk, and a superior smirk.

"Where?"

"Why ask me? I am only a woman, and 'tis best for me to not concern myself with male pursuits."

The floor beneath Rogan felt as if it were made of sand and he was sinking, sinking. "Male?"

"Indeed."

He fought for control. "Your Grace, Aunt Anna, this male is asking you, where is my sister and how is her disappearance a male pursuit?"

"What a shame to find you are typical of your gender," she remarked, her expression one of annoyance and appreciation combined. "Like all men, you expect that because

I am a woman I exist to serve you in some way. When, dear Nephew, is a woman to know when to keep her mouth closed, and when to open it? One man demands silence; another demands information. I am afraid that you simply cannot have it both ways." Anna fluttered her eyelashes demurely and then lifted conniving eyes to meet Rogan's. "I know my place. Perhaps 'tis time you learned yours."

Her silk skirts rustled as she turned to leave, the gold beads encrusting her gown twinkling in the afternoon light. Before she could take two steps she gasped at the crude grip of her nephew's hand on her upper arm. Her teacup smashed to the floor, splattering tea everywhere as he turned her bodily until she faced him. Her mouth gaped open with fear and indignation as he bent down to stare at her, nose to nose.

"This man is her brother and protector. You will tell me," he instructed very, very quietly. "Now!"

She jumped at the final outburst, her eyes going wide. Recovering her poise somewhat, she glanced down at the hand that crushed the sleeve of her gown. "And again, like a typical male, you resort to violence and intimidation to settle a matter. Fine," she spat, "I will tell you. But you will let go of me first."

Rogan released his grip immediately, and Anna smoothed her silken sleeve, sniffed primly a few times, and then swept across the room so she could take a seat on the divan. She did not speak until she was completely composed.

"'Tis twice today that my routine has been disrupted. First my morning nap by Simon, and now my tea by my rude nephew. It seems all the males under this roof are nothing more than rutting bulls, sniffing after the latest pretty face."

"Simon took Kieran?"

"Took? She went willingly with him. My maids inform

me that, whilst I returned to my napping, he offered Kieran a ride into the city, to which she readily acquiesced."

The room spun as his gut was stabbed with icy swords of fear. In that instant, he was transported in front of his parents, trying to explain how he had allowed his sister to be lured away by a man such as Simon.

The image was replaced with the vile and degrading things Emeline had told him Simon preferred.

Rogan spun on his heel and ran back to Kieran's rooms where Emeline sat patiently waiting for his return. As he informed her in a rush of what he'd learned, Emeline followed Rogan into his rooms. He handed her paper and quill, slammed an inkwell down on the table. "Write the locations of all his land holdings."

Rogan stripped off his soiled clothes and reached into his armoire, pulled out black breeches, and began to dress. As he buttoned a clean black shirt, Emeline's mind raced to recall all of Simon's many properties; brownstones, town homes, estates and cottages. The man accumulated properties the way some dogs collected fleas. She penned the locations, giving landmarks and directions, wracking her brain to try to remember them all, certain she was forgetting a few. Where would Simon take Kieran? she kept asking herself. What if he went to an inn or a tavern? But no, she told herself, Simon didn't take Kieran because he wanted her. He had taken Kieran because he wanted Emeline back. With that thought in mind, she turned her face up to Rogan's.

"Trade me for her," she said.

Rogan paused in his dressing and glanced up. "Don't be absurd."

"'Tis why he took her. To punish you for taking me."

"It does not matter why. He took her, and he'll pay."

"Trade me, Rogan," she repeated, thinking of the things Simon would do to Kieran. "She cannot handle herself with him as I can. Trade me, and then when Kieran is safe, come back for me."

Rogan tucked his shirt into his breeches and slipped into his knee-high black boots, fastening them as he spoke. "I told you once before, I don't send women to handle business between men. She is my sister. I will get her back, and while I go, you'll stay here, aye?"

"But 'tis me he wants."

Rogan slid his dagger into his boot, checked the priming of his pistols, buckled on his pistol belt, and then over that, his sword belt. With a swirl of black cloth he draped his long cloak over his shoulders, its thick, heavy folds masking most of his weapons. He crossed the room, grabbed the framed map of the city from the wall, tore open the back and extracted the map. He stood before Emeline, looking every inch an angel of death, his eyes brutally cold, his mouth set in a firm, grim line. He reached out and cupped her chin, waited until she met his eyes with her own.

"I don't care what he wants. Kieran is my family, and he will answer to me." He took the paper from Emeline, read the long list of properties with a sinking feeling in his gut. So many. Where to start? His cloak flared around his calves as he headed for the door. He yanked it open and paused, turned to her once again. When he spoke his voice was as cold as his eyes. "I mean what I say, Emeline. You are my wife now; you will listen to me. Stay here at the mansion, lock the door behind me, and wait."

Emeline did as she was told. She locked the door to Rogan's rooms and leaned against the cool wood. Worry for Kieran had Emeline's belly tensed as she thought about Simon alone with her and the many implications that could have. Simon loved nothing more than to frighten a woman nearly senseless. He would rape Kieran's mind long before he would violate her body.

A tremulous sigh escaped her lips as she leaned her head back, sagging against the door. The irony of the situation did not escape her; she now belonged to a different man and was locked behind different doors. This time, however, the threat of rape hung over someone else. The thought was scarcely a comfort.

The silence in the room filled her ears with its monotony, far too reminiscent of the many weeks she'd spent locked away for Jeffrey's use, and before that, the rooms in which Simon had imprisoned her. Those rooms had been different than the Bradburn mansion. There, Simon had kept her in a room with boarded windows, because he would not risk her throwing herself to her death or breaking the glass to use as a weapon or a method of suicide.

Yes, Emeline thought sadly, Simon thought of everything, and he would take special delight in the challenge of breaking Kieran. Hopelessness was his specialty.

The sudden thought came into her mind though, clear as water and just as refreshing: *Simon did not break you.*

Like a trickle of water that wells into a stream, new feelings overwhelmed her, emotions as unaccustomed to Emeline as jewels but far more valuable: pride and esteem for herself. She closed her eyes against the force of those emotions, even as tears of relief stung her eyelids. She had been broken once, but not beyond repair. The pieces were coming back together, rejoining and fusing, making her whole.

After a while the trembling stopped, and she pushed herself to stand upright, on her own power. The rooms were where Rogan had been staying, and she saw little signs of him everywhere. She wandered through the rooms, looking at his things, leather-bound books written in languages she did not know, more books, these in English, though they were written about subjects of which she knew nothing. Her mother, Madeline, had seen to Emeline's education, but it had gone no further than the subject of England, and so Emeline turned the pages of Rogan's book with some initial interest.

With a sigh she set down the book. She could not concentrate. A restlessness took her, an impatience to be doing something to help. But Rogan had given her an order, and as his wife, she would obey.

He had left the doors to his armoire open, and in a wifely manner she began to straighten his clothes, lifting the sleeves of his coats to breathe his scent as it still lingered on the fabric, clean and masculine. His dirty clothes lay in a puddle of cotton and linen on the floor, and she gathered them up and held them to her face, buried her nose in them and inhaled deeply. The scent recalled their lovemaking, spicy from bathwater and their bodies. Desire awakened in her once again, her body tingling with the memory of moving on his body, the sensual rush of pleasure and power combined.

A discreet knock sounded on the door, breaking her reverie, and Emeline dropped the clothes back to the floor as she went to the door.

"Who is there?" she asked.

"Molly, milady."

Emeline recognized the voice of the young maid with whom she'd entrusted her note to Rogan. She opened the door to allow Molly to enter, locked it behind them as the maid came into the room, her feet scudding the floor as she walked in slippers too large for her feet. Emeline waited patiently as Molly shifted her weight nervously, causing the skirts of her homespun gown to swing like a bell over her ankles. Molly did not meet Emeline's gaze, but instead her eyes darted around Rogan's rooms while she scratched the side of her nose, resting finally on the bed.

"''E's gone. I 'eard the kitchen 'elp talkin', an' they said 'e'd gone ter find 'is sister."

"That's correct." Emeline waited for Molly to elaborate. When she did not, and instead stood staring at the bed as if it was of extreme interest, Emeline prodded further. "Is there something you need?"

"I would 'ave taken the note ter 'im fer free."

"Oh."

Another long silence fell between them until Molly finally brought her gaze around to meet Emeline's.

"Ye gave me a foin gown."

"I did."

"Why did ye do that? I would 'ave been 'appy with much less."

Emeline paused before answering, finally deciding on the truth of why she had given Molly one of the costlier Jeffrey had purchased her. "Chamber maids don't earn very much. A generous bribe seemed most likely to ensure your silence."

Molly glanced at the bed again before she dragged her attention back to Emeline. "I 'ated ye, before. Ye, so loverly and so sad. What did ye 'ave to be sad fer, I'd be thinkin' as I carried out yer piss and shite. Ifn I'd been born lookin' like ye, I'd be workin' on me back an' livin' as a princess, instead o' doin' the work o' a common maid, an' a chamber maid, at that. Not walkin' about wit my angel face all amopin'."

"Things are not always as they seem," Emeline said.

"Humph," Molly snorted in response, as if to say she did not need a lesson in the inequity of appearance to worth. "An' yet, ye escaped only ter return." She wrinkled her nose as she looked up at Emeline, tearing at her ragged nails with her grubby fingertips. "I got the money fer the dress. Buried it in a secret spot."

"Good. I hope the money serves you well."

"Anyways, I came 'ere to thank ye."

Emeline nodded her acceptance and opened the door as a signal for Molly to go. But instead of leaving, the chamber maid strolled over to the pot to check its contents, found it empty, and then casually went to the foot of the large bed, ran a finger along the carvings of the footboard as she stared down at the soft sheets and silk coverlet.

"Is there anything more you want to say, Molly? I fear I am not inclined to take visitors now, as Lady Kieran is gone and I am quite worried. Perhaps we could continue this at a more opportune time." Emeline opened the door wider.

"Humph. *Lady* Kieran," Molly muttered. And she began to saunter towards the door, a look of superiority stamped on her grimy face.

Servants knew everything that went on in a house, and information was their currency. Curious at her attitude, Emeline closed the door.

"You do not care for Lady Kieran?"

"Care? Isn't my job to care about 'er, but only to clean 'er pots."

"Yes, but you have formed an opinion. What is it?"

A shrewd gleam came into Molly's eyes even as her fingertips resumed their picking, ripping off pieces of her fingernails and cuticles until little cracks welled with blood, though she did not seem to notice.

"Well," Molly began, her tone hushed and gossipy. "*Lady* Kieran is too 'igh and mighty ter spend 'er days lookin' or talkin' to the lowly maids. Sure, an' she'll speak wit her attendants, but the ones 'oo come ter clean? Oh, we don't exist at all."

"I am certain she meant no rudeness. She has been quite ill."

"Not so ill lately. Spendin' 'er days washin' 'erself an' groomin' 'er 'air," Molly countered, reaching past Emeline to rest her hand on the knob. It seemed she was no longer concerned with impertinence; she treated Emeline as she would a peer and pulled the door open, not waiting to be dismissed. She turned her head long enough to remark over her shoulder as she left, brows raised and a smirk twisting her lips. "It's not all o' us wot can't read, you know. Me friend, Jane, 'oo cleans the hearths, knows all her letters, an' she read the letter in the package Lady Kieran's mum sent her."

Molly leaned in and narrowed her eyes for effect. "'Ad *Lady* Kieran ever taken the time ter speak to the lowly, she would 'ave known better than to run off wit the likes o' Lord Simon. An' 'ad she taken the time ter unwrap the bundle 'er mum sent 'er, she might 'ave a bit o' protection against 'im, maybe a chance at savin' 'er virtue, just as 'er good mum was warnin' 'er. But *ladies* don't speak to servants. An' *ladies* often git what they deserve."

Molly did a little jig before scudding down the hallway, swirling her skirts as she disappeared into the maze of the mansion. Emeline closed and locked her doors once again, but this time her mind spun with what Molly had told her.

Emeline waited a few moments, as long as she could bear it, before she opened her door and peeked out into the hallway. She listened hard for approaching footsteps. The corridor remained empty and silent, save for the creaking noises of the manse and the occasional muffled voices drifting up from the lower level as the servants conversed while as they went about their duties.

She stepped into the hall; the floorboards squeaked under her feet as she crossed the space and entered Kieran's rooms. She closed and locked the door behind herself and leaned against it, her heart pounding. Gathering her composure, she began searching the room for a bundle sent by Camille, intended for her daughter.

The armoire proved fruitless, bearing nothing but gowns and shoes and the coordinating accouterments. She peeked under the bed, saw nothing but an expanse of immaculate hardwood. The bathing alcove, too, proved fruitless; her snooping yielded naught but the expected soaps and oils beside the copper tub.

Emeline stood in the center of the bedchamber, nibbling her thumb as she looked around in a circle. Her eyes alighted on a small, brown leather traveling trunk that sat beneath a window. She saw that its lid was closed, the shiny brass latches securely hooked. But it was not locked.

She went and knelt before it, her blood pounding in her ears. Her fingertips ran across the leather, felt the striations and texture of it, traveled the brass and reached for the latches.

Camille packed this trunk, Emeline thought. Wrapped bundles for her daughter and secreted them inside.

As she lifted the lid, the woody scent of fragrant cedar filled her sinuses, mingling with the rich smell of the leather and odd whiffs of oils and spices. Emeline unpacked the trunk, removing packages of saffron and long vanilla beans, sacks of coffee and cocoa beans. Puzzled by the contents, Emeline set them aside and withdrew a few bolts of fine silk, immaculately wrapped in muslin to protect the gossamer fabric from being pulled or torn.

All alone at the bottom lay a parcel. Wrapped in thick, black leather and securely wound with a braided thong, the oblong package bore a single piece of parchment, upon which were written two words in elegantly simple handwriting:

For Kieran.

With hands that trembled, Emeline reached deep into the trunk and lifted the bundle, knowing that it had to be what Molly had spoken about. No doubt the servants had opened it while Kieran slept, snooping as they always did in search of information that could prove useful.

Camille herself had prepared this trunk for her daughter, and most especially this leather package. Emeline held it to her breasts, closed her eyes and pretended for a few precious moments that it was she Camille had sent the package for, one Englishwoman to another, both daring to reach for lives they had not been born to live.

But that fleeting moment passed. The parcel had been intended for Camille's daughter, who was now in danger. And so Emeline unwound the thong and unwrapped the leather.

"Sweet Jesus and all that's holy," Emeline whispered in awe. She lifted the contents and held it up in the fading afternoon light.

A dagger: its blade an insidious wink of well-oiled steel, the hilt and pommel black and unadorned. It had a sheath of black leather, fitted with straps and buckles, and at the top it possessed an odd steel catch the likes of which Emeline had never seen.

Wrapped beneath the weapon lay a letter. Still clutching the dagger, Emeline paused only for a second before opening it, reading the words Camille had intended only for her daughter's eyes:

> *My Kieran,*
> *We are alike, you and I. You cannot know the extent of it, and well you should not, for is it not the way of young women to find the ways in which they are not like their mothers? I know those truths very well myself, my love, and so I need you to know that the many times we have disagreed were a joy to me, for I saw you making your own way.*
> *By now you'll have found the dagger.*
> *Suffice it to be said, dearest daughter of mine, that once upon a time, I made my own way as well.*

When I was a girl, my grandmother, Elizabeth, left me a letter before she died, and its cryptic nature haunted me for many years. I will not be cryptic here.

I was raped, Kieran. Afterwards, I wore this dagger for a long while, until the loving care of your father and the healing nature of time caused me to feel strong enough to put it away.

I give it to you now with this admonition: wear it. Fasten it under your skirts; you'll see the clasp your father had fitted for me, it can be worn hilt-down and is easily released into your palm with only the flick of your thumb. Strap it on, practice pulling it, and wear it at all times. Tell no one you have it; a woman allows her men to protect her, but there are times when a woman protects herself.

Men will want to bed you, Kieran, simply because of how you look. 'Tis their nature, and most will try to seduce or woo you to their beds; you'll know this already. But there will also be men who will believe they can take what is not freely given. They may try to force you down, may even succeed despite the dagger beneath your skirts. Nothing in this life is certain.

With that said, I follow with a further admonition: stay close to your brother. London is not like Barbados, not in the slightest. Keeping close to Rogan will guarantee that the dagger will not be needed.

I wish I could have taken a moment to do this in person prior to your leaving, but I know how likely the moment would have turned to something other than what I intended it to be. Again, there is nothing in my heart but acceptance of that fact; you are a willful girl, spoilt, and headstrong. I, too, know something of that as well.

I smile as I write this, for I know that as you read my criticisms your face will be drawn in a defiant scowl.

Ah, my dearest daughter, you are also sweet and kind, thoughtful and generous. You've grown well, Kieran, and I could not be prouder of the young woman you are, and the grown woman you will become.

'Tis my hope that you will tire of London and return home. And your home it shall always be, waiting for you when you choose to reclaim it. We are here, Kieran, your father and I. Always.

With Love,
Mum

P.S. The spices and silks are to be given as gifts to your aunt and uncle. Though I sent letters to this effect, please tell them your father and I are thinking of them fondly.

The letter drifted from Emeline's fingers as she sat, stunned. It seemed Camille spoke to Emeline in the letter, with understanding and forgiveness. Fragments of herself that had only just begun to come back together healed a little more.

The sun had begun to set, casting long blue shadows through the room, the light fading more and more as night threatened. In Kieran's rooms, Emeline did not want to risk lighting a candle and calling attention to her presence, so it was time to go. With infinite care she repacked the letter in the bundle, placing it in the trunk and replacing the bolts of silks and spices until it looked as it had when she opened it.

Emeline got to her feet, lifted her skirts and strapped the dagger to her thigh, buckling the black leather straps just above the rise of her stocking on the stretch of naked, creamy skin. After a few fumbling tries she figured out how to release the catch, finding it easy just as Camille had written. In a few fluid motions, she could withdraw the dagger and have it glittering from her palm.

The power of it inflamed her, tightened her nipples, heated her blood. She reached under her skirts, tossed the catch and pulled the knife, practiced brandishing it. As she did, she envisioned Simon in front of her: thrusting the knife between his ribs, piercing his heart and spilling his blood. And she felt her womanhood grow hot and damp.

Giddy with the feel of empowerment, she decided to wear it until Rogan returned with Kieran. Emeline slid the dagger back into its sheath and flipped the catch closed.

And then she dropped her skirts and stood just a bit taller.

Chapter 22

Jeffrey stood in the doorway to Kieran's rooms, watching Emeline. With skin-prickling awareness, she turned and faced him.

"I was told you'd returned." Jeffrey's manner was composed, but his eyes were not. They shimmered with something Emeline could not name. "Rogan informed me of your nuptials. Many felicitations."

"Thank you." She watched as the shadows of night shifted, grew longer, reached to envelop him.

He leaned against the door frame. "I admit, I will miss your companionship."

The awkwardness of the situation had Emeline twisting her fingers together. Her former lover-turned-uncle watched her with glistening, pale eyes, and in the dimness she read him as she had before, saw his longing and knowledge combined. It was there with his anger of her rejection. "You will find another mistress."

Jeffrey stiffened. "Of course I will. I am the Duke of Eton. I can have any woman I desire. Perhaps this time I will take more than one, maybe three or four. I can have a harem, if I wish it." He preened, ran his hands down the front of his jacket while he sniffed with annoyance. "No

one denies me anything. I certainly deny myself nothing.
I will indulge whatever whim strikes me. And Lord knows,
you are not the only woman who has pleased me. There
will be many more to follow in your wake."

Emeline saw beyond his pretensions. His pride had
taken an enormous blow, and her desertion of him for
Rogan fueled his fears and insecurities. But his feelings
aside, she had far greater concerns. "I hope we will be able
to put our former . . . association behind us, Your Grace."

Jeffrey laughed. "Oh, you are droll, Emeline. Look at
you, all manners and charm. As if you and I do not know
what lies beneath. Perhaps you have fooled young Rogan
with such a display, but I am older. Wiser. I know a slut
when I bed one."

No, her conscience asserted, *with Rogan you are yourself. Only Rogan sees the real person inside.*

But a dissenting voice spoke to her as well: *What of
when society reviles you? What of when you cannot give
him heirs? He will grow to hate you when his lust has
worn off.*

Emeline squeezed the thoughts back, beat them down.
"You never knew me at all. You only knew what I showed
you. Nothing more."

"Your bedroom tricks were intriguing," Jeffrey agreed.
"I grant that. Have you done that thing to Rogan yet? The
thing with your tongue on his—"

"Stop."

His laugh was cruel, his eyes cold. "Ah, a blushing
whore. You are priceless, Emeline."

"Yes," she answered fiercely. "I will never be bought or
sold or bargained for again."

There was a plaintive valor in the way she spoke, and
Jeffrey was struck by it. Was at last able to name the thing
about Emeline that had drawn him to her from the start:

Emeline possessed herself, in a way that neither Simon nor Jeffrey ever could.

For a moment, Jeffrey was still. Except for his eyes. They roamed over her, feasting, memorizing, remembering. And then his posture slumped; his anger faded. That quickly it had spent itself; he could not be contemptuous of her, in his own way, he'd cared for her. He turned to leave, speaking over his shoulder rather than facing her beauty any longer. It hurt too much to see her and know she did not want him, had never wanted him. Self-pity welled again, so hard his heart hurt. "For the time that I spent with you, you made me happy."

"Your Grace."

The supplicating sound of her voice had him turning, hopeful. She'd moved closer to him, so that only a few feet separated them. He nearly got lost in her eyes, her scent.

"I'm sorry," she said simply.

Jeffrey sighed, then nodded, accepting the inevitable. He pinched the bridge of his nose, and with visible effort, composed himself. When he spoke, it was with every bit of his dignity. "Very well, Lady Emeline. You can rest assured, I will speak of our *association* to no one, and I will instruct Anna to follow suit. Any rumors will be staunchly denied. The last thing our family needs is another scandal."

Our family.

Emeline inclined her head. "My deepest thanks, Your Grace."

Jeffrey turned and walked away, leaving Emeline to her thoughts. For all his odd proclivities, Jeffrey had not been unkind to her. Indeed, the night she'd been forced to leave with him had turned out to be the end of Simon's grip on her, the start of new beginnings.

As Emeline crossed the hallway to return to Rogan's rooms, a ruckus drew her attention. Drawn by curiosity, she moved to the top of the stairs, leaned over the banister, straining to see or hear. Jeffrey was down there, but he did not see Emeline as he stood waiting, obviously aware that the person who ran crying through the halls of the mansion was headed toward him.

Emeline watched as a young woman came running into view. She wore the plain homespun of a servant, her mousy brown hair tumbling around her shoulders in complete disarray, eyes wide, wild, and weeping. The maid spotted Jeffrey and came to a stop and appeared to attempt to remember her manners, but could not contain herself.

"I need to see Rogan Mullen," the maid burst out, and then regained a bit of her decorum. "Your Grace. It is an emergency."

"He is not here," Jeffrey answered abruptly, made to move by her.

Getting nowhere, obviously frustrated and breathless from running and crying, she looked up to Emeline with huge, wet eyes. She had a piece of paper clutched in her hand, and she waved it to Emeline as if it were an explanation. "His sister. My mistress. Miss Kieran. She's been taken."

"Simon," Emeline stated. It wasn't a question, but a prompt.

"Aye! Yes. He took us for a ride, but then dropped me by the street. He gave me this letter and a few shillings. Told me to hail a carriage and come back here. 'Give this note to Rogan Mullen.' He left then, with Miss Kieran screaming for him to stop." The maid stopped and gasped for breath. "But I was robbed, and they took my money. I had to walk, but I don't know the city, milady. I couldn't find my way back. I walked for hours, trying to remember the way. Nothing looked familiar. Finally a nice man, a fruit vendor, took pity on me. I told him where I'd been staying, and he brought me here."

"What does the letter say?"

"I can't read, milady," the maid said, as if it were a shameful confession.

Jeffrey snatched the letter from her and read it aloud.

> *Rogan,*
> *Your sister and I will be waiting for you. Your little lover will know the address. Ask her where to find us, and be sure to bring her along. Do not make me wait long; your sister is far too lovely to garner much in the way of restraint.*

"That's it?" Emeline demanded.

"'Tis all it says."

Emeline turned her attention to the maid, wondering why Simon said she would know the address. Why not just name the property? "Do you know where Simon dropped you?"

"No, milady. I can't be sure." The maid paused, thinking. "The Strand?"

As if with magnetic impetus, Emeline and Jeffrey locked eyes. The Strand. And both of them suddenly knew where Simon had taken Kieran.

Emeline's arms went heavy, her knees weak. It was the only address she hadn't put on the list, had completely forgotten about, because it was a property Simon hadn't purposefully acquired, a property he had very little interest in. Emeline had spent years consciously trying to wipe the memory of that place from her mind.

Long ago it had been Emeline's home. She'd been born there, and in the sheltering circle of her tiny family, had been happy there. And she'd been lost there, too, in a poker game where the winner had been decided long before cards had been dealt.

"When is the next meeting?" Emeline asked Jeffrey.

"Tonight. Oh God." He looked sick.

Kieran. Simon would take her there, to their disgusting, perverted meeting. Without a trace of doubt, Emeline knew that Simon would take especial delight in letting Kieran see what the men did with the whores, letting her wonder if those same acts would happen to her in a matter of seconds, or minutes, or hours. Her fear would be his aphrodisiac, she knew, the scent of sweat and terror that would gather on Kieran's skin would be like perfume to him.

The waiting is worse than anything else, she thought. Worse than the actual violation, worse than a beating, worse than pain. Those things are reality. But the waiting is time to ponder what might be, what could happen, what it would feel like. It sickened Emeline's soul to think of Kieran like that now.

The dagger Camille had sent burned like a brand against Emeline's skin. Burned like her conscience. How could she not have known where Simon would take Kieran?

If Simon gave her over to the lords, Kieran could well be praying for death by the early hours of morning.

Emeline could possibly help Kieran, though. Her hand touched the bulk of the dagger through her skirts. Rogan's admonition rang in her conscience, as well: *I mean what I say, Emeline. You are my wife now; you will listen to me. Stay here at the mansion, lock the door behind me, and wait.*

But Rogan would not know where to find his sister.

There was only one thing to be done. "Send men to each of Simon's addresses," she instructed Jeffrey. "Have each of them carry the message of where Simon has likely taken Kieran. They will all take a post and wait for Rogan to arrive, and when he does, they can send him to the house on the Strand. Hurry. Now."

"Done." Jeffrey turned on his heel, rushing away to carry out Emeline's orders.

She turned her attention to the maid. "You wait here. If Rogan returns, tell him what has happened."

"What will you do, milady?"

Emeline did not answer her, already on the move. She raced to Rogan's rooms where her bag lay on the floor, still unpacked from her attempt to flee. Emeline yanked out her warmest cloak, went to Rogan's armoire and pillaged it for money, stuffing her pockets with coins. And then, feeling around at the bottom of her bag, her fingers brushed against the metal she sought. Emeline withdrew the key to her childhood home and slid it into her bodice.

She rushed down the stairs. The maid hurried after her. "I'll come with you, milady. It's not safe, you venturing into the night alone."

"And will you protect me as you did your mistress?" Emeline snapped. At the stricken look on the maid's face, she softened her tone as much as she could manage. "Stay here. You'll be no help to me, anyway."

The maid tugged at Emeline's cloak. "Milady, please."

Emeline pushed her hand away, kept moving through the maze of the mansion. Her decision was made. She would go and see if she could help Kieran while Jeffrey's men scattered to find Rogan.

In a few minutes she was outside the mansion, rushing to the stables. She saw a ragtag bunch of men, servants and stable-hands and gardeners, all snatched from their duties and gathered before Jeffrey near the out-kitchen. She kept to the shadows and entered the stables. After a few well-spent coins and well-chosen words with the stable lad, she was saddled on a small paint while the others waited as Jeffrey and an attendant rapidly penned missives to be handed to Rogan. Wheeling the mare around, Emeline pulled the hood of her cloak up over her head to hide the brightness of her hair and the look of her face.

With both hands gripping the reins she leaned forward and urged the mare to run, not caring now if she was seen. The mare, cooped in the stables far too long, took her head with that bit of encouragement. The sound of the hoofbeats echoed off the cobblestones and rang out into the darkness, followed by a few shouts for her to stop, to come back.

And in Emeline's chest her heart thundered. Kicking the mare, she let the horse completely have her head, and went galloping off into the damp night, the hem of her cloak snapping and flapping behind her like a banner.

Simon did not want to hurt Kieran. He had not intended on taking her, and so did not even have a plan of what to do with her. But she was the means to an end. He would get Emeline back, and would see to Rogan in the process.

For those things to transpire Simon needed Kieran, his only ace in a game that had somehow turned against him. He would not have had to be so hard on the girl, if she hadn't tried to fight him, tried to escape. Simon needed the girl to cooperate, to wait the situation out, to simply sit still and be quiet.

Kieran had not acquiesced to those requirements. As a matter of consequence, Simon had been forced to coerce her.

There is no better method of control than fear. So Simon saw to it that Kieran knew what it was to be afraid. To languish in its panicked clutches, eyes rolling whitely, skin tingling and sweating, heart hammering.

Perhaps he'd gone too far, he mused. The girl was not so much frightened into submission as she was completely terrified out of her wits.

Only the rarest of women possessed Emeline's brand of mettle.

Simon sipped his gin and laid down his cards with a flourish, besting the last two men who had come to the house that night; the rest had already come and gone. He tipped back in his chair, balancing on the two rear legs as he checked on Kieran. Sure enough, she was still balled in a heap on the floor, curled into the fetal position in an effort to hide her nudity.

He shrugged and turned back to the other men. "Who wants to play another hand?"

"I'm finished," Samuel, the Duke of Westminster said. He slapped his hand on his thigh and stood up. "My lust is spent and my purse is empty. Another fine night in our house of lords."

"I suppose I'm leaving then," Arthur, the Duke's cousin, said nastily. They'd ridden together, and Arthur was in no mood to see the evening end.

"Come along, Arthur." Samuel reached for his cloak. "If you're a good lad, I'll bring you next time."

The two men continued to bicker as they donned their outerwear. They passed to bade Simon goodbye, opening the door, their words dying on their tongues as they gaped in surprise.

Emeline stood on the landing, a key in her hand. Behind her stood The Bull, posted by Simon for protection, looking quite unsure of what to do.

Samuel and Arthur turned to Simon, and Samuel winked broadly before they stepped between Emeline and The Bull, and took to their carriage. They rumbled away and Simon rushed to greet his stepdaughter as she stepped across the threshold.

The night was no longer liberation. It was rage and fear and desperation. Somewhere in the city of London, Simon had Rogan's sister.

The stallion beneath Rogan could not gallop fast enough. Rogan kicked the beast's sides, urging it on, faster, faster as his imagination provided full-color detail of what Kieran might be suffering.

Rogan remembered her as a little girl. He'd been seven

years old when she was born, old enough to be past the point of seeing Kieran as a menace. No, he'd been thrilled; she'd been more like a new toy than anything else, and her presence had made their family even happier. Rogan recalled her following him around like a puppy, always asking "why" as if he knew all the secrets of the island and the world beyond.

Rogan tried not to think about what might be happening to her now. It was too horrible, too real. He vowed over and again, a silent thread of words running through his mind: *If he touches her, I will kill him slowly. I will cut him up while he is alive to feel it.*

The third property was a dignified brownstone with two lanterns burning a beacon of welcome on either side of its shiny black door. It was a pretty house, sedately charming, the location listed in Emeline's fluid handwriting. Rogan thundered to a stop in front of the steps, careless of the flowers crushed beneath his stallion's hooves. He swung down from the saddle and was in front of the door in an instant, thumping his fist on the door.

After much banging on the door he saw the bobbing, yellow glow of a single candle being carried to the window. Lora peeked out and then pulled back. Soon enough he heard the sound of the door being unlocked. Lora pulled it open, dressed in her nightclothes. In the soft light she looked younger and far less worldly. Her expression was puzzled, and she'd clearly been awoken. "What are you doing here?"

"Simon took my sister. Where is he?"

"He did what? Your sister?" Lora rubbed a hand over her eyes. "Pardon?"

"There is no time for explanations. Tell me where Simon is."

As she grew more awake her eyes took on their habitual mien of sly cunning, and she swept her gaze over his appearance, pausing at the hilt of his sword protruding from the folds of his cloak. "Rogan," she murmured appreciatively.

"You look positively . . ." her gaze moved to the bulge between his legs and then up to his face, "murderous."

Rogan laid his hand on the door and pushed it all the way open. He stepped close to Lora, stared down at her with absolute seriousness. "I should hate for this meeting to turn ugly, Lora. I have never been a man to threaten a woman, but then, never before have I been this angry. I tell you, you will never meet a more dangerous man than the one before you now."

Lora tilted her head back and smiled up at Rogan, a true smile, full of genuine enjoyment. "No needs for all this blustering, love. You may not realize that a woman's heart beats in my chest. I cannot resist a man who protects his sister. 'Tis sweet, Rogan, and altogether appealing." She sighed and pressed her hand to his chest. With a deliberate motion her thumb brushed over his nipple. "I will tell you where Simon is most likely to be." Lora reached up and touched Rogan's cheek, her finger skimming along his jaw. "And if you tell Simon 'twas me who told you, I will murder you myself."

Emeline clung to her control, shaking with it, her belly trembling like her hands, like her legs. Beneath her skirts Camille's dagger waited, and beneath her outwardly calm veneer a storm swirled, violent and black with hate. She wanted to slice him, watch him bleed. She wanted to make him pay for Madeline's suffering and death by inflicting his own. But first she needed to see to Kieran.

Emeline knew she must dissemble; she reached deep for apathy to veil her true feelings, the guise Rogan had stripped from her. She needed it now more than ever.

With an insouciance she did not feel, Emeline swept into the house that had once been her home. The air swirled with smoke and stank of spilled semen and whore's perfumes, mingled with musky male sweat and gin. The familiar stench made Emeline's skin crawl.

Simon could not conceal his delight or his surprise at her unexpected appearance. He leaned out the door and looked around; there was no sign of Rogan. Odd, Simon mused, that she would have come alone. His note had meant to lure them both, together. Simon spoke to The Bull. "If he arrives, kill him. Remember what I told you: finish him and you'll be back in Africa by month's end."

The Bull said nothing. He patted the back of his breeches where a dagger was sheathed and hidden beneath the tail of his shirt. His eyes glistened in the light of the outside lantern. Simon nodded with satisfaction and The Bull retreated back into the shadows to wait and watch.

Emeline heard Simon's words. She knew with every beat of her heart what she needed to do: Protect Kieran, protect Rogan. Sacrifice herself, if it came to that.

Her resolve hardened. She would not allow Simon to hurt the one she loved, or his family. And she would also protect Camille by protecting Kieran and Rogan, the best she could.

Simon withdrew back into the house, closed the door and turned the lock so it was once again securely bolted. He slid the thick, oak bar into the cuffs bolted into the wall. He turned to Emeline, content that they were secured from Rogan for the time being. Rogan would not get past The Bull too easily. "Dearest daughter of mine, you came back to me."

Emeline made a purring sound in her throat, neither confirmation or denial. She glanced around, her composure cool and unaffected. "Where is Rogan's sister?"

"So that's why you came, is it?" Simon's lips flattened, but when he spoke he sounded offhand. "Oh, she's been watching. Learning. Waiting her turn. I'm spent for now, I'm afraid. You know, I'm not as young as I used to be." He swept his hand around the house. "Your timing is impeccable. I sent the whores away an hour ago and the last of the lords have left. We can be alone."

Emeline removed her cloak and hung it on a hook, a not so subtle indication that she was in no hurry to leave. She went to the table that held the liquor and poured herself a glass of burgundy wine, turned to face Simon as she leaned a hip on the table, took a sip and regarded him over the rim of the goblet. "So we are."

"Where is Rogan?"

"I do not know, actually."

"You lie."

"Perhaps." Emeline's lips curved upward. "You taught me well, after all."

There was something in her gaze, a promise combined with a dare. It inflamed Simon. His obsession with Emeline began and ended in the same place: he wanted her passion, in all its manifestations. He took two steps closer to her, closing the gap between them.

"I missed you." Simon raised his brow and smirked. "Dare I admit I worried?"

"What worried you?" With the tip of her finger, Emeline skated the top of the goblet, then dipped in and caught a drop of wine, brought it to her lips. "Did you fear for my safety?"

"I did. I feared I would never see you again."

"But I am here. Now."

"You are," Simon breathed. He took a step closer as she bit her bottom lip. "Tell me why."

"I'm here for the girl."

"And what of Rogan? Where is he; why isn't he here?"

"You will not believe me, so why should I tell you?"

A small sound from the other room caught Emeline's attention. She inclined her head in question. Simon waved his hand as if it were a trivial matter.

"Is she hurt?"

"She is fine. Unmolested, for the most part." Simon

shrugged, as if to indicate his own helplessness in the matter. "She would not listen, and the situation escalated. 'Twas only meant to frighten her, but one of the lords got carried away with his excitement. . . ."

Emeline forced her steps to be even and slow, and she wandered through the room as if moved by mild curiosity. She hid her gasp of dismay behind a sip of wine.

Kieran lay naked and curled on the floor, her dark auburn hair streaming around her body, dirty and matted in places. Emeline's gaze roamed over the slim figure, inspecting her. She saw no smears of virgin blood on her thighs or bruises on her skin. They hadn't hurt her physically.

Kieran lifted her head slightly, gazed at Emeline with ravaged, tired eyes. Eyes that had seen too much.

Emeline turned to Simon, her unaffected demeanor in place despite the shivering of her soul. "How predictable. Is this not the precise way you 'initiated' me?"

"She brought it on herself."

"So you say." She kept her tone dismissive. "Well, you have me now, so why not let her go."

"Have you? I do not have you. I never had you."

"I am what you want, why you took her. So here I am. Send her on her way so we can be alone. There is much for us to discuss."

"Convince me."

The words made Emeline sick, but she showed no true emotion. Her mask was in place, and it smiled. "Not in front of the girl, Simon."

"There is nothing she hasn't seen at this point."

"Perhaps you don't understand what I am saying. Listen well." Emeline stepped closer to him, laying her hand on his chest. "This is not a negotiation, and it's not a game where the winner takes all the spoils. This is a trade, plain and simple. Me for her. If you want me, all of me, you will have to let her go."

Simon chuckled, grabbed her hand and pressed a kiss to her knuckles, and then slowly took an erotic nip of her skin. "You are not in a bargaining position, my dear. You are here, and so is Kieran. My man is posted at the door, and your puppy has less of a chance of surviving that encounter than you do of reclaiming your innocence. Cease your attempted seduction of me, Emeline. I know you hate me. I've always known it. You are far too disingenuous and I see right through you."

She'd expected this response, counted on it. Beneath Simon's words and demeanor lay his need for dominance, of all types. Emeline knew what Simon wanted more than anything. He wanted the thing he'd never been able to wrest from Emeline: her self-possession. And so she offered it to him.

"I know about my mother, Simon."

He raised his brows, puffed his chest, ready to explain, but Emeline raised her hand.

"I went to Bedlam. I know she passed months ago." The words burned, a vitriolic acid in her mouth. From the corner of her eye she saw Kieran, and she knew Rogan would be coming soon. She also knew the man lay in wait for Rogan, with orders to kill him. Emeline scrambled, trying the only thing she could think of that might make Simon take her and leave so Rogan would follow rather than confront Simon's men. "You do realize what this means, Simon. You are finally free to marry me."

"You are not devious enough to carry out this pathetic attempt of a ruse. You would never marry me, not for any reason."

"Call my bluff. We can do it now." She took his hands and held them in her own. "You can finally bind me to you. Forever."

"You think I am so easily manipulated? Emeline, my darling, dear thing, you know that I know you too well to be taken in by this little display. Now tell me, why did you come here alone, and where is Rogan?"

Emeline forced herself to look confused, distraught. When she spoke, it was with resignation; the sound of a woman whose scheme has been exposed. "'Tis inevitable that I will have to tell you: I tried to kill Rogan. I lured him to the carriage house, armed with the poison mixed in wine. I hoped that it would be strong enough to kill both of us, actually. But I faltered; I was afraid. He misread the confusion in my eyes. He grabbed me, then, and began kissing me. He became impassioned. He pressed his lust on me." Emeline looked away, as if humiliated. "And when it was over, he begged forgiveness. Offered to marry me."

Simon grew very still; he studied her every nuance. "Go on."

"Well, I did not know what to do, but I worried for my mum. So I left with him, still armed with the wine. He took me to an inn and pressed himself on me again and again." Emeline pursed her lips in disgust. "He is a libertine, a rogue, a blackguard. I waited until he slept, took his money, and I fled. I went to Bedlam to see my mum.

"And then I returned to the mansion; I had nowhere else to go, and I thought I would tell Jeffrey of what Rogan had done to me, let him deal with his disgusting nephew. I saw the maid as she arrived, found that she had a note intended for Rogan. I took it from her and came here myself." Emeline held Simon's hands tighter, squeezed them. She hoped the hatred in her voice would be mistaken for jealousy, that the flashing in her eyes would appear like desperation. She was a player once more, immersed in the part she had hoped to never play again. "You don't need Kieran. You need me. You've always needed me."

Simon dropped Emeline's hands and pushed her away. But she read the uncertainty in his eyes before he said, "I can't believe you. I never could. You lie as you fuck: without remorse."

"We are linked, Simon," Emeline insisted passionately. "You cannot mean to throw me over for this girl. You cannot tell me I mean so little to you. You need me. You want me."

"I have no patience for this, Emeline. Tell me the truth."

"I shall tell you. This is the truth: you cannot break me." Emeline dropped her lashes over sly eyes, the look of the gauntlet being tossed down. "Kieran is already destroyed; see how she lies there on the floor, scared out of her mind. But you have never, ever broken me, and well you know it. You cannot beat me down; you never could. I am stronger than you."

"No more of your games, slut. I am not your fool."

She disregarded his words, his denials. She spread her arms wide open, thrust her chest out, a posture of seductive defiance. "Take me, Simon. Try and break me."

Simon knew Emeline was trying to buy time, just as he knew Rogan was likely on his way to the house. He was neither stupid or senseless.

But the fact was, he did not need Kieran. And God, he did want Emeline, like he wanted food, water, and breath. He'd always wanted her, from the very first time he'd laid eyes on her, a young girl of twelve working beside her mother in a little shop near the Thames. He craved her, obsessed over her, longed for her. And now she stood before him, full of dare and allure. As much as he hated it about himself, he was powerless to turn away from her offer. He had to see just how far she'd go.

"Fine." Simon crossed the room to where Kieran's gown lay in a heap, picked up the bundle of wrinkled green fabric and tossed it to Kieran. "Get dressed and get out."

Kieran scrambled to her feet and fell, finally grabbing onto a chair to aid her to stand. She struggled to pull on her garments, her hands shaking too much to manage clothing herself. Emeline went to Kieran's side, began sorting the garments, took the shift and shook it out, helped Kieran dress. As she tied Kieran's corset, Emeline leaned forward, spoke gently into Kieran's ear.

"Run East. There is a small livery company on the corner, not too far up, on the left. The owners are good people; the man is called Archie. Tell him I sent you and you won't need money."

Kieran's entire being was a trembling mess. She nodded as best she could while Emeline laced her gown, and she asked shyly, "Who are you?"

Her question stung Emeline more than she would have thought. Rogan had not mentioned her to his sister. *He is ashamed of you*, her conscience taunted. Emeline pushed the thoughts away, and grabbed Kieran's cloak off the floor, swung it around the quivering girl's shoulders. Of course Kieran would not know who she was, she told herself, consoled herself. It didn't matter if Kieran did not know her.

Emeline knew who Kieran was, and that was enough. She was Camille's daughter, and the dagger intended for Kieran was strapped to Emeline's thigh.

Who are you, Kieran had asked. It should be an easy question to answer. It wasn't. A multitude of responses assaulted Emeline's mind: Simon's pawn; your uncle's mistress; your brother's wife. Your replacement. She was all those things, and more. More than she could ever have dared to pray for.

"I am Emeline," she finally answered. And her voice was strong and sure.

Chapter 23

Kieran tried to run away from the house, took two steps and fell to her knees on the landing just outside the door. Behind her, she heard the lock being slid into place. The beam slid across the door, and she knew Emeline was now bolted behind closed doors, alone with Simon.

A sobbing whimper, of relief and guilt and fear in unison, welled in her throat and escaped. The night spread out around her, a vast bowl of darkness and danger in which she was exposed and vulnerable.

Go East; Archie; you won't need money.

She struggled to regain her feet, but her legs gave out again. She was crying openly now, huge gasping sobs. With all of her remaining strength, she put her feet under her and tried to stand, wanted to run. And her legs were useless. She crumpled back down to the landing in a heap.

Out of the darkness a black hand gripped her arm. She screamed as he emerged, a man as black as the night itself, his eyes an unearthly glow in the light of the tallow lantern outside the door.

The man hauled her to her feet, and then handed her a scrap of linen with which to wipe her face.

"Quiet," the man said.

In the dimness Kieran struggled to see him. He smiled at her, his teeth a white beacon in the darkness, his face set in an expression clearly meant to put her at ease despite the sheer menacing size of him. He relaxed his grip on her arm, but did not let go.

"You will be good with me," he said.

His accent was strange, thick, and slow, as if he labored to form each tentative word, his cadence was not of the islands where she'd grown up. Still, she knew he was trying to tell her that she would not be harmed by him. Kieran managed to relax a tiny bit, and her logs regained some strength. He was no longer the only thing holding her upright.

She opened her mouth to speak, her throat working, but could only produce more breathless sobs. Together they became aware of a distant, drumming sound, growing closer until they both knew what it was. The sound of the approaching horse was like thunder ringing off the cobblestones, echoing from the buildings that lined the street.

On the back of the fast-encroaching stallion rode a man dressed entirely in black, his cloak flapping behind him like the wings of some great, descending beast. He was big, imposing, ominous, his face obscured by the darkness, his form limned with moonlight.

Rogan yanked on the reins so hard the stallion reared up, his hooves pawing the air before they dropped back to the cobblestones with the resounding clash of metal striking stone. He saw them both on the landing, lit by the lantern, his sister and The Bull.

And The Bull's hand, which had pounded Rogan to the end of his endurance, was wrapped around his sister's arm, gripping it.

"Set her free," Rogan commanded as he leapt from the horse's back. He was braced for a fight, ready for a war.

Kieran crumpled again at the sound of her brother's

voice. "Rogan." Her sobs picked up where they'd left off. "Rogan, I'm so sorry."

"Kieran, be silent." Rogan's tone was both a warning and a command.

She stopped speaking, stopped sobbing.

Rogan approached the house cautiously. His eyes, well adjusted to the darkness, took in every shadowed corner as he scanned for possible danger.

The Bull dropped Kieran's arm, his body tensed.

But Rogan was not watching The Bull. Instead he wondered why his sister was outside. Why had Simon let her go? And then his gaze fell on the small horse tethered to the post; the paint from the Bradburns' stables.

And instantly, he knew why. Emeline.

"Where is she?" Rogan asked.

Kieran tried not to cry, but her breaths were hitching, hiccuping. "She traded herself for me, Rogan. Took my place."

Hysteria edged her voice, the sure promise of a breakdown imminent. Rogan struggled to get her to focus. "How long ago?"

"Not long, I don't think. I'm not sure."

"Are you hurt, Kieran?"

"No." She started to cry again. "Yes."

Rogan climbed the steps and took his sister, his eyes meeting The Bull's as he lifted Kieran into his arms. He broke the contact, turned his back, and carried her to his waiting horse, that poor beast lathered and foaming at the mouth. He hugged her, hard, before he lifted her into the saddle and reached into the folds of his cloak, pulled out a pistol and pressed it into his sister's shaking hands.

"If anyone comes near you, shoot him, Kieran." Rogan glanced once at the gun wobbling in her slim hands. She'd been taught to handle weapons, but was clearly in a state. Rogan sighed heavily. "And try not to shoot the horse, aye?"

Rogan turned to face The Bull. The last beating had

taken him to the end of his tether, shown him the bottom of the pit of his endurance, and just looking at The Bull made his body hurt. He climbed the steps, recalling the flushed excitement on Simon's face as he'd leaned over the balcony while Rogan was battered past his ability to stand. Rogan put the pieces together. Aristocratic patronage indeed.

"You told me you fought for freedom," he said to The Bull.

"I lose," The Bull replied, gesturing to his knee in a way clearly meant to indicate his had touched first. He spread his giant hands in a helpless gesture.

"My wife is in there." Rogan pointed towards the door. He spoke plainly, one primal man to another. "My woman. Let me pass."

The Bull did not reply. He only shook his head and moved to block the door.

Simon heard the hoofbeats and ran to the window. He peeked through the a gap in the drapes, angling his eye through a crack in the shutter so he could see out onto the landing, where Rogan approached The Bull.

Behind Simon, Emeline silently reached under her skirts and flipped open the catch to Camille's dagger. The pommel slid into her hand. She withdrew it from beneath her gown and held it, hidden in the folds of her skirt.

Simon had his back to her, his wide shoulders hunched forward as he peered outside. Her hand ached from squeezing the handle. In her mind a thousand questions swirled like an eddy: How much force would it take to kill him? Would she have the strength? Could she live with herself as a murderer after the deed was done? Could she live with herself as a coward if she faltered, knowing Simon lived while her mother rotted in a grave?

A man like Simon was thick with flesh and muscle and bone; it would not be easy to stab to his heart.

And neither was murdering him the simple matter she had thought it to be.

She'd wanted to kill him for so long, had fantasized and dreamed of it, and now, with his back to her and a knife in her hand, she trembled with its imminent reality.

Murder.

She was terrified to kill him; petrified not to.

How could she let him live, after all he'd done? her mind demanded.

And how could she thrust the knife in his back, with all the hubris of naming herself executioner? her heart countered.

Tears rolled down her cheeks, and she sobbed in silence, wanting to do it, and hating herself for her inability to complete the act. His back seemed as wide as the room, a wall of flesh, a mountain of a man. And in her mind flashed image after image; Simon pressing on her when she was too young to know what he was doing; Madeline, young and pretty and laughing; Simon forcing Emeline to commit vile acts that sickened her very soul, using her mother to manipulate her; Madeline, raped and bleeding, still managing to encourage her daughter to survive.

Emeline raised the dagger.

Standing between him and Emeline was once again a locked door, this one guarded. Rogan loved her. He knew that now. For too long he'd beaten himself up over his part in Orianna's death, so intent on suffering for penance. And then Emeline had taught him the meaning of strength, the value of forgiveness. She'd shown him what it truly meant to face his pain with boldness, to expose it, lay it out, naked and unveiled, where the sunlight could help it heal.

And in doing all of that, Rogan realized he could love again. Just like Emeline, courageously.

"I need my wife," Rogan said to The Bull, hoping to reason with him. He pulled out his remaining pistol and leveled it at The Bull's head. "I do not want to kill you. You are an honorable fighter. But I will kill you if I must. Let me pass."

The Bull's face was unreadable, impassive. He glanced at the gun, and then the house behind him. Something that looked like disgust passed over his features. He reached behind his back and withdrew a dagger, grabbed it by the hilt and buried it two inches into the door frame. And he moved aside.

Rogan did not hesitate. He ran to the door.

"Noooo," Simon moaned, as he watched The Bull relinquish his weapon, and then ultimately step aside. He swung away from the window, ready to grab Emeline and make a dash for the rear of the house where he had a carriage waiting in the back alley. "We must go, Emeline. The game is lost."

And then he froze, staggered.

His sweet little girl stood before him, a shimmering sharp dagger gripped tightly in her upraised hand. Her hair streamed around her shoulders in disarray, her face set in grim lines that belied the tears coursing from her burning blue eyes. She looked frozen, bloodthirsty, terrified, and infinitely enraged, like a medieval marauder set with a sudden pang of unwanted conscience.

To Simon, she had never looked more beautiful. A rose with a shining silver thorn.

In that instant Rogan was at the door. He braced his stance wide, fired rapid shots into the locks. Splinters flew and sparks shot into the night as the bullets struck the iron lock. Rogan dropped his empty pistols and began bodily throwing himself into the door, even as a carriage rumbled to a stop behind him. The locks had given, but the door was also barred, and he threw himself into it over and over, the hinges groaning as they took his weight again and again. This time no barrier would keep him from Emeline.

Jeffrey opened the door of the carriage and called to Kieran, who slid from the stallion's back and ran to seek refuge in her uncle's presence, relieved to see footmen and guards riding atop and on the back, all heavily armed.

But Rogan paid no attention, animal instinct in full command as he thrust his entire being into the splintered oak door. He scarcely glanced up when The Bull began throwing himself into the door beside him, the combined weight and strength of the men working to yank free the cuffs that held down the oaken beam.

The noise outside broke Emeline's trance. Rogan was coming, breaking down the door that kept her from him; her time was now. With a shriek of anguished fury she leapt forward, the dagger pulled back for a strike. She wanted blood. Simon's blood. It was so much easier to come at him while he faced her, when the look of his patrician face conjured every nightmare she'd ever suffered.

Simon braced himself for her attack, dodged to the side as she came at him. With a fast, hard swipe at her back, he knocked her into the wall. Emeline's face hit, her breath left in a rush. Dizzy but determined, she turned and went for him again, this time wielding the dagger like a sword, swinging it wildly, hoping to slice him.

With a quickness that belied his age, Simon grabbed a chair and swung it at Emeline, knocking her to the floor, the dagger thrown from her hand. Emeline was too dazed to regain herself. He scooped her up and threw her like a rag doll over his shoulder, ran through the house to the back, where his carriage waited in the alley. A crash sounded behind him as Rogan came flying through the battered door and broken beam, and then footsteps as he ran behind him, covering the gap.

Simon burst outside, wheezing, wild and desperate. He tossed Emeline into the carriage and vaulted himself in behind her, screaming for the coachman to drive.

Rogan was outside in a blink. He launched himself onto the back of the carriage, grabbed the footman and tossed him to the ground as the conveyance lurched into motion and began to pick up speed. He gripped the handle with his right hand, and, muscles bunched and tensed, leaned over the side, trying to reach the handle of the door despite the bouncing wheel.

Inside, Simon reached around in the darkness, hoping to find something that could be used as a weapon to knock Rogan off, when Emeline came to. She scrambled on the floor, reached for the handle and pushed the door open. Simon reached for her as she tossed herself from the careening carriage, heedless of the danger.

She hit hard, her breath escaping in a *whoosh* as she landed on gritty cobblestones. Rogan was yelling something, his voice echoing and ringing off the brick buildings.

Dazed, she finally managed to hear him clearly.

"Go through the house to the front!"

Emeline jumped to her feet and did as she was told, running through the house that had once been her childhood home. She dashed outside to find Jeffrey's carriage waiting, and without hesitation, she jumped inside.

Rogan held tight as the carriage rounded a bend and took to the Strand. He'd all but gotten hold of the handle when shots rang out.

Both horses kept going as the wooden tongue that

hitched them to the carriage was shattered. With a yelp the driver was pulled to the ground as the reins were wrapped around his wrists. The horses pulled him until he disengaged himself and scrambled to his feet. He took off at a run. The carriage wheeled crazily, out of control, and Rogan leapt off just before it crashed into a tree.

Simon opened the door, braced for a fight, his eyes gleaming with fear and rage. He'd ripped a piece of the windowsill free and brandished it like a cudgel. He didn't take more than two steps before another two shots barked, and he crumpled to the ground, bleeding from wounds to his head and chest.

Jeffrey gave the sign to his marksmen as he alighted his carriage and walked over to his nephew. In the moonlight the jewels and gold stitching on his jacket shimmered, like his eyes. He looked down at his dead cousin with an expression of resignation, and then turned to Rogan. "He brought this on himself, you know. I cannot be expected to live in fear of assassins lurking around every corner. But even still, 'tis a shame. Bloody shame, really, what greed will do to a man."

Jeffrey took a few steps back, so Simon's seeping blood wouldn't dirty his shoes. He smoothed his sleeves, and then sniffed. "All right then."

And he turned to leave.

"Uncle."

When Jeffrey turned back, Rogan held out his hand. Surprised, Jeffrey shook it.

"You know," Rogan mentioned as they walked back to where the carriage waited, "if you'd only needed a clear shot, I don't suppose we couldn't have just lured him outside."

"The door was thick, wasn't it, boy?" Jeffrey laughed.

"The door was thick, aye."

"Right, well, it serves you right. She was mine."

Rogan turned back to where Simon lay in a bleeding heap on the street. "What will happen here?"

Jeffrey shrugged. "Ah, well, all of the peers know he was out to kill you, and *me*, thanks to your clever warning at Parliament. And of course, there is the note Simon penned, meant to entice you here to your death, at which time I saw the need to protect my lineage. They will understand that I was forced to hire guards, as would any man of sense. 'Twill be no matter, I can assure you. Simon was not well-liked in the House of Lords, but my reputation is impeccable." Jeffrey stood a little straighter, squared his shoulders. "I am the Duke of Eton. I will not be terrorized."

Behind them, like ghouls emerging from the shadows, urchins crept to the crashed carriage, stealthily stripping it of all its value.

Careless to the theft and satisfied for the moment, Rogan once again began walking to his uncle's carriage, noticing for the first time that the night was clear and cold, the air crisp and thin, the sky beaming with moonlight and sprinkled with thousands of stars.

As the two men approached Jeffrey's carriage, in an off-hand manner, Jeffrey remarked, "I shall send for Lora first thing in the morning. Skilled seduction, Simon had said. How very intriguing."

With that, Jeffrey hopped into the carriage, a slight spring in his step.

He left the door ajar, and when Rogan looked inside, both the women were gone. One of the marksmen pointed in the direction of the house.

Rogan motioned for his uncle to wait and went to seek out his wife and his sister alone, but stopped for a brief moment when he spotted The Bull.

The Bull sat on the landing, his legs spread, large hands dangling between his knees. He met Rogan's gaze.

"What is your name?" Rogan asked, and then gestured

to himself. "I am not 'The Duke.' I am Rogan Mullen." He pointed to the black man, who watched his every movement with the intensity of a man who understood little of the language, ascertaining meaning from body language and tones as much as words themselves. "You are not 'The Bull.' Your name. What is it?"

The man who had been stripped of his family and tribe to be sold as a slave, been beaten and transported like cargo, who had been freighted on stinking ships, crowded in shoulder to shoulder in horrific living conditions, and endured more humiliation at the hands of strangers than he thought he could ever bear, looked into the eyes of the man before him, and smiled. It was the very first time any white man had treated him as a man, and not a slave. A human, and not a beast to be bought and sold. A person. With a name all of his own.

"Nilo," he said, his deep baritone ringing with pride. He thumped his chest with his fist. "Nilo."

"You have choices," Rogan promised him. "You helped me protect my wife, and I will help you go where you want. I have a ship."

"Africa not good." Nilo shrugged and spread his hands. "No tribe. No family."

Rogan gestured to the carriage, where his uncle waited, along with guards and footmen and drivers. A veritable entourage. "Go with us if you want. We'll figure the rest out later."

Rogan left Nilo to his decision and entered the house through the shattered door, searching room by room for Emeline and Kieran.

He found them in an upstairs room. The window had been left open and the night breeze stirred the gauzy curtains. Emeline sat on the floor, a dagger and an old box clutched to her chest. Kieran knelt beside her, her arms wrapped around Emeline's shoulders as they wept.

Rogan hovered in the doorway, silent, watching his little sister hold his wife. He knew women's business when he saw it, and did not interfere.

"Thank you," Kieran said to Emeline. "Thank you for coming for me."

"This was my house," Emeline clutched the box to her chest. "This was my room when I was a little girl. And he would bring me back here and . . ."

"It's over now," Kieran said softly.

"This was my house. My home." Emeline looked around the dark room, familiar and yet strange, its dimensions fractured by her tears. Once, a long time ago, it had been her childhood refuge, a place where she had fancied herself a lady-in-waiting and dreamed of the day her prince would come.

Instead, Simon had come into their lives. The room had become a torture chamber like no other, where what was good and safe was twisted and deformed into something monstrous. Emeline gripped the box even harder, held it tight to her chest along with Camille's dagger. "This was my home," she repeated.

Kieran smoothed Emeline's hair, and pressed a kiss to her head. She shushed her and rocked her, a slow sway that soothed them both.

"Don't worry," Kieran said gently, her cheek pressed against Emeline's hair. "Your home is with us now."

Emeline brought her eyes to meet Kieran's and searched them for a moment, before she nodded and leaned into the embrace. Kieran held her until both their tears dried, and then she stood up, reached down to help Emeline to her feet. They both turned and saw Rogan standing in the doorway. In the darkness of the room, his face was unreadable.

"Come here, Kieran."

She ran to her brother and he grabbed her, held her tight in an embrace that was gentle for all its intensity.

"I'm sorry, Rogan." Her words were muffled in his chest.

"*Ná bac, sidhe gaoithe.*" He spoke against her hair as he held her. In his mind he said a silent prayer of gratitude and thanks. "*Ná bac.* You'll do."

"I don't know why I didn't listen. I was stupid. Foolish."

"Enough. It will wait until tomorrow." Rogan patted her back. "Go wait with Uncle Jeffrey, Kieran. I'll be along directly."

Kieran nodded and shuffled from the room, left Rogan alone with Emeline.

Rogan stood in front of his wife. He reached out and took the dagger, held it up in question.

"Your mum's."

He raised his brows but said nothing, and then tapped the box Emeline held, again in tacit query.

"My mum's."

Emeline opened it, and out wafted the scent of musty, dry flowers, like potpourri that had long ago lost its perfume. "My mum's flowers." She held up a summer daisy, pressed flat and browned with age. "She would not have wanted them left behind."

Emeline looked around the room one last time as she placed the flower back in the box. She closed the lid and latched it before meeting Rogan's gaze once again. "I shall never return here."

"No," Rogan agreed, "this is not your place."

But there was something in his voice. He sounded different. Harder. Perhaps even a little cold.

Before she could speak, Rogan took her by the arm and led her from the room, down the stairs and outside, into the night. He tethered the small paint to the back of the carriage, and then leaned into the confines to speak to Jeffrey, glad to see that Nilo waited inside, as well.

"We'll ride behind you," Rogan said to his uncle. "Emeline and I have much to discuss."

* * *

Rogan swung up into his stallion's saddle and lifted Emeline into his arms in front of him. With a call of readiness, the strange retinue began the journey back to the mansion.

The ride through the streets of London seemed surreal under the light of the moon. The worn cobblestones of the streets gleamed like polished metal, the shop fronts dark holes in ghostly buildings that rose around them like fortress walls. Every so often they would hear rushing footsteps, unseen street urchins slipping down alleyways, the winding, hidden passages that laced the city like a ribbon.

Unsettled and nervous, Emeline was stiff in his arms, holding herself away from him. Finally, her back ached so that she was forced to lean against him. His hard chest was warm, and the solid, real feel of him made her feel oddly ashamed. When she spoke, her voice was small.

"Are you angry with me?"

"For leaving?" His voice was still cold. Distant.

"For disobeying."

She felt him shift his weight beneath her, heard him clear his throat.

"You did as you felt you must, aye?"

"Yes. I did."

Rogan was silent for a while, and when he spoke, the sound of his voice startled her.

"You took her place?"

"Yes."

"So you put yourself in the position of being violated by him. Again."

Emeline could feel the tension in his body, heard the subtle change in his tone, as if he struggled to not sound accusing.

Between her legs she burned as if branded by Simon. "Not quite."

Another shift of his voice, annoyance creeping in, despite his best effort. "What does that mean, *exactly*, Princess?"

"I went armed. I was going to kill him," Emeline answered bluntly. And then the rest poured out, bitter and fast. "And if he violated me, so what? What would you have had me do? Stand by, safe and unharmed in the mansion, while I knew full well that Simon would hurt Kieran, and take what little innocence she had left? I saw no need for her to know the nightmares, for her marriage bed to be stained with it, for her to spend the rest of her life reliving it. Of course I traded myself for her; he'd already raped me many times, once more would have made little difference to me. But to Kieran it would have meant everything."

Jealous rage slammed into Rogan. His arms tightened around her as he envisioned Simon between her thighs, as he once had been. His gut burned; it made him sick to think of her submitting to Simon, using his lust for her to provoke him, giving herself over to his power.

And then the full weight of what she'd done sank in, deeper than his pride or his jealousy. She'd sacrificed herself, always thinking herself stronger than those around her. His Emeline, willing to be violated rather than to allow it to happen to another. He knew she felt as if she could endure it, and so she ought to. It was why she'd prostituted herself to Simon all those years, bargaining with her sex to save her mother from further harm. It was why she'd run off, traded herself for a girl she'd never met, and allowed the man she hated more than life the opportunity to hurt her again. The knowledge that it protected Kieran was enough for her to endure anything Simon might do to her.

Rogan thought of the woman he held in his arms, warm, beautiful, and fearlessly fierce. A woman of savage strength coupled with the most tender compassion he had ever encountered.

Rogan was silent, so much so that Emeline began to wonder if he would ever speak to her again on that matter, or even any other. Degradation threatened once again, as she was forced to consider that he might truly think her a whore. Only pride had Emeline holding back from saying more, from begging for his understanding. She beat the shame back with the pride, refused to give in to guilt's downward spiral. She had done the only thing she knew how to do, bargained with the only power she had. If it was not good enough, there was nothing she could do about it now.

Finally, Rogan did speak.

"I will not question your motives again. You did as you thought you must." This time his voice was gentle. His lips found her forehead in the darkness, and he pressed a tender kiss to her skin. "Thank you for protecting my sister."

He understood.

The realization tingled in her blood like bubbles in champagne, filled the secret folds of her heart until she felt it would burst with joy. He understood not just what she had done, but why she had done it. He understood *her*.

His words released her, and like a bird she felt as if she could fly. No bars of shame surrounded her, no locked doors barred her, no barriers held her back. It seemed to her that he'd opened her final lock, untied the last tether, and she was truly free.

Rogan understood her, down to her essence, saw the woman beneath the lure and the beauty. And that kind of understanding was her heart's one true desire.

Chapter 24

Clouds began to gather in the night sky, obscuring the stars and the moonlight and deepening the veil of night as the group approached the mansion. Inside, candlelight burned, signaling that the occupants were still awake.

Leaving Nilo with the driver to see to his needs, Rogan and Jeffrey escorted the women to the front door. The door was locked, but when Rogan knocked upon it, it was opened almost immediately. The butler looked as if surprised to see them all, a long brass candle snuffer dangling from his hand. He appeared weary, but his bow remained stiffly formal as he greeted them.

Rogan pulled his sister close, wrapped his arm protectively around her shoulders as Jeffrey addressed the staff.

"Send for my valet. And I am a touch peckish. Prepare me a light repast," Jeffrey instructed. "I am off to pen a missive to the magistrate. I will need a man to deliver it."

Jeffrey turned and headed in the direction of his office. The butler bowed again, turning to Rogan. "And you, my lord? Your needs?"

Running footsteps echoed down the hallway, and Kieran's maid burst into the foyer. "Mistress, thank God."

Kieran sagged and Rogan held her upright.

"Jane, thank you for finding my brother," Kieran said. The words made her cry.

Jane drew close to Kieran, her face twisted with sorrow. She gently touched Kieran's matted hair as her eyes traveled over her lady's countenance. What she saw had her own eyes tearing. "My lady, what did they do to you?"

"I cannot speak of it; I shall never speak of it. I only want a bath and my bed," Kieran answered, tiny sobs breaking her words.

"Of course, of course, my lady." Jane wrapped her arms around Kieran, ushering her to her rooms.

Rogan let his sister go reluctantly, but knew that in Jane's care, she would be well met. He addressed the butler. "My sister needs a bath, as do Emeline and I; please arrange for hot water to be brought to both our rooms, and give my apologies to the staff for our lateness."

Anna swept into the foyer, brushing past Kieran and Jane without comment. The normally serene expression on her face pinched with annoyance as she spotted Emeline.

"You're back," she stated flatly. "I shall see your rooms are prepared once again."

Rogan reached out and clasped Emeline's hand, pulled her closer to his side as he met Anna's eyes with an even regard. "No need, Your Grace. Emeline will be staying with me in my rooms until we seek out our own home. We have been married."

"She is your wife?" she gasped, her knuckles pressed to her mouth. Her brown eyes darted from Rogan to Emeline and then back again. "You did not, Rogan. You would not be so foolish. So utterly careless."

"I do not answer to anyone, least of all, you." Rogan gave his aunt a look that warned her to hold her tongue. "I married Emeline, and she is now my lady. You, and everyone else, would do best to accord her the proper respect."

"That tramp cannot take my place. She is common. A . . .

low, vile . . . 'Tis obscene!" Anna rallied, leaned forward and hissed at him like an angry cat. "Listen to you, informing *me* what you'll do, as if you know what position you hold, as if you understand even the slightest bit of what you're inheriting. All you've managed to accomplish is to prove that you do not know what you're doing here in England!"

Rogan folded his arms on his chest and grinned down into her reddened face. "'Tis my birthright, and I'm a quick study. 'Tis as if I'd been born to it, don't you think?"

"You do not even know the difference between a gentle-born woman and a common slut. You have brought shame on an ancient title you do not even understand."

"Shut up," Rogan ordered tersely. "Do not speak in my presence until you can show my wife her due. Fail to do that, and suffer the consequences." He clutched her arm and pulled her close. "Emeline is family. Your family. Accustom yourself."

Rogan let go as Anna gasped and held both hands to her mouth, whirled on her heels, and began running up the stairs. In her haste she did not mind the hem of her gown and she tripped, sprawling face down on the steps as she sobbed. Her maids rushed to attend her, lifting her arms and helping her the rest of the flight until they disappeared on the upper level, the sound of her harsh weeping fading as she made her way to her suite of rooms.

Rogan turned and faced his wife. Around them the mansion was dark, save for the candles that burned in the main foyer, casting wavering shadows around them and bathing the area in rainbow prisms as the golden light reflected off the crystal chandelier that hung above them. Finally silence reigned, and they were completely alone.

Emeline had remained still and silent through the entire ordeal. The look on her face was inscrutable, as if a curtain had dropped behind her eyes, concealing her every feeling and thought. She looked distant and removed, and he hated that indifference more than her sadness or her anger, for it seemed as if she was held away from him again, veiled with the safety of her apathy to shield her from the weight of other's opinions.

"I am sorry for that, *anamchara*."

"I will need to accustom myself. 'Tis how all the peers will react."

The wooden sound of her voice echoing in the cavernous foyer pained his heart.

"Nonsense." Rogan took a few steps closer so he could touch her. He stroked her face, cupped it in his hands. "They may wonder how I managed to convince such a beautiful woman to marry me."

Emeline closed her eyes, her exhaustion complete. His words were meant to comfort her, but in her heart she knew them to be lies, and his words did not alter the truth of the matter: she was still a woman of common birth, who had no reputation, no social standing, and no right to the title of duchess. "You cannot fight everyone who speaks the truth."

"The truth? Look at me." When she did not, Rogan pressed her further. "Look at me, Emeline."

Emeline opened her eyes and met his, the connection so instant and powerful she felt it to her bones, as if he could see inside her, beneath her skin where her blood raced through her veins to her heart, the way a river rages to the ocean. He knew her in ways she could not understand and struggled to accept.

Rogan dropped his hands from her. His eyes swept over her from face to feet, and he realized that he now saw so much more than the gold of her hair, the beauty of her face, the promise of pleasure radiating from her sapphire eyes, and the luscious lure of her tall, curvy frame.

She stood before him, her gown tattered and stained, the ratty box of flowers she'd carried all the way home still clutched to her chest, her arms wrapped around it. He saw her for who she was, and also for who she was not. He saw Emeline. "You are as uncommon as any woman I have ever known."

She wanted to believe him, but Anna's tears rang in her mind. Had Emeline been an innocent girl of lofty birth, Anna would have welcomed her and taken her under her wing. Rogan had not been raised in England; he did not understand how deep certain prejudices ran and the importance of a woman's reputation.

But still, she wanted to believe him. Wanted it so much it hurt like broken bones.

Emeline tried to gather her apathy around her like a blanket, to hide in the folds of it where nothing could reach her.

Yet, her desires would not be denied. She wanted more. They had been awakened in her and would not be set aside. She challenged Rogan, full on. "What of when they revile me?"

He heard the life coming back into her. Defiance is a form of passion, and it meant her defenses had been penetrated.

"I will scorn them."

"And when they gossip about me?"

"We will carry on, and they will tire of the subject."

"What of when they speak the truth, and all will know you are not the first man in my bed? Will you be embarrassed to call me wife?"

A grin tugged at his lips. He fought it, wanting to maintain the solemnity the situation called for, but the absurdity had his lips pulling into a grin. "You cannot be serious."

"They will say all that, and more," she insisted, now riding high on the waves of her unleashed emotions. "They will say the children I bear are not yours. Men will boast to each other that they have bedded me. If I am capable of bearing children, they will suffer my disgrace, branded as bastards even when they are born of lawful wedlock. And if I am barren, it will be claimed I am infertile because the Lord punishes whores. You will see. It will happen."

"Orianna. You'll remember I told you she was a gypsy?"

Emeline stopped, his sudden change of topic and the easy way with which he spoke about his first wife combined to take her completely by surprise, stunned speechless. She nodded.

"Well, they're all thieves and tramps, you know. A Godless tribe, without any regard for the lives of decent people. Can't trust a single one, and they'll rob you blind the moment you turn your back." Rogan leaned against the wall and folded his arms in front of his chest, grinning. "Oh, aye, and don't even chance to have one around a child, because they'll steal your baby, too."

"I see your point, but—" she began, ready to argue with him, but he interrupted.

"No, Princess, I don't think you do. Listen to me, aye? I've never done anything for the approval of others, save my parents, and that's as it should be." Rogan's grin faded and the look on his face softened, grew far away. "I married Orianna because she was funny and mysterious, bold and opinionated. And aye, she was beautiful, too. But there was so much more to her than only that. She made me laugh, and she could make me so angry that I wanted to punch holes in walls. We fought and we loved and we talked."

He tilted his head to the side, remembering. "Aye, we talked all the time. I think I could have spent the rest of my days talking with her, and not felt that one of them was wasted."

One of the candles in the wall sconce beside him guttered and died, and its loss of light cast his face half in shadow. Around the foyer more began to expire, the flames stretching high before dying out, the prisms on the wall fading as they went out, one by one. As if influenced by the failing lights, Rogan dropped his voice.

"Do you think I ever cared what others thought of our marriage? Did they lie in bed with us in the darkness and share our secrets? Did they know for even a moment what it was like, to have a soul-deep connection that makes earth and sky make sense? All the wonders of the world made sense to me when I was loving her."

Rogan shrugged then, and smiled at Emeline in the dying, flickering candlelight, not his reckless grin, but a slow curving of his lips that made Emeline think of velvet and aged whiskey. "And now there is you. My beautiful Emeline, my princess, my *anamchara*. Do you think I will give any regard to gossip and the opinions of others? If you do, you do not know me at all."

"I do not want to be your burden. Can you understand that? I don't want to be the reason you are not accepted."

He laughed a bit and reached for the box she clutched, took it and set it beside them on the floor before he grabbed her hand and pulled her close against the length of his body, only a few candles remaining to light them.

"Love isn't burdensome, Emeline. 'Twas trying to live without it that weighed me down, but you freed me from that. Reached into my heart and healed me. I'm not fighting it anymore. I'm not fighting anything anymore."

Bringing her eyes up to his, she felt her heart stop, then start thudding, hard. "What are you saying?"

"I'm saying I love you, Emeline."

"You love me?" The thought staggered her imagination. "But I am . . . and you . . ."

He cut her off before she could say anything more. "You are wonderful, and I am besotted." And then he continued on, as if her mouth were not gaping open. His arms tightened around her. "And if it gets to be too much, being here in England, and you aren't happy, we can always just take the money and go home."

"Go?" Emeline was floundering, trying to make sense

of what was happening. Had he just talked about how much he had loved Orianna and then followed it up with a casual 'I love you, Emeline'?

"Sure," Rogan went on, "I didn't come here for a love of England. It won't trouble me to leave if my wife isn't satisfied with the life we're building. I've no need to be called duke, but the wealth is mine, and I'll claim it." His grin grew more careless, wild and untamed, and mischief was heavy in his voice. "Then again, it might be a high time, the two of us together and turning the aristocracy on its arse with our common ways. I think we should stay, for a bit. It could be fun."

Emeline forced herself to remember that she was getting more than she had ever dreamed possible. She needed to be grateful and stop wanting more. And it was so easy, anyway, to let him hold her as he did. Her heart was full of feeling as she rested her head against the curve of his shoulder, breathed in deep through her nose so she could inhale his scent, loving the heat and essence of him.

Rogan stroked her hair. "And if it isn't fun, we'll go home to Barbados. My mum would love that."

The idea of it captured Emeline with its promise, images Rogan had described to her coming back, this time with Camille and Patrick there to welcome them, their son and his wife. Already Emeline could feel their acceptance, it was warm, solid, and strong around her in the form of Rogan's embrace. And over and over in her mind, like a mantra, *he loves me, he loves me.*

"I've never been on a ship." With his arms around her, Emeline could see them traveling the ocean together. When he held her like that, everything seemed possible. She saw moonlit waves and starry skies over an endless horizon. She saw them making love while the rocking of the sea cradled them. "Is it very wonderful?"

"No. Aye." Rogan thought about his father, his

grandfather, and the Mullen men before them. The sea was in them, like blood, and he could not separate his love from his hate of it. "It is like all of nature, relentlessly merciless, but also very beautiful."

Two more candles sputtered out, leaving Rogan and Emeline in the light of a single flame that burned nearby in a wall sconce, the tiny blaze casting them in a halo of gold as it prevented the darkness from completely engulfing them.

"The lights are dying," she observed. "There is only one left."

Rogan bent and lifted the box that lay by her feet, handed it to her as he reached up and pulled the candle from its holder. "'Tis our cue."

Rogan paused outside the doors to his suite. The wavering candlelight under Kieran's doors and the muffled sound of weeping filtered into the hallway, and he handed Emeline the candle. "Go see to your needs, *anamchara*. I must see to my sister's."

Emeline nodded, her chest tight with affection and sympathy for Kieran. "Do you want me to come with you?"

Rogan paused, considering her offer. His sister was like Camille, and rarely wept, least of all in front of others. "I think maybe I should go alone."

"As you wish."

Emeline waited as he knocked, holding the candle for him to ward off the darkness of the hallway. At the sound of his knock, Kieran's weeping immediately ceased, the quiet tone of her voice calling out, inquiring who was at her door. Rogan replied, and entered at his sister's soft invitation.

All alone in the empty corridor, Emeline stifled the pang of guilt that nearly kept her from leaning against the door, listening. She heard the low timbre of Rogan's voice speaking in Gaelic to his little sister, words the meaning of which Emeline could not understand, but spoken in tones that were universally comforting.

The bonds of blood reached deep, and with a sense of sadness, Emeline recognized that now that Madeline was gone, she truly had no family left who shared her lineage. Pulling away from the door, she entered Rogan's rooms and lit the candles, grateful that the staff had thought to light the fire.

Steam drifted from the bathing alcove, candlelight spilling out to form a wavering rectangle of light on the floor, and Emeline suddenly could not wait another moment to bathe. Simon's scent seemed to cling to her skin and hover in her nostrils, and she wanted it gone from her, once and for all, secure in the knowledge that he could never, ever touch her again.

She set her ancient box aside, stood and paused as she looked down on it for a moment, her fingers resting on the scarred and nicked wooden exterior. And then she turned and left it behind, entered the bathing chamber and gasped a bit with delight at the candlelit oasis of comfort.

A thick curtain of burgundy velvet swagged over the entrance to the alcove, and Emeline released the drape from its hook and let it hang closed, confining the warmth of the hot water to the little bathing nook. Candles had been lit around the room, on wall sconces and in floor pillars, and enclosed as it was, the tiny space glowed with dreamy, steamy light like a magical, hidden grotto.

Emeline piled her hair atop her head and secured it with combs, too tired to care that tendrils slithered free and escaped to hang in long waves down her back. Slowly she removed every piece of clothing, letting them drop carelessly to the floor in a puddle. Naked but for Camille's dagger, Emeline placed her foot on the wooden steps that led to the tub and looked down at her thigh, knowing that the knife had once been strapped to Camille's leg, as well.

In the candlelight, the black leather sheath shone like

polished onyx, the dagger's hilt thick and hard against the softness of her skin, making her look delicate but feel strong. With feelings that wavered between satisfaction and regret, she unbuckled the straps and set the sheathed dagger aside.

She climbed the little wooden steps and sighed as she slid into the copper tub that had been filled nearly to the rim, the warm water like a lover's caress on her skin. A table beside the tub supported lumps of soaps along with vials and jars of salts and oils, and Emeline lifted the stoppers and sniffed each one, finally settling on an oil that smelled of honeysuckle, the fragrance putting her in mind of her dream cottage far away in a small, perfect village that existed only in her imagination.

With a slow motion, she drizzled the oil into the water, watching the arc of the liquid drop until it hit and pooled on the surface of the water. Oil and water do not mix, she thought, like commoners and aristocracy.

With a defiant thrust, she stopped the bottle back up and set it on the table before swirling the oil into the water, long, spiraling swishes with her hands, the beads of oil blending, melding, until she could no longer tell where one liquid stopped and the other began. Momentarily satisfied, she lathered a flannel and washed every inch of her skin until the clean fragrances saturated her sinuses. Once clean, Emeline leaned back against the copper tub, her head resting on the curved lip, and closed her eyes.

A faint waft of cool air touched her shoulders just before long, deft fingers slid into the mass of her hair, releasing its weight from the combs. Golden waves spilled to the floor, draped over the copper of the tub, the hair and the metal gleaming with the patina of polished coins in the candlelight. Emeline opened her eyes and met Rogan's gaze as he stood above her, his fingers rubbing tiny circles on her scalp.

"I did not hear you come in, my lord."

"I did not want to startle you."

"Is your sister well?"

"She will be, in time." He shrugged a bit, thinking of his sister's teary, swollen face. "I wish my mother were here. She would know better than I what to say, how to comfort her."

His fingers drifted lower, rubbing her neck until it felt as if her muscles were melting into the water, her head floating above her shoulders as if by sorcery.

"I would love to meet Camille."

"You will, one day."

"Will you tell her what I was before you married me?"

The question gave Rogan pause, turned him instantly angry. He looked down on his bride in the steamy, flickering light, unable, despite his annoyance, to keep from noticing how the bath water turned her skin to rose gold, her breasts rounded and floating, the water curving around her body as he wished to do. Her eyes were turned up to his, full of promises and contradictions, questions and secrets and honesty. She radiated an intense allure, bruised and wounded but also strong and savage. Emeline was plain and beautiful, complicated and simple. She was also very naked in his tub.

"Do you wish me to?"

The husky timbre of his deep voice made her shiver. He loomed over her dressed entirely in black, his face as handsome as a Celtic fable, and his eyes as hard and green as emeralds under brows that slashed thick and black, drawn down into a scowl. As easily as the written word she read his expression, anger and arousal combined; a dangerous combination, she knew. But she did not fear him, and that fact made her skin grow hot and damp in a way that had nothing to do with the warmth of the water.

"No, my lord. I do not."

"Never ask me again if I will betray you."

Emeline bit her bottom lip and nodded, unable to

speak. He continued to awaken her in every way, and it hurt as it healed.

"Can you think of yourself as my wife?" he pressed, not willing to let the subject rest simply because of her nakedness and the lust it provoked. He reminded himself once again that he chose what kind of man he would be. "I am willing, aye, and proud, but are you? Answer me, because I would know where we stand."

His questions shook her to the core. He had raised her feelings from the dead, and now he probed her darkest fears. The way he spoke to her had her heart thudding harder and faster. There was lust in his eyes, more familiar to her than anything else, burning brightly in the golden, misty light of the alcove, its gleam brighter than his annoyance. He contained it though, with disciplined restraint that Emeline found intensely erotic. Caught between his anger and his passion, Emeline found it easier to respond to the latter.

She did not answer his questions.

With achingly slow, deliberate strokes, she trailed her hands through the water, up and over her arms, leaving little silvery beads in the wake of her wet fingers, shivering in the candlelight as they rolled from her skin like liquid drops of moonlight. She slid her hands to her breasts, caught and cupped them close, her nipples peeking through her parted fingers. Emeline heard Rogan's breath snag and hold. She squeezed her breasts together, and then released them once again to sway in the water, hearing his breath hiss out in time with her motions. All the while she had her eyes closed as if suspended in the moment, and then Emeline opened her eyes, caught Rogan's gaze, and held it.

"I see your desire for me, my lord."

She rose from the tub, the water streaming from her rosy skin in rivulets, steam rising from her body. The candlelight turned her to pure, glistening perfection, as luminous as pearls, as lustrous as gold.

"You are enticing," he agreed. But he did not reach out for her.

"Will you take me?"

"Do you wish me to?" His voice sounded deeper, rougher.

"Yes. I do."

"You are using your sex in an effort to distract me."

"Yes." Emeline shifted her body so that her breasts thrust forward, drawing his eyes to the pink-tipped peaks of her nipples. "'Tis what I have to offer you, and you want it. I am yours. Take me."

Still, he did not touch her, though he stood only a pace away. Rogan's eyes swept leisurely down her body, to where her thighs were circled with water and then back up, pausing at the dark gold triangle of wet hair, her flat belly, her full breasts, and then finally her face. He met her gaze with his, unwavering. "What will you be, frightened temptress or fearless wife?"

The question caught Emeline off guard, broke her rhythm. It made her want to grab a cloth and cover her nakedness. Her throat burned with a lump that made breathing difficult; her eyes began to burn. She did not want to answer his questions, because she would be forced to admit that she did not know if she could separate the two.

And so instead she deliberately leaned forward and grabbed hold of the rim of the tub, hearing the seethe of Rogan's breath as she did so, knowing it gave him the full view of her breasts as they hung down, round and ripe, and also the curve of her back and the round swell of her buttocks. She lifted her leg out of the water and shook it, setting her breasts to swaying, and then the other as she withdrew from the tub.

"Enough of your seduction. Answer me," he rasped.

"I want your desire." Emeline took a step closer to him, so that the heat of her body touched his, and his scent filled her, as compelling and complex as the man himself.

"And what of yours?"

Emeline leaned against him, lifted her mouth to his, ready to stop his uncomfortable questions with the answers that came much more easily, those of passion and pleasure.

Rogan grabbed her arms and pushed her firmly back. His entire body was hard and hot for her. He could not have her so close, or he would lose his resolve and take what she so lavishly offered. He held her still, his eyes boring into hers. "I will not have you trading sex over honesty. I'll have all of you, or none at all."

His hands were tight around her arms, banding her in a grip from which she knew she could not break free. Still, there was no violence in his strength. His control aroused her as nothing else; it meant she was safe to lose her own. Safe to be truthful, safe to be passionate, safe to come undone in any and every possible way.

Truly and completely aroused, Emeline leaned her head back, unconsciously exposing her neck to him in a primitive display of surrender.

"I am all these things, my lord: I am brave and also afraid. I want you to cherish me as your wife, and yet I still want you to use me as your whore. I desire your lust and your love, and I am foolish enough to crave both, but I am suspicious of your motives when you give them to me. I am jealous of the way you love Orianna and I want it for myself, but I also do not feel worthy of it. I want all of you, and it scares me so much I want to push you away. But I long to pull you close and hold you forever, as tender as a mother, but also as sensual as your lover."

Her voice broke and her heart pounded, but she pressed on, giving him her truth in all its convoluted glory. "I am woman and girl, victim and willing participant, cunning slut and innocent prey. I am damaged but I am strong. Broken but healing. And most of all, I am very sorry for you, my lord, because you seek to discern what even I cannot. There is only one thing about myself that I understand, that I know for certain."

"What is it?"

She brought her head back up with a snap, looked him straight in his eyes, burning green meeting midnight blue. "I want you."

Rogan tenderly cupped Emeline's face in his hands, stared into her eyes searchingly until finally he nodded, once. "I believe you do."

She laughed a little, a short sound of relief more than anything else, and Rogan bent and lifted her into his arms, cradling her close to his chest as he carried her to the bed and laid her down, stretching her long form on the silken coverlet.

"Your honesty is worth more to me than your seduction," Rogan said, "and 'tis far more arousing."

He sat beside her on the bed and trailed his finger across her body, from the elegant bones of her neck and shoulders to the supple curves of her breasts, waist and hips, and down the length of her legs to the tips of her toes. Her knees fell slightly apart, goose bumps raising on her skin and tightening her nipples, her entire body shivering and shimmering with sensation.

"This is how I want you," he said. "Open to me in every way. Your mouth, your arms, your heart, your thighs, and all your secrets and truths, every part of you open to me and to no one else. You are mine, now."

In the light of the fire and candles, his eyes burned darkly green, and Emeline was caught willingly in the web that was Rogan Mullen.

"I am yours," she vowed.

"Say it again."

"I am yours."

Rogan kissed her, his lips so soft against hers they felt like nothing more than a sigh. Their breath mingled and the kiss deepened, and once again Emeline was falling and spinning, his mouth on hers turning the entire existence of an outside world to nothingness.

He pulled away and stood before her, his hands on the buttons of his shirt. He unfastened them as he watched her face. Rogan slid out of the black shirt, unlaced his boots and shucked them as well. With the same deliberate motions, he untied the laces of his breeches.

"You stripped for me. Stripped yourself bare and asked if I could want more than your body, your beauty, your sex. Could I see beyond the attraction of you and see what lies beneath. You'll remember this?"

"Yes."

"'Tis my turn to ask you." Rogan slid his breeches from his hips and let them drop to the floor, used his foot to sweep his clothes and boots aside as he stood before her, completely naked. "What am I to you, Emeline?"

Emeline's eyes slid over him like honey, slow, savoring every bit of him. From the handsome lines of his face and the striking color of his eyes and hair, her eyes traveled the wide, muscled chest, and hard belly. His arms bulged with sinewy strength, and his legs were long, ropy with thick muscles and dusted with black hair. Her eyes were drawn back to the center of him where his penis stood erect, hard, thick, and ready. But he did not move towards her, was not ruled by his lust. He would control it, she knew, for as long as she needed him to, a restraint that was as sexual to her as the most intimate touch.

"You are my lover and my friend, my husband and my lord." She would have reached for him, but she controlled herself as he did, waiting, trusting. "You are my everything," she finished simply.

"Something lingers in your voice," he urged her, "like an unvoiced desire. Tell me what you think but do not say, Emeline."

She did not hesitate to answer his demand for truth, because she lay before him naked and open, her body, heart, soul, and mind, just as he wanted. "I want what you gave Orianna. I want all of you."

"All of me."

"Yes. I want the kind of passionate love that you gave her. I want your whole heart. I want it all."

"And you are bold enough to ask for it."

"Yes." An edge of intensity took her tone. Now that she had laid bare her deepest desire, there could be no going back. And so she raised her chin a notch.

"You are jealous enough to covet it."

"I am."

Rogan took two steps closer, so that the side of the bed touched his thighs and Emeline's heat caressed his skin. She lay stretched out before him, all silken curves and secret hollows. She met his gaze with a smoldering intensity that matched his own, her needs exposed, as naked as her body. The hunger in him had reached epic proportions, a dark urgency that rolled like a storm through his blood. "I do love you. I say it now, plainly. I love you, Emeline."

"Prove it."

A slow smile spread across his face at her tone, husky, full of challenge. His was a need that spanned darkness and light, sun and moon, earth and sky. He longed for her the way he longed for life, the way he had once longed for a fight, like compulsion and need combined, a lust so great it became like suffocation to not touch her.

Slowly he extended his finger and ran it down her body once again, tracing over her every detail, watching her skin shiver in his wake. He reached the tip of her toe and then traveled back up her foot, over her ankle, around the shape of her shin and the bump of her knee, and finally up her thigh until he reached the center of her heat. He held his finger there, just at the opening of her, the damp heat of her sending a thrust of fresh lust through him. She was hot, ready, willing. And completely unabashed.

Emeline held his gaze and spread her legs apart, and with a smile as wicked as Jezebel's slid down, impaled herself on his finger, then gasped with decadent delight, her eyes locked on his. Slowly she moved on him, up and down.

A low, deep sound tore from his throat. Never before had he known a woman to be so boldly sensual. It took his breath away. "You are wondrous."

"And you are taking too long." She reached her hands up to grab his shoulders. "Give me what I need, Rogan."

The hot, wet softness clutching around his finger gave him no doubt of her readiness, that the urges that pumped through him were driving her, as well. He wanted to kiss her, to hold and caress her, to use his fingers and tongue to drive her insane with urgency and pleasure. But that would wait. For now, he would simply possess her.

In a fluid motion, he was on top of her, feeling her hands slide down his back and clutch his buttocks. She opened to him with no hesitation, wrapped her legs around his, matching his passion with her own.

"I need you," she demanded breathlessly. "All of you."

He did not know if she spoke of his heart or his body, but he could not hold back any longer and he slid inside her heat, filling her until he had nothing left.

She clamped around him, a tight wet softness that caused pleasure so intense it nearly ached. He moved inside her, and in the light of candles and fire she burned beneath him, golden goddess and steamy seductress in one woman. Her fingers dug into his skin, gripping and raking him as she came completely undone, her cries and gasps of delight filling his ears as she moved beneath him, shamelessly gazing into his eyes, watching him watch her pleasure.

She was all around him, her scent, her heat, the sweet clenching shudder of her release. And Rogan was falling into her depths, drowning, dying, breathing, coming.

They lay entwined in the bed, the candles long since expired, and only the light that of the fire. The fire burned low, molten red embers glowing beneath logs that crumbled to ashes even as small flames ate away at what remained.

Rogan held Emeline close against his body, the length of her pressed to his skin so he could not know completely where he ended and she began. In the silence of their room and the privacy of their bed, he stroked her hair as they talked quietly in the darkness.

"I never dreamed I could do this again," he confessed.

"I never dreamed I would have this at all."

Held against him, where life seemed elementally simple and complete, Emeline saw the image of her mother on her father's lap once again, the shining happiness of her eyes, the pink that rode high on her cheeks. *Marry for love*. Emeline's arms tightened around Rogan.

I did, Mum, she answered her silently.

"I loved Orianna with my whole heart," Rogan said, still stroking Emeline's hair.

She stiffened beneath his touch, and heard him laugh quietly.

"Listen, *anamchara*, aye? I loved her without heed. I never thought she would die. I never thought about anything. I just rushed, headlong, into it." Rogan shifted so that he could look into Emeline's eyes. "Hear me well, Emeline. The love I feel for you isn't that heedless, careless love. 'Tis something maybe a bit deeper. I love you despite knowing you can die, that I can die, and that anything can happen. I love you beyond caution.

"But I can't give you what I gave Orianna, because the fact is, I'm not that man any more. Instead I'm giving you the man I am today, and God willing, many tomorrows to come."

Rogan pressed a kiss to her lips, and in doing so, they inhaled each other's breath, their vital essences mingling as one. "Every minute, every hour, every day. I'll savor them with you. For as long as we both shall live."

Emeline pulled back so she could look at him. "Say it again."

He smiled at her grave solemnity. He'd have the rest of her life to teach her something different; he'd begin with showing her that being in love could be pure fun. But that lesson would wait, because for now he wanted her to understand it, to know it the way she knew the most basic of all truths.

"I love you, Emeline."

"Again."

"I love you, Emeline."

She *was* like a flower, and he'd never trouble himself to mock the comparison again. Yes, he thought, she was his slow-blooming rose, so soft and fragile and tenacious, and yet possessed of thorny troubles. But in the light of his love, she bloomed a bit more. Her smile deepened, grew radiant, and her skin glowed so dewy soft in the firelight that she was incandescent, luminous. She took his breath away, she did. His beautiful Emeline. His soul-friend. His soul-mate.

This time when Rogan spoke the same words, his voice was full of wonder, of tenderness. "I love you, Emeline."

Emeline reached up and cupped Rogan's face. A multitude of things she wanted to say filled her heart to bursting: that she would be a faithful and true wife, that she was so grateful for the man he was, that she would love him until death. But those were promises one lives up to, and she vowed he would never be sorry he came to her door. For now, though, Emeline spoke the plain truth of the matter, so simple, and yet, it was everything she had ever dared to hope for. "I believe you do."

Epilogue

Kent, England, 1775

On the rolling green hills of the eastern English countryside, down winding narrow roads and across sheep-dotted pastures, stood a charming Tudor manor. Built in the time of Henry VIII, it was rumored that the property had been commissioned by the king himself as a gift to one of his lovers.

Emeline had dreamed of a cottage. Rogan had managed slightly better than that: It had miles of property hedged with stone fences, its own game lands, several ponds, stables to house fifty horses, and inside the twenty-room house itself, a complete staff to take care of whatever a person might require. Attached to the manse by way of iron and glass doors was an enormous glass solarium designed simply for growing things, no matter the season.

No more scraggly grass on a windowsill, Rogan had told her when they toured the property. No, she would grow fruit trees in January, if her heart fancied it.

As it turned out, Emeline found that she fancied many things. She enjoyed learning, and hired a tutor to come for daily lessons. She found a love of painting and horseback riding. She discovered the joy of crewel, tapestry, and needlepoint, taught to her by her sister Kieran. In fact, Emeline found there was utter satisfaction to be had in life, and would often find herself humming and smiling as she went about her daily routines.

One particular June day, Emeline, finished with her daily lessons, changed into an old gown and disappeared into the solarium for a few hours of planting and pruning. The hour approached tea time when she was finishing up, cutting roses and slipping them into a vase of water for a centerpiece in the front foyer.

A maid burst through the iron and glass doors, breathless. "My lady, the master has returned."

"Today? He's not due back until tomorrow!" Emeline's hands flew up to her hair. "Is he inside yet?"

"No, my lady, the carriage has only just arrived."

Emeline wasted no time. She tugged off her gardening gloves and ran through the house, past the library and up the curving staircase, and burst into the chambers she shared with Rogan. She called for her maid as she glanced in a looking glass and, with considerable dismay, confronted her appearance.

"Oh Rogan," she murmured, looking at her braided hair that had pieces escaping, and her dirt-smudged face. She wore a plain muslin gown suited to gardening, not greeting her husband, who returned from a week-long stay in London to conduct his business. Returned a day early. She added, "I fear I do not look like the lady of the manor this afternoon."

She knew he wouldn't care, but she did. Like her mother before her, Emeline strove to look her very best for her husband each day. It was a matter of her pride.

Her maid rushed into her rooms and the two women got to business. In a matter of minutes, Emeline had her hands and face washed, her hair brushed and dressed high with carved, gold combs, and was dressed in a silk day-gown of soft, buttery gold. She slipped into matching shoes as she put on the newest jewelry Rogan had gifted her with, a pair of earrings that were crafted of gold and sapphires and diamonds, along with a matching necklace and ring.

"You're lovely, my lady. Now hie yourself downstairs. Your lord will be looking for you."

"He will," Emeline agreed with a smile, as she gave herself a final inspection in the mirror. She saw her own color rise, turning her pink with expectation at seeing Rogan. Her lover, her friend, her husband and lord. The past six days without him had been endless.

She descended the stairs at a ladylike pace and swept into the foyer just as he walked through the front doors. And her heart did its usual trip, her belly did its usual flip. It wasn't possible for her to look at him and not feel extraordinarily happy. God, he's handsome, she thought, and her gaze traveled over every inch of him with greedy delight.

"My lord," she said softly. "You are home a day early."

He grinned, and his eyes did the same as hers, taking in all of her details. He crossed the room and took her hands in his, looked down on her with an expression of warmth and love and something more. "Is that acceptable, my lady?"

"Better than acceptable. I missed you so."

"And I you. The days dragged without you, Emeline." Rogan pulled her close into his arms and pressed a kiss first on her lips, and then on the hollow behind her ear. He pulled back and smacked his lips together in contemplation. "Soap and water, and the faintest hint of soil and flowers. I interrupted you in the solarium."

"I was just finishing up, anyway."

"Uncle Jeffrey sends his best regards, as does Lora." Rogan did not mention Anna; they never spoke of her.

"And I also brought something home for you and Kieran. Where is she?"

"She's out riding. And Rogan, truly, you do not have to bring me back a gift every time you go to London."

"I shall bring you as many gifts as it pleases me, and I'll hear nothing more about it. And anyway, 'tis for the best that Kieran's out. I wanted to give you your gift privately." His manner was completely casual, but knowing him as she did, she could feel his excitement. She wondered what kind of thing he could have purchased her; the last bit of jewelry had been quite extravagant, and yet he hadn't been like he was now.

"Hmm." Rogan patted his pockets as if he had forgotten where he'd placed something. "Perhaps I left it in the carriage. Come with me to get it, *anamchara*."

She put her hand in his and let him lead her to the front doors. He opened them, and there on the landing stood a man and a woman, both smiling at her. Emeline glanced at Rogan and then back to them. Her eyes were drawn to the woman, whose green eyes were identical to Rogan's.

"Camille," Emeline said in awe. "You are here. In England."

"I came to meet my new daughter," Camille replied. "And so I say, welcome to our family, Emeline."

Tears filled Emeline's eyes, fractured her vision, and then spilled down her cheeks. She glanced up to Patrick for a second, smiled a tremulous smile as she saw Rogan's face, thirty years older. And then she looked back to Camille, absorbed every detail of her, from her wavy silver and black hair neatly coiled beneath a stylish hat, to the trim figure dressed in elegantly chic traveling clothes. She is so beautiful, Emeline thought, but not simply in appearance. No, she radiates a gentle strength.

"Camille." It was all she could say.

If Camille noticed Emeline's shock or her lack of

manners, she did not show it. Instead she entered the home and took Emeline's hands in her own. "Rogan tells me you and I have quite a bit in common."

Emeline glanced back to Rogan, who stood beside his father. He grinned at her with such joy it filled her heart to bursting. "Better than jewelry, *anamchara*?" Rogan asked.

She dashed away a few tears with the back of her hand and matched his grin with a smile of her own. "Better than anything."

"Patrick and I could not wait to meet you," Camille said to Emeline. "I fear my brother's feelings may have been injured that we cut our visit short to come here. But we have daughters in the countryside, I reminded him, and one we have not met yet."

"Daughter," Emeline whispered.

"I hope you don't mind my calling you that."

"No," Emeline answered quickly. "No, I do not mind. Please do so."

Rogan turned to his father. "Da, you need to see my horses."

"Aye, son, I'd like that."

Rogan put his hand on his father's shoulder. "And later tonight, we'll sit out on the terrace, aye?"

Patrick grinned at his son, the pride on his face so beaming that Emeline had to look away. *I want to give Rogan a son,* she thought for the millionth time. *I want Rogan to have this moment someday.*

Camille looked around the foyer. "Will you give me a tour of your lovely home, Emeline?"

"Of course. Please follow me."

The men went off to admire the horses as the women toured the home. As they were in the solarium, Kieran came rushing in.

"Mum!"

Camille spun around as her daughter threw herself into

her arms, and the two embraced as they never had before. Tears coursed down Kieran's cheeks and she sobbed freely, gripping her mother so tight that Camille gasped for air. Finally, she relented and let go, met her mother's eyes. "Mum."

"You got your England, my Kieran."

"I missed you."

"And I you, my Kieran." Camille smoothed Kieran's hair with a gentle hand, studying her daughter's face as if she had never seen it. "Is all well with you?"

"Mum." Kieran took her mother's hand and kissed it, hard. "I missed you, Mum, and I'm so sorry I gave you such troubles, and I'm so very, very sorry for every time I argued with you, and also every time I—"

"Shhh." Camille pulled Kieran in close. "You have always been my joy."

Kieran let her mother hold her and she wept, tears of regrets and happiness and relief, and Camille smoothed her hair and patted her back in the warmth of the solarium. "That's it, love, and you're better for shedding the tears. I know, my Kieran, it's painful to think of what you would change if you could, but it's part of life, and of growing, to learn from it. Now come, love, today is a day of celebration."

Kieran nodded and dried her tears, reached out and grabbed Emeline's hand and pulled her into the embrace with Camille. The three women held for a moment, and then Camille stepped back and swept her eyes across the two girls.

Camille looked proud and happy. She looked beautiful.

"We need tea," Camille announced decisively. "And cake."

Emeline laughed and led the way.

Sometime around midnight, Camille and Patrick lay in their bed, limbs entwined. The night was too warm for a fire, and only a single candle illuminated them.

"Thirty-one years," Patrick murmured in Camille's ear. "Thirty-one years and you are back in England. How are you finding it?"

"I'd forgotten it was so green," Camille replied. "All my memories of it seemed gray and rainy."

"Perhaps we should stay a while and make new memories here."

"Perhaps. Will you want to go home to visit Ireland, as well?"

"Home?" Patrick said, and chuckled. "Home is with you, Camille. It always was, from the moment I met you."

Camille smiled and wiggled even closer to him. Thirty-one years of marriage had not changed her need for his skin against her own. She loved his scent, his feel, his essence. The simple pleasure of being with him. "Rogan is happy," she said.

"He is. And it pleases my heart to see his healed."

"But Kieran. There is something amiss with her. I do not like the look in her eyes," Camille said.

"Aye, I saw it, as well. We will keep a close watch on her."

"Yes. I think we shall stay a while. Kieran needs me, but so does Emeline."

Patrick nodded his agreement. "Emeline is a lovely girl. She fair glows with her love for Rogan."

"She does," Camille whispered. "It lights the room."

"You lit the room. 'Tis your spirit, Camille. The children bask in it. I bask in it."

"'Tis all because of you." Camille held Patrick, her fingers brushing down his back, and she cupped his buttocks, pressed her pelvis to his. "Everything I am, I am because of you."

"We are magic together," he said, kissing her lips.

Alone in her bed, Kieran cried softly into her pillow, hoping the sound would be muffled enough that no one would hear her. As good as it had been to see her parents and to spend the evening with her family, Kieran was weighed with a terrible secret burden; she could never speak to anyone about what had truly happened in the house of lords that night. Her family must never know, and so each day became a struggle to appear normal. Her only daily peace was her riding when she could ride far enough ahead of her chaperone to have solitude enough to not have to mind the pain and horror that would show on her face.

It isn't easy, she thought, to be alone. And yet, it was how she vowed she would always remain.

The warm night air sighed through the open windows in Rogan and Emeline's bedchamber. They did not bother with candles, but instead kept the drapes open so the moonlight could illuminate them. They lay without covering, naked in the silvery light. Rogan caressed Emeline's arms, her waist, her belly, and then back up to cup her face.

"I shall never grow tired of touching you," he swore. "You are beautiful beyond my words, Emeline."

Emeline shifted so she could look up at him. The pale white light of the moon made him look as though he was sculpted of marble. "'Tis you who is beautiful."

"I was proud to have you by my side this day. Proud to introduce you to my parents."

Emeline lay in his arms and thought of the day that had just gone by, the most idyllic day she could have ever dared to imagine. Camille had even taken a private moment to talk with her, to tell her that while she could never replace Madeline, she very much wanted Emeline to think of her as a mother, and to feel free to come to her as she needed. Emeline felt like she had a family now, nearly perfect in its completeness. But for one thing.

"Rogan?"

"Hmmm? What is it, my love?"

"I want to give you a son."

"You shall. Someday."

"That is just it; what if 'someday' does not come. What if I cannot?" Her voice grew very small. "What if I am barren?"

"What if you are?"

"That's it?"

"That is it," Rogan said definitely. "I will not lie, I think children are a blessing. But I did not marry you for heirs, Emeline."

"You married me to keep me safe," she reminded him.

"Aye, and how am I doing with that, then?"

She smiled. "Very well, my lord. I am safe in your arms."

"And are you happy?"

"I am. Blissfully so."

Rogan gazed down on his golden wife who lay naked beside him, her skin glistening in the silver light. He wanted to tell her that sons did not matter to him; but that would not have been the truth, completely. Rogan did want sons, but he did not want them at the price of Emeline's life. Women died in childbirth, and he would trade his unborn children for the life of his wife, without question. Nothing meant more to Rogan than Emeline: her health, her safety, her happiness. He wanted her by his side, always.

But Rogan had learned a few things about himself, and about Emeline, as well. One was that he would not spend his days in fear, but would love Emeline as if each day were their last. That was Orianna's gift to him; she'd taught him a lesson in gratitude. Rogan was grateful for every minute of joy Emeline brought him.

Another thing he'd learned was that his beloved Emeline was a woman of fierce passions. She wanted to give Rogan the gift of children, and no words from him would change her desire.

Rogan lay his hand on her flat belly, and told Emeline what he truly believed. "They will come. I know it. They will be created in love, and born into the safety of the home we have made. They will come, Emeline, make no mistake. And until that happy day, we will not worry about it, aye? Trust your body, trust your heart, and trust my love."

"I do trust you."

"Do you know what would truly please me more than anything?"

"What?"

Rogan grinned, wickedly, naughtily. He lowered his mouth to Emeline's ear and whispered a request that had her toes curling, her body shivering with sensual anticipation. She pulled back, flushed with heat. "Is that so?"

"Aye," he said, and he pulled her to him. "It is so."